# TALISMAN

## DAVID EVANS

## ABOUT THE AUTHOR

Born and brought up in and around Edinburgh, David Evans graduated from Manchester University and had a successful career as a professional in the construction industry before turning to crime ... fiction that is and writing thereof.

*TALISMAN* is the third in his Internationally Best Selling Wakefield Series.
*TROPHIES*, the first in the series, along with *TORMENT*, the second in the series which was shortlisted in 2013 for the CWA Debut Dagger Award are also available.
A fourth in the series, *TAINTED*, will follow.

His other novel currently available is *DISPOSAL*, the first of a planned series set in the Tendring area of North Essex.

Find out more by visiting David's website at
www.davidevanswriter.co.uk
or follow him on Facebook at
www.facebook.com/davidevanswriter
and Twitter @DavidEwriter

# ACKNOWLEDGMENTS

I have been privileged to meet some amazing people, without whose help, encouragement, support and above all friendship got me through some occasions when it would have been easier to walk away and do something else with my time.

First and foremost, I have to say a huge thank-you to Sally Spedding who was the first in the publishing industry to take my writing seriously. I owe her a great debt for all her continued support and encouragement.

Heather Adams did an inspired editing job which improved the story's telling.

I am fortunate to have a great little band of writing friends and I would like to thank Sarah Wagstaff, Jan Beresford, Julie-Ann Corrigan, Manda Hughes, Lorraine Cannell, Glynis Smy and Peter Best, all of whom are talented writers in their own right and have made some significant contributions.

I am also fortunate to have the input of Colin Steele, ex-Detective Superintendent of the Essex Murder Squad and Tom Harper, ex-Principal Crime Scene Coordinator for the Kent & Essex Serious Crime Directorate. Both have given their time and guidance generously. Also, thanks to Dr George Pontikis for his medical assistance. Any residual errors here, are all mine.

Nichola Ellis and Val McMunn for providing some initial inspiration.

Finally, Ger Nichol for just loving the series.

*Mum & Dad,*

*who gave me everything I needed*

DAVID EVANS

# TALISMAN

**David Evans**

# 1
## Thursday 16<sup>th</sup> August 2001

The hood is put over his head, shutting out the light. This is the final act. His wrists and ankles have been shackled to the frame that is bolted to the wall. His excitement grows, clearly visible, as he anticipates what is to come. Will it be whips, or canes? Leather; he loves leather. The belt is his favourite. Or will nothing happen at all? That would be the cruellest deed. Another set of footsteps enters the room, coming steadily towards him. What is this? His mouth is forced open and something made of sponge forced in. He nearly gags. Tape then covers the lower part of his face. This is new. He never expected that.

After a minute or so, he hears the door close. The key is turned. The sounds of feet on the stairs. He wants to shout out but the object in his mouth stops him. He can't work out what is happening; what might happen. After another few minutes, he is sure he hears the outside door closing. This isn't funny. His other senses become more acute. There is no sound at all now. He is positive he's alone. But surely this can't happen. This is a huge turn-off. He struggles with his arms and legs. It's no good, they are too well restrained. And then he smells it. Only very faint at first but after a few seconds, he is sure. Smoke. Not cigarettes, but something burning. It grows stronger.

He can't feel any heat. But he is sweating. He tries twisting his hands in the restraints, first one way, then the other. He can't get either thumb through. His feet have no chance, the heels catching against the shackles. Shit! This isn't happening. Suddenly, he relaxes. Of course, this is the chosen way of torturing him, pleasuring him; letting him think he is going to die, restrained in a fire. He

9

can't hear anyone, but they must still be in the room; keeping quiet. He can't work out how it is being done but it must be some sort of smoke machine. That's it. Yes.

No. He hears crackling sounds from the room below. He doesn't imagine that. He tries to yell again, but convulses with the object in his mouth. The automatic reaction is a deep breath through the nose. This is when he first catches the unmistakeable stench of acrid smoke. He tries to calm himself but it is no good, his body fights for oxygen. The more it does, the more choking poisonous smoke it draws in. A small explosion and the sounds of broken glass.

He composes himself once more. Sleep is coming.

He is a boy again, back in the bedroom of his parents' house where he grew up. His elder brother is with him. They are playing, their voices muffled. He can't make out what his brother is saying, but it's a rough game. He isn't frightened when his brother sits on his chest. What's that he's saying? Sounds like, 'Tell me what it feels like. What happens afterwards?' He feels himself nod. Then the pillow comes over his face. He struggles, then the feeling of falling down a deep hole. The light at the top is fading and growing smaller. It has almost disappeared when he hears his father's voice, shouting. He can't make out what is said but the weight of his brother is gone and he can breathe again. That was how he remembered the incident; only this time, his father doesn't come. This time the deep hole swallows him until the light is extinguished.

Before he can hear the sirens, it is over.

# 2
## Six Weeks Earlier
## Thursday 5th July 2001

Wakefield; lying at the heart of the world-famous rhubarb triangle; home of the Empire Stores catalogue and the National Mining Museum. A fine, warm sunny day had dawned but over Wood Street Police Station, dark clouds formed.

In his office on the first floor, one of West Yorkshire's finest, Detective Inspector Colin Strong was contemplating the news. Disappointment, anger and shock were the emotions running high in his system. Disappointment that, after nearly nine months as Acting DCI, the permanent promotion had failed to materialise. Anger at the thought that it may have had something to do with the actions he took in trying to protect his old boss, Cunningham. And shock at the candidate who had been drafted in for the position, a graduate entry fast track high-flyer by the name of Rupert Hemingford. Thirty-six years old, single and late of the Cambridgeshire Constabulary. Detective Chief Superintendent Flynn had called Strong up to his office that morning to break the news. Flynn's words from last August sped through his mind. 'Who knows, play your cards right and it could be yours permanently,' he'd said to him. Well it was obvious now that he hadn't played his cards right.

"I'm sorry, Colin," Flynn said, "I know you'll be bitterly disappointed but the top brass thought it appropriate to bring in some fresh blood ... shake things up a bit."

"It'll certainly do that," Strong had managed in response. He didn't say much else.

Sitting at the desk in his office next to the CID room, he festered. Finally, he stood up, put on his suit jacket and made for the door. He needed to use some energy as well as have time to think. Exiting through the main doors, he turned left, down the steps onto Wood Street and headed towards The Bullring. Unaware of the warm sun on his shoulders, he walked down the street, lost in thought. Fresh blood, ha! Forty-three years old and feeling passed over. *He* was a university graduate too, but he'd put his time in on the beat initially, before making his way through the ranks in CID. Although it was never mentioned, Strong suspected that evidence he had discovered to overturn a young man's conviction for sexual assault, and Cunningham's retirement in the fall-out, had not done him any favours.

He caught his reflection in a shop window as he passed by the side of the cathedral. He still had all his hair, light brown with no grey, didn't need glasses, but there was a slight slouch to his walk. Imperceptibly, he pulled himself straighter to his full six feet and headed for The Ridings shopping centre. Through the doors, down the steps and along the mall, a name caught his eye. Laura Ashley. Laura? Yes what will Laura say? Married for twenty years this year. Laura was deputy head teacher at a primary school in Morley. She'd probably be more disappointed for him than he was.

He found himself in Morrisons, standing in front of the cigarette counter and heard himself asking for a packet of his favourite cigars. Only he'd given up for, how long was it now, almost a year? He paid for them, put them in the inside pocket of his jacket and left, desperate to smoke one. But the illogicality of his purchase snapped Strong from his self-pity. He couldn't allow the failure to gain permanent promotion to be reflected in his failure to remain smoke free. He would keep the packet unopened as a reminder of how long he'd given up and just how close he'd come to failing. With that thought, he strode purposefully back to the station.

Returning through the main doors and into the reception area, a youth and a woman he took to be his mother were at the desk signing paperwork with the sergeant. Strong was about to tap in the key code to gain entry to the main building when the door opened.

DS Kelly Stainmore appeared. "Ah, guv, I was just looking for you."

Stainmore, one of his best detectives, looked worn out. Short blonde hair framed a face that had begun to look older than her thirty-four years. Dark shadows below her eyes and skin that appeared leathery made him think there was some underlying health problem. She also seemed to have gained weight in recent weeks.

"What's up, Kelly?" he asked, passing through the open door.

She followed him down the corridor. "Got a call about a sudden death."

"Where?"

"Normanton."

When he reached the door to the car park at the rear, he turned to face her. "Tell me what you know on the way. Do you want me to drive?"

"Er, yeah. Don't mind."

"Then you can tell me what's up with you as well."

She hesitated for a second then followed him to his Mondeo.

The journey to Normanton, a former mining town and railway junction to the east of the city, took fifteen minutes. At the beginning, all Stainmore contributed was the address. She was silent for the next ten minutes. Strong felt he had to probe. "Come on then, Kelly, what's on your mind?"

She continued to look out the window. At first, he thought she was going to ignore him altogether. Finally, she replied. "Have you ever thought you were going nowhere?"

He gave a sardonic smile but said nothing.

"Oh, ignore me. I'm fine." She turned to face him. "No, really I am. I'm okay."

He knew she wasn't. "Look, Kelly, we've worked together for what, five years? If you ever need to talk about anything ..."

"I know."

The remainder of the journey passed in silence. They turned into a street with red brick terraced houses on both sides and drew to a halt behind the marked police vehicle already there.

"You go in," Strong said, pulling his mobile from a pocket. "I need to make a call."

"Thanks, guv," she said with irony, paused a moment, then got out.

# 3

Belinda Chamberlain collected coppers. No, not policemen, she didn't have a fetish for men in uniform. She'd saved pennies and two pence pieces, ever since she never had two of them to rub together in her student nurse days. That was before she met Charlie, or Charles as the stuck-up sod insisted everyone call him now. She blamed his parents, alliteration gone mad. It was only as his career began a vertical trajectory did he think Charles Chamberlain sounded far more professional. She had to agree it looked better on the brass plate outside his offices but it did rankle when he insisted she call him by his full name as well.

He was studying for a law degree when she met him in a nightclub in Leeds, over twenty-seven years ago now. She was with a couple of colleagues, student nurses, out on the town, rather the worse for wear; he was with a group of fellow students. Three years later, they were married, she a staff nurse at Leeds General Infirmary, he articled to a legal practice in Wakefield. A daughter was born soon after, Grace, now twenty-three and working in an accountants' office in Southampton, after graduating from university there last year. Six years later a son, Anthony, now seventeen, arrived. He'd just completed his AS Level exams at QUEGS, the prestigious Queen Elizabeth Grammar School, a short walk away in the city.

She'd had a relaxing morning, bit of a lie in, a shower, cooked breakfast, and was preparing for a late shift at the hospital. Her shoulder length blonde hair had been dried, brushed and swept up onto the top of her head. The pennies and two pence pieces were stacked in ten pence piles on top of the chest of drawers in the bedroom. About to bag up another pound's worth, she realised she'd already used her last plastic coin bag. Spares were kept in her bedside drawer but, when she opened it, there were none. When she thought about it later, she could never explain why, but she walked round and checked Charlie's side. No plastic bags; just a couple of paperbacks, a pot of skin cream and a plastic pop-out paracetamol pack. He was the one who 'suffered' from headaches these days. She shuffled them to the side and spotted below an official-looking brown envelope. Intrigued, she pulled it out and looked inside at what appeared to be old legal documents. She tipped them partly out and read, 'LAND CHARGES ACT'. She was about to put them back when another document slipped clear. This was marked, 'CONVEYANCE'. But this one spoke of a freehold property having been transferred from someone she didn't know to C M Chamberlain. The address was Leeds Road in Outwood, no more than a couple of miles away, and it was dated July 1998, nearly three years ago. She was stunned. The only property she thought they had an interest in was where they lived now; St. John's Square, a stylish 3-bedroom apartment in an elegant Georgian block near the centre of Wakefield. She carefully replaced the documents, leaving the drawer exactly as she'd found it.

Abandoning the coins for the moment, she wandered through to the lounge and gazed out of the tall windows across the wooded green to St John's Church. Why would Charlie have bought another property without telling her? The man was becoming more and more surreptitious. When they first married they shared everything. Slowly, as his career began to take off, he told her less and less. She didn't even know how much money they had. Her salary went into a joint account and the bills were paid from there. But, when she thought about it, she didn't have a clue what other savings they had. Charlie looked after all the finances. She would have to change that. And she'd also have to find out about the Outwood house. Just then, the sun broke from behind the clouds, put the church spire into perfect silhouette and streamed in through the lounge windows. Exactly, she said to herself, I'll talk to him tonight.

# 4

The contents of the bath resembled pea and ham soup. Stainmore hadn't seen many bodies in her career. If it wasn't for the remains of the two forearms and hands tightly gripping the edges of the bath, she wouldn't be sure she was looking at one now.

Kitted up in standard issue white coveralls, latex gloves and a face mask in place, she was standing in the bathroom of the mid-terraced house.

"I've never seen anything like this," she said quietly, almost to herself. "Any initial thoughts, doctor?"

Dr Andrew Symonds, one of West Yorkshire's regular medical specialists, drew a deep breath behind his mask and considered a response. "For what it's worth, I've never come across anything like it either."

Stainmore studied the scene again. The head had dropped forward into the water, the hair floating on the surface. The remains of numerous candles stood around the edge of the bath, all burned down to the end. A whisky tumbler, stained dark brown, lay within reach of the right hand. She looked back to the doctor. "Anything to arouse suspicion?"

"Nothing obvious," Symonds responded. "But how the Hell we strain this off …"

"One for your scientist associates then."

"They'll be delighted. Do we know who it is?"

Stainmore flipped open her notebook. "Housing Department gave the name of the tenant as Denise Whitaker, aged fifty-eight."

"It could be her, I suppose. We won't know till we get those remains out of here."

Two workmen from Wakefield District Council's Housing Maintenance Team had called the police nearly two hours earlier. They'd had no response to a number of requests to gain entry to the property over the previous few weeks. Legally obliged to conduct the annual safety check on the gas appliances, the uniformed constable sent to accompany them had forced the front door. The odour led to the dreadful discovery in the bathroom.

Apart from the forced entry, there had been no other signs of disturbance that the constable could see. The two workmen had been told to wait in their van on the road outside. Stainmore had spotted it on her way in and had approached them.

"Have you two been in the house?" she had asked.

The younger one, about twenty, was in the passenger seat and looked ashen. His older colleague, balding with two day's beard growth responded, "No, the copper told us to stay here while he checked the house. Is it bad?"

"We're dealing with a sudden death," was all she'd told them before heading inside.

Stainmore left the bathroom, removed her mask and walked into the main bedroom. The curtains were drawn and the bedside lamp lit. A double bed appeared freshly made, turned down ready for its occupant who would never again slide between the sheets. On the bedside table, a novel lay opened flat, waiting for the story to be resumed. A drinks coaster and alarm clock lay by its side. Protruding from underneath was a card with a strange symbol. She pulled it free and read, 'Talisman Club'. It didn't mean anything to her so she put it back and opened the drawer. A few creams and ointments, loose change and a purse were inside. But it was some other objects that puzzled her. She picked up one of the half dozen or so sponge balls, the size of a small apple.

"Bollocks," Strong said, startling her.

She turned to see him standing in the doorway, dressed in a forensic suit similar to her own. "What?"

"They're false bollocks. And there are a number of these in the bathroom cupboard too." He held a sponge phallus aloft in a gloved hand, like he'd just won a trophy. "Denise has been living as a man for some time. Denis, the neighbours said, according to the constable downstairs."

She walked over to the wardrobe and opened both doors. Male suits, shirts and ties were on one side, whilst a small number of female jackets and trousers were on the other.

Stainmore shrugged. "Takes all sorts, I suppose." She closed the doors again. "You've spoken to Dr Symonds, obviously?"

"He's passing it on to Forensics to get the body out." He put the piece of sponge on the bedside table next to the book. "First impressions?" he asked.

She shuffled a few items on the dressing table, appearing not to hear.

"Kelly, I said first impressions?"

"Sorry, guv. I was just thinking … how could someone go unnoticed for over a year? In this day and age."

"You'd be surprised how many people in this country never see anyone else from one week to the next. Loneliness is a big problem."

"Like when they say you can be alone in a crowded room, you mean?" She turned to face him and seemed to recover her professionalism. "No sign of forced entry – apart from us, no disturbance in any room, no obvious sign of anything missing or intrusion. So, unless anything comes out in the PM, I'd say it was just another tragic case of someone dying alone and unnoticed."

"And if she didn't have gas, she could have lain there forever." Strong scratched his temple. "Despite that big pile of mail behind the front door. You'd have thought someone would have started to wonder …"

"I'll bag it up and go through it all back at the station."

"Okay, Kelly, take a statement from those two in the van. I'll have a quick look round before we go. But, I agree. Inform the Coroner's Office and we'll log it as unexplained, pending the PM."

# 5

Warm summer sun presented the Yorkshire Post building in its most flattering light. Normally, the concrete panelled structure looked dull, grey and depressing. With its digital clock visible to trains approaching from the south and the west, it had been a Leeds landmark since it opened in 1970.

At his workstation in the newsroom, Bob Souter was studying his computer screen, reviewing what he'd written. He had settled in well as Crime and Home Affairs Correspondent since his move from the Glasgow Herald in January last year. A number of exclusive headlining stories had eased his transition. The Deputy Editor, John Chandler, had been his boss previously at the Sheffield Star, and it was his approach that had coaxed him to return south.

Things had been fairly quiet on the news front for a few days. He'd had a bit of fun with John Prescott, the MP for Hull who'd straight jabbed a bloke after having had eggs smashed on him; a brawling MP was always good for a headline. Then there were serious concerns over the imminent rise in petrol prices and whether the psychological ceiling of £4.00 a gallon (87p/litre) would be broken. At the moment, though, he was reworking some agency news to keep the hunt for Damilola Taylor's murderer on the front page when the phone on his desk rang.

"Souter," he said.

*"Is that Bob Souter, used tae be on the Glesga Herald?"* enquired a male voice with a strong Glaswegian accent.

"It is. How can I help you?"

*"Ah unnerstan' ye hae a new retail park development just near Leeds aboot tae be announced?"*

Souter had heard rumours that something was in the offing, involving land owned by Wakefield District Council, but so far nothing official. "You have something of interest on this, Mr er …"

*"Ah'd rather you didnae know whae this was. It's safer that way."*

"For you or me?"

*"Maybe baith. Just check oot the developer. If he's cairryin on like before, he'll hiv some important people in his pocket. He disnae like tae lose."*

"I don't think anyone's mentioned any developer yet. Who are you talking about?"

*"Brogan. Kenny Brogan. He rins Thistle Developments up here. Nasty bastard."*

"What exactly do …" Souter stopped, the caller had hung up.

Phone back in its cradle, he ran both hands through his dark hair, scratched his scalp and considered the conversation. For 'up here' that can only mean Glasgow, he thought. The best person to give him the industry low-down on Thistle Developments would be Sandra, Sandra McKenzie. That might be a bit awkward, bearing in mind their two-year involvement and subsequent acrimonious split about eighteen months ago. She was an architect he'd met at a barbecue, not long after he'd joined the Glasgow Herald. Later that night, they'd ended up in bed. As he used to say, it was lust at first sight. Within a short time they'd moved in together. It was blissful for a while and he began to think that she might be the one. God knows, he'd made a mess of plenty of relationships before that. Then she found herself a new position with a larger architectural practice. She began working more hours and late evenings, but he discovered she was having an affair with the principal, Frank Buchanan. All that coincided with the phone call from John Chandler offering him a new position of his own, back in Yorkshire. Serendipity.

He wheeled his chair backwards to check behind the low partition to the next workstation. It was empty. Janey Clarke would normally be there. A smart young woman of twenty-six, she was a promising journalist whose work had impressed him. He was about to ask someone else where she was when she walked back into the office.

"Looking for me, Bob?" she asked.

He stood up. "Yeah, Janey. You've been following that story on the new retail park just off the M62, haven't you?"

"The Lofthouse scheme, you mean? Yes. Why?"

He stretched his six feet two frame and heard a few cracks from his back.

"That sounds painful," she quipped.

"Sitting at these desks for too long. Anyway, how far down the line is it? I mean, have they appointed a developer or anything?"

"Not as far as I know. It got initial planning approval last month. It goes back in a few weeks for some referred matters, I think they said. It's a bit controversial and it was quite a fiery meeting. Apparently, there's a lot of funding floating around on that one. It's on old mining land and there's grant money from the EU for cleaning up the site, as well as some central government funding."

He resumed his seat. "So it might be fairly attractive financially?"

Janey nodded "Not quite sure how it works but with all those money sources, there's always someone involved who's likely to trouser something they shouldn't."

He raised his eyebrows then turned back to his desk.

"You heard something, then?" she persisted.

"Maybe," he said over his shoulder. "Need to check a few things first."

She held out her hands in a show of exasperation and was about to respond but her desk phone rang, so she sat down to answer it instead.

Souter took out his wallet and found the business card he wanted. He read Sandra McKenzie's name then lifted the phone and dialled her office number.

*"Buchanan Associates, how can I help you,"* came the nasal-sounding West Coast accent of the female receptionist.

"Could I speak to Sandra McKenzie, please?"

*"Ah you mean Sandra Buchanan? I'm afraid she won't be in until this afternoon. Can I take a message and get her to call you?"*

Souter hesitated. He was thrown by the news that she had presumably married Frank Buchanan. "Er, no. No message. Thanks."

He slowly replaced the receiver as his thoughts drifted back two years to a period in time when he thought she might consider becoming Mrs Souter. Before he could explore the memory further, *Scotland The Brave* struck up from the mobile phone in his trouser pocket. He retrieved it and saw that Alison was calling.

What the fuck are you thinking, he told himself then answered the call. "Hello, sex bomb," he said in quiet tones.

*"Whoah, down boy. I hope you've been taking your medication,"* Alison chuckled.

God, he loved it when she laughed. It was such a turn-on for him. He'd met Alison in February last year. A year before that, she'd been involved with someone he was investigating. Later, their relationship blossomed. Last summer, Alison had also been very understanding when he met Sammy Grainger, a young street girl who had approached him for help in finding her missing friend. Initially suspicious, Alison had taken her in and even helped find a job for her with the firm where she worked.

"Hi," he said. "Everything okay?"

*"Of course. I just wanted to let you know that Sammy's calling round tonight. I thought it might be an idea if both she and Susan came for a meal. My place."*

Although they were in an intimate relationship, Bob and Alison valued their independence and, for the time being, had decided to keep their own accommodation. She had a cosy stone-built terraced house in Ossett, about five miles to the west of Wakefield whilst he retained a one-bedroomed modern flat near Westgate railway station.

Susan Brown and Sammy had become good friends following Susan's accident last year. She was now in her first year studying Broadcast Journalism at Leeds University and the girls shared a flat together.

"Sounds good. I haven't seen them for ages."

*"About seven then? You haven't got any ground-breaking scoops on the go that means you'll be working late?"*

Souter laughed. "I wish. No, it's all very quiet just now. I'll see you then."

When the call ended, he sat for a moment and thought how lucky he was. He loved Alison. She was gorgeous. Why did he even think back to Sandra?

He leaned forward again, picked up the phone and dialled another number.

*"Ritchie,"* another Scots voice answered.

"Charlie, how's it goin', my man," Souter responded, dropping into a Scottish accent.

*"Bob! Bloody Hell, long time no hear."*

"Indeed."

*"So what are you up to? Any interesting stories?"*

"Actually, there is something I'd like to pick your brains on," he replied.

# 6

Colin Strong turned the key in the lock of his modern 3-bedroomed detached home and opened the door. Amanda came bounding down the stairs and hugged him.

"Hi, Dad. Mum told me your news. But in my opinion, you're still the best policeman ever."

She was eighteen and in that nervy period of having just finished her A Levels and hoping the results would be good enough for her first choice of university.

Strong pulled his head back then kissed her forehead. "Thanks. Appreciate that."

"Dad." Graham emerged from the lounge and joined in a group hug.

"Hey! What is all this? I'm fine. I'm a big boy now, you know," Strong responded.

"Tell me about it," Laura smiled, arms folded, standing in the kitchen doorway.

"Oh, please. Too much information." Amanda made a face in mock disgust.

He chuckled. "Seriously, I'm okay."

"Come and sit down," Laura said. "I'm making spag bol. Be about half an hour."

Amanda disappeared back upstairs whilst Strong took off his jacket, fetched a beer from the fridge and joined Graham in the lounge.

"How's the job?" he asked, sitting on the settee next to his son.

"It's okay, for the summer, I suppose." Graham, at twenty, had completed his second year at Hull University, studying History. He had managed to find a position at The National Mining Museum about seven miles away.

"I thought you said it'd be useful for your studies. The mining industry, an important part of the Industrial Revolution."

"It is. It's just I was hoping for something a bit more challenging than working in the cafeteria."

Strong laughed. "At least it's a job."

Graham nodded then studied his father. "Dad, are you alright? With this situation at work, I mean."

Strong puffed out his cheeks. "Well, there's not a lot I can do about it. But, it's disappointing, to say the least."

"When does the new bloke come in?"

"Beginning of the month."

"Are there no other opportunities for you? Leeds maybe?"

"I've got a good team here. I won't make any kneejerk decisions but … I suppose there might be other openings."

"There's bound to be good teams elsewhere. Look at me. We had a good football team at school. I didn't think we could get that same camaraderie again, but the lads at Uni, from all over, we all gel together."

Strong smiled at his son. "Graham, you should be studying philosophy."

The pair laughed.

Half an hour later, they were all seated around the dining table. This was the first time they'd been together as a complete family since last Christmas.

The conversation had drifted through Graham's time at Hull and the choices Amanda had selected for her university courses. They'd finished the meal and Graham and Amanda had departed to do their own things. Laura made a mug of tea for them both and brought the subject back to her husband. "So how have the rest of the team taken the news; Luke, Kelly?"

"It's not been formally announced. But I'm a bit worried about Kelly. There's something going on I don't know about."

"What do you mean, 'something going on'?"

"Health wise, I think." He took a drink. "She looks washed out. I think she's bulked up a bit too. And when we went to that unexplained death today, it seemed as though it affected her. She was a bit distant at times."

"Well you can't sort everyone's problems out, Colin. You've got enough on your own plate with what's going on for you."

He sat back in the chair. "No, I know. It's just that she's a good officer and if there's something wrong and it can be sorted … well, you know what I mean. What if one of your teaching staff showed some worrying signs? You'd be concerned, wouldn't you?"

Laura sighed. "I know. Has she not given any clue?"

"I've offered; said if there was anything troubling her, if she ever wanted to talk to anyone, I'd listen …"

"Nothing?"

"Not yet."

"No doubt she will when she feels ready."

\*   \*   \*

Souter let himself in to Alison's house with his key, the front door leading directly into the living room.

"Hello, Bob." Susan looked up from the settee where she was reading a magazine.

Sammy waved, sitting on the floor by the fireplace, flicking through Alison's CD collection.

Souter smiled, returned the wave, then turned to Susan. "How's the leg?"

The twenty-five-year-old had broken her left leg when she tumbled into a deserted building's basement nine months ago. It was Souter who had found her.

"Just about back to normal, thanks." Her attention returned to the article. "Got signed off from physiotherapy last month. Back to see the consultant in a few weeks and that should be me clear."

"That you, Bob?" Alison shouted from the kitchen.

"'Tis I."

"Great timing. I'm about to dish up."

"Smells good." He looked to Sammy. "Your job working out okay?"

Sammy was twenty with long blonde hair. She looked far healthier than when she'd first come to speak to him in the Yorkshire Post offices last year. She'd overcome her lifestyle problems successfully, with the help of Alison and himself. "Great, yeah. They're sending me on a course next week. Dire Straits any good?" She held up the *Brothers In Arms* album.

"Of course," he said. "Another milestone in your musical education."

She stuck out her tongue.

"Come through, you lot!" Alison yelled from the back room.

Souter led the way to the kitchen diner, bottle of wine in hand. He gave Alison a hug and big kiss then joined the others sitting down at the table. As he opened the wine and began to pour four glasses, the bass riff of the first track, *So Far Away From Me*, closely followed by Mark Knopfler's distinctive lead guitar kicked in.

With gloved hands, Alison placed the Creuset pot onto the wooden mat on the table, before returning with a couple of Pyrex dishes full of steaming vegetables. "Get stuck in," she instructed.

"This's lovely, Alison," Sammy said, dishing up the goulash onto four plates.

Over the course of the next half hour the conversation drifted effortlessly from recent news stories, concerns over more cases of CJD and having a laugh at the expense of John Prescott. Then there was the knowing look Sammy gave Alison when she mentioned the case of the fifty-six-year-old woman who had just given birth to twins.

"Any more of that and I'll stop your pocket money," Souter joked.

By the time he was asking Susan how her Journalism course was going, he was feeling warm and mellow, so grateful he knew these three women and could enjoy their company.

"Actually, I was wondering, Bob ..." Susan hesitated.

"Yes," he replied slowly.

"I was wondering if ... if there might be a chance of ..."

"Oh, for God's sake, Susan," Sammy interrupted, turning to Souter, "She wants to know if there is any chance of a job at the Post for the summer."

"Thanks, Sammy, I was coming to that." Susan looked put out.

"Honestly, you'll have to sharpen up your questioning techniques if you want to survive in journalism." Souter laughed. "I thought you were going to ask that. I'll have a word tomorrow and let you know. When could you start?"

"Anytime you like." Susan broke into a broad smile. "Thanks, Bob."

"Well, I can't guarantee, but ... I'll see what Chandler says."

\*   \*   \*

Kelly Stainmore sighed heavily and uncorked another bottle of Frascati. She poured a generous measure into her glass, pulled a large cardigan around her and returned to the lounge. The previous bottle stood empty by the side of the low coffee table. She'd meant to take it back into the kitchen but felt she had a bad case of CBA – can't be arsed. Even she was starting to become concerned about her moods. A mournful tune on the music centre didn't help, but it matched how she felt.

She hadn't eaten, didn't feel hungry. Besides, she'd put on some weight recently, she'd get something later. Her thoughts kept returning to the scenes she had witnessed that afternoon in the terraced house in Normanton. Denise Whitaker. What a sad and lonely end. Nobody missed her. Nobody, it seemed, cared. What if something similar happened to her tonight; undetected heart condition, say. Who would miss her? True, she'd probably be found quickly. She couldn't imagine the DCI not sending someone round when she failed to turn up for work; no answer to their calls on her mobile. Mobile? She didn't remember seeing a mobile phone in Denise's house or any bills for one in the pile of mail. She'd check on that when she was next in. Phone records too for any land line.

So here she was, thirty-four years old. A fairly successful career so far, if you thought Detective Sergeant was a reasonable rank for someone of her age to have attained. She took a drink of her wine, stood up and looked out onto the street below. The trees lining the road were in full leaf and the last of the day's sunlight dappled through the lounge window. Another sip. No, she didn't think she'd be missed. Well, a day or two maybe. Apart from her mum and dad. Her two brothers wouldn't give a shit. She hadn't seen them in years.

Mum; she'd seemed a little tired last time she went over to Huddersfield. There again, she was fifty-nine. She wondered if she'd retire next year or carry on. Her mum loved nursing and had worked at the Huddersfield Royal Infirmary since it opened in 1965. Dad was a couple of years older and still drove buses in the town. They seemed content with one another. They kept each other going. Who would keep her going? That dark feeling again.

Another gulp of wine. Had she really drunk three-quarters of a bottle before this glass? She looked at the empty bottle on the floor. Well yes, she had opened that one the night before and had only one glass out of it. She was easily getting through a bottle a night, sometimes more. And it didn't seem to affect her any more. No, she'd need to do something about it. She'd have a free night tomorrow and see how long she could remain AF – alcohol free. Okay, decision made. Feeling happier already, she went back to the kitchen, refilled her glass and took another slurp.

*   *   *

Charles Chamberlain was sitting in the leather easy chair in the lounge, watching television when Belinda came home. She'd finished her shift at ten. Hungry, she made straight for the kitchen.

"Have you eaten?" she shouted from there.

"Got myself a Chinese on the way home. Knew you were on a late."

Sounds of dishes being moved in the kitchen, the microwave door being closed then the hum of power as it was switched on. She appeared at the doorway. "Have you seen Anthony?"

"Came home about an hour ago. Been at Simon's after school. He's up in his room."

The microwave pinged and she returned to the kitchen.

"Good shift?" he asked, once she'd reappeared with a bowl of soup and some crusty bread on a tray.

"Not bad. You had a good day?" She sat down on the black leather two-seater settee.

"So so." His attention had drifted from the television. He put on some reading glasses and picked up the TV section of the newspaper.

She studied him; dark hair thinning slightly and the beginnings of a paunch. All the trappings of a successful business, she supposed. "Anything interesting on?"

"Not really." He turned the TV off and opened out the sports pages.

They were quiet for a few minutes. Eventually, she spoke. "I was just wondering ..." She took a spoonful of soup then a bite of her bread.

"Mmm?"

"How much are we worth? Do you know?"

"We're comfortable." He stopped reading and looked up. "Why are you interested? Do you want to spend on something?"

"No ... I was just curious." Another spoonful of food. "We used to talk about it, but I've no idea where we are now."

"I can give you a summary if you like."

"That would be interesting." More bread. "I mean, is it all in cash in savings accounts or do we have stocks and shares or …?"

"Cash savings mostly."

"I was going to say, property too?"

"Property? We have this place but it's mortgaged."

"So we don't have anything else then?"

"What are you talking about, Belinda?"

She was gaining in confidence. "Nothing you want to tell me? Outwood, maybe?"

He folded up the newspaper angrily. "Have you been …? It's an investment. Why were you rooting through my drawer anyway?"

"I thought you might have had some coin bags."

"Not you and your bloody pennies again."

"Anyway, why didn't you tell me about it?"

"I thought it would be good for Anthony."

"Anthony? So what about Grace?" She calmly scraped the last spoonful of soup from the bowl. "Or is there another property somewhere with her name on it? Not that Anthony's is on the Outwood one."

He stood up. "For Christ's sakes, Belinda, what does it matter? It's just an investment."

"So you said." She rose and made for the kitchen. "I'm just surprised you didn't think it worth mentioning, that's all."

"It's no big deal." He spoke louder. "But seeing as you're so interested, I'll sort out a list of all our investments. Tomorrow all right for you?"

She turned to face him at the kitchen doorway. "Bloody Hell, Charlie, what are you getting so pumped up about? I was only asking."

"And I'm only telling. And don't call me Charlie. I'm off to bed, I've a busy schedule tomorrow." He turned and left the room.

Belinda disappeared into the kitchen, surprised at the way the conversation had gone. She opened the fridge and poured herself a glass of white wine. "That went well," she said quietly to herself.

# 7
## Friday 6<sup>th</sup> July 2001

Early the next morning, Strong walked up to DCS Flynn's office and knocked on the door.

"Come," the voice from inside said, so Strong entered.

"Ah, Colin," Flynn greeted from the other side of his desk. "Sit down, please." He indicated one of the two chairs in front of him.

Strong sat down.

"Look, I'm sorry about the news I had to break to you yesterday." Flynn closed the file in front of him and put his pen down. "I did try and support you but I was over-ruled. For what it's worth, I think you've done an excellent job in the role."

"Thank you, sir." Strong studied his boss. He felt he was being sincere, convinced that Flynn had always backed him. "What I wanted to discuss is … well you know what I feel about the team. They've supported me every step of the way too, sir."

The Detective Superintendent leaned back in his chair, elbows on the arms, hands clasped together on his lap. "You want to be the one to let them know, is that it?"

"Exactly. I think they deserve to hear it from me."

Flynn stood up and walked to where his coffee machine was steaming on top of one of the glass-fronted units. "I didn't think you'd want to handle this any other way. Coffee?" Flynn lifted a cup and saucer.

"Thanks. One sugar, sir."

Strong watched his boss pour out two cups, place them on the desk then sit in another chair alongside him.

"How do you feel about it, Colin?" Flynn asked, after they'd both sampled their coffees. "And drop the 'sir' in here. This is just between us."

Strong sat back and looked to the ceiling for a moment before facing Flynn. "I'd be lying if I said I wasn't bitterly disappointed. Like you, I thought I'd filled the role pretty well. The team have done well too."

Flynn nodded.

"But, tell me this," Strong took a deep breath. "Just between us … did the situation with Jack have anything to do with this?"

He could see a slight reaction on Flynn's face from his reference to former DCI Jack Cunningham, his predecessor in the role.

"One or two on the panel were aware of his history," Flynn responded.

"Come on, you know I'm not asking what they thought of Jack. The fact you've answered how you have tells me everything."

"Look, I know you did everything you could to cover for his failings, it's just some of the older school …"

"Like Halliday?" Strong was referring to DCI Frank Halliday who had been Cunningham's mentor in his early career and had initially resented Strong for what he saw as betraying him, whereas, the opposite was true.

Flynn nodded once more. "Well … Have you heard about Frank?"

Strong shook his head.

"Passed away last month. Pancreatic cancer, I'm afraid. So he didn't have a long retirement. But, yes. I'm afraid there may have been some legacy from Jack's actions that some don't fully understand. I know you tried your best to keep his weakness, shall we say, from being exposed but you had to get to the truth on that trophy case last year. At the end of the day, Jack doesn't blame you. He would support you one hundred per cent."

"I know he does, he's told me himself. Thanks for the coffee." Strong rose to his feet. "So when can I tell the troops? Not particularly about Hemingford, I'll let you do that at the appropriate time, but that I won't be carrying on as DCI?"

Flynn also stood up. "I'll leave that entirely up to you. You're in the best position to time it right." He held out a hand and smiled.

Strong shook it, face impassive. "Thanks."

\* \* \*

About an hour later and ten miles away on the Newsroom floor of the Yorkshire Post, Bob Souter was typing away at his computer keyboard. After last night's conversations with Susan, he'd bumped into John Chandler on the stairs and asked him if there would be an opportunity for her to have some work experience through the summer vacation.

"Is that the young woman you rescued from the basement last year? The one who wrote some of that article with you later on?" he had asked.

"That's her."

"I'll ask the boss and get back to you." 'The boss' referred to the editor and Chandler's response had been as good as Souter could have expected.

Reporting on a recent spate of car thefts in the Adel area, he was about to pick up the phone and call his DC connection at the local police station for an update, when it's chirruping beat him to it.

"Souter," he answered.

*"Is that Big Bob who thinks he's still only twenty-one?"* Alison giggled.

"Hello gorgeous," he said, leaning forward onto his desk and lowering his voice. "How are you?"

*"I'm fine. But listen, I've got a bit of news."*

"Well this is the newsroom." He smiled into the mouthpiece.

She chuckled again. *"This isn't for public consumption."*

"What isn't?"

He heard her take a breath. *"How would you feel about me working away for a few weeks?"*

"Where do you mean, 'away'? And how long would be 'a few weeks'?"

*"How about our New York office and, say, six weeks?"*

"New York? That sounds brilliant for you, Alison." He leaned back in his chair, swivelled round and looked to see if anyone was within earshot. "But when exactly?"

*"Wouldn't be until the end of August, going through September but my boss just asked me this morning if I'd be interested."*

"Well of course you'd be interested, wouldn't you? I mean, an opportunity like that." None of his colleagues were nearby. He turned back round to face his computer screen. "Could I come with you?"

*"I don't know, it's only an initial conversation I've had. But you couldn't get that much time off could you?"* Alison sounded surprised.

"Not six weeks, no. But I could come over near the end and we could have a little holiday there before you have to come back?"

*"I'll find out a bit more and we can talk about it later."* Again laughter in her voice. *"I just wanted to see what your reaction would be."*

"Sounds great. We'll talk later then."

\*　\*　\*

Strong slipped unnoticed into the CID room and stood for a moment to study those members of the team at work. What he'd said to Flynn earlier was true. They'd given him every bit of support they could have over the past few years.

Detective Sergeant Jim Ryan was sitting at his desk with his back to him, on the telephone. Ryan and Stainmore were the two DS's in the team. Thirty-four, slim, with receding fair hair, Ryan couldn't be more pleased with life. He'd become a father nineteen months ago and was loving every moment he could spend with his little girl. Strong was proud to have been asked to be one of her godparents.

Detective Constable Malcolm Atkinson sat at the adjacent desk and was intently studying his computer screen. Atkinson was the most recent addition to the CID team, twenty-five years old, a keen and intelligent lad, Strong thought.

With a drawer to a filing cabinet open, DC John Darby was rummaging through some files. Darby was thirty-seven, originally from Nottingham and had the unfortunate habit of making the most amusing comments without realising he was doing so.

Kelly Stainmore was sitting at her workstation facing away from him. Several files were open on her desk but she was staring at the window, deep in thought.

Strong was about to make his presence known when Detective Constable Luke Ormerod entered. Ormerod, at thirty-nine, was his most experienced officer. Short and stocky with thick black hair and a caterpillar moustache, he should have been a Sergeant by now but he spoke his mind and wasn't too concerned who heard. That probably had held his career back. However, he seemed satisfied with his lot and Strong couldn't imagine the team without him.

"Morning, guv," he said cheerily. "Everything alright?"

"Well, I need to speak to everyone." He looked round the room. "Where are the others?"

Ormerod quickly assessed who was in. "Trevor is out talking to the second hand car dealer on Doncaster Road who's had three cars driven off his forecourt in a week, and Sam's downstairs interviewing a shoplifter nicked in Primark in The Ridings."

DC's Trevor Newell, originally from Lincoln, a tall slim lad of twenty-six and Sam Kirkland, a chunky thirty-four year-old from Leeds, completed the team.

"What's wrong, guv?" Ormerod asked, a puzzled expression on his face.

"All right, Ladies and Gents, listen up please." Strong walked to the centre of the room, then glanced back towards Ormerod. "Just shut the door, will you, Luke."

Strong waited until Ormerod had closed the door. "I just wanted to say that I've appreciated all your support over the past months since I filled the role of Acting DCI." He paused for a moment. "I'm afraid that's coming to an end soon and I'll be back to Detective Inspector." There were slight mutterings. "We will be having a new DCI taking up the post at the beginning of the month. I'll let Detective Chief Superintendent Flynn tell you about that at the appropriate time but I thought you deserved to know this bit of news from me."

There was a palpable feeling of shock in the room. It was Ormerod who finally spoke. "That's not right, guv. We all know you're the best man for the job. You know this patch inside out." He held his arms wide and took in the whole room. "Everybody here thinks the same as me. We're all part of your team."

Again, mutterings of agreement.

"Absolutely," Ryan added.

"I really appreciate that but I'm afraid the powers that be have decided they want an external appointment. Now, I'm sure you'll give the new man all the support and encouragement you've given me when he arrives." Strong looked at his colleagues as they reacted to the news. "Okay, that's it for now."

# 8
## Tuesday 10<sup>th</sup> July 2001

Three days later, news of a blockage on the M1 on her usual route into the hospital threw Belinda into a bad mood. She'd struggle to make ward handover on time. Sister would no doubt take great delight in ticking her off. Nothing for it but to take the old road to Leeds through Outwood.

As she suspected, traffic was heavier than normal on the alternative route; temporary road works also added stop, start for several miles. Just as she drew to a halt once more, she glanced off to the left and noticed the houses. She was trying to remember the number on the conveyance form she had seen a few days before when something else caught her eye.

A black BMW was parked on the side, about thirty yards in front of her. She squinted to get a clearer view just as the traffic moved another few yards. At a halt again, she could finally see the number plate. No doubt, it was Charlie's. Her heart rate rocketed and she felt nauseous. She studied the front doors and focussed on a mid-terrace with a white front door and black numbers. She was sure that was the address. But what was he doing here at this time of the day? He should be in his office.

A loud honk from the car behind startled her. Traffic had moved forward. She put her car into gear and slowly moved off, giving the scene one further sweep. Fifty yards on and the traffic stopped once again. She adjusted her mirror to focus on Charlie's BMW. She was puzzled. After the discussion they'd had a few nights back, Charlie had indeed provided a list of their investments. Things looked very healthy. But there was something niggling away at her about his whole attitude. There were things he wasn't telling her. Again, as the traffic moved off, she put her mirror back in position and began thinking about what to do.

*   *   *

Stainmore entered the CID room, a manila folder under her arm and a polystyrene cup of coffee in her hand. She removed her coat threw some keys onto her desk and lowered herself into the chair at her workstation on which the bundle of mail retrieved from Denise Whitaker's house sat.

"Everything all right with you, sarge?" DC Luke Ormerod asked from the next desk. Ormerod was the only other officer in the CID room that morning.

"What? Oh yeah, fine, Luke. Just been back out to Normanton."

He turned his swivel chair to face her and noticed her thick cardigan. He looked surprised, it was the middle of summer. "Your unexplained death?"

"Yep." She took a drink of her coffee. "Been looking for anything to give us a clue on relatives, but I'm struggling."

"What about bank accounts, anything there?"

She pointed to the pile of envelopes on her desk. "Everything on standing order or direct debits. Various allowances in, housing benefit, that sort of thing; rent, water, electric, gas etc. out. If those workmen hadn't had to gain entry, she'd have still been there. Regular money in to cover all the outgoings. Missed by no one. Makes you wonder how many other poor sods are out there now; dead; nobody knowing, nobody caring."

"Wow, we are in a down mood today, aren't we?"

She shrugged. "No, not really, just makes you think, that's all." Both hands around her coffee cup she took another sip, looking at Ormerod over the lip. "Also called in and spoke to the coroner's officer on the way back. He's thinking about placing an ad in the Wakefield Express." She drained the cup and dropped it into the bin by her desk. "Anyway, it doesn't appear she had a mobile either and I've just got the land line records from BT." She pulled out some pieces of paper from the manila file. "Last call out on Friday 26th May last year. Since then, only twelve calls in, and eight of those were from overseas call centres, we think."

"What about the other four?"

"Just going to check those out now."

Ormerod stepped over to Stainmore's desk. Quietly, he said, "I've not really had a chance to talk to you, Kelly, but what do you reckon to the guv dropping back to DI?"

Stainmore swivelled in her chair and tapped her teeth with a pencil as she gave the question some thought. "I think he's pretty pissed off," she finally said. "I mean, he's done a good job since Cunningham went. As he said the other day when he told us, we've all supported him."

Ormerod was about to say something else but Stainmore jumped in, "So I'm going to check out those other numbers now."

A split second later, Ormerod understood when he realised Strong had just breezed into the CID room.

"Ah, Kelly, you're back," Strong greeted. "Anything interesting from Normanton?"

"Just telling Luke here, guv. Nothing much of anything. There was a stroppy letter in the mail pile from her dental practice. She must have missed an appointment, and they wanted her to rearrange. I passed the details on to Dr Symonds. I'm assuming he might need dental records for identification. I mean, we're all assuming it was Denise in there."

Strong nodded. "It would be embarrassing if it was someone else."

She picked up a second set of keys, a Yale and a deadlock and began to study them. "I wonder what these are for?"

"Where were they?" Strong enquired.

"On a hook in her hallway along with her house keys. But they don't fit any locks at her place, back or front."

She put them down again. "Anyway, what news from forensics?" she asked.

A grin appeared on Strong's face. "I think they secretly enjoyed the challenge. They got a local plumber in to disconnect the bath, draw it out and then drain the contents off. After that, they were able to lift the body into a bodybag."

"I'd have thought it would have disintegrated." Stainmore said.

"Actually, the part of the body below the water is better preserved than that above. A process called adipocere, apparently. A bit like mummification."

Stainmore screwed up her face.

"Initial toxicology shows nothing suspicious and the PM's taking place tomorrow," Strong continued.

"I presume you'll want me to attend?"

"Please Kelly, you may as well follow it through." From Stainmore's desk he picked up a card she'd brought in with the other paperwork. "What's this? *Talisman Club*? Never heard of it."

"Me neither, guv. Found it on the bedside cabinet."

He turned and showed it to Ormerod. "Mean anything to you, Luke?"

Ormerod took the card and flipped it over. He shook his head as he gave it back to Stainmore. "No and I don't recognise the symbol either."

"Probably nothing," Strong dismissed, then began a discussion with Ormerod. "Those distraction burglaries, any developments there?"

Stainmore studied the mysterious card for a few seconds before placing it back in the file, pulling out the BT information and picking up the phone.

Ten minutes later, she knocked and entered Strong's office where he'd returned after talking to Ormerod.

"Yes, Kelly," he said.

She approached his desk. "Maybe something and nothing, guv."

He looked up from his paperwork. "If you're puzzling, it's probably something. You know, coppers' instinct."

"One of those numbers that called Denise Whitaker's land line last June ..."

"Go on."

"When I rang it, it was answered by the office of Charles Chamberlain Associates."

He leaned back in his chair. "The commercial legal practice?"

"Yes. Only the receptionist said she'd never heard of a Denise Whitaker, or Denis for that matter, and she definitely wasn't a client. She told me she'd worked there for the past four years."

"But your gut feeling is telling you ...?"

"Not sure." She shrugged. "Like I said, probably something and nothing. Might even have been a misdialled number. One other caller was the local paper. Said they were conducting a sales initiative around that time, you know, free paper delivery for a six month subscription, one from the dentist prior to that letter I was talking about and one from her doctor's surgery. Again, I've passed that on to Dr Symonds."

"And no relatives coming out of the woodwork?"

"Not so far. I'm just ringing round the likely solicitor's practices that might have had Denise as a client, from the point of view of a will."

"Well, if that draws a blank, and the PM comes up with nothing suspicious, then I think you've wasted enough time on the case."

\* \* \*

"I've had a word with the boss," Chandler said, referring to the paper's editor, "and he's agreed to take your friend on for the summer, subject to interview."

"That's great, John," Souter responded.

Mid-afternoon and Chandler had wandered onto the newsroom floor at the newspaper's headquarters.

"She'll have to muck in with anything though, copying, general office duties," he went on. "She won't be let loose reporting. She can shadow you and Janey for a while."

"I'm sure she'll be delighted with that, thanks. Who'll interview her and when?"

"Get her to call Selina in HR and we'll sort something out. I've emailed her to expect a call."

The phone on Souter's desk rang as Chandler took his leave.

"Hello?" Souter answered.

*"Bob, my man,"* came the Glaswegian voice from the earpiece.

"Now then, Charlie," he said, recognising his friend from the Glasgow Herald, "how's life in the far north?"

*"Ah'm no' that far north, cheeky bastard, otherwise ah'd 'ave been on The Orcadian in Orkney or The Shetland Times!"*

"I'm sure you'd have fitted in well as a southerner from Shettleston," Souter chuckled. "Anyway, what nuggets do you have for me?"

Ritchie's tone grew serious. *"Tread carefully, Bob. This Kenny Brogan is one evil bastard from what I can make out. Nothin' sticks tae him. 'Teflon Kenny' somebody called him."*

Souter picked up a pencil. "But he has a record of getting himself in on the action though?"

*"Thistle Developments have a reputation of securing some lucrative projects, aye. They've made some big money up here. But always reekin' of dirty money. A lot of construction people I've spoken to wouldnae touch anythin' they're involved with. They've got their feet under the table with some big council developments and word is they have some influential people in their pockets. Always interested in stuff that has European funding too."*

"So this retail development would sound right up their street," Souter pondered.

*"Absolutely. And word here is they're attracting too much of the wrong sort o' attention so they're lookin' at*

*things further afield. This Yorkshire project would be their first foray south o' the border."*

"So where did Brogan get his influence and money from?"

*"Well he's a smart cookie. Took a Business Studies degree at Strathclyde University. That's where he met his missus. Dropped on lucky there too. Some minor aristocrat, Lady Morag Hamilton. Her faither died soon after they got spliced."*

"Convenient." Souter was taking shorthand notes.

*"And she copped for a shed load o' money plus some big estate near Dalmellington."*

"Dalmellington? That's Ayrshire, isn't it?"

*"Aye. In the middle o' bloody naewhere. But on top o' that, her brother's an MEP, so ye can imagine, he's got more contacts than a telephone exchange. You know what those bastards are like wi' their snouts in the trough. Bloody gravy train, I wouldnae gie them the steam aff ma tea!"*

Souter smiled. "Not a big EU fan then, Charlie?"

*"Make me boak."*

"So word is Brogan is expert at working the system?"

*"Got a PhD in it. And he's an expert at exploitin' people's weak spots for his own ends."*

"Anything concrete?"

*"Too careful for that. But there were strong rumours he was behind that Stuart Williamson scandal last year."*

"Was that the financial guy from the city council that committed suicide? Jumped off the Erskine Bridge?"

*"That's the fella. Smeared the bugger's reputation afterwards wi' rumours he was intae rent boys and such. Then they discovered all sorts o' irregularities, especially wi' development projects. He ended up carryin' the can. Brogan was involved in some o' those projects too but nothin' stuck tae him."*

"Thanks for that, Charlie. And if you discover anything else ..."

*"I'll let you know. And one more thing, he has a heid case as a sidekick. Name o' Kennedy, Wullie Kennedy. I think he's done time for GBH and such."*

Souter was silent for a moment as he wrote down the last details.

*" But ... remember what I said,"* Ritchie added, *"tread carefully."*

"See you, mate." Souter ended the call and reread the notes he'd taken. Brogan had certainly got his interest.

\* \* \*

When Belinda arrived home, just after half past ten, Charlie was out.

"Said something about a meeting at the golf club," Anthony informed her.

She looked round the hallway. "What happened to that bin bag full of clothes I meant to take for recycling?"

"Dunno. Maybe Dad took it," he suggested then disappeared back to his room.

In the kitchen she made herself a bacon sandwich and a mug of tea, then sat down in the lounge. Fortunately, her shift had been busy, not allowing her to dwell on the sighting of Charlie's car near the house. But now, in the quiet of the room, she began to ponder. Her thoughts took in the investments he'd told her about. There were a couple of savings accounts in joint names, kept below the government's guarantee level, plus two ISA's in separate names, and finally the Outwood house which he claimed to have bought for £55,000. All that seemed fairly believable but she wasn't convinced he was telling her everything.

She finished her supper and walked into their bedroom. Opening Charlie's drawer again, she rummaged through, looking for the envelope. Nothing. The crafty sod must have moved it. Not surprising, though.

A yawn surprised her. She had to get up for an early shift tomorrow. Back in the lounge, she collected her mug and plate and took them to the kitchen. When she returned to the bedroom, she began to get ready for bed. She hoped Charlie wouldn't be too late or noisy to disturb her.

Slipping between the sheets, she picked up a book and, sitting up, began to read. She must have nodded off, because the next thing she knew, she opened her eyes to find Charlie stripping out of his clothes and putting on his pyjamas.

"That backside looks a bit red," she said spontaneously.

He pulled the bottoms up quickly. "Been sitting on it all day," he said, climbing into bed.

"Busy day in the office then?"

"Yep." He leaned over and switched off his bedside lamp.

"No break then; you weren't out and about anywhere?" She was wide awake again.

He yawned. "No, just boring paperwork and a couple of meetings, that's all."

"And to top it off another meeting at the golf club?"

"Mmm." He lay on his side with his back to her.

She looked down at him. "Still, at least you'd have had a drink there?"

"Managed a pint, yes."

"So you weren't out of the office all day then?"

He turned back to face her. "What is all this? The Spanish Inquisition?"

Again, she surprised herself remaining calm. "Did you hear about the accident on the M1? It was shut when I set off for work."

He rubbed his face with his hand. "I know this might be fascinating information but what're you getting at?"

"I had to take the alternative route into Leeds." A puzzled expression grew on his face and she continued, "Up Leeds Road through Outwood."

"Oh, I see." His perplexed features changed to anger.

"So I was just wondering how I came to see your car parked up outside *your investment*."

"I didn't realise you were keeping tabs on me. You can get trackers fitted you know, then you'll always know where I am. And if you must know, I'd nipped out to check on the place. As a responsible owner I need to make sure there are no leaking pipes, the power hadn't tripped, boring stuff like that. Is that okay?" He held her gaze for a few seconds then turned away. "Now, if you don't mind, you're not the only one with a busy day tomorrow."

She studied him for a few more minutes before turning off her own bedside lamp and settling down in the bed. The bastard was lying – again. And she was wide awake, probably would be for hours now. He wouldn't have admitted he'd been there if she hadn't challenged him. And she wasn't sure she'd had the full story from him, even now. Maybe he did feel it was so insignificant, he'd forgotten that he'd nipped out of the office. No, she was sure there was more to it than that. She'd find out but she'd have to be as sneaky as he was. Her mind turned events over for some time. He was breathing deeply now, in that initial descent into a deep sleep. Finally, after what seemed like ages, sleep overtook her as well.

# 9
## Wednesday 11<sup>th</sup> July 2001

"You look a bit pasty," Ormerod greeted Stainmore as she put her bag down by the side of her desk.

"Just been to the weirdest post-mortem I've ever had to attend."

"Of course, the body in the bath."

She sat down in her chair. "What was left of it."

Strong sauntered in and joined in the discussion. "Everything all right, Kelly, you look a bit tired."

Stainmore looked round at the otherwise empty CID room. "Anyone else like to contribute to how shit I look?"

Ormerod grinned.

"Sorry," Strong said. "Just concerned, that's all."

She held up her hands and shook her head. "No, I'm sorry. I didn't mean to bite your heads off."

"So what were the findings?"

"Natural causes. Evidence of a heart attack."

Strong nodded. "Heart, eh?"

"Yes. That tied in with her medical history, Dr Symonds confirmed. Apparently, she was on medication for high blood pressure as well. You'll also be glad to know dental records confirmed it was Denise Whitaker, fifty-eight years of age as reported by Housing."

Strong leaned against the adjacent desk and nodded. "So, natural causes."

"Actual cause of death, though, was drowning," she continued. "Head dropped into the water and, well …"

"That's not surprising. Forgot to say when you were out, Kelly, Denise's GP surgery rang for you and I took it. I think they were embarrassed. Her own GP retired last April and the new one only lasted three months before he moved south. So, her third GP in five months wasn't aware of her as a patient. Hence she wasn't missed."

Stainmore rolled her eyes. "Great. God help us if we ever become ill and need to count on our doctor."

"Anyway, that's it then," Strong concluded. "Case closed. What else have you got on now?"

She sighed and shuffled some paperwork around before pulling out some sheets. "I've got the Donaldson rape case coming to trial next week and then there's these distraction burglaries that Luke's been working on for the past two months."

"You'll need to be on the ball for that next week." He leaned in closer. "You're okay with your evidence though, aren't you?" Stainmore nodded and he turned his attention to Ormerod. "But we've got to get to the bottom of those distractions, Luke."

"I know, guv."

"Okay." Strong headed for the door. "I'll catch up with the rest of the team later."

When he'd gone, Ormerod turned to Stainmore. "You're not one hundred per cent happy with the Whitaker case, I can tell."

Stainmore picked up the mystery set of keys and began fiddling with them. "No," she said, "Not entirely." Focussing back to her colleague, "I just want to check on a couple of things first before I hand it all back to the Housing Department."

The phone on the desk rang and she answered. "Oh, hi Jason," she said, listened for a few seconds then continued, "No, go ahead with that and I'll let you know if I get anywhere with it." A few more nods of the head as she listened to what Jason was saying, punctuated by several 'yep's' before she brought the call to an end. With a loud sigh, she replaced the handset.

"You sound exasperated," Ormerod said.

"No ... I mean, he's a nice lad but ..."

"Who was that? Your new best friend, Jason?"

"He's the coroner's officer I'm dealing with. He's one of those guys who tells you everything in the minutest detail. Anyway, the ad will be in the paper this week."

*   *   *

Susan was delighted with the chance to work with the Yorkshire Post newspaper. She'd made the call the following morning to Selina in HR and arranged to come in for an interview at the end of the week.

Souter, meanwhile, had picked Janey Clarke's brains about the Lofthouse Retail Development.

"Why do I get the feeling you know more than you're telling me?" she asked.

"I just think it would be something interesting for Susan to get involved with when she comes here for the summer." He'd told her about Susan's upcoming interview and what Chandler had said about shadowing Janey and himself. "Nice bit of local politics," he concluded.

"I still think you're up to something." She turned back to her desk.

Of course you do, Souter thought. I'd be a bit disappointed if you didn't, you being an aspiring journalist.

The retail scheme was returning to the full Planning Committee the following week and the outstanding matters were expected to be passed without too much opposition. Souter had dug back through their records and identified one or two of the main players, as far as the Council was concerned. The Head of Planning was Michael Pitchforth, married with three children and had been in post for nearly ten years. The Leader of the Council was the Labour councillor, Bernard Faulkner. He was married but did have a bit of a reputation as a ladies man. It was his aim to drive this project through.

He'd also put in a call to his friend DS Ron Boyle of Strathclyde police following the conversation he'd had with Charlie Ritchie. He wanted to find out a bit more about Kenny Brogan but, more importantly, his supposed muscle, William Kennedy.

His computer pinged, indicating new mail. When he opened it up, he found it was from Charlie Ritchie.

*"Just thought you might be interested in who you're dealing with,"* he wrote. Attached were two picture files. When he opened them up, he discovered photos of Kenny Brogan, short fair hair, about five foot six inches tall, looking dapper in an expensive looking overcoat, striding in to offices, obviously in Glasgow.

His desk phone rang and Patricia on reception announced it was a Mr Boyle returning his call.

"Ron, thanks for calling back," Souter said.

*"No problem, Bob. How's that new bird of yours? Still not found you out yet?"*

"We've been together for over a year now." Souter laughed. "And there's nothing to find out."

*"Right,"* Boyle said in a disbelieving tone. *"Anyway, you wanted a heads up on a couple of names."*

I'd appreciate that."

*"Well, I'd just caw canny with these two, if you know what I mean,"* Boyle warned.

This was becoming a recurring theme, Souter thought. "What do you mean, Ron?"

*"Slippery wee bastard is our Brogan. Lots of reputation but we've got nothing on him. Too clever for that, but loads of rumours about dodgy building deals with his company, Thistle Developments."*

Souter tapped his pencil on a pad. "I've heard that. He's looking to do something down here which is why I'm doing some checking."

*"The other one, Wullie Kennedy, is a real psycho. Apparently he went to school with Brogan but thick as shite. Wiry but deceptively strong and violent with it."*

"Not a good combination then?"

Boyle laughed mirthlessly. *"I'd say the worst. He's got some serious form, ABH, GBH, robbery with violence. But since Brogan seems to have taken him under his wing, he hasn't brought himself to our attention."*

"So how long has he been working with Brogan."

"*These past two years. Ever since Thistle started to move up the leagues.*"

"Obviously Brogan feels Kennedy serves a purpose though?"

"*I would say so. I mean there have been rumours about Thistle's dealings up here. Opposition to some of their projects mysteriously evaporating, if you get my drift. But nothing we can get involved with. But if they're muscling in down your way, I'd be very careful how you go, Bob.*"

"That's the second word of caution I've received from up your way, Ron. Appreciate your concern."

Souter ended the call, made a few notes, put his jacket on and left the newsroom.

# 10
## Tuesday 17<sup>th</sup> July 2001

On several occasions during that week, Belinda chose the Outwood route to the hospital. Charlie's car was nowhere to be seen. Then, on the Friday, the roadworks had altered and traffic in her direction was diverted by way of a couple of side streets while work continued on the main road. After turning left down the first street, she was following the signs, about to turn right. A black car parked on the street straight ahead caught her eye. Surely not?

She was in a traffic flow, unable to stop, so followed the diversion back onto the main road. However, instead of following the road to Leeds, she turned back towards home. The way Charlie had reacted the week before persuaded her to take another look.

She turned back into the diversion again but this time drove straight on, slowly past the black BMW. Definitely his car. A quick three-point turn and she passed the car again. She checked her watch. No time to do anything today, she needed to get to work, but she was determined to find out what was going on. Next week, she'd use this route regularly and give herself more time.

She didn't have long to wait. The following Tuesday, the diversions and roadworks had all been removed. No sign of his car on the main road so she turned down the side street as she had done the week before. There it was again, parked in the same spot. She'd given herself an extra half hour to get to work so she parked on the opposite side.

She felt herself seethe, the adrenaline flowing. As she walked up the street to the main road, she tried to calm herself. Deep breaths. She needed to be in control. Right at the top and two doors down, she was standing outside the house with the white door and black numbers. The first ring on the bell went unanswered. At the second push, she heard footsteps on a staircase. The door opened partly and there stood her husband, a shocked look on his face.

"Belinda. What are you doing here?"

"I could ask you the same question. Mind if I come in?" She made to bundle her way past him and into the house.

He held the door firm. "I was just heading back to the office."

"But I'm sure you can spare a few minutes to show me round, seeing as it *is* our investment."

This time he sighed and swung the door wide. "If you insist."

She stepped straight into the living room. "How come you're here again anyway?"

"Well ... they came to read the meters, so I had to make arrangements to be here for that."

She turned and faced him. "They've been then, have they?"

"Yes, about ten minutes. Look, I really have to get back." He looked at his watch. "I've got a meeting at the office."

Belinda began a slow walk around the room. "Just as well the meter reader came when he did." She stopped and looked at the framed print of Rievaulx Abbey hanging above the fireplace.

"Er, what? Yes, I suppose so."

She strolled around the leather settee, rubbing a finger along the back. "Because normally, you can wait in all morning or all afternoon for them." She was back up close to him. "Normally, they give you a window of four hours or so."

"Well, anyway, he's been now, so I must get back. And you need to get going if you're going to make your shift too." He opened the front door. "Where are you parked?"

"Just across from you. You can walk me down, if you like."

Relief spread over his face. "Yes. Yes, of course. Come on then."

They set off back down the side street in silence until they reached Charlie's car.

"Well, I'll see you tonight," he said, leaning forward in an attempt to give her a quick peck on the cheek.

She moved her face away, said nothing and walked over to her own car. Her anger was simmering just below the surface, but she was determined to remain controlled. As she performed another three-point turn, she saw her husband wave and smile to her as he sat in the driver's seat, mobile phone to his ear. Arrogant bastard, she thought. At the top of the road she turned left to head towards Leeds but pulled in about fifty yards further on. Something wasn't right. She could sense it in the house. Charlie was too keen to get her out of there. And as for all that bollocks about meter readers and meetings back at the office, well, she just didn't believe a word of it.

Her nearside door mirror afforded an unrestricted view back down the pavement. She was about to drive away when a figure in a black coat appeared. She was a bit too far away to be sure that the woman had come from the house but there was no mistaking who it was; Anita Matthews, Charlie's personal assistant and family friend.

She suddenly felt cold; and sick. Her stomach was turning upside down. Anita walked in her direction then turned down the street where Charlie was parked. A couple of minutes later, his BMW appeared at the junction, Anita in the passenger seat. With a break in the traffic, the car turned right towards Wakefield.

She struggled to breathe. Tears welled in her eyes but she made a great effort to hold them back. After a few gasps, she managed to regulate her breathing. She dabbed her eyes with a paper tissue and checked for mascara smudges in the mirror. Another glance at her watch and she set off for the hospital.

*  *  *

Strong strode into the CID room, sheaf of papers in his hand and began to address the officers present. "Okay team, listen up," he said in a loud voice.

Attention focussed on Strong as he approached a display board on the CID room wall. "This pair, I'm assuming they're the same, are seriously getting on my tits now." He pointed to two nondescript Identikit images before fixing a photograph of an elderly man to join the three elderly women already up there.

"After a gap of five weeks, our distraction specialists have struck again." He indicated the latest picture. "Frank Parsons, eighty-three year old widower and late of the Green Howards." Strong looked round the room. "And I know this, how? Because our enterprising distractors have walked away with old Frank's Second World War medals, along with his life savings of fifteen hundred pounds."

The detectives let out a collective groan.

"So, Luke, you've been on this from the beginning. Take us through what we know because Flynn wants our full attention on this."

Ormerod stood and approached the board. In turn, he ran through the sequence of robberies. "Florence Harvey, widow, seventy-six was targeted on 19th April at her semi-detached home in Hemsworth. Two men, one around forty, stocky with a thick moustache, wearing overalls and a cap, holding a clip board, told her he was checking on water pressure and could he test the kitchen taps. Younger assistant, shorter, slim, dressed in jeans and black sweat shirt comes in behind and sneaks upstairs. She didn't clock him until he was coming down again. The older one spins her a story about his apprentice having a weak bladder. Calm as you like, they wander off down the street. After they'd gone, she checked upstairs and found the three hundred pounds she'd put by for her grand-daughter's eighteenth birthday present had gone."

"No sightings by the neighbours?" Strong asked. "No strange vehicles seen in the immediate vicinity?"

"Nothing." He pointed to the second photo. "Victim number two, eighty-one year old widow, Hannah Williamson living in a bungalow in Walton visited by two men on April 25th. Similar routine – testing water pressure, the older guy talks his way in whilst his younger compatriot sneaks in to the bedroom. This time the contents of her handbag were rifled and one hundred and fifty pounds gone along with some gold and silver jewellery. Again, no indication of how they'd arrived or left. Thirdly, eighty-two year old Winifred Haywood targeted on May 3rd. Unfortunately, Winnie is in the early stages of dementia, so it was a bit more difficult getting an account of her encounter. Her daughter was visiting her flat in Sandal when she saw our two walking down the road, away from her mother's front door." He indicated the images of the suspects. "Those are the best likenesses she could provide when she tried to think back. It was only when she went into the flat and found Winnie in a state of confusion that the daughter started to piece together what had happened. Of course, by this time Little and Large are nowhere to be seen. Daughter thinks about twenty pounds had gone from the drawer in the dresser that she'd put there two days before. Also her mother's gold watch, a present from her late father has disappeared."

"These items have genuinely gone, Luke?" Strong put in. "Not doubting the daughter but people with dementia do hide things."

"No, she's not that bad, guv. Besides, the daughter searched the whole flat."

"Okay, so after some time off, our friends decide to return. So, where have they been in the meantime. Luke, have you checked with other forces, South or North Yorkshire, Greater Manchester?"

"On it."

"Can we revisit the neighbours of all four victims. Did they see anyone suspicious, maybe matching the descriptions of … I like that, Luke … Little and Large. Any strange vehicles parked nearby, not necessarily at the time of the distractions. They may have been recceing the places. Okay, you all know the routine. Let's have a big effort on this one. We all have, or have had parents or grandparents that could be vulnerable to this sort of crime. Let's get these shits before they have the chance to upset somebody else's mother or father."

Strong paused at Stainmore's desk on the way out. "Everything okay, Kelly?"

"Yeah, guv. They reckon Thursday for my evidence."

"The rape trial?"

She nodded.

"Good."

He'd begun to walk on when Stainmore added, "Oh, Denise Whittaker, I've got her GP surgery ringing back with next of kin details and I'm waiting on a couple of solicitors to get back to me."

"Well don't waste too much more time on it," Strong said before indicating the display board. "These scum are our priority."

\*   \*   \*

About a hundred yards from Wood Street police station, Souter, Janey Clarke and Susan walked up a few steps and into Wakefield Town Hall, following the directions for the Council Chamber. Up the stairs, they entered through some double doors and found themselves at the rear of the chamber, raised up from the main council area. Three rows of solid oak panelled seating were set aside for the public. About a dozen or so people, sitting in ones and twos, were already there when they entered. Souter, Susan and Janey sat on the rear row towards the centre.

As he settled onto the uncomfortable seat, Souter, influenced by the surroundings, allowed his thoughts to drift. Whitewashed walls with exposed stone details to the stained glass feature windows and doorways gave a citadel feel to the light and airy space. He took in the chamber itself. On a podium, like some throne, large wooden seats were placed before a long desk with a lectern built in. The councillors themselves were treated to padded wooden seats with armrests. Around twenty or more of them had begun to congregate, men and women of all ages. He imagined meetings of the last century where only men would have been present. Victorian characters with large mutton chop whiskers, top hats and morning coats perhaps. The building would have hardly changed in all that time. If only it could speak, what kind of secret deals and skulduggery had gone on in decades past? More to the point, what underhand shenanigans were going on now?

After a few minutes, he was brought back to the present with a request for the assembly to stand as the chair of the meeting took his seat on the podium like some High Court judge. The chair, a tall, bordering on obese man with thinning dark hair and rimless glasses, announced that he was the Leader of the Council, Bernard Faulkner. Souter knew he was fifty-two and imagined too many social lunches and charity dinners had contributed to his appearance. The slightly shorter, slim figure of the Head of Planning, Michael Pitchforth, accompanied him onto the dais. According to Souter's information, he was fifty-seven and looked healthy for his age. A full head of white hair and a deep tan helped with that analysis. Whilst remaining on their feet, a prayer was said, reinforcing the ethereal atmosphere.

The meeting proper began with a few building projects briefly discussed and, for the most part, approved. Fifteen minutes in, the double doors behind Souter opened and a shortish, well-dressed man quietly entered the chamber and took a seat in the front public row, near the door. Kenneth Brogan had arrived. Souter watched his body language. Confidently, Brogan relaxed in his seat and his gaze swept round the councillors present before his attention fixed on Faulkner and Pitchforth.

A councillor from the floor was speaking but Souter spotted the signs of recognition of Brogan by both men on the podium. Finally, the Lofthouse development was announced. Faulkner outlined the potentially huge advantages of such a scheme to the council, not least regenerating old mining land and bringing it back into use. Once he'd concluded his contribution to the meeting, it was Pitchforth's turn to address the council. He confirmed his department had scrutinised the proposals and were very much in favour of the scheme going ahead.

"What's in it for you?" came a voice from the floor. Laughter followed, along with other shouts, some in support of that comment, others obviously annoyed with the intervention. Souter shifted his attention quickly between Faulkner, who was attempting to bring the meeting to order, and Brogan, who was slowly shaking his head. Pitchforth looked uncomfortable.

Eventually, calm reigned once more as Faulkner responded by saying that it was in the interests of Wakefield as a whole that this scheme was approved. More mutterings, waving of arms and shaking of heads from some of the councillors finally died away. After a few speeches from the floor in support as well as against, the proposed scheme was voted on and approved. With that, the meeting formally ended.

Souter watched as Brogan stood, gave an almost imperceptible nod towards the two men on the podium and turned to leave. As he got to the double doors, Souter impeded his exit. "Mr Brogan," he said.

Brogan looked him up and down. "Who are you?"

"My name's Souter. I'm a journalist with the Yorkshire Post."

"So?" He looked as if he had smelt something distasteful. "What do you want with me?" he asked in an educated Scottish accent.

"I just wondered if you had a reaction for our readers on this afternoon's vote."

"Why would I?" He moved forward to barge past Souter. "If you don't mind …"

Souter stood firm. "So your company doesn't have a vested interest in the outcome of the approval of the Lofthouse Development then?"

Brogan put the palm of his hand into Souter's chest and pushed him to one side. "Excuse me," he said, making his way out of the chamber.

Souter followed. "No truth in the rumours that Thistle Developments are earmarked for the project?" he shouted after him.

Brogan turned and took a couple of steps towards him, "What was your name again?" he calmly asked.

Janey Clarke and Susan were standing behind Souter at this point. "Robert Souter," he answered.

Brogan nodded. "Souter. The Yorkshire Post." He pointed a finger at him. "I'll remember you, Robert Souter."

They stood motionless and watched him walk away.

"Who's that?" Janey asked.

"Oh, just some ..." Souter paused, "... psychotic delusional."

Janey looked puzzled; Susan seemed unnerved.

\*   \*   \*

"No, I just felt in need of a pint," Souter said, once Strong had returned with the beers. "I was in a council meeting over the road from you and I thought, we haven't had a meet up for a bit."

They were sitting in the Black Horse on Westgate. One or two office workers were winding down from a day talking on their phones or glued to the screen, tapping out texts. Early doors custom.

"Not surprised you needed a drink." Strong sipped his beer. "Can hardly be riveting stuff at these meetings."

"Oh, you'd be surprised. The challenge is to make it sound interesting for the readers, even if it's only filling obscure column inches." Souter proceeded to down half the pint in one hit.

Strong watched him put his glass back on the table, lean back and close his eyes for a few seconds. "Everything okay, Bob?"

He opened them again. "What? Yeah, sorry, Col. It's just I'm thinking … well, it's coming up to the anniversary."

"What, you and Alison?"

"No. Adam."

"Shit. Sorry." Strong felt bad. Of course, Bob's son, taken to Canada by his first wife when she left him just before he took the job on the Glasgow Herald. "It must be … what, two years now?"

"Two years next month, the fifth."

Strong sat in silence, remembering the day his friend had called him, distraught at hearing the news of Adam's drowning.

Souter looked unfocussed at a space on the far wall. "He'd have been nine last Christmas. Growing up into a great lad." Snapping himself out of his reverie, he lifted his pint. "Anyway, can't dwell on that now."

Strong nodded, not entirely convinced. "That was a nice piece your paper put about our body in the bath case last week, by the way," he said, after a pause. "Kelly thought your reporter hit the right tone."

"That was young Janey. She's good. Nothing suspicious about that, was there?"

"Don't think so. Mind you, the PM was a new experience for Kelly."

"I can imagine." Souter smiled.

Strong leaned forward, as if about to take him into his confidence. "Have you ever heard of a 'Talisman Club'?"

Souter's brows furrowed. "No," he said after a few seconds. "Can't say I have."

"Not one of your poncy Leeds establishments?"

Souter laughed. "As if I'd know if it was." Another slurp of his beer. "Where did you hear the name?"

"Oh, it was just a card that turned up somewhere, that's all. Nobody in the team had heard of it either."

Souter drained his glass. "I'll get you another and you can tell me what's occupying your team at the moment."

"Just a half for me. I've got to drive home."

*   *   *

During the journey home from her shift, Belinda felt sick. She'd never been anxious about going home before, but what she'd witnessed that morning had turned her emotions upside down. She parked her car next to Charlie's so she knew he was in.

"Hi Mum," Anthony greeted, as she closed the front door behind her. "Dad's in the lounge. I'm off to bed. I've got an interview for a summer job tomorrow."

She hugged him close. "Of course, Waterstones. Best of luck for that." She pulled his head down and kissed his forehead. "Goodnight, Son. I'm sure you'll do well."

"Thanks." He looked at her with a puzzled expression. "Are you okay?"

"Fine, yeah. Just a difficult shift, that's all."

He turned and climbed the stairs, not noticing her sweeping the back of her hand across her eyes to wipe away some moisture.

She took a deep breath, entered the lounge and closed the door.

Charlie was sitting in his favourite chair, whisky on the side, watching the television on low volume.

She studied him for a second. "So what have you got to say for yourself?"

He looked up slowly. "What do you mean?"

She walked over to the settee, put her bag down but remained standing. She wanted to have all the psychological advantage that she could. "All that crap this morning about meter readers. You were there with her, weren't you?"

His best bewildered look. "Who?"

"Don't give me that innocent shit. I saw her."

He rose to his feet. "Look, I don't know what you think you saw but whatever it was, it wasn't."

She fiddled with her wedding ring. Slowly and deliberately, she said, "I saw Anita leave the house and then you drove her away. She was in the front seat."

He turned away and stood in front of the false fireplace. "It's not what it seems."

"Seems pretty plain to me." She folded her arms and the thought struck her that a psychologist would have a field day with her body language. "How long has this been going on?" Continuing her train of thought, she paid close attention to his actions.

He threw his arms wide in a gesture of innocence. "There's nothing going on. Okay, okay, she was there. But I didn't want you to see her because I knew that's what you'd think. Believe me, there's nothing going on between us. She's just our friend."

"Our friend. *Our* friend!" she exploded. "How do you make that out? She used to be my friend but not anymore. And I can see she's more than just a friend to you."

He took a step forward. "She's not. This is why I tried to keep it quiet. I knew you'd go off like this."

"Well can you blame me? You've just lied and lied. Ever since I discovered those deeds. And for all I know you've been lying to me for years."

Another step forward and his face had turned red. "Christ's sake, Belinda, will you just shut the fuck up and let me get a word in!"

"Don't you dare talk to me like that."

"Look." He grabbed hold of her upper arms. "You're not listening to me."

She struggled. "Let go!"

He shook her then raised his hand. "Just listen …"

"Dad! What's going on?" Anthony was at the door, a shocked look on his face. "What are you doing to Mum?"

Charlie froze then slowly released his grip and turned to face his son. "Nothing … nothing, we were just having a discussion."

"I could hear you in my room. Didn't sound much of a discussion to me."

Belinda moved away from her husband, towards the kitchen.

"Just mind your own business, Anthony," Charlie said.

"You were going to hit Mum."

"No. No, I was just trying to calm her down. I would never hurt your mother."

"Whatever."

Charlie looked from Anthony to Belinda then back again. "I'm going out."

"Where do you think you're going at this time of night?" Belinda asked. "You've had a drink."

"Anywhere. I don't care." He shoved his way past Anthony and Belinda heard the front door open then slam.

Anthony rushed to his mother and put his arms round her. "It's okay, Mum," he said.

From outside they could hear a car fire up and drive away.

# 11
## Wednesday 18th July 2001

*"Belinda … can we talk?"* Charlie sounded contrite. She had no doubt he'd practiced that tone before he rang.

Anthony had set off for his interview and she was sitting gazing out the window onto St John's Square when her phone rang. She remained silent.

*"Look, I'm sorry. I didn't mean to get angry last night."*

She took a deep breath. "You did though. And Anthony had to witness it."

A moment's silence. *"I know. I'm ashamed."*

"You've got some making up to do with that boy. I'm not sure you can make things right with me though."

*"Belinda, don't say that. Look, can we meet up? I know it's your day off today. Howsabout that new Italian place on Northgate? Bit of lunch maybe?"*

"I'm not hungry. Besides, it'll take more than a bit of lunch."

*"Whatever you want. Just a coffee then. Let me explain."*

She gave it a bit of thought. At least it was in public and somewhere neutral. "Okay," she said quietly.

*"Twelve?"*

She checked her watch. "All right."

*"See you then."*

She felt tired; hadn't slept much last night after the big argument. Anthony had made her a hot drink before she insisted he went to bed. He needed to be fresh for this morning. It was only a part-time holiday job, but he loved books and was excited at the prospect of working in a bookshop. Charlie hadn't returned. God knows where he'd spent the night. Probably with his trollop; she'd begun not to care. Their marriage had been dying for years. She'd thought long and hard about what she should do. Anthony was her priority now. She needed to guide him through his exams and on to university, if that's what he wanted to do. She knew she'd have a battle on her hands if she went down the divorce route, Charlie being a lawyer. He'd have sharp friends who specialised in divorce. What was she saying – if – more likely to be when, the way she was feeling at the moment.

But then, she didn't need to make any rash decisions. For the time being, she felt she had to gather evidence. She wandered through to the bedroom. She'd have to be clever; at least as clever as Charlie. She looked round the room, taking in her bedside unit, her chest of drawers, still with piles of pennies and two-pence pieces on top; the dressing table and the large wardrobe, his chest of drawers and finally his bedside cabinet. Another glance at her watch. It was a five minute walk to their rendezvous. Just gone eleven now, so a comfortable forty minutes to carefully search through his things. What she was looking for she wasn't sure, but she'd know if she found anything of use.

She started with his bedside cabinet. It was as she had left it a few days before; no documents relating to Outwood. Next, the chest of drawers. She pulled out the drawers one at a time and carefully felt all round, below his underpants in the top one and his socks in the next. Nothing unusual, but there again, she was the one who put those items in there after washing. The bottom drawer contained scarves, gloves and winter woollies. At the back, her hand touched a small cardboard box. She pulled it out. Condoms, large. Ha, that was a joke. But why would he have condoms? She'd been on the pill since Anthony was born. Bastard. That meant only one thing in her view.

Next, the wardrobe, his side. She rummaged through the pockets of his suits, jackets and coats, looking for receipts, notes, anything. Nothing. And then she felt something solid in the pocket of a suit jacket. Keys for a Yale and a deadlock on a ring with a tag. She pulled them out and read the small label. *"Leeds Road"*. Had to be. She glanced at her watch again; eleven-thirty.

She quickly closed the wardrobe doors, making sure everything was as she had found it then made herself ready. If she got a breeze on, she'd have time to call in on the shop near The Bullring that mended shoes and cut keys.

\*   \*   \*

Strong was in his office when Detective Chief Superintendent Flynn's head popped round the door. "Colin," he said.

"Morning, sir," Strong greeted.

The rest of Flynn followed, closing the door behind himself. "Sorry we haven't had a chance to catch up since but I was wondering how the troops took the news?"

Strong put down his pen and leaned back in his chair. "Disappointed, I think."

"Understandable. They've been with you a fair while." Flynn remained standing. "Did you tell them when DCI Hemingford was starting?"

"Beginning of the month. But I didn't say who it was or anything about him."

Flynn nodded. "I'll introduce him to the team then."

A knock on the door preceded the appearance of Kelly Stainmore.

"Oh, sorry, sir," she said and was about to close the door again.

"That's all right, Kelly. I was just leaving anyway," Flynn said. "I'll catch you later, Colin."

Flynn departed and Stainmore approached Strong's desk. He leaned forward. "So, what news?" he asked.

"Denise Whitaker. Her surgery gave me a name of next of kin. Then Bennetts, one of the solicitor's in town, came back with the same information. Denise has a son, Patrick and he's the sole beneficiary of her estate apparently, such as it is."

"Is he anyone of interest to us?" Strong closed the folder on his desk.

"Bit of petty stuff years ago, shoplifting, but nothing significant. Apparently, he's a porter at Pinderfields."

"Must live locally, if he works there. Still, one for the solicitors to sort out now." Strong stood up and opened the top drawer of his filing cabinet before placing the folder from his desk into one of the files. "Any developments on those distraction burglaries? Flynn never mentioned them but I'll bet he will next time I see him."

"Jim found out there'd been two in and around Barnsley in the period between Winnie Haywood in Sandal and Frank Parsons in Ackworth. Similar descriptions, same MO."

"Any further information from there that helps us?"

"He's getting the DS in charge to email the files as we speak."

Strong closed the cabinet drawer and faced Stainmore. "Has anyone checked to see if there's anything to connect our victims," he pondered.

"How do you mean?"

"I don't know … do they all have meals delivered, by the same people, say? Do they have carers visit from the same care company? Do they play bingo at the same hall? Just another avenue to explore."

"Okay, I'll look into that, guv."

"Thanks, Kelly." Strong sat back down in his chair as Stainmore left his office.

\* \* \*

"Come on then, who was that you challenged at the meeting yesterday?" Janey Clarke was standing, hands on hips, trying to look her most formidable.

Susan stood behind her, a slight smile playing on her lips.

"I thought you were on top of this story, Janey?" Souter responded.

"Obviously not." She turned to Susan. "Do you know more about this?"

"Hey, I'm just the trainee," she said.

"Right," Janey said in a condescending manner. "Well I'm off to court now. On my own. So have fun, the two of you." With that, Clarke put on her jacket and left the newsroom.

Susan pulled up a seat and sat down next to Souter. "She has a point, though. She was supposed to be covering the Lofthouse Development story. I think I'd be a bit teed off if another journo hijacked it."

Souter turned to face Susan. "I haven't 'hijacked the story', as you so dramatically put it. I just haven't told her all I know." He paused a second. "Look, if she was any sort of journalist, she'd know who that was yesterday." He shook his head. "No, sorry, that was unfair. Janey's good at her job. It's just …"

"You think this could be a bit dangerous, right?"

"Well … no, not really."

"Come on, Bob. I was there too. That was a threat. He might not have said anything threatening, but it was meant as such."

Souter rubbed his face with both hands. "You're right. It was a bit of a warning, I suppose." He thought for a moment, then drew his chair closer to Susan. "Okay," he said, "that man was Kenneth Brogan. He owns Thistle Developments." Over the course of the next few minutes, he told Susan all he'd heard about Brogan's rumoured involvement with the Lofthouse Project.

"So you think Faulkner and Pitchforth could be on the take?" she asked when he'd finished.

"That's what I intend to find out."

"So how do we do that, then?"

"We? We? What do you mean 'we'?"

"You'll need some assistance on this. Someone to watch your back."

"Don't even think like that, Susan. Now, promise me you'll keep what I've just told you to yourself."

Susan held his stare for a second then nodded. "Alright. But don't take any risks."

He smiled. "I won't. Now, what else are you working on?"

She pulled out her notebook.

* * *

It was ten past twelve when Belinda entered the restaurant. She wasn't going to rush to meet. In her handbag were two sets of keys to Leeds Road. Charlie was at a table for two against the side wall. There were only four other people in the place. He stood as she approached. He was about to lean forward to kiss her but she swerved away.

"I don't think that's appropriate, Charlie, do you?"

He winced and she wondered whether that was due to her rebuttal or the use of his name. Either way she didn't care and he didn't comment.

"Thanks for coming," he said when they'd sat down.

She gave a slight nod and then the waiter approached.

"Something to drink?" he enquired, handing menus to Belinda, then Charlie.

"I'll just have a cappuccino, thanks. I'm not hungry," she replied.

"Me too," Charlie said.

The waiter bowed slightly, took back the menus and headed to the counter.

"Belinda," Charlie began, "I'm really sorry for reacting like I did. I shouldn't have."

She said nothing.

"I can understand why you were suspicious and annoyed. But you must believe me, there is nothing going on between Anita and me."

She looked away, not wanting to see him lie as well as listen to it.

He reached for her hand but she pulled away. Taking a deep breath, he continued, "The reason she was with me was that she helps me clean the place."

"Oh, she's a cleaner now, is she? I can't imagine Anita as a Mrs Mopp, but there again, maybe that's your fantasy."

"Look, it's true. The last cleaner I had never came back, not even to collect her wages. That was over a year ago. I'm not letting it out. I don't want anyone else in there. We try and do that once a week, just to keep things fresh."

"Huh," she snorted. "I can imagine."

He pulled his mobile phone from his pocket and placed it on the table. "Look, give her a ring if you don't believe me."

"Right," she said sarcastically. "And I don't suppose you haven't worked on her script overnight then?"

He looked incredulous. "No. I … I just don't know what else I can say."

The waiter returned with two coffees and put them down on the table.

She watched him retreat before asking, "So where did you spend last night?"

"At the office. I slept on the couch in reception." He smiled. "I had to make sure I was up and about before the receptionist turned up."

Belinda had noticed the change of shirt and fresh tie since last night. "And your clothes?"

"I keep a spare set there in case of emergencies." He lowered his voice. "I could do with coming home to change my underwear, though."

She ignored the comment, added some brown sugar to her coffee, stirred it and lifted the cup.

He sat back in his chair. "How's Anthony? Did he get off okay this morning?"

She put the cup back in the saucer. "Yes, no thanks to you."

"I'm sorry. I'll speak to him tonight."

"Is that when you come back for a change of underpants? And for what it's worth, I told Anthony you'd left early this morning, something about an early meeting."

"Thank you."

"See, I can lie too. But I don't want to. Certainly not for you."

He leaned forward, arms on the table. "Please Belinda, I am not having an affair with Anita, nor anyone else for that matter. You must believe me."

She drained her coffee and checked her watch. "I have to go. I want to be in when Anthony comes home." She stood up. "What time will you be turning up for some clothes?"

"But ... look ... er, about six."

"Six it is."

She walked out of the restaurant, pleased she had made him squirm for a change. She certainly wasn't going to roll over that easily. There may be some truth in what he'd told her but she still felt there was more to know. In the meantime, she'd play it cool.

# 12
## Monday 23<sup>rd</sup> July 2001

It was early the following week before Belinda felt ready to check out the Outwood house for herself.

Charlie had indeed returned to their home in St John's Square for some fresh clothes on the evening of their lunch-time meet. He'd spent some awkward time with Anthony, who had given him a disinterested reaction when he tried to reassure his son that all was well between his mother and him. Anthony didn't even mention that he'd been successful with his job interview and was starting today. Belinda, for her part, had presented a frosty atmosphere, before he left to spend another night on the office sofa. Not until the following evening did she allow him to return, only on the proviso that he slept in Grace's bedroom.

She was on a late shift and had given herself time to call in. Driving up Leeds Road, she passed the house and turned left down the now familiar side street. Carefully checking for signs of Charlie's BMW, she pulled in to a gap between a Ford Ka with a dented wing and an old Triumph 2000. Charlie had told her he was off to Manchester for a meeting that morning, but she couldn't believe a word he said anymore.

She got out, locked her car and, with a check to her coat pocket to feel the spare keys she'd had cut, set off back towards the main road. Turning right at the top, she approached the familiar white front door. With a glance left and right, she pulled the keys from her pocket and selected one for the deadlock. It slipped into the lock but wouldn't turn. A brief moment of panic, then she tried the other. This time, the key did turn. Next one of the Yale keys. Right choice first time on this one. She pushed down on the handle and the door opened. A moment's hesitation. Taking a breath, she stepped inside, closed the door and listened. She half expected to hear footsteps from above, voices, laughter, but all was quiet.

She put the keys back in her pocket and looked around the room. The curtains were closed but thin enough to allow in sufficient light. An imitation coal fire was set into the fireplace on the right hand wall. On the mantle, the mechanism of a small carriage clock, spinning one way then the other caught her eye. As on her previous visit, her attention was drawn to the framed print of the abbey ruins hung on the wall. The unusual thing that had struck her before was that it was similar to one hanging in their sitting room at St John's Square. An imitation leather three-piece suite took up most of the room whilst a second-hand dresser was against the wall opposite the door. A passageway led from the left hand side of that wall. The carpet seemed a cheap thin option from one of the national chains. No photographs were on display, giving an impersonal feel.

Stepping through the passage led to a rear kitchen diner. Stairs led up to her right and she would explore them shortly. Another comfortable but old three-seater settee was in this room with no sign of a dining table. The cheap carpet ended at the kitchen area where sheet plastic flooring took over.

The kitchen itself was fitted out with basic white melamine floor and wall units. The stainless steel sink and drainer was empty. Through the window above she could only see a brick wall. The half-glazed rear door was to the left hand side and she saw the same security arrangement as the front; a deadlock and a Yale. She wandered over, unlocked it and looked out.

A metal bin stood in the corner of the unusually clean rear yard, surrounded by a six foot high brick wall with a timber gate for access. She couldn't resist stepping out and lifting the bin lid. Empty.

Back inside, door locked and secure, she opened the cupboards. The only contents were a few cheap looking mugs and drinks glasses. Some tea, coffee and sugar were in another. Below the sink, only some cleaning materials.

Ambling to the connecting passage, she paused and looked up the stairs. If there was anything to see, it would be up there she told herself. Slowly, she climbed the steep flight. At the top, was a door to her right. She turned the handle but it was locked. Digging out the spare keys from her pocket, she tried both deadlock keys. It was worth trying but neither, as she suspected, fitted. She bent down and strained to peer through the keyhole. Pitch black. It either had a cover on the inside or a total blackout curtain fitted to the window.

Turning to her left, a short corridor led to a door facing her with another door to her right. She walked ahead and chose the door facing. A bright and airy bathroom, toilet, bath, shower and wash basin looked clean and fresh. The obscure window looked over the rear yard, she guessed.

Leaving the bathroom, the last remaining door was opened. It revealed a narrow bedroom with a single bed taking up most of the floor space. The curtains to the window were closed. The mattress was covered only by a black silk sheet and a single pillow, clad similarly. She was about to close the door again, but hesitated. Dropping to her knees, she looked under the bed. Not even dust. She almost missed it. Looking again, she saw something small towards the wall. Shuffling down the side of the bed, she put her hand underneath and felt something small and tube-like. She grabbed it at the second attempt and brought it out. It was a 35mm film container. Everything had been wound back into it, so she suspected it was an exposed roll. She slipped it into her pocket, then made sure the bed was as she had found it. Closing the door, she made her way to the top of the stairs. Before descending, she tried the locked door once more. No surprise; same result. Whatever he was hiding, she was sure it would be in there.

Downstairs again and into the living room. A large television with video player below was sitting on a unit in one corner next to the window. With trepidation, she opened the cupboard. About a dozen pornographic videos were lined up. She took in the titles and wondered if Anita shared her husband's tastes? Presumably, during her 'cleaning sessions' she must have seen this collection. She felt sick. Closing the door again, she turned her attention to the dresser. Quite a few bottles of wine and spirits were in the bottom cupboards. Checking the drawers drew a blank. Unconsciously, she rubbed a finger along the top of the mantelpiece where the carriage clock stood. No dust. At least they do do some cleaning, she thought. But she'd had enough. Checking her watch, it was time to go.

\* \* \*

Sammy and Susan had become good friends the previous year when Sammy visited Susan in hospital after her accident.

Sammy had been brought up in a children's home after her mother failed to cope; drinking and a succession of men friends, one of whom had taken an unhealthy interest in Sammy. After she left the home, she drifted into street prostitution. She'd met Bob Souter last year after seeking help to find her friend who'd gone missing. Souter, and then his girlfriend, Alison, helped her out. She was a bright girl with a talent for computers. Alison had arranged for a successful job interview where she worked. Sammy was indebted to Alison and Bob for having faith in her and giving her back her self-respect.

Susan was rescued by Souter after she had fallen through a rotting floor into the basement of a remote farmhouse. She didn't like to dwell on it but she felt it was not an exaggeration to think that, if he hadn't discovered her when he did, she may not have survived. She had also had a difficult few years prior to the incident; her mother a cancer victim when she was fourteen and her father developing dementia. Eventually, he had to go into a home. Only then could Susan concentrate on her A levels. Finally, last year, she began her Broadcast Journalism course at Leeds University.

After a lengthy stay in hospital, Susan had to give up the family home in Wakefield and the two girls decided to share a rented flat on the outskirts of Leeds.

It was just after six o'clock when Sammy turned the key in the lock and smelt the aroma of the pizzas warming in the oven. Susan had called her to say she'd be in first and would have something ready for them to eat when Sammy got in from work.

Half an hour later, they were sitting on the old comfy sofa in front of the TV, meals on trays on their laps.

"These are really nice, Suz," Sammy said between mouthfuls of Four Seasons.

"They were on offer at the supermarket, so I thought, for quickness, you know."

"Mmm. So how's the job going? What's it like to be on the front line of news reporting? Is Bob looking after you?"

"Well," Susan managed before an errant piece of pepper made good its escape from the segment of pizza she was about to put in her mouth. "Sod it," she said, picking it up off the knee of her trousers.

Sammy laughed. "I bet you didn't want that bit anyway."

"You know that council meeting we went to last week …"

"In Wakefield, to do with that M62 Retail Park thingy?"

"Yes. Well, I didn't tell you but there was a strange incident as we were leaving."

"How so?" Sammy asked.

"Bob collared this bloke on the way out. He told me today that he was rumoured to be the developer in line for work on the scheme."

"And?"

"Well, I didn't hear the start of their conversation but I was a bit uneasy with the way it ended." With prompting from Sammy, Susan related her view of the encounter and what Souter had told her, in confidence, the following day.

"Wouldn't surprise me if those councillors had their fingers in the till." Sammy said. "They're always into that, aren't they? Little kick backs from all their fancy schemes. Only this one is quite big, isn't it?"

Susan nodded. "Yes, but I'm just wary that Bob might be ... I don't know. I'd hate for him to be ruffling the wrong feathers, if you know what I mean."

Sammy looked straight at her friend. "Have you had one of your feelings again?" She knew she sometimes had premonitions, for want of a better word, about things not being as they should. Ever since she'd heard her mother's voice asking her to keep an eye on her father just after her mother had died.

"It was the way that Brogan bloke looked as he spoke those words to Bob. I just think we need to be aware, that's all."

"And you think Bob might need our help."

"How do you mean?"

"I don't know exactly," Sammy said, "but I'm sure we'll think of something."

*   *   *

Bennetts, Denise Whitaker's solicitor, had given Stainmore the home address for Patrick, her son. Still disturbed by what she'd discovered of Denise's death and the fact the woman had been ignored for over a year, she decided to pay him a visit.

Patrick Whitaker lived in a flat in a block of four on one of Wakefield's council estates. The front garden was unkempt, an old fridge and a settee gave the only relief to the weeds that grew there. He could be at work but she'd decided to call by in any event.

About to ring the bell, she paused. A thought struck her and she pulled out the mystery set of keys she'd found in Denise's house. There was no deadlock but she tried the Yale anyway. Not surprisingly, it didn't fit. Keys back in her pocket, she did ring the bell. After about a minute, footsteps could be heard on the stairs inside. The door, on a safety chain, partly opened and a youth of around twenty appeared.

"Yes?" he said, nervously.

"I'm looking for Patrick Whitaker," she announced.

"What's it about?"

Stainmore looked at him quizzically. "Are you Patrick Whitaker?"

"No. No, he's me dad."

"Is he in?"

"Who wants to know?"

"Look, this is about Mr Whitaker's mother." She pulled out her warrant card. "If he's in, I'd just like a quick word."

The door closed and she could hear the youth shout up the stairs. "Dad, it's police about Gran."

After another pause, she heard the safety chain being removed and the door opened wide.

"Come in," the lad said.

Stainmore followed the youth up the uncarpeted staircase to a hallway and was led along a corridor to a sitting room. A taller, heavier man with thinning dark hair, who appeared to be in his early forties was standing in the middle of the room. "Frank says you're police. Something about my mother?"

She showed the man her identity and asked if he was Patrick Whitaker, son of Denise.

"It's okay, Frank," he said to the lad. "You can leave us alone."

The boy turned and closed the door behind him. Whitaker indicated the settee. She sat down whilst he sat in one of the two armchairs. As they did so, the sounds of Frank's footsteps could be heard on the stairs before the front door slammed shut.

"I'm afraid I have some bad news for you, Mr Whitaker. Your mother was found dead in her house twelve days ago."

Whitaker looked shocked. "What? Nearly two weeks? How?"

"According to the post mortem, natural causes. A heart attack, we suspect."

"They've carried out a PM?"

"It's usual in these cases." She studied him for a second. "There was an advert in last week's Express asking for her relatives to contact us or the Coroner's Office. Did you not see it?"

Shaking his head, he reached into his pocket and pulled out a packet of cigarettes and a lighter. He offered one to Stainmore, who refused. "No, I don't get the paper." He lit up and, after an initial puff, he spoke again. "Who found her?"

"Council workmen needed to carry out the annual gas check."

He looked at her with a puzzled expression. "So how long had she been dead?"

"Some time." She didn't think he needed to know the full details for the time being. "Could you tell me the last time you saw your mother?"

He appeared to wince. "Things have been difficult." He lifted an ashtray from the floor and held it in his lap. Another draw on his cigarette. "It must have been January last year."

"So, over eighteen months?"

He pointed a finger at her. "Look, don't judge me. If you've done some digging then you'll know she wasn't what you'd call a typical mother."

"I'm not judging anyone, Mr Whitaker." She paused a beat before continuing, "Are you referring to her lifestyle?"

"Huh. If you can call it that," he snorted.

"Is that why you weren't in regular contact?"

He took a deep drag and blew the smoke out violently. "How would you feel if you discovered your mother wanted to be a bloke? Had done for some time. Christ, it's weird."

"And your father, he's not on the scene?"

"He died eight years ago. They'd been divorced for about ten before that." He gave an ironic chuckle. "Fuck! What would the old bastard have made of that? He marries a woman who, it turns out, wants to be a man."

Stainmore said nothing, allowing the man to continue.

"She was serious about it, you know?"

"About what?"

"Having an operation. Constructive ... I almost said reconstructive, surgery. But how can you reconstruct something that was never there?" He laughed again, stubbing out his cigarette hard in the ashtray before placing it back on the floor. He looked to the ceiling then rubbed his face with both hands. "The last conversation we had, she said she'd got a plan, and soon, she'd have her wish."

"And that was last January?"

"No. we spoke on the phone about four or five weeks after I saw her."

"So what did you take her to mean when she said she'd have her wish?"

"I don't know, the operation maybe? But she'd told me before it would cost at least ten grand."

Stainmore thought back to the contents of the terraced house in Normanton. Nothing she saw there would lead you to suspect the occupier had a spare ten thousand pounds. From what the solicitor had said, the whole estate wouldn't amount to much more than the cost of the funeral. "Did you have any indication as to where she might obtain that sort of money?"

Whitaker shook his head. "The house was rented from the council, Dad left three eighths of sod all and I'm not sure if she'd enough saved for a half-decent send off." He looked directly at Stainmore. "I mean, fifty-eight. You'd expect to make a good few years after that, wouldn't you?"

"And you never spoke to her again after that last telephone call in ... February last year?"

"It would have been March. But no, we'd had words ... heated. I left it up to her to contact me." He laughed nervously. "To be honest, the next time I expected to hear from her ... I was thinking some fella might turn up."

Stainmore was silent for a second. "Did she work? As you said, fifty-eight wasn't old."

Whitaker looked away and hesitated to respond.

"Look, I'm not interested if she was earning a few bob on the quiet and claiming benefits. I just want to get a full picture of Denise."

"As far as I know, she did some part-time cash in hand jobs over the years. The last thing she'd been doing though was a bit of cleaning for some bloke with money. I've no idea who or where."

\* \* \*

Strong was sifting through the resultant reports from the detectives and uniformed officers who had conducted door to door enquiries in the area of the six known distraction burglaries. In all, there were sightings of a suspicious van seen in the vicinity of two of them around the times that the offences were committed. Unfortunately, there was no number plate information, not even partial. Finally, he gathered up the paperwork, rose from his desk and walked into the CID room.

Ormerod and Darby were the only two officers there.

"Luke, John," Strong began, "you've seen these latest reports from near where these distraction cases occurred?"

"I visited Walton and Sandal," Ormerod said, "Kelly went to Ackworth and John, you visited Hemsworth, didn't you?"

"That's right, guv," Darby confirmed. "Meanwhile, Jim Ryan got hold of the South Yorkshire notes where they had two cases in Barnsley."

"Have you cross-checked any of them?"

Ormerod and Darby looked at one another before Darby answered. "Well, we've all seen all of the reports, if that's what you mean."

"Are you talking about the white Transit van, guv?" Ormerod added.

"There is that, although that's a bit sketchy. No, I mean, does anything strike you as odd?"

Again Ormerod and Darby exchanged puzzled glances.

"Have a look at this." Strong sat down at a nearby desk and began to spread out the sheets of paper he'd brought with him.

The other two detectives gathered round.

"Take the first known case, Florrie Harvey in Hemsworth." Strong pointed to one sheet. "She lives in a community of old people's bungalows."

"That's right," Darby agreed.

"Similar for old Frank Parsons in Ackworth." Another sheet indicated. "The two in Barnsley, similar."

"That's not the case for Mrs Williamson in Walton or Winnie in Sandal, though," Ormerod commented.

"But there are a lot of elderly people living round and about both of them though, isn't there?" Strong persisted. "I mean some of those would have been spoken to in this round of door to door?"

"Go on, then, guv," Ormerod encouraged, "you're obviously on to something. What's there that we haven't seen?"

"That's exactly it, Luke. It's what isn't there that's interesting." Strong leaned back in the chair. "If 'Little and Large' were speculative, areas where a large elderly population lives are where you'd expect this to occur."

"And it has," Darby uttered.

"Yes, John, but, if that was the case, I would expect to see other reports of **attempted** distractions ..."

"I get it," Ormerod said. "You think each of these victims was targeted in some way?"

"Right," Strong agreed. "That being the case, there must be some connection between the victims. Did Kelly mention last week, we should look into that?"

Darby shook his head and Ormerod answered, "No, guv."

Strong sighed. "Okay, let's look at all the victims again. Get as much detailed background from them as possible and see if we can't come up with something."

\* \* \*

Belinda stared at the film tube standing upright on the desk at the nurse's station. What secrets were hidden in there? Did she want to know? Of course she did; she had to. She'd done not much else but mull those thoughts over in her mind since she came on shift

"Penny for them, Belinda?"

She looked up to see Helen, the ward HCA – Health Care Assistant, smiling at her.

"Sorry, I was just wondering what gems were on here." She picked up the film and turned it around in her hand then put it back down.

"Only one way to find out." Helen leant over the desk, took the film and examined it. "Can't you remember what you took?"

"Just found it in the back of a cupboard. Must have forgotten about it."

Helen handed the tube back to her. "But what's really puzzling you, Belinda? You've been distracted for a while now, not just today."

"Oh, nothing really. Worrying about Anthony and his exams, I suppose. You know he's got himself a little part-time job for the summer?"

"I didn't, no. Where's that?"

"Waterstones in Wakefield, so it's handy for him to walk to. He started today."

"Good for him."

"And then there's Grace in Southampton. She seems to be enjoying her job after she graduated from there last year."

"Do you think she'll ever come back north?"

"Who knows."

Helen raised her eyebrows. "But nothing else worrying you?"

Not only was she a good HCA, she was also perceptive. Belinda decided to move the conversation on, putting the film tube back onto the desk. "You're quite right. There's a place in Wakefield I know. I'll take it in there tomorrow before I come in."

Further probing by Helen was cut short by the ward phone ringing, giving Belinda the opportunity to avoid the issue. "Orthopaedic Ward," she announced.

# 13
## Wednesday 25<sup>th</sup> July 2001

*"They've firmed up the dates when they want me in New York and some other details,"* Alison said.

"So shall I come up to yours after work?" Souter responded.

*"I thought I could come to you for a change."* Alison lowered her voice. *"I thought you could take me to that new Italian place on Westgate to celebrate."*

"Okay … so you'll be staying over."

*"See you later."* She giggled and was gone.

Souter was left with a broad smile on his face, only to be interrupted by Susan approaching his workstation.

"What's the latest news on the Lofthouse project, Bob?" she asked.

He wasn't quick enough changing expressions. "Not sure."

It was her turn to grin. "What are you looking so pleased with yourself about?"

"Nothing to concern you, young lady. Anyway, Janey has her finger on the pulse of Lofthouse."

"It seems to have gone quiet, according to her. I was just wondering if you'd managed to dig up anything on Faulkner or Pitchforth?"

"Not had much of a chance. I've been tied up with other things."

"So what if I could find out some confidential information for you?"

Souter looked puzzled. "What are you on about?"

She pulled up a chair and sat down next to him. "I've just been chatting with Billy Wilkinson earlier." Billy Wilkinson, Post photographer and font of all knowledge on all things technological.

89

Souter gave her his full attention. "Oh, yes."

"He was explaining to me how … people might be able to …" she hesitated, "listen in to mobile phone messages."

Souter shook his head. "I know he's a gadget geek, but that can't be legal."

Susan raised her eyebrows. "No idea, but who would know?"

"Christ's sakes, that's not the point." Souter stood up and looked round the newsroom to check no one could overhear the conversation.

"Come on, we need something to give us an advantage. Billy's explained how to do it. It's relatively easy. All we need is their mobile phone numbers, and you remember, I'm quite good at that, and hope they've not altered the pre-set code to access their messages remotely."

"It's not right, Susan. I'm not condoning this."

"And then Sammy could hack into their emails. She told me she could do that."

"Sammy? You've told her about this too?" Souter shook his head and gave an exasperated gesture. "I told you to keep all this to yourself. Now I find you've discussed it with Sammy. Billy knows about it and God knows who else."

"No, Billy doesn't know. We were just having a conversation about modern technology when it came up. And I thought, this might be just what we need."

"Like a bloody court case, you mean. That's where all this eavesdropping will end up."

"Okay," Susan said. "Have you got a better plan of finding out what these characters are up to?" She stood up and stormed off, passing Janey who had just come in.

"Aw," Janey said, "you haven't upset your little prodigy, have you?"

"Piss off," Souter retorted and returned to his computer screen.

\*   \*   \*

Strong had handed another report into Flynn's office. The man himself was out. That was one thing he wouldn't miss about being a DCI. Loads of paperwork. The job was becoming wrapped up in it. Striding down the corridor to his office, he became aware of hilarity coming from the CID room. He approached the door and paused.

"That looks bloody painful," Darby could be heard saying.

"But have you seen her?" Ryan asked. "She looks as if she's really enjoying it."

Strong silently peered in to see Darby, Ryan, Newell and Kirkland grouped around a desk, picking up various photographs, turning them one way then the other and putting them back down again.

"Is that a bloke in stockings and suspenders?" Kirkland wondered.

"Either that or a butch bird," Darby said.

"He's a big lad," Newell remarked.

Darby took the picture from him. "What are you on about, Trevor? He's not even average."

Guffaws of laughter followed Kirkland's quip of, "Right. You'd need both hands to find yours."

Strong had quietly approached the group. "Gentlemen," he interrupted, startling the detectives. "Something I should know about?"

Newell and Kirkland drifted away to their respective desks as Ryan and Darby became serious.

It was Darby who spoke. "Just had the manager in from Magic Snaps, guv. He was a bit concerned about the contents of a roll of film a customer brought in to be developed the other day. We were just er ... checking it out." A smirk appeared on his face.

Strong looked down on the desk. "Oh yes," he said, picking up one of the pictures. "So now you've all had the opportunity to review the evidence, what do you feel?" he asked the whole group. "Is there evidence of criminal behaviour?"

"What he's doing to him is definitely criminal," Darby said, with a broad grin.

Strong shot him a disapproving glance then concentrated on the twenty or so colour prints that were on the desk. He singled one out and studied it for a few seconds. "This character here," he said, "the one that appears to be shackled to a frame. He doesn't seem too happy about his situation. And look at this," another photo selected, "his backside looks in a bit of a state. Or is it she?" He looked at Darby. "Who brought the film in?"

Darby consulted a notebook. "A woman, guv. Belinda Chamberlain. No address, just a telephone number."

"Give it a ring and see what you can find out. Be tactful and discreet. Don't arouse any suspicion."

At that moment, Ormerod and Stainmore came into the room. Ormerod, at least, looked excited.

"We think we've got it, guv," Ormerod said.

"Good for you, whatever it is." Strong sat down at a spare desk. "Grab a pew and tell me all about it."

"We think we've found a link," Ormerod began.

Ormerod and Stainmore sat in two chairs opposite Strong. Stainmore looked disinterested, he thought. "Everything okay, Kelly," he asked, for what seemed to be the umpteenth time in recent weeks.

"I'm fine, guv," she responded. "Just want to get these bastards."

Ormerod took up the conversation. "Kelly, John and myself," He gestured towards Darby who, by now was on the phone. "have been back to speak to all the distraction victims." He flipped open a notebook. "Florrie Harvey had a knee replacement a few years back and regularly attends Pinderfields for outpatient appointments." He paused to look to his boss before continuing, "Hannah Williamson was rushed into A & E a week before she was robbed. Suspected heart attack, but it turned out to be just a panic attack. Pinderfields again. Winnie Haywood is also a regular attender at Pinderfields outpatients. And ten days before Frank was targeted, he'd been taken into

Pinderfields A & E after a fall at home. Fortunately, he suffered nothing major, just a few cuts and bruises."

"So, the hospital is a common factor," Strong pondered. "Not unusual for people of that age. Not all the same departments either."

"No," Ormerod agreed, "But it's something."

"You're right, Luke. So I'm assuming you're off down there next?"

Ormerod looked to Stainmore who had said nothing so far. "We were thinking, who could they have met whilst they were there?" she said. "Nurses, doctors, porters, ambulance staff, although not for the outpatient women, but they could all have had the same ambulance car driver home. And he, or she, would certainly know where they lived."

"See if you can get as much info about the times of their visits," Strong said. "It'll mean speaking to various members of staff, including admin. If you come across any awkward sods that claim patient confidentiality or some other old bollocks, let me know."

Strong stood to leave when Darby called across. "Belinda Chamberlain, guv," he said, "must work on the Orthopaedic Ward at Leeds General. That's the answer I got. Not on duty till this afternoon."

"Okay." He thought for a moment. "Kelly, we might take a trip into Leeds later, so let Luke head down to Pinderfields now. It might be useful to have a female presence when I speak to this, Belinda Chamberlain."

\* \* \*

In the Horse and Trumpet pub on The Headrow in Leeds at lunch time, Souter, Susan and Sammy sat around a table with a drink in front of each of them. Sammy had called Susan that morning and suggested she bring Bob to have a chat. They'd eaten the burgers that Souter had bought and were discussing what to do about Susan's idea.

"This is crazy," Souter said. "I can't believe I'm even considering it. You can't just listen in to private messages."

"Look, it might not work," Susan suggested. "There might be no messages left on any of their phones. But I can't see how anyone would find out."

"Famous last words."

"Oh come on, Bob," Sammy joined in. "How else do you suppose we can get inside this story?"

"The pair of you are ganging up on me. If ever this gets out, I had nothing to do with it."

Sammy smiled. "We'll take that as a yes, then."

"No time like the present." Susan stood up.

"Where are you going?"

Susan raised her eyebrows. "The ladies, where else?"

Sammy and Souter watched her disappear towards the rear of the bar.

"Be brave, Bob," Sammy said. "In life you have to take a few risks."

"Easy for you to say."

She grinned and leaned in closer to him. "I'll think of something to track down their emails too. There's bound to be more useful information from them than any voicemails."

"One day, this will be illegal, if it isn't already," he said, voice low.

Souter looked all round to see who was at the adjacent tables. Most were engrossed in their own conversations thankfully, although there was one solitary drinker, dressed in a black leather jacket at a table nearby. He seemed to be concentrating on his newspaper crossword.

A few minutes later, Susan returned with a smile on her face.

"Don't tell me, Faulkner's had a call from the Queen and he's up for a knighthood?" Souter said.

"Well, he's not as smart as he thought," Susan announced. "He hasn't changed his security code from the default setting when he got his phone."

"But how did you get hold of his number?"

"Easy. Just rang the council offices. Chances were the bloke would be out to lunch, expanding his girth. Spoke to his secretary and said I was calling on behalf of my boss who had spoken to him last week about a meeting they'd arranged. We would have to change and could she give me his mobile for them to sort it. Easy peasy."

"So what did you find out?" Sammy asked.

"Nothing. Well, nothing of any interest. There was only one message, from his wife, asking him to pick up some milk on his way home."

"Hold the front bloody page," Souter said. "I can see it now, 'Councillor in dairy scandal."

Sammy punched his arm. "At least we know we can access them," she said.

"Exactly," Susan concurred. "All I need to do is monitor the voicemails and wait for something interesting to be left."

*   *   *

Belinda was on a late shift. Tomorrow, would be similar, so she planned to call in to the photographic shop near the market in Wakefield before she came in. She had said nothing further to Charlie. That had been easy because there had been little conversation between them lately, not since the big row when she'd challenged him over Anita being in the Outwood house with him. She'd said nothing to him about her subsequent visit there. She was intrigued but also apprehensive about what might be on the roll of film she had found in the small bedroom. She'd also given some thought about what might be concealed behind the locked bedroom door.

She was at the nurse's station, lost in thought when Helen drifted past, turned around and spoke. "Did you ever get those pictures back, Belinda?"

"Sorry?"

"That roll of film," Helen persisted, "Did you take it in to be developed?"

"Oh, yes. I'll pick it up tomorrow morning before I come in."

The HCA approached the desk and studied her colleague earnestly. "Are you sure you're okay?"

"Just a bit tired, that's all," she said.

At that moment, Strong and Stainmore entered the ward and approached the nurse's station.

"Hello, can I help you?" Belinda asked.

"I'm looking for Belinda Chamberlain," Strong said.

"I'll see you later, love," Helen said and wandered off to one of the side wards.

Belinda looked puzzled. "Well, you've found her."

Strong took out his warrant card discreetly and showed it to the nurse. "I'm Detective Chief Inspector Strong from Wakefield CID and this is my colleague Detective Sergeant Stainmore. Is there somewhere private we could chat?"

Belinda's expression changed from puzzlement to shock. "What's happened? Is it Anthony? Not Grace? Tell me it's not Grace?"

"Anthony? Grace?" Strong repeated.

"My son and daughter."

"No, it's nothing like that, Ms Chamberlain. We just need to have a quite word, in private, if you don't mind."

"It's Mrs Chamberlain," she responded. "I'll just need to get one of the other nurses to cover for me, then we can use Sister's office. She's not in until later this afternoon."

In the office, door closed, Belinda sat nervously on one of the seats.

"Mrs Chamberlain," Strong began, "did you take a roll of film in to Magic Snaps in Wakefield to be developed?"

Belinda coloured. "Is that what this is about?"

"Did you take the photographs themselves?"

She shook her head. "No. I've no idea who did. And I've certainly no idea what's on them."

"So where did you get the film?"

She looked down onto her lap. "I … I found it."

"Where? In the street?"

96

"No." She looked up at Strong. "I found it in a house. A house that my husband owns." She stiffened.

Strong sat back and exchanged looks with Stainmore before resuming. "And your husband's name?"

"Charles Chamberlain."

"Would that be Charles Chamberlain, the commercial lawyer in Wakefield?"

Belinda nodded.

"So you maintain that you have no knowledge of what was contained on that roll of film?"

She looked shocked. "Of course not. Why?"

Strong ignored the question and continued with his planned line of questioning. "I wondered if you might recognise some of the people pictured?" He looked to Stainmore who produced an envelope from her bag. He pulled out the first photo and passed it across to Belinda. "These have been selectively printed from the negatives to show only the faces or decently recognisable body parts, if you know what I mean."

The first photograph showed a man's face in obvious ecstasy. Belinda handed it back. "I don't recognise him," she said.

Next, a woman laughing. "That's Anita." Belinda's brows furrowed. "Anita Matthews." She looked up at Strong. "I knew the bastard was having it about with her."

"Your husband?" Strong asked.

"Supposed to be a family friend; his PA. Huh!" She leaned forward. "Do you know, she used to babysit Grace and Anthony when they were small."

"I'd have to check," Strong said, "but I don't think she was … indulgent, shall we say."

"Doesn't matter, she was there."

A few other photos depicted two men and another woman Belinda didn't recognise and two other men she said were business clients of her husband's whom she'd met on a couple of occasions at social gatherings. Two more showed the same man plus what appeared to be someone else's back.

She paused, looking close to tears. "This one," she said, "That's Charlie's back. You see this mole ..." She pointed to part of his anatomy. "... that's definitely him." She wiped her eyes with the back of her hand and looked defiantly at Strong. "You don't sleep with someone for twenty-odd years and not recognise their back."

"Okay, thank you Mrs Chamberlain. You've been very helpful."

"Will you be talking to Charlie?"

"We just need to establish that all participants were of legal age and consenting."

"I'll kill him," she said. "Bringing all this to my door." She looked between Strong and Stainmore. "It's just ... I wanted to choose the moment when I challenge him. He doesn't know I had access to the house and found the film."

\* \* \*

Souter drove into his allotted space in the underground car park of the apartment complex near Wakefield's Westgate railway station. He was running late, the table at L'Italia was booked for eight. Looking forward to seeing Alison, he was interested to hear exactly when she would be returning from America. He planned to organise tickets for himself to join her in New York for the last two weeks of her secondment. As he leaned into the boot to retrieve his briefcase, his mind was already picturing their time in bed together after their meal.

With all those thoughts buzzing around his head, he wasn't aware of someone lurking in the shadows of the car park. He never managed to straighten up out of the boot before an almighty blow was delivered to the back of his head. His legs gave way and grey fuzz clouded his vision. An arm came round his neck and the grip tightened.

"Souter, ya bastart," his assailant yelled in his ear in a guttural Glaswegian accent. "You are seriously pissin' some people aff."

The arm yanked tighter at his neck. "You listen and you listen good," the voice continued. "You'd better leave digging around that Lofthoose site. Naebody wants tae hiv you proddin' intae somethin' that disnae concern ye. You hear me?"

All Souter could do was mumble incoherently.

"Because we ken where ya live. An' we ken where your friends live. Do you get ma meanin'?"

Another weak mumble then he felt his legs being lifted off the ground. He was bundled into his own boot and the lid slammed shut. After that, all was blackness.

# 14

Alison drove into a visitor's space on the other side of the car park and noticed Souter's car as she got out and made for the stairs. She loved Italian food and was looking forward to trying the new restaurant. At least he was home, she thought, and not delayed because an important news story had broken. That had occurred in the past.

Ever since the incident last year when she surprised him in his apartment with Sammy, he had vowed there would be no secrets. Not that there was anything to hide on that occasion anyway. To that end, he had given her a key to the place. She had given him a spare set to her house in Ossett in return. She put the key in the lock and opened the door. "Only me!" she shouted as she entered. "If you're in the shower, I'm coming in," she laughed.

Silence greeted her.

"Hello? Bob?"

No response.

She walked through the lounge and checked the kitchen, then into the bedroom and finally the bathroom. No sign. In fact, looking round, it didn't appear that Souter had returned at all; there was no briefcase or discarded jacket. Strange? She was sure that was his car in the space downstairs.

Locking the front door behind her, she walked back down the two flights of stairs to the car park. Definitely his car. She walked over and looked inside. Trying the driver's door handle, it opened. Stranger and stranger, she thought. She closed the door again and walked back to her own vehicle. About to get back in, she paused. Perhaps he'd just nipped to the shop; a bottle of wine for later and he'd forgotten to lock the door. Pulling out her mobile phone, she rang his number. After a few seconds, faint strains of Scotland The Brave could be heard. Only it sounded as if it was coming from his car. Back across the car park once again. It was coming from the boot. Perhaps it had fallen out in there and he hadn't realised.

She felt for the boot catch and squeezed.

It clicked open.

*   *   *

Strong entered the waiting area of Pinderfields A & E and scoured the collection of walking wounded and attendant friends and relatives. Alison was sitting on her own on the back row, head down. He walked over to her. "What's happened, Alison?" he asked.

She looked up, relief in her eyes. "Colin, thanks for coming." She stood up and he gave her a hug. "He's been attacked."

Strong put his arm around her shoulder and gently eased her back into the seat. "Can you tell me what happened? Take your time."

She wiped her eyes with the back of her hands and related the events of earlier in the evening. After phoning for an ambulance, Alison had called Strong at home and he had notified Wood Street. Uniforms were first on the scene but he'd also spoken to Luke Ormerod, asking him to get involved. He was at the car park, along with the SOCO officers, investigating the scene.

When she'd told him as much as she knew, he asked what the medical staff had said about his condition. "He was beginning to come round in the ambulance," she responded, "but he wasn't making much sense. They've sent him for a scan."

"Is there anyone I can call for you?" Strong asked.

"I've rung Sammy. You remember Sammy?"

Strong nodded.

"And she was coming in with Susan."

"How are those two?"

Alison began to relate their stories when a nurse approached.

"Ms Hewitt?" she said. "Mr Souter is back from his scan and asking for you."

Alison stood. "Will you come in with me, Colin?"

"Of course."


Souter was lying on the trolley in a bay in A & E with a sheet over him, still feeling nauseous.

Alison approached and reached for his hand before stroking his forehead and sweeping his hair gently back. "Oh Bob," she said. "What have you got involved with?"

He smiled at Alison's concern then focused on his friend standing behind her. "Hello, mate," he said.

"Now then, Bob," said Strong. "This is a bit of a mess you've gotten yourself into, isn't it? Any ideas who might have attacked you and why?"

Before he could respond, Alison followed up with a question of her own. "Is this anything to do with that council development scheme you've been working on? Lofthouse? And that unsavoury developer?"

Souter gave a bewildered look.

"Susan told me about when you confronted him at the council meeting the other week."

"I don't know," Souter said. "I didn't see who it was. I was just leaning in the boot to fetch my case when I got walloped on the back of the head. Things went hazy and I had the feeling of being lifted off the ground. After that … I woke up in the ambulance with you."

"Whoever it was, they didn't say anything?" Strong asked. "No words of warning?"

"Like I say, I don't remember anything really"

Alison spotted a doctor nearby and went to speak to him. Meanwhile, Strong leaned in closer to his friend. "Come on, Bob," he said quietly. "They must have said something."

"No, I'm telling you, Col."

"What about anything else? Sounds? Smells?"

Souter thought for a minute. Leather. A leather sleeve. A jacket. His thoughts went back to the pub in Leeds. The man studying his crossword. He was wearing a leather jacket.

"Well, Bob? Anything?" Strong repeated.

"No. Sorry, mate."

"And what about this Lofthouse thing Alison mentioned?"

With no time for him to answer, Alison returned. "The doctor says there's no lasting damage that they can spot on the scan, but you'll be staying in tonight."

Souter felt disappointed.

"Routine for head injuries," Alison went on. "You probably have some concussion. And we can always have that Italian later."

Before anyone could say anything else, a trolley was wheeled into the next cubicle. Strong thought he recognised the woman accompanied by a youth.

"You'll be okay, Mum," the boy was saying. No real privacy was afforded by the curtain.

"All right," Strong said, "I'll get off and see how Luke's getting on at the car park. You take things easy and I'll be back tomorrow for a statement."

Before he could say his goodbyes to Alison, a man stormed into the department and approached the woman who had just been brought in to the next bay.

"Belinda. Belinda, darling," he said.

"Get away from me," Belinda responded. "I don't want to see you."

"But ... I didn't mean ..."

"Leave Mum alone, Dad," the boy said. "You've done enough damage already."

"But you don't understand. I'm not leaving."

Strong decided it was time to intervene. He stepped outside of the curtain surrounding Souter and faced the man. "I think you should go, Mr Chamberlain," he said.

The man looked him up and down. "Who are you? What the fuck's it got to do with you?"

"You're seriously upsetting the patients in this unit, not to mention the hard working staff. Now," He flashed his warrant card. "I'm DCI Strong and we can continue this conversation at Wood Street if you want to, I don't mind."

A look of contempt passed over the man's face as he appeared to weigh up the situation. Finally, he turned towards Belinda. "I'll see you later," he said. One final glare at Strong then he left.

Strong turned to the woman and saw the swelling around her eye and the cut on her forehead. "Mrs Chamberlain," he said. "Did he do that to you?"

Anthony, who had been watching events unfold between Strong and his father, jumped in before his mother could respond. "Yes, he bloody well did."

"Anthony!" Belinda said. "Don't say that. You weren't there."

"Maybe not this time, but I've seen him raise his hands to you before now. You can't let this carry on."

Strong took out a card and gave it to Anthony. "Now's maybe not the right time, but if your mum wants to talk …" He turned to Belinda. "Give me a call."

She gave him a weak smile and he walked away.


Ten minutes later, Alison had gone to get herself a hot drink, when Susan and Sammy rushed in. The curtains had been pulled around the adjacent bed. Anthony had disappeared somewhere and a nurse was suturing Belinda's cut head.

"I knew that Brogan was trouble when you confronted him at the Town Hall," Susan opened up.

"Who did this to you?" Sammy asked.

"Just forget about it," Souter said.

Susan folded her arms. "Oh no, you don't sweep this under the carpet. This is serious."

He tried to raise himself up. "I do know that. Which is why I'm telling you to forget about it."

"Did they say something to you?" Sammy joined in. "When they hit you and bundled you into the boot?"

He groaned, lay back down onto the pillows and closed his eyes.

"You're scared, aren't you?" Sammy persisted. She leaned in and lowered her voice. "I know you too well, Bob. You need to tell us. You never let me down and I trust you. And I hope you know that I," she glanced at Susan, "that is we, would never let you down either, and that you can trust us."

A little moisture ran from Souter's left eye and he quickly swept it away with his hand.

"They threatened you, didn't they?"

He opened his eyes and tried to pull himself up. Susan propped another pillow behind him. "I'm not bothered about me," he said.

"Alison?" Susan queried. "Did they threaten Alison?"

"Not as such."

"So what did they say?" Susan's voice scarcely above a whisper, aware others might wig in on the conversation.

Souter sighed and realised they needed to know. "Only that as well as knowing where I live, he also knows where my friends live."

Susan exchanged glances with Sammy as Souter paused.

"And by that, I'm assuming they meant Alison. And you two."

The curtains swished by the end of the next bay and a nurse pushed out a dressings' trolley.

"Thanks nurse,"

The nurse turned, smiling. "Just look after yourself, Belinda, she said.

"I'll try my best."

Susan looked at Sammy then peered around the curtain.

"Belinda?" Susan said, surprised. "It's me Susan Brown. You remember I was on Orthopaedics last year.

"Hello, Susan, yes I do. How's the leg?"

"As good as new. I've got one last appointment with the consultant next week and that should be it. But it was thanks to you and your team that everything's okay. Anyway, never mind that, what's happened to you?"

"Oh, I just had a bit of a tumble, that's all. Nothing to worry about."

Sammy was standing behind Susan. "Hi Belinda," she said. "How are the kids? Grace and … Anthony, isn't it?"

"Hello, Sammy. How are you? Yes, they're fine."

"That looks a like fair tumble you've had. She's done a good job on the stitches though."

Involuntarily, Belinda put a hand to her head. "I'm just a bit tired now."

"Of course," Susan said. "Come on, Sammy, let's leave her to get some rest. Hope you recover soon." She bundled Sammy away from the bed and pulled the curtain back into position.

Sammy gave a questioning look and silently mouthed, 'I don't believe her.'

\* \* \*

At the underground car park to Souter's apartment block, Scenes Of Crime Officers were tidying their kit away when Strong appeared.

"Anything interesting?" he asked Doug Norris, a man he'd worked with often in the past.

"Not a lot," he said. "A few prints from the door handles and the boot but they'll probably match the victim or his girlfriend." He looked over into the far corner where Ormerod was bending down. "We found his briefcase though. Luke has it bagged up. Again, a few smudges but nothing for us to work with."

"Okay, thanks Doug." Strong walked towards his DC.

"Found it open in the corner here," Ormerod said when his boss approached. "Not forced, so either it wasn't locked or whoever opened it knew the code. Nothing forensics could get from it."

"Yeah, Doug said."

"So, I'll let your friend have a look at it and see if he can identify if anything's missing."

"I'll take it in in the morning, Luke. I want to see his face when I show him."

"Not telling you all he knows, then?"

"No. He claims he has no idea why this has happened."

Ormerod shrugged. "Must admit, it seems strange. Robbery wasn't the motive, unless he had something in the case. He still has his wallet apparently."

"I'll see what I can find out tomorrow. You get off home, Luke."

"Don't fancy a pint, do you, guv?"

Strong checked his watch. "I'd like to, but I need to get home."

\*   \*   \*

Alison returned with hot drinks in two polystyrene cups.

"Oh, hi," she said when she saw Susan and Sammy. "I didn't know you were here, or I'd have … here, you have these, I'll get some more."

"No, we're fine," Sammy said. "You and Bob have those."

"Sure?"

Susan shook her head. "Yeah, we're okay."

Alison passed a cup to Souter and sipped from the other. "I don't suppose he's told you what really happened?" she asked.

"Only that someone jumped him when he was reaching into the boot," Susan responded.

Alison's expression was disbelieving. "After what you told me about the work you've both been doing on the Lofthouse scheme. Are you sure you couldn't have upset the wrong people?"

Susan and Sammy looked at each other. "I don't see why," Susan finally said.

"Nothing to do with this Scottish developer bloke then?" Alison persisted.

"It was just a bit of a frosty exchange really," Susan said.

"Frosty? I thought you said he was a bit threatening."

"Well … no. More like a bit of posturing. But anyway, nobody would resort to violence over some planning issue."

Souter, quiet throughout this exchange, drained his tea and held out the empty polystyrene cup. "Look, I'm really tired," he said.

"Subtle as ever, Bob," Alison quipped, taking the cup from him. "All right, we'll leave you alone now." She gave him a lingering kiss and a big hug. "I'll see you tomorrow." Susan and Sammy waved and they all left.

Again, he was alone with his thoughts. And then, he remembered the patient in the next bay.

"Belinda?" he called through the curtain. "Hello, it's Bob Souter. I don't know if you remember, I used to visit Susan on your ward last year?"

"I do," she responded quietly. "I wouldn't have known your name but … it was you who rescued her, wasn't it?"

"Well, I found her."

There was silence between them for a while.

"What happened to you?" she asked.

Souter sighed. "I just upset someone, that's all."

"I know the feeling."

Another pause. "Susan said you'd been cut and bruised."

"It's nothing."

Souter slowly swung his legs over the side of the trolley, steadied himself and walked over to the curtain. He popped his head round. "Do you mind?" he asked, indicating the barrier between them.

"No, it's better than talking to a sheet of material." She gave a weak chuckle.

"Doesn't look like nothing to me," he said, getting back onto his trolley.

She looked across at him. "Your someone must have been pretty upset too, the look of you."

"It's a mystery," he sighed.

"Right," she murmured.

But he knew he hadn't convinced her either.

# 15
## Thursday 26<sup>th</sup> July 2001

Next morning, Strong finally tracked Souter down to the Male Medical Ward where late the previous evening, he'd been found a bed. One of the cleaning staff let him through the doors and onto the ward. A check of the chart on the wall revealed which bed Souter should be in and, as he approached, he saw the curtains drawn around it.

An old gentleman sitting up in the next bed spoke. "I think 'e's gerrin' dressed," he said. "They said 'e could go 'ome, lucky bugger."

Strong gave him the thumbs up and peeked through a gap in the curtain. Souter was fully dressed and putting on his shoes.

"Come on, no time to laze about in bed all day," Strong said.

"Hello, mate. Managed to track me down then?"

"I'm a detective, remember. Anyway, they've signed you off as fit and well, I assume."

"I can't stay in here, Col. It'd drive me do-lally."

"I thought you'd be in your element, all these lovely nurses tending to your every need."

"Have you seen any?"

"Not yet. The ward cleaner let me in."

"They're all about seventeen stone. Talk about a caring profession. How can you take them seriously, telling you about all the things you should and shouldn't do to stay healthy when they're that size."

Just to quash Souter's argument, the curtain was pulled apart and a lovely dark-haired, slim nurse in her mid-twenties appeared.

"Off already, Mr Souter," she said in a delightful soft Irish brogue. "I'll miss ya."

Strong looked from the nurse to Souter.

"Ah, well," he said with a shrug, "I lied."

"If you've got your friend here to help you, I'll leave you alone," she said.

"Thanks, Mairead." Souter smiled.

"See ya, Bob."

Ten minutes later, they were sitting at a table in a corner of the hospital cafeteria. Strong had offered to buy his friend a cooked breakfast.

"Very generous of you, Col," Souter said as he began cutting up a sausage.

"Shut up, I wanted one as well." Strong smiled and dipped his bread into a fried egg.

His initial hunger slated, Souter indicated the briefcase that Strong had brought with him. "You found it then?"

Strong nodded, mouth full of bacon.

"And you want me to see if there's anything missing."

Strong pointed his fork at him. "You know what? You should have been a detective."

Souter grinned. "I've said it before, not a lot of difference between our jobs."

"Was it locked?"

"I don't bother. There's never anything that valuable in there normally," Souter responded.

"How about last night?"

Souter paused between mouthfuls to give the question a bit of thought. Strong wondered if it was more for his benefit.

"No," he finally said. "But let's have a look?"

Strong pulled the briefcase from the plastic evidence bag and passed it over. "Won't surprise you to learn that forensics got nothing of any use from it."

Souter flicked both catches and opened the case, gave it a cursory look, rummaged through some papers, then closed it again. "Looks just as it was when I left the office. Where did you find it?"

"In the corner of the car park."

Souter became surprised. "Well I was leaning into the boot to get it out when I was attacked, so whoever it was must have been interested enough to have a look. Probably thought I'd got credit cards or something in there."

"But if you were being mugged, Bob, they'd have had their hands in your pockets after your wallet. Are you sure they didn't say anything to you?"

Souter looked serious. "I've told you, I can't remember too much about it. But I certainly can't remember whoever it was saying anything."

Strong held his friend's stare for a second then continued his breakfast.

Souter took a slurp of tea then leaned back in his seat. "How did you know that bloke from last night … Chamberlain?"

"Charles Chamberlain you mean? Respected commercial lawyer … or so he'd like us to think."

"Oh, that's him," Souter said. "I didn't know he was Belinda's husband."

"You know Mrs Chamberlain?" Strong mopped tomato juice from his plate with the last piece of toast.

"Well, it's more that Susan and Sammy do. I've met her a few times. She was on the Orthopaedic Ward where Susan spent most of her time in the LGI. Susan had a lot of good things to say about her and Sammy always had a natter when she went in to visit."

Strong washed down his toast with a mouthful of tea.

Souter continued, "I had an interesting chat with her last night after everyone had gone."

"Oh yes."

"He's not as upstanding as you might think."

Strong smiled, images of the photographs flashing through his mind. "Oh I don't know about that."

"You know he smacked her last night?"

"She told you?"

Souter looked around to make sure no-one was listening, deciding how much to tell his friend. "She told me about the photos."

Strong raised his eyebrows and leaned forward.

"She knows you haven't spoken to her husband about them."

"Not yet, anyway," Strong confirmed.

"She thinks he's having it off with his PA amongst others. In that house she knew nothing about until the other week."

"Did she mention any of the other participants?"

"No, I didn't probe too much."

"Not like you."

"I do have some empathy with people you know. Besides, I like her. She was always very pleasant when I visited the ward."

"So, one last time, you can't recall anything your attacker said to you?"

A surprised look passed across Souter's face and he exhaled deeply.

"And you've no idea why anyone would attack you?" Strong went on.

"I've told you, Col. It's a complete mystery."

"No stories you're working on that might be upsetting anyone? Alison mentioned something about Lofthouse and a developer."

Souter stood. "Look, I need to get into work. Thanks for bringing my case back. And thanks for the breakfast. I owe you one."

*   *   *

Strong made his way out of the hospital, more convinced than ever that Souter was holding back on him. Mention of Lofthouse and he'd clammed up. He'd ask around back at Wood Street.

Lost in thought, he walked through the main doors and automatically turned to check no one was close behind should he let it go. Surprised, he saw Belinda Chamberlain approaching.

"Hello," he said. "How are you feeling this morning?"

"Better, thanks," she said. "How's your friend?"

"Just been let out too. Your lad not come to meet you?"

"Anthony? I made him stay at his friend's last night. I wasn't sure when I'd be discharged."

Light drizzle had begun to fall. They walked together for a few yards in the direction of the car park before she stopped by the taxi rank queue. About half a dozen people were waiting.

"Look, don't hang around for a taxi," Strong said, looking to the sky. "I can give you a lift."

"It's okay," she said, "I'll be fine."

"Honestly, it's no trouble." He smiled. "I'd be neglecting my duty if I didn't see you home safely."

She looked to the queue then back to Strong. "It's not that far. Thank you."

Finally settled in the car, seatbelts on, he looked round to reverse out of the space.

"So where are we headed?" he asked.

"St John's Square."

"Very nice." He drove off, heading for the exit.

She said nothing and looked out of the window.

"They've done a neat job on that cut," he said. "That cheek'll look colourful for a few days though."

Again, she didn't respond.

"Sorry," he went on. "What do I know? You're the nurse." He glanced across.

This time she smiled. "You don't need to have any medical training to predict I'm going to look a mess for a while."

They came to a halt at the lights to exit onto Aberford Road.

"I haven't spoken to your husband, you know … about those photos."

"I know. Thanks."

"So, was this sparked by you confronting him about them?"

"Yes."

The lights changed and he pulled away.

"So how did he explain them?"

"Just a bit of fun, apparently. Ha! Fun? He still insists there's nothing going on between him and Anita, his PA."

"But she's in the photos?"

"I know. Apparently, it's her thing."

Strong paused for a second. "And what happened to you stemmed from this same argument?"

"It all seems to be one big argument these days." She turned her head away and looked out of the window. After a few minutes silence, she spoke again, "Bob told me you'd spoken to him last night."

"Did he now?" Another pause before Strong made one more attempt. "You don't have to put up with it you know."

She ignored his comment. "Did he tell you what happened to him?"

"Who? Bob? We know what happened."

"But he didn't tell you why?"

"He told you?"

"Not exactly. But I heard enough. He was talking to Susan and Sammy."

"Anything you can tell me?"

By now, they were travelling up Wentworth Street.

"Anywhere just here will be fine," she said.

Strong drew to a halt by St John's Church.

"Thanks again," she said, opening the door and stepping out. Before she set off, she leaned back in. "The only thing I can tell you was the name 'Brogan' was mentioned." With that, she shut the door and walked off.

\* \* \*

Belinda put the key in the lock, nervously opened the front door and listened. The only sound was the comforting tick of the clock on the mantelpiece in the lounge. Satisfied there was no one in the house, she stepped inside, closed the door and leaned back against it. After a few seconds, she began to walk down the hall but the mirror on the wall drew her eyes. She instinctively touched her stitched forehead, then lightly stroked her cheek. Immediately the tears began to flow. She couldn't stop them. She didn't want to. There in the hallway, she finally crumpled onto the floor.

She'd seen a side of Charlie she never knew existed. Was this his true nature? Were the last twenty-seven years a lie? Had she ever really known him? Those questions had played around in her mind all of the previous night. Again and again she came back to the most pressing question of all; what was she going to do now?

The noise of a key entering the front door lock shocked her out of her angst. Still sitting on the floor, she leaned hard back against the wall and held her breath. She wished the wall could swallow her up. Slowly the door opened. Keys struggled to be released from the lock and then Anthony appeared. Her body relaxed in pure relief.

"Mum? Why didn't you tell me you were coming home? What are you doing down there?" He closed the door, dropped his bag on the floor and rushed over towards her. "He's not here, is he? He hasn't hurt you again?"

Belinda shook her head and wiped her eyes with the backs of her hands. "No. He's not here. But what are you doing here? I thought you'd be at work."

"Half day today." Anthony sat on the floor alongside his mother and put an arm around her shoulders, pulling her towards him. "It'll be okay," he said. "We'll sort it."

She looked up at him. "How? How can we sort this mess?"

"For a start, he's not coming back in here. We'll change the locks."

"But this place is his."

Anthony pulled his arm away and faced her. "It can't be just his? It must be yours too. You've put as much into this house as he has, probably more. You were always here when I was growing up. You made this a home."

Belinda looked at her boy, wise beyond his years. Her tears began to fall once more. "Oh, Anthony," she managed through sobs. "I'm so glad you're here."

They held each other for a few minutes before he stood and helped her to her feet.

"Come on," he said, leading her through to the lounge and sitting her on the settee. "I'll make you some tea."

Belinda wiped her face. "Thanks."

He paused at the kitchen door. "Have you spoken to Grace?"

She shook her head. "I don't want to distract her. She's got her job in Southampton. She doesn't need to know all this."

He took a step back into the room. "She does, Mum. She will find out what's been going on … what Dad's really like."

"Not just yet, eh? Now where's my tea?"

He frowned then made his way into the kitchen.

While Anthony made them both a drink, Belinda pulled out her mobile phone and checked the screen. It was on 'silent' and there had been three missed calls, all from Charlie.

"I hope you're not thinking of ringing Dad?" Anthony appeared with two mugs.

"He's been trying to call me."

He gave one mug to his mother and sat down cradling his own. "I hate him."

"Don't say that Anthony."

"It's true Mum. I wish he was dead. He's spoiled everything."

Belinda sat rigidly on the sofa. "I know you're angry, but I know you don't mean that."

"Don't I?" He put his mug onto the table and stood up.

"Anthony?"

"We'll see."

"Anthony!"

He ignored her and stormed out of the room. A few seconds later, the front door slammed.

# 16

Strong parked in Wood Street station car park. Up in his office, he collected the pack of photographs and made his way to the CID room. The office was empty, apart from Darby typing on his keyboard. "Is Kelly not in?" he asked.

Darby glanced towards Stainmore's desk then looked up at Strong. "Think she's gone to the bog, guv."

"Can you do something for me, John?"

"Sure."

"Can you see what you can find out about a proposed development on the old Lofthouse Colliery site?"

Darby nodded. "Okay."

"And when Kelly gets back, tell her …" He stopped as she appeared behind him. "Ah, Kelly, come with me."

"Where are we going?"

"To rattle a cage."

They left Wood Street station on foot and headed for town before turning off to the right down several narrow streets and walkways. Names associated with the capital and the legal profession, like Chancery Lane and Crown Court. They walked between some interesting Georgian and Victorian properties housing recruitment consultancies and estate agents. Crossing various side streets, they finally arrived at the offices of Charles Chamberlain Associates. Pushing open the glass door, Strong approached the reception desk, Stainmore close behind.

"Good morning," the attractive young receptionist greeted.

With a discreet flash of his warrant card Strong asked to speak with Mr Chamberlain.

"I'm afraid he's in a meeting at the moment and said he wasn't to be disturbed."

"That wouldn't be with his PA, Ms Matthews, Anita, would it?"

"... er, yes, but ..."

"I'll just go straight through." Strong strode towards a door to the side of the reception counter.

"But wait ... you can't ..."

Stainmore caught up with him before the receptionist could move from behind her desk and they found themselves in a short corridor, glazed partitioning down one side and several doors leading off. The first door was open revealing a meeting room. The second had Chamberlain's name on it, the venetian blinds closed in the screen at the side.

Strong knocked as the receptionist appeared at the end of the corridor.

"Wait," she cried.

Too late, Strong opened the door and discovered Chamberlain and an attractive woman in her mid-forties sitting opposite one another at a table. Their held hands sprung apart when the door opened.

"What? ... Who? ... Oh, it's you," Chamberlain said.

"I'm sorry, Mr Chamberlain," the flustered receptionist said from behind Strong. "I told them you were in a meeting ..."

"That's okay, Kate. This man is a policeman, I believe. I'm assuming the young lady is police too."

On cue, they both produced their warrant cards.

"We'd like a word, Mr Chamberlain," Strong announced, "... if you don't mind."

The woman stood to leave. "I'll be in my office," she said.

"Oh no need to leave on our account, Ms Matthews."

"It's Mrs," she retorted.

"Still ... we'd like you to stay as well."

Anita exchanged bewildered looks with Chamberlain and slowly sat back down at the table.

Chamberlain leaned back in his chair. "Look, if this is anything to do with my wife, it won't involve Anita."

Strong ignored the comment and glanced round at two spare seats against the office wall. "May we?" he asked.

Chamberlain exhaled noisily. "If you must."

Once Strong and Stainmore were seated around the table, Strong produced the wallet of photographs. "I wondered what you'd like to tell me about these?" He took out the first picture and placed it on the table in front of Chamberlain. It depicted a man in his fifties with an ecstatic expression on his face.

"Really, Inspector," Chamberlain protested, "this has nothing to do with my assistant here."

A second picture was placed on the table. "Sure about that?" Strong looked directly at the woman opposite. This time, no mistaking a laughing Anita Matthews looking downwards and appearing to be topless, although no naked breasts were on view.

She blushed and looked away.

"So, Mr Chamberlain … again, what can you tell us about these photographs?" Strong dealt the contents of the wallet onto the table like a pack of cards. "As you might be aware, these are selected views. The originals displayed … how would you describe it," he looked to Stainmore, "more details?"

"Certainly more flesh," Stainmore agreed.

"Okay. This is just a bit of harmless fun between consenting adults," Chamberlain said. "It shouldn't have even been brought to your attention."

"But it has. And now that it has, we have a duty of care to ensure that it is what you say it is. And by that I mean that it does only involve adults …"

"God's sakes, man," Chamberlain interrupted. "We're not into under-age."

"… and that those adults were consenting and no crime was being committed," Strong continued.

"Well there wasn't."

"We'll need the names of those participating," Strong persisted.

"I don't think so," Chamberlain retorted. "This was a private gathering of friends and what we get up to in private is nobody's business but ours."

"I was hoping for a bit more cooperation from you, Mr Chamberlain." He looked to Anita. "What about you, Mrs Matthews. Are you prepared to help us?"

"As Charles just said, this is a purely private matter."

"And what would Mr Matthews say about this?" Strong waved a hand over the photographs. "Or is he one of those participating?"

Anita pulled back, her expression turning stony. "That would be difficult. Bill died ten years ago."

"I'm really sorry about that." Strong looked from Anita to Chamberlain. "But we do need to check your version of events."

Chamberlain stood, walked to the door and held it open. "I've told you what those photos were about. I don't need to tell you anything else. If you really thought there had been a crime committed, you would have arrested me. Unless you plan to do that, I'd like you to leave. I have work to deal with."

Strong looked to Stainmore, then Anita as she also stood up.

"Just one other thing," Stainmore said, folding her arms and remaining seated. "Do you know a Denise Whitaker?"

"What? Who?" An exaggerated puzzled expression formed on Chamberlain's face.

Anita, by contrast, looked away.

"Denise Whitaker."

Chamberlain made a point of giving the question thought. "No, I don't think so. She's not a client, I'm sure. I don't recognise the name."

Strong had been studying Anita. "What about you, Mrs Matthews?"

She looked edgy. "It's not a name I've heard before."

After a moment's awkward silence, Strong gathered up the pictures and placed them back in their wallet. "If you're sure."

"Anita will see to back to reception," Chamberlain said.

Strong and Stainmore rose and walked towards the corridor. "Oh, by the way," he said, pausing by the door, "how did your wife come by those injuries?"

"She drinks." Chamberlain looked from Strong to Stainmore. "Sometimes she has accidents. Good day." With that he closed the door and walked over to his desk. Picking up the phone, he dialled a number. After a few rings, a male voice answered.

"Giles, it's Charles," he said. "Are you well? ... Good ... Listen, I have an irritating problem I think you could help me with ..."

At the end of the corridor, before Anita could open the door into reception, Strong placed a hand on it. "We will identify everyone, you know. It would be easier if you cooperated. We could handle things discreetly."

She looked pointedly at his hand on the door, waited for him to release it then opened the door. "You know your way from here," she said.

He held her gaze for a second then stepped through into the reception area, Stainmore in his wake.

Outside, making their way back to Wood Street, Strong finally had the opportunity to ask Stainmore, "What was all that business about Denise Whitaker?"

"I just thought I'd throw it in and see what reaction I'd get," she said, both hands in her coat pockets. "Remember I told you I checked her phone records and there was a call from his office?"

"That's right, yes, you said. You thought it might have been a misdialled number but your instinct's telling you something else?"

"Just thought it was worth a punt." She stopped and looked to her boss. "Did you clock the reactions though?"

"Oh, yes. She, for one, knows more than she's telling. Very nervous when you mentioned the Whitaker name."

"And he was definitely hiding something too." They resumed walking as Stainmore continued, "And at the end of the day, I still haven't found out where the other set of keys is for."

Strong said nothing.

"Are you really going to track down and visit those guys?" she asked.

"No. It's not worth it. They all look well above the age of consenting adults. I just want to make the bastard sweat a bit."

Stainmore smiled. "Not just any old bastard though, an arrogant bastard."

That brought a chuckle from Strong. "That's the first time I've seen a happy expression on your face for some time, Kelly. Is everything alright with you?"

"Yeah. Just feel a bit tired, that's all."

"Have you been to see a doctor?"

"What was all that about his wife's injuries?" she asked, ignoring his question.

"I saw her in A & E last night. She was in the bay next to Bob."

"You didn't buy that drinking story then?"

"Not in the least." He glanced towards her. "I can usually tell when drink's involved. No, I think he's slapped her about after she told him about those photos."

"So what the Hell's he liable to do now?"

Strong didn't answer. He hoped Chamberlain wouldn't be stupid enough to repeat his actions. There again, he could never be sure.

\* \* \*

As Souter emerged from the stair doors onto the news floor of the Yorkshire Post, a spontaneous round of applause broke out. He'd already had enquiries as to his well-being from Patricia on Reception, but this reaction brought a huge grin to his face. He held up a hand in acknowledgement.

"Trust you to make an entrance," Janey Clarke said, a smile on her face. "But don't think I'm going to give you any special treatment." She sat down behind the screen at her own desk.

After a few seconds, normality reigned; he sat at his workstation and fired up his computer.

Susan appeared. "How are you, Bob?" she asked.

"Bit of a dull headache, but no different from a good session on the beer."

"What's the plan of action now?"

He looked over his shoulder and gave her a smile. "You don't fancy getting me a nice coffee while this thing comes to life, do you?"

Susan raised her eyebrows. "Only this once because of what happened." She began to walk off to the small kitchen. "I won't be making a habit of it."

Various pinging noises indicated new emails and he reviewed the headings. Finally, one from about an hour earlier caught his attention. It was from Charlie Ritchie on the Glasgow Herald.

*'Managed to get an image of Brogan's heider, Kennedy. Hope of use',* the message said.

He clicked on the attachment and a photograph filled the screen. His heart rate quickened as he studied the subject. The character appeared to be around five feet nine inches tall, slim and yes, as Ron Boyle's description, he looked a wiry little sod. His dark thinning hair looked greasy and he had a face only a mother could love. Souter recognised the location as Glasgow's Sherriff Court. No doubt he was making one of his regular appearances. He was giving two fingers to the photographer. But it was how he was dressed that struck Souter; jeans and a leather jacket. Leather. He zoomed in on the face.

"Who's that ugly looking bugger?" Susan asked, placing a coffee on his desk.

He jumped. "Don't sneak up on me," he hissed.

"Come on then, who is he?"

He turned to face her. "You don't recognise him?"

She shook her head slowly. "I don't think so. Should I?"

"Remember when we were in the pub yesterday …?"

"Mmm, yes."

"I think he was sitting at a nearby table pretending to do a crossword."

She looked from the screen to Souter. "I don't remember. But you think … no, let me guess, you know he was the one who attacked you?"

"I didn't see who it was. But look, the leather jacket. It was a leather sleeve that was around my face. That and an uncouth Glaswegian accent." He looked closely once more at the screen. "I'm sure that was him in the pub." He clicked the file closed and turned around. "It would make sense."

\*   \*   \*

Chamberlain put the phone down, a wry smile on his face. His expression dropped when the door opened and Anita entered.

"Why didn't you tell me she'd found some photos?" She angrily strode over to his desk. "When were they taken? It must have been at least a year ago."

"I don't know Anita. But old Geoff's been dead for six months, and he was pretty prominent. I recognised that scar."

"And why did that female detective start asking about Denise? I thought you'd sorted that. How come her name has come up again?"

"I have … I mean, I did." He banged a fist on his desk. "I don't mean it like that. I thought she'd dropped out of our lives too. Only …"

Anita looked alarmed. "Only what, Charlie? What's changed?"

He sighed heavily. "You didn't see it, then? In the paper?"

"Just bloody tell me, what's going on?"

"She was found dead in her house over a week ago."

124

Anita covered her mouth with both hands, then slowly let them drop. "How?"

"Natural causes, I think. But she'd been dead for months, maybe even a year."

"Don't tell me you had something to do with it."

Chamberlain's eyes blazed. "Of course not."

"Only you did say you'd sort the problem after she started to want money from you for that operation she wanted."

"I told you I persuaded her to leave me alone."

"Weird woman. She was a crap cleaner as well." Anita walked around the meeting table. "But how did the police make the connection? I didn't think there was anything to tie her to Leeds Road or the club."

"I think they were just fishing. If they'd got anything to link her and those bloody photos, they'd have said so."

"Shit, what a mess." She slumped into a chair. "So what exactly did you tell Belinda?"

Chamberlain rubbed his face with both hands. "Only that ..." He broke off as the sounds of a commotion were heard from the corridor outside. He stood and walked round his desk. "What now?"

The door burst open and Anthony stormed in.

"Anthony? What ..." Chamberlain was cut short as his son landed a punch on his jaw. Off balance, he stumbled to the floor.

"That's for what you did to Mum," Anthony said.

Anita screamed.

"And you can shut up too."

The receptionist appeared at the door. "I'll call the police," she said.

"No. Wait, it's okay," Chamberlain said, getting up. "I'll handle this."

"What, like you handled Mum?" Anthony stood defiant, fists up. "I'll do it again."

"Anthony ... look, calm down." Chamberlain held both hands up in front of himself, like a cowboy confronted by a gunslinger. "Sit down a minute and let's talk."

"There's nothing to say." He pointed a finger at his father. "You come near Mum again and I'll kill you."

"Anthony, don't say that to your Dad," Anita said.

The boy turned to face her, a disgusted look on his face. "And you're just a whore. Don't you ever talk to me again."

"Hey, don't speak to Anita like that."

"Like what? How else would you describe someone you're paying to shag?"

Chamberlain took a step towards him and raised a fist but Anita stepped in front of him.

"No!" she yelled. "He's your son."

"That's it," Anthony responded. "Hit me. Like you hit Mum."

For what seemed like an age, they all stood motionless, holding each other's stare. The tension in the room was palpable. Slowly, Chamberlain dropped his arm.

Anthony's anger also appeared to subside. "But she's wrong. I'm not your son and you're not my father. Not any more." He let out a low groan. "Pathetic," he said then turned and walked out of the office.

# 17
## Friday 27<sup>th</sup> July 2001

Darby sighed, leaned away from his desk and rubbed his eyes. "This is such a tedious exercise." He was trawling through sheets of paperwork listing staff allocations from Pinderfields Hospital going back months. "I'm going for a pasty. Anybody want anything?"

"No, you're alright," Stainmore responded from the next desk.

"Fetch me a coffee back, will you?" Jim Ryan called out. "Milk, two sugars."

"See if they've got one of those steak pies," Trevor Newell piped up.

"I fancy a sausage roll," Luke Ormerod added.

"Bloody Hell, I was only being polite!" Darby protested.

"Wayhay!" Ryan, Newell and Ormerod exclaimed.

Grumbling, Darby made for the door to be met by Colin Strong.

"Ah, John," Strong said, "are you headed for the canteen? Can you bring me back a tea?"

"Anybody would think I've got 'mug' tattooed across my forehead," Darby mumbled on his way out.

"Something I said?" Strong wondered aloud.

Ryan looked up, a broad smile on his face. "Don't worry, guv, he just got stitched up to bring us back some food."

"How's the search going? Anything standing out yet?" Strong referring to the hospital staff correlation exercise.

"Not as yet, guv," Ormerod replied. "John, myself and Kelly have shared it out in the first sweep."

Stainmore looked up from her paperwork. "I thought I had someone here. A nurse on duty in the right areas for the first three victims' visits but was off-duty for the next two."

"From John's reaction just before you came in, I don't think he's got anything yet either," Ormerod added.

"Is there anything else that links the victims or is it just coincidence that they all have strong connections to the hospital? I mean, it's hardly unusual for elderly people to be visitors to the major hospital in the area. I don't want us to focus on only one avenue here if it's not correct."

Ormerod responded, "Well I'm also sifting through likely candidates with past experience who might be out on the streets at the moment, but most are still banged up." Indicating Ryan sitting at the desk behind, he continued, "Jim got hold of the notes from the two cases in Barnsley and again, both of those victims have connections with Pinderfields."

"Alright. Keep at it."

Detective Chief Superintendent Flynn appeared at the door. "Colin, a word please," he said, before disappearing back along the corridor.

"Headmaster's study," Ormerod quipped.

Strong looked to the ceiling before following his boss.

\* \* \*

Souter was putting the finishing touches to an article for the weekend edition when Susan pulled up a spare chair and sat beside him.

"We've booked a holiday, Sammy and me," she announced. They'd met for lunch and she'd just returned. "Do you think Mr Chandler would mind?"

Souter looked at her incredulous. "Are you serious? You've booked a holiday *before* asking for any time off?"

"It's only for a week."

"When?"

"19th August."

He looked at the calendar pinned to the workstation screen. "That's only three weeks away."

"Yep. It was a late deal to Majorca."

He spun round in his seat to face her. "Chandler might well tell you you can take as much time off as you want."

"You don't think he would, do you?"

"Do you realise I called in a favour to get you this summer job?"

Susan looked down on her lap. "I do, yes. But I really need a break after these last few months, starting the course, Dad and everything."

Of course, Souter thought, the poor girl has had a tough time this year, her father dying a few months ago. For the second time, it could be said. She'd already lost him some years prior when the dementia took him. Before he could say any more, his desk phone rang. He snatched it from its cradle and barked a response. "Souter."

*"Mister Souter,"* came the guttural Glaswegian accent. *"I hope you paid attention to whit you wis told the other day."*

"Who is this?"

*"Let's just say Ah'm lookin' efter yir best interests. We wouldna want tae see ye get hurt; or mair tae the point, yer lovely lookin' friends, now would we?"*

Involuntarily, Souter glanced at Susan who looked concerned at his reaction to the phone call.

'Who is it?' she mouthed silently.

Souter turned back to face his computer screen. "Look, I don't know what you're frightened of but you must be scared of something if you're resorting to …"

*"You don't fucking get it, do ye?"* the Scots voice interrupted. *"It's you who should be scared. Now, if we have to speak to you again, you'll be sorry you didnae listen tae me."*

Souter opened his mouth to respond but the line had gone dead. Slowly, he replaced the handset.

"Was that who I think it was?" Susan asked.

Souter's brows furrowed. "Is Janey doing any more on the Lofthouse Development story, do you know?"

"I don't think so. It was, what, ten days since that Planning Meeting. She only reported on the fact that it was given approval. So unless the council release any more information, I don't think there's anything more to say. Was that your friend in the leather jacket then?"

Souter nodded. "Not a word to anyone."

Susan looked offended.

"I mean it, Susan. Especially Alison." He leaned back in his chair and sighed. "You don't think they could have found out that you've been listening to Faulkner's messages do you?"

"Wouldn't have thought so. There's only you, me and Sammy who know I've done it. Besides, there wasn't anything of any interest. I haven't even checked them for about a week."

"Do it now."

"Sure?"

"Yes. Let's see what there is." As Susan began dialling numbers, he thought of something else. "What would be really useful is if we could do the same thing for Brogan's phone."

Susan put up a hand to interrupt. "Sounds like he's on holiday. This is a Scottish voice asking him to call him back when he returns."

Souter held out a hand for the phone. "Here, let me listen to that."

"Hold on, I'll get it to repeat." Another number pressed on the keypad and she handed the phone to Souter.

He listened then gave it back. "That was Brogan," he said. "I'm sure of it."

Susan looked inspired. "There's one other person I haven't tried," she said and began dialling a number.

Souter was puzzled.

After a few seconds, she began to speak. "Planning please, Michael Pitchforth." Another pause. "Yes please." She listened and began to write down a number then hung up. "Got it," she said, a pleased expression on her face. "Now let's see if he's as careless as Faulkner." More dialling and then a broad smile spread over her face as she listened before ending the call.

"You got access to his voicemails too?"

"That's the good news," she said. "The bad news is there are no messages, but I'll keep a close eye on both now."

Souter shook his head. "I can't believe it's so simple. It must be illegal."

Susan stood. "And now, as I feel invincible, I'm going to see Mr Chandler about that week's holiday."

\* \* \*

By the time Strong arrived at Flynn's office, the Superintendent was seated behind his desk. "Come in, Colin," he said. "Shut the door and take a seat."

Strong did as asked. "Something wrong, sir?"

Flynn studied Strong for a moment. "Charles Chamberlain," he finally announced.

"Ah."

"Indeed. How much of a fishing exercise have you been conducting?"

Strong relayed the details of the photographs brought to his attention, his interviews with Mrs Chamberlain, the confrontation in A&E and his visit to Chamberlain's office the day before.

"But there's no evidence of non-consensual or under-age activity?" Flynn asked when he'd finished.

"It doesn't appear so, sir."

"And Mrs Chamberlain hasn't actually made a complaint of assault against her husband?"

"No."

Flynn stood up and walked to the window, looked to the street below for a second before turning to face Strong. "Assistant Chief Constable Wadsworth asked me to have a word."

"Wadsworth?"

"Giles, yes. He wondered if your persistence in this might be construed as harassment. He doesn't feel unnecessarily upsetting a prominent lawyer in the town would help the cause."

Strong smiled … ah, the cause. "And which cause would that be, sir? The force or the Lodge, or possibly both."

"Now Colin, I'm only passing on ACC Wadsworth's concerns here. It doesn't do any good to upset the powers that be, especially …"

"Especially as I've been passed over for the permanent DCI position."

"Look, I know you're upset with that. But you're not doing yourself any favours by provoking the wrong people."

"The wrong people?" Strong stood up and took a step towards Flynn "Maybe I should have accepted Jack Cunningham's invitation all those years ago and joined. I might even have had your job by now." He put up both hands and waved Flynn away. "No, I wouldn't have been able to live with myself. At least I can sleep easy on a night."

"Colin. Calm down."

"Calm down? I'm perfectly calm. I had every right to investigate the contents of those photos. And if Giles's 'brother' turns out to be a wife-beater then that's perfectly alright then is it?"

"Just don't do anything hasty."

He turned, walked to the door and opened it. "By the way, I wasn't planning on doing any more digging on those photos. But I will if Mrs Chamberlain wants to press charges." He left and closed the door before Flynn could respond.

On the way back down to his office, he felt for the comforting outline of the cigar packet in his jacket pocket.

# 18

Souter pulled up in the street about twenty yards from Alison's front door. He'd driven past once already, checking other parked cars for any signs of life; anyone possibly keeping an eye on the place. He didn't want to admit it but that call this afternoon from Kennedy - and he was sure it was Kennedy - had unnerved him. Just what was so important that he had to be warned off? Was the development that lucrative for Brogan? In any event, Alison was too important for him to be putting her in jeopardy.

Again, he looked up and down the street before letting himself in to her house.

"Is that you, Bob?" her voice came from the kitchen.

Savoury aromas were wafting through the room. "Smells like you're cooking up a storm."

She appeared at the doorway smiling, a glass of red wine in her hand. "Oh, just something I've thrown together."

He put his bottle of wine on the coffee table and walked towards her. "Come here," he said, a huge grin on his face. He put both arms around her, pulled her close and kissed her. "I've not had a chance to thank you for coming to my rescue."

She laughed. "Head feeling better then?"

Both hands dropped to her bottom, squeezed and pulled her closer. "Much," he said.

"Nothing wrong with your friend either," she giggled and pulled away.

He stood leaning against the door frame and watched her bend down and open the oven door. "Home-made pizza," she said over her shoulder.

"And for afters?"

"Down boy."

Whilst Alison fettled around in the kitchen, Souter nervously walked around the sitting room. He checked the street again from the window before lifting the telephone receiver and listening for any unusual clicks and tones.

"What are you doing?" Alison took him by surprise.

"I just … well, I was making sure it was working okay."

"And the glances through the window?"

He looked down at the floor but said nothing.

She moved closer, put her arms around him and kissed the top of his head. "This attack has shaken you up. More than you're admitting, hasn't it?"

He raised his head, feeling sheepish. "I'm more worried that you're okay."

"Me?" She looked incredulous. "What's it got to do with me? Unless … Is there something I should know about? You still haven't told me about this Lofthouse story you've been working on."

He shook his head. "No, it wasn't that. I was only concerned that you might have been affected by finding me … having to go to hospital with me … you know."

She kissed him on the lips. "Come on, silly boy. I'm absolutely fine. Let's go and eat. This is ready now."

During their meal, Souter asked about Alison's possible trip to New York.

"Yeah," she said, "I was going to tell you all about it when we were at L'Italia the other night, but you didn't make it, remember?"

"Cheeky sod." He grinned. "I might have had a bang on the head but my memory hasn't gone."

"Anyway, they want me to fly out on the second of September. It's a Sunday. The office manager will meet me at JFK and show me round. I'm going by Virgin, isn't that great?"

"Get you, JFK. You'll be talking like a native in no time."

"I doubt it. I couldn't disguise my accent."

"And you'll be based in one of those towering buildings?"

"The World Trade Center, yes."

"So how long will you be there?"

"The return ticket will be for Sunday October the fourteenth. So, if you can, you could fly over for the first two weeks in October."

"So you'll be away ... what, six weeks."

"Yep, but I could see you for the last two."

"But I won't see you for four weeks. That's the whole of September. How am I going to manage?"

Alison pulled a face. "You'll be fine. And Sammy and Susan will keep an eye on you for me."

"I've never been to New York, so that'll be great. I'll ask Chandler tomorrow." He topped their glasses up with the Italian red he'd brought with him. "But you'll never guess, Susan only went to see him today to ask for a week off in three weeks' time."

"I know. Sammy requested that too. They're off to Majorca. They'll have a great time."

"But this is only a summer job for Susan. I thought she'd be pushing her luck but Chandler agreed."

"She has had a lot to cope with over the last year or so. And Sammy needs a break too. She's blossomed really well. When I think about the first time I saw her ... you and her together in your flat. I can't tell you."

Souter smiled at the memory. He had ordered Chinese food for them both when Alison knocked on his door unexpectedly. "I thought you were the takeaway delivery. I'm so glad you took care of her. She deserved a bit of luck."

A mischievous expression grew on Alison's face. "But would you have, though? Sammy, I mean?"

"Come on, Alison, what do you take me for?" He was incredulous. "Of course I wouldn't have. She was vulnerable. She'd come to me for help. I wanted to help. Look how she's turned her life around."

"I know. I'm sorry." She looked down to their empty plates. "Now, about afters." She picked the plates up and took them to the sink. "I've got some cheesecake, if you fancy it."

His face broke into a broad grin. "That's not all that's on offer, is it?"

She grinned coyly, took hold of his hand and led him upstairs.

An hour later, they lay exhausted and naked on the bed. Darkness had fallen outside and the room was lit by the orange glow of the streetlamp over the road.

Alison gently fondled him. "Glad to see the knock on the head hasn't affected other parts."

He looked down and smiled. "Not with you."

After a few seconds, he rose and padded into the bathroom. When he returned, he couldn't resist looking out of the window onto the street.

"There is something bothering you, isn't there?"

He turned and smiled at her. "Just paranoid, that's all. After what happened last week."

"And you've no idea why it happened?"

"No," he said and looked away.

She swung her legs off the bed and reached for her dressing gown. "I don't like it when you lie to me, Bob." She slipped her arms into the robe stood up and tied it at the waist. "I had enough of that with my previous." She walked past him and out of the bedroom.

\* \* \*

"Won't it be great, Suz? I've never had a real holiday before, certainly never abroad," Sammy said dreamily. "I just hope my passport arrives in time."

"Should do." Susan was studying the screen of her mobile phone. "Have you really never had a holiday?"

Sammy stretched out on the settee in the sitting room of the flat they shared and closed her eyes. "We did some sea-side trips when I was a kid. Before ... Well, it was all Mum could afford. I remember Blackpool once. She took me on the Big Dipper. I threw up and she got really annoyed with me. She took me back to the guest house where we were staying and left me in bed while she pissed off out enjoying herself." She sat up and looked at her friend. "It hasn't rung, you know," she said.

Susan brought her head up. "No, I know. I was just looking at something. Anyway, your mother just left you on your own? How old were you?"

Sammy lay back down. "She did that all the time. I must have been about nine. And then she comes back pissed with this bloke in tow and I had to listen to a load of old bollocks they were talking. That was until the landlady found out and threw us out."

"What? In the middle of the night?"

"Wasn't the first time."

"So what did you do?"

"Pitched up at the railway station and waited for the first train in the morning. We were due to leave that day anyway."

"So this will be your first trip abroad?"

"Yeah." They were both quiet for a minute as Sammy turned her head to observe her friend, once more concentrating on her mobile phone. "What the Hell's so fascinating?" she finally asked.

"I'm going to check the voicemails again," Susan answered.

"Is that the councillor bloke you and Bob were talking about the other week?"

"I'm on to two of them now, the Council Leader and the Head of Planning."

"And have you learnt any more, other than that guy's shopping habits?"

"Shush!" Susan grabbed a pen and opened a notebook.

Sammy closed her eyes again as her friend began scribbling.

After a couple of minutes, Susan put the phone down. "Well that is interesting," she said.

"What is it this time?" Sammy commented, eyes still closed. "Does he need to get a loaf of bread on the way home today?"

"Faulkner is actually on holiday."

"You learned that from his voicemails?"

"No, I knew that a couple of days ago. But the interesting thing is, he's obviously been having trouble with his PC. That was a voicemail from the IT department. They were letting him know they would be down to look at it on Monday."

Sammy sat up on one elbow. "You're not thinking what I'm thinking, are you?" A broad smile spreading over her face.

"Do you think you could?"

"If I can get access, I don't see why not. Just have to choose the best time that's all."

"Let's do some serious thinking," Susan said.

\*   \*   \*

The previous morning, when Belinda was released from Pinderfields, she felt grateful that it coincided with her off duty. In addition, her own GP had given her a sick note for five days. She wouldn't want any of her own patients in Orthopaedics to see her face as it was.

Anthony had been quite attentive earlier but she'd finally persuaded him he couldn't jeopardise his little summer job on her account. He'd rung her in the afternoon to say that he was meeting up with his schoolmate, Simon, and they planned to go into Leeds to the cinema in the evening and could he stay over. She told him that would be okay and she would be fine. She wasn't sure she would be but she couldn't stifle the lad because of her problems with Charlie.

She'd made herself have a lie in before finally getting up and running herself a bath. Normally she'd shower every day so a nice long soak was a treat. She'd lazed around all day, tried to read a book but put it down then made herself something to eat, although she didn't feel hungry. It was half past eight and she was finding it difficult to concentrate on a film she was trying to watch on the television when the noise of a key being placed in the front door lock disturbed her.

Her heart rate quickened as she heard the door open then close.

"Hello? Belinda?"

Shit! Charlie.

He strode into the lounge where she sat on the sofa.

"Ah, you *are* here."

"What do you want?" she asked disdainfully. "A change of clothes or do you want to knock me about again?"

"Come on, Belinda. You know it was an accident. I didn't mean it."

"Sure. Of course I do. I tell myself that every time I look in the mirror."

His demeanour hardened. "Look, you know the pile of crap you've brought down on top of me; poking around my business, taking that film to be developed. I've had some shitty detectives round to the office trying to imply all sorts of nonsense."

"And that's my fault ... how?"

He stood rigid for a moment, holding her gaze. Finally, he appeared to deflate, sat in an armchair and let out a deep breath. "How did we get to this?"

She sat up straight. "You really don't know?"

He leaned back and looked to the ceiling but said nothing.

Belinda relaxed a little. "Was I really that boring? No, don't answer that. I saw what you and your friends were doing on those photographs." She studied him intently. "What was it? A thrill you felt you couldn't get from me?

"I don't know. It's like a drug, I suppose."

"Oh, so I need to feel sorry for you now, do I? Some addict that needs help? Or will some hot-shot psychiatrist tie it all back to what happened to Jeff?"

He stiffened. "Don't you dare bring my brother into this."

"Why not? It was you that told me all about those weird incidents when you were growing up. Trying to smother you, wondering what it would be like to die. And then he goes and does it. Stark bollock naked with a plastic bag over his head."

"Shut up, you stupid woman!"

Silence hung in the air for a split second as they both studied one another.

Eventually, Belinda spoke. "I'm sorry, Charlie, I shouldn't have …"

"No, I'm sorry." He stood. "I shouldn't have come. It's too soon."

"It'll always be too soon."

"Did Anthony tell you he came to see me at the office yesterday?"

She shook her head.

"I know you're both hurting and I'm truly sorry. I only came to say I'm going away for the weekend – on my own. I just think it would be a good idea. Get some distance … well, anyway. I'll be back on Monday. We can talk then."

After the front door had closed, she curled into a ball on the sofa and began to sob.

# 19
## Monday 30<sup>th</sup> July 2001

Strong dashed from his office, paperwork in hand and literally bumped into Stainmore. "Sorry, Kelly, I was just … Is everything okay? You look on another planet."

"I was. Have you got a minute?"

"Sure." He held out the file. "Let me just take this upstairs and I'll be right back. Sit down and wait."

Five minutes later, they were facing each other across Strong's desk.

"What's troubling you?" he asked.

"I didn't tell you but, last Monday, I called in to see Patrick Whitaker, Denise's son."

Strong raised his eyebrows. "Did you now?"

"Yes. I'm sorry, I should have told you."

Strong waved her apology away.

"Anyway, he seemed to hint that his mother was looking forward to a sex-change operation. When I quizzed him on how she might be able to pay for it, he didn't know but he said that 'she had a plan and would have her wish'."

"Any idea how?"

"Well, I've been thinking … and I know this is all circumstantial, but when I pushed him, he said she'd latterly done some cleaning job for a … quote, 'bloke with money'. So that coupled with the phone call on the records, I just thought I'd fly a kite with Chamberlain when we went round there. But then, with his reaction, I'm wondering whether Denise knew what went on in that house? Maybe details of who attended and her silence might be worth the ten grand she reckoned she'd need to 'have her wish', as Patrick said."

"It's a theory," Strong agreed. "But take it on a stage further, and this could be serious."

"I know."

He stood up, walked over to the window and stared out, hands in his pockets. After a minute, he turned back to face Stainmore. "What would be your next move?"

"Back to see Chamberlain and press him on the telephone call."

"No, let's leave him for a minute. Anita Matthews is your best way in. She looked decidedly shaken when you threw in that little cracker on Thursday." He sat back down. "See if you can organise a meet somewhere away from Chamberlain's offices."

"Okay, I'll sort that. I'm assuming you'll want to come with me."

"That depends. If you think you'll get more from her on your own, woman to woman, so to speak, then go for it."

Stainmore headed towards the door. "I'll let you know," she said.

When Stainmore returned to her desk, Ormerod approached, a strange smile on his face. "Kelly, your new secret admirer is downstairs." She looked puzzled. "Jason, your little coroner's officer."

She pulled a face. "Ha, bloody ha. Is he downstairs now?"

"Desk called up five minutes ago."

Jason Manningham was twenty-eight years old but looked much younger. Stainmore thought he looked like he should be in a boy band. Tall and thin, he struggled to give shape to the suit he was wearing. His shirt looked about an inch too big on the neck and his dark floppy hair was neatly coiffured.

"Jason," she said in greeting, holding out her hand. He shook it limply.

"Hi Kelly," he responded. Was it her imagination or did he seem to be nervous? "I was just wondering if you were any nearer completion of your investigation into Denise Whitaker?"

"Oh, yes. You're still holding the body. Not literally, you understand."

He gave an exaggerated laugh.

It was her turn to feel nervous. Why? This was stupid. "I haven't yet concluded all my enquiries."

"That's fine. It's just I had her son, Patrick contact me last week and he was wondering what to do as regards a funeral."

"That's fair enough. There's a few more things I need to check and I'll be in touch when I'm happy."

"Okay, thanks," he said.

* * *

Souter shook his head as he spotted Susan appearing on the newsroom floor.

"What's with you?" she said approaching his desk.

He swivelled on his chair. "You."

"What about me?"

"I can't believe you managed to sweet-talk Chandler into giving you the week off."

She swayed around and made a pout. "Well, when you've got it, you've got it," she said, looking for a smile from him that wasn't there. "Anyway, that's not the only thing though, is it? I can tell. You're looking particularly grumpy this morning." That comment finally drew a smile. "So come on," she encouraged, sitting down next to him at a spare seat.

"It's nothing."

"Bob," she said, eyebrows raised, "it's not nothing. So, come on … spill." She leaned closer and waved her hands towards her as if attempting to draw the information out of him.

After a delay, he reluctantly responded. "Well … it's my fault really. Alison got a bit upset on Friday."

"Why? What have you been saying?"

"Nothing. I suppose I'm still nervous after that phone call on Friday. I let it get to me."

"But you must have done or said something if she got upset."

He sighed and leaned towards her. "I was just nervous when I was at her house, looking out onto the street, checking her phone, you know. I didn't say anything, that's the point. I wanted to but I didn't want to upset her. In the end that's just what I did. She knew there was something I wasn't telling her."

"She's a big girl, you know. You should trust that she can handle whatever you tell her. The worst thing you can do is keep things from her, for whatever reason."

He took a breath and looked around the newsroom. "I know. She told me she didn't like people lying to her, she'd had enough of that previously. But I didn't lie. I just didn't tell her everything. Anyway, have you been vigilant? Nobody watching you or hanging around the flat?"

She shook her head. "No. I think you're building this up too much. After all, what's at stake in this development? It's got the go-ahead but we don't know that Brogan is going to be involved. Not for certain."

"What about Sammy? Has she mentioned anything?"

Susan looked him in the eye. "Bob, talk to Alison. Tell her all that's been going on. She'll understand. You'll find there's really nothing to worry about."

He broke into a grin. "Thanks," he said.

"Wow, this is cosy," Janey Clark quipped as she strutted over to her desk next to Souter's. "Oh, did you know ...?" she continued, "This is a very rare week."

Souter and Susan exchanged puzzled looks. "How's that?" he said.

"This is one of only two weeks in the year when there aren't any discount deals from national furniture or bedding stores."

Souter snorted a laugh.

"So I thought I'd do a piece on that."

\* \* \*

Anita Matthews' house was a neat semi-detached on a quiet residential street in Durkar, to the south of the city and not far from the M1 motorway. It was just after one o'clock when Stainmore rang the front door bell. Chamberlain's office had informed her that Anita had a day off and passed on her home telephone number. Initially reluctant to meet, she had finally agreed to a lunch-time visit from Stainmore.

After a short wait, Anita answered the door and waved Stainmore inside. She led the way straight down the hall and into the kitchen. A seat was offered at the breakfast bar.

"Thanks for agreeing to see me," Stainmore said, settling onto the uncomfortable seat.

"I didn't have much choice did I?" She filled a kettle and switched it on. "Tea? Coffee?"

"A coffee would be nice, thanks."

The woman sat down opposite Stainmore. "So, what do you want?"

"I'm not here to give you a hard time over those photographs." Stainmore held up both hands. "As you said, what consenting adults get up to in the privacy of ... well, somebody's home, is up to them. But I do think you know a bit more about another matter I'm investigating."

Anita stiffened. "And what would that be?"

"The name Denise Whitaker clearly meant something to you when I mentioned it last week."

The kettle clicked off and she rose to put some instant coffee in two mugs.

"Who was she?" Stainmore pulled out her notebook and pencil.

Anita paused for a second, facing the window, before opening the fridge and fetching out the milk. She held it up as a question to Stainmore.

"Please," she said, "no sugar."

Finally Anita returned to face Stainmore over the breakfast bar, drinks in front of them. "She cleaned for Charles," she eventually offered, "at the Leeds Road house."

"So why did you say the name meant nothing to you the last time we talked?"

She took a drink of her coffee, avoiding eye contact. "I … I don't know. I suppose it was because Charlie … I mean Mr Chamberlain had said he didn't know her."

"And why would Mr Chamberlain deny any knowledge of her? I mean, he must have known she cleaned for him. Presumably you didn't organise this?"

"You'll have to ask him that." Her expression had hardened again.

"You are aware of what happened to Denise?"

"Only when Charles told me."

"When was that?"

Again, hesitation from Anita. "After you called last week."

Stainmore sipped her coffee and remained silent for a second. "Okay, so when was the last time you saw Mrs Whitaker?"

Anita smiled nervously. "Sorry. It's just … I assume you know of her situation?"

"What situation do you mean?"

"She was … a bit … strange, shall we say."

"Shall we say she was hoping to change her gender?" Stainmore responded.

Anita looked down. "Well, yes."

"So, again, when was the last time you saw Denise?"

Anita screwed up her face as if in thought before answering. "Maybe last January? I don't really know. I do know she let Charles down early part of last year - April, May time."

"In what way, let him down?"

"Well, she never turned up to clean the place. He said there'd been no word of apology, no notice that she was leaving, nothing."

"Didn't that concern you?"

"I didn't think too much of it. After all, I didn't actually employ her."

"So what did Mr Chamberlain say when she suddenly stopped working for him?"

She shrugged. "He thought she'd had a better offer somewhere else. Maybe she got a job for more hours or paid more money."

"But he didn't try and find out why?"

"Not as far as I know."

"So it wasn't you who rang her home number from the office on …" Stainmore made a point of referring to her notebook. "… June 6$^{th}$ at 10:23?"

Anita hesitated. "No. I never had her contact details."

"Then it was most likely Mr Chamberlain who made that call?"

"I've really no idea. You'll have to ask him."

"We will." Stainmore closed the notebook. "Well, thanks for your time Mrs Matthews." She stood. "That has been helpful. I'll see myself out."

As Stainmore turned to close the front door behind her, Anita was still sitting at the breakfast bar staring into her coffee mug.

\* \* \*

"Charlie, it's me."

*"Is everything okay?"*

"That policewoman who came to the office last week. How did she get my home number?"

*"Not from me. Why? Has she called you?"*

"More than that … she's just been here."

*"What did she want?"*

"Asking about that oddball cleaner you had. The one found dead."

*"What did you say?"*

"Just that. She was your cleaner for Leeds Road and she was an oddball."

Chamberlain exhaled noisily. *"What else did she ask?"*

"When was the last time I'd seen her. I said about January last year but she'd let you down by not coming back."

There was silence for a short while before Anita spoke again. "Charlie ... tell me the truth ... did you have anything to do with her death?"

*"Christ, Anita, what are you saying? Of course I didn't."*

She looked out of the kitchen window, her eyes misting. "But you went to see her though, didn't you. That last night after she'd called you."

Chamberlain said nothing. All she could hear was him breathing.

"You said you were going to sort it."

*"She was okay when I left."*

A tear fell down her cheek. It was her turn to be quiet. She'd known Charlie for years. For the first time, she was beginning to feel uncomfortable. She remembered his distracted state of mind the day following his visit to her house.

*"You do believe me, don't you?"*

"Why did you call her in June?"

*"I didn't ..."* Chamberlain hesitated. *"Oh, right. That was how they made a connection. Phone records. I just thought ... I hadn't heard from her and ... I ... I just wanted to make sure that what I'd said to her had sunk in and she wouldn't be pestering me again."*

"But she didn't answer."

*"No."*

Anita slowly put the phone down. "She was probably already dead," she said quietly to herself.

\* \* \*

"You've never been satisfied with what happened to Denise Whitaker from the off, have you?"

Stainmore was sitting at a table in the canteen at Wood Street Police Station opposite Strong. She'd paid for their coffees and told her boss the gist of her earlier conversation with Anita Matthews.

"Why lie about not knowing who she was?" she said, referring to Chamberlain. "It's not as though he'd drop himself in it about what went on in his secret house. We already knew that thanks to his wife taking that roll of film to be processed."

Strong scratched his ear. "It's more than that, though, I can tell."

Stainmore instinctively looked around then leaned in closer. "I had a quiet word with Dr Symonds ..."

Strong mirrored her moves. "And?"

"Although the PM showed she'd suffered a heart attack, the cause of death was officially drowning."

"That's what you said the other week. Go on."

"The assumption is she suffered a heart attack while sitting in the bath and that led to her head dropping forward into the water and hence, drowning." She paused to drain her coffee cup. "What if someone held her head below the water and during that period she suffered a heart attack?"

"But there was no sign of forced entry. She appeared to have been relaxing in her bath ..."

"So someone she knew? Someone she thought she could trust? Someone who might have had a key?"

"Christ, Kelly, that's a huge leap to get to that."

"That's why we need to speak to Chamberlain again. Despite what he said, they knew each other. I'm wondering if that set of keys she had was for his other house, if she did indeed clean for him. If so, the question is, did he have a key for hers?"

"You two look as if you're plotting something." Luke Ormerod was grinning, holding a tray with a meal and a drink.

Strong looked up. "No, we're just talking about ... well, it doesn't matter. Come and sit down, Luke."

"If you're sure."

"Don't be daft," Stainmore agreed. "You can tell us how the search for likely suspects at Pinderfields is coming along."

"Ah, well ..." Ormerod placed his food plate, cutlery and mug of tea onto the table before looking round for the tray trolley. "Back in a sec."

Once he'd sat down, free of tray, he began, "We've identified five people so far who were at work at the hospital on the last occasion each of our victims attended."

"Have you finished the trawl?" Strong asked.

"Not quite, but I'm hoping to see it through today."

Stainmore joined in. "So who are they?"

Ormerod finished chewing a mouthful of cottage pie before answering. "There's a junior houseman, from Ghana, a female nurse from Rothwell, a male midwife from Huddersfield way, a services engineer from Selby and a porter from here in Wakefield."

"Well, no racism intended but I'm assuming the houseman is black, so we can eliminate him." Strong looked to Stainmore then Ormerod. "I doubt any of our victims would have needed to see a midwife, and unless the nurse was in direct contact with all of them, I think we're realistically prioritising looking at the services engineer and the porter."

A forkful of chips had followed the pie into Ormerod's mouth. "Exactly what I was thinking, guv."

"You're not really enjoying that, are you, Luke." Strong grinned and stole a chip from his plate.

"I'm absolutely starving," he responded.

"So you'll be tracking down those two then?" Stainmore added.

"Ah, now there's the thing." Ormerod pointed to Stainmore with his fork. "The porter is someone you might already know."

"Who?"

"Patrick Whitaker."

# 20
## Tuesday 31st July 2001

"So the new man starts tomorrow." Stainmore was making conversation as she and Strong retraced their steps of a few days ago, back to the offices of Charles Chamberlain Associates.

"First of August, yes."

"Any idea what he's like?"

Strong shook his head. "No more than the little Flynn told me. He's a graduate entry, thirty-six years old and comes fresh from the Cambridgeshire Force."

"Says it all," Stainmore quipped.

They walked on in silence for a few more minutes before she spoke again. "We have a definite appointment to see Chamberlain then?"

"Called this morning just to make sure he would be there. Receptionist put me through." He checked his watch. "Ten-thirty he said."

"No doubt Mrs Matthews will have filled him in on our discussion yesterday. Plenty of time to get their stories straight."

Strong looked at his DS, a mock surprised expression on his face. "Kelly, what are you saying? You think they may be fabricating something between them?"

"Perish the thought, guv."


"Mr Chamberlain, please," Strong addressed the receptionist he'd by-passed last week.

"Ah, yes," she said, and then with a hint of irony, "He is expecting you."

A few minutes later, Chamberlain, Strong and Stainmore were seated around the table in the meeting room next door to Chamberlain's office. The receptionist had brought a cafetiere of coffee, milk and sugar along with cups, saucers and spoons for three.

All smarm, Chamberlain asked, "So, how can I help you?"

Strong had decided to let Stainmore take the lead in this morning's questions.

"Denise Whitaker," she began, "have you had a chance to reconsider your answer from the last time we met?"

He leaned forward and pushed down on the handle of the cafetiere. "Well, obviously, having had a chance to think about it, of course I remember Mrs Whitaker. I just didn't put two and two together before, that's all." He poured coffee into three cups and slid two across the table to the detectives. "I thought you were referring to a client."

"So having thought about it, what can you tell me about her?"

He shrugged a surprised expression. "Not a lot really. She was a woman who cleaned the Leeds Road house for me."

Stainmore held out the set of keys she'd retained from Denise Whitaker's house. "Can you have a look at these. Are they for your Leeds Road house?"

Chamberlain reached into his trouser pocket and pulled out his own set of keys, took hold of the ones Stainmore offered and compared them. "Yes," he said. "These would be the set I gave to her so she could let herself in. Can I have them back?"

"In due course," she said, taking them back. "Mrs Whitaker, was she any good?"

"She was a cleaner, sergeant. Not a lot to it. It wasn't as though anyone lived there, so the workload wasn't particularly heavy."

Strong leaned forward and added a spoonful of sugar and some milk to his drink.

Stainmore's eyes never left Chamberlain. "When was the last time you saw her?" she continued.

Chamberlain gave a show of giving the question some thought. "Oh, it must have been ... early part of last year? ... maybe January, February, something like that."

"And where was that?"

"At the house. I'd arranged to meet her to pay her some wages."

"And there would be some record of that, of course?"

He laughed nervously. "Really, this was an informal arrangement. For all I knew she was claiming benefits or some such. I just paid her cash in an envelope. It wasn't worth formalising things."

Strong had taken a drink from his cup and placed it back on its saucer. "Is that something you do often, Mr Chamberlain?" he asked. "Paying cash in hand for services."

He looked sharply at Strong. "Look here, she was just a cleaner. It was more for her benefit than mine. But no, inspector, it is not something I do frequently or even condone."

"But obviously, this arrangement came to an end. Can you tell me about that?" Stainmore resumed.

"She just stopped coming. I mean, I left her wages in an envelope tucked below the clock on the mantelpiece, like I'd done before ... and the next time I went, it was still there and it was obvious she hadn't been to clean."

"Did that not concern you?"

"No, not really. I just thought she'd had a better offer and moved on. To be honest, I began to realise I didn't need a cleaner. So I just let it go."

"And how long had she cleaned for you?"

He puffed out his cheeks. "Ooh ... about a year, I think."

Stainmore looked surprised. "So she cleans for you for a year and then one day she fails to show and you don't appear concerned."

"Well, no."

"And you didn't try and call her?"

"I honestly can't remember."

"So if we said her telephone records showed that she was called from these offices on 6$^{th}$ June last year, that wouldn't have been you, would it?"

"It might have been. Yes, I remember now … I wanted to confirm she wasn't coming back."

"And what response did you get."

Chamberlain looked puzzled. "Nothing. There was no answer."

"Did you know where she lived?"

"Not exactly. I think she lived in Normanton. I may have had her address when she first started but I've no idea where I put it."

"So you wouldn't have had a key to her place?"

"Her house?" he flustered, "No. Why would I have a key to her house?"

"Or her flat," Stainmore said quietly.

"Er … yes. I mean, no."

Slowly she leaned forward and picked up her coffee for the first time.

Strong picked up the initiative. "Have you heard of something known as the *Talisman Club*, Mr Chamberlain?"

A flustered expression appeared on Chamberlain's face. "Talisman? No. I can't say I have."

Stainmore looked at her boss as she put down her coffee cup. "Is that a denial similar to the one you gave us last week when I asked you about Denise Whitaker?"

"I've told you, it means nothing to me."

"What sort of car do you drive," Stainmore threw in.

Chamberlain looked puzzled. "Car? Is that relevant to anything?"

"Just curious."

"A BMW 5 series. Black."

Strong stood. "Well, thanks for your cooperation Mr Chamberlain. I hope you won't find our visit necessary to report to ACC Wadsworth."

Chamberlain opened his mouth to reply but said nothing.

Stainmore followed Strong's lead and made for the door.

Hand on the handle, he turned to look at Chamberlain. "By the way, how is Mrs Chamberlain? No further relapses, I hope."

"Er, no. She's recovering well, thank you.

On the short walk back to Wood Street, Strong and Stainmore assessed the responses they'd heard from Chamberlain.

"He's lying again, guv," Stainmore said.

"He wouldn't make a very good poker player, that's for sure. Nice touch that," Strong replied, "throwing him off balance when he appeared to assume that Denise lived in a house."

"I'll bet he's been there. Would it be worth asking the neighbours if they'd ever seen his car outside? Would be a bit flash for there. Someone might have noticed."

Strong shrugged. "Not after all this time, Kelly. Even if one had been spotted, there'd be no proof it would have been his. Besides, he could have known she lived in a house from the newspaper reports of her death."

"You're probably right."

They paused while they let some traffic pass before crossing Wood Street and heading for the Police Station.

"But he knew what the *Talisman Club* was all about, though," Stainmore added, climbing the steps to the building and holding open the main door for her boss.

\*   \*   \*

"Have you seen Susan this morning?" Janey Clark sounded frustrated.

"Earlier on. Why? Have you lost her?" Souter was working on a story about the political and economic effects of bumper High Street sales for July when she interrupted his thoughts.

"She was supposed to be coming with me to the court for this afternoon's session, that's all." She was noisily packing a bag at her workstation. "Waste of time, that girl," she said under her breath. Then at normal volume, "Is she doing something for you that you've not mentioned?"

"What? No … I mean, she might be researching some background material we were talking about the other day. Not sure, though."

Janey gave big sigh and heaved her bag over her shoulder. "Well if she does show up, tell her to meet me in Court Two at the Crown Court."

"Will do," Souter said to her disappearing back. Once she'd gone, he picked up his mobile scrolled down and rang Susan's number.

\*   \*   \*

About ten miles away in Wakefield, Susan sheltered in a doorway opposite the Town Hall. She was on a reconnaissance mission. Totally unofficially, but she felt it had to be done. She was hoping she wouldn't be missed back in the offices of the Yorkshire Post. With a bit of luck, Janey would think she was with Bob and vice-versa. She'd been inside the Town Hall building to check her quarry, what she looked like, and hoped she would be the sort of person who likes to leave her workplace for a break at lunchtime.

A few minutes later, the woman emerged from the doorway and skipped down the steps onto the pavement, checked for traffic and made her way down Wood Street.

Susan checked her watch and followed.

Her phone rang just as she was passing the Police Station.

*"Susan, where are you? Janey's been looking for you."*

"There's just something I have to do, Bob," she answered.

*"Listen, don't take the piss. I called a favour to get you in here. Don't be letting me down."*

"I won't."

*"Well, whatever you're doing, it was a bit of research for me but get yourself in to Court Two at the Crown Courts as soon as you can. Janey's expecting you."*

She was about to say thanks, but the line had gone dead.

*       *       *

As Susan Brown answered her phone on the street below, Kelly Stainmore was in the CID Room a few yards away searching her desk drawer. She found the number she was looking for, picked up the phone and dialled.

"Ah, Doctor Symonds," she said when it was answered, "It's DS Stainmore here. I was wondering, about our body in the bath, Denise Whitaker ..." She paused as he greeted her. "Your initial findings were that the cause of death was drowning but there was evidence of a heart attack first?" She listened as the doctor confirmed the assessment.

"What I was wondering was ... could she have had her head held under the water and effectively been drowning and that caused her to panic and suffer a heart attack? I mean could it have been that way round?"

Another pause as she digested the medical opinion given.

"But it is possible?" She took a breath and listened again. "Okay, okay. But you couldn't rule it out either? ... Alright, thanks doctor." Thoughtful, she replaced the receiver.

"Not the right answer?" Ormerod asked from the adjacent desk.

"Not any sort of answer, Luke. It would be impossible to tell apparently, especially after the time lapse since death, which occurred first; heart attack or drowning."

Ormerod put his pen down, stood up and walked over to his colleague. "This one doesn't seem right to you, does it?"

She leaned back in her chair and looked to the window. "Oh, I don't know. Maybe I'm seeing something that isn't there. Or maybe it's because I've taken a dislike to this Chamberlain character."

"The one whose wife discovered that roll of film?"

She turned back to her colleague. "You know he assaulted her after that, don't you?"

He leaned on her desk, arms folded. "So I heard. But she didn't report it, though."

"How many of them do?"

"But are you thinking there's a link with Denise Whitaker?"

She sighed. "It was just that one call on her phone records from his office. I throw in her name; his initial denial. Now, he admits she did cleaning for him. So who knows, Luke. What else is he keeping quiet about?"

"But it sounds like you've no evidence ... just a feeling."

"Yeah, I know." She suddenly leaned forward. "Anyway, what are you up to?"

He walked back to his desk. "Well, I was about to head off to Pinderfields. The distractions."

"You got something?"

He shuffled some papers in a file. "I was going to question Mike Samson, the services engineer. According to his firm, he's supposed to be conducting some maintenance work in the plant rooms today. Fancy coming along?"

She gave the invitation a moment's consideration. "Why not." She stood up and pulled her jacket off the chair back. "What about Patrick Whitaker though? The porter. I thought he was on your list?"

Luke was already making for the door. "He's on holiday for a few days. Gone fishing in the Lakes, so his boss tells me."

The Estates Manager's office gave Ormerod the information he required. Mike Samson should be in a separate outbuilding behind one of the ward blocks. They followed the directions and saw a single storey flat roofed building with a white van parked outside. Ormerod and Stainmore exchanged glances.

"White van," Stainmore said.

"A Mercedes Sprinter, not dissimilar to a Transit," Ormerod added. "Let's see what he's got to say for himself."

Walking around to the front of the building, a pair of louvered doors were wide open. As they approached, a tall stocky figure in blue overalls and yellow hard hat emerged.

"Mr Samson?" Ormerod enquired.

A wary expression immediately appeared on his face. "Who wants to know?"

"I'm DC Luke Ormerod and this is my colleague DS Kelly Stainmore from Wood Street CID. I wondered if we could have a quick word."

"What's this about? I've got to get this equipment back up and running otherwise the hospital will give me stick."

Ormerod turned to the road. "Is that your van, Mr Samson?"

"Yes. What of it?"

"You had it long?"

Samson shrugged. "About two years, why?"

Ormerod flipped open his notebook. "Can you tell me where you were on Thursday 19th April this year?"

"I'll have to check my diary. It's in the van."

"If you would."

Samson walked to the van, opened the passenger door and flipped open a briefcase that was in the footwell. Rummaging through the pages of an A4 book with much writing, he stopped at 19th April 2001. "Pontefract Hospital," he said. "I do maintenance work at various hospitals around and about."

Ormerod asked about 25th April and 3rd May. On the first date, Samson was on site at Pinderfields and on the other, back at Pontefract. Finally, he mentioned the most recent, 16th July.

"Easy," Samson responded, "I was in Corfu. Two weeks, fantastic. Just got back to work last week."

Ormerod could see the days in the diary scored through with 'HOLIDAY' in bold letters.

"Thanks Mr Samson," Ormerod said. "If we need to contact you again, what's the best way?"

"Here." The man pulled out a business card and held it out to the detectives. "Mobile's on here. Now if that's all," he indicated the building, "I really need to fire this equipment back up, if you don't mind."

# 21

Belinda was soaking her tired body in a hot bath at the flat. She shouldn't feel fatigued but ever since she'd discovered the Outwood house, her energy levels had diminished. She needed to re-charge her batteries but everything that flowed from that discovery had acted like a drain.

She'd already come to one decision; she was finished with Charlie. There could never be any trust there again. Okay, so he earned mega-bucks but she'd never been interested in money. Fine, it was good to have and she certainly enjoyed living in a smart part of town. But she'd struggled to make ends meet when she was a student nurse before she met him and that held no fear for her now. She knew that traits inherited from her mother helped in that respect.

Anthony was her top priority now; and Grace. Her daughter seemed quite settled down south, so she wasn't as anxious over her future as her son's. But she'd have to get some professional advice. She thought of Karen, one of her nurse colleagues whom she'd trained with. She now worked on the Critical Care Unit at the hospital. It must have been three years ago when Karen went through a messy divorce but she remembered her saying how her solicitor had done a great job with the settlement. Maybe when she got back to work next week …

She closed her eyes, slid beneath the water and lost herself in the feeling of complete relaxation; the water enveloping her. She was a child again, back in the comfort of her parents' council house in Halifax. Safe, warm. She pushed herself back up into the sitting position and quickly opened her eyes, aware of another presence.

"Glad to see you're nice and relaxed," Charlie said. "At least one of us can."

Instinctively, she wrapped her arms around herself. "What are you doing in here? Get out!" she shouted.

"There was a time when you'd invite me in." A thin smile played around his mouth.

"I was younger and more naive then. Now will you please leave."

He shrugged and left the room. "I'll wait for you out here."

She pulled the plug, stood and began to dry herself on the towel. As she stepped over the side of the bath she paused and took some deep breaths. She could feel her heart racing. She could do without this stress. She was feeling vulnerable. Anthony wouldn't be home just yet. But then she relaxed. What was she worried about? It was only Charlie.

A few minutes later, a bath robe pulled tight around her, she walked through the lounge, past Charlie sitting on the sofa, and into the kitchen. She filled the kettle and switched it on before returning to stand in the doorway. "Do you want a drink?"

"Time was I'd pull that chord free and open up that robe," he smirked.

"But now, all you'd want to do with it is tie me up. I've seen the photos, don't forget."

He stood up, his face twisted in anger. "You've created all sorts of shit for me. Why couldn't you just mind your own business? The police have been round to the office again this morning asking all sorts of questions."

She pulled herself straight and tensed. "I'm surprised you haven't got your mate Giles to call them off."

This deflected him. "Hasn't bloody well worked."

"So you have tried then? I can only guess he's not one of your flagellation gang."

He flinched and pointed a finger at her. "Don't you … It's …" Once more, he softened. "Look, I was only involved with this because these guys are into all that. I thought it would be a good lever."

"Blackmail you mean?"

"No, not that. But it might lead to new business opportunities. It's useful to have influential people that would be willing to do you a favour."

Belinda broke into a smile. "So let me get this straight, you only organised all these ... entertainments to help promote the legal practice?"

"Well ... yes in a way."

"And you didn't get any enjoyment from it?"

He stiffened and took a step towards her. "That's not what it was all about."

"Bollocks!" She screwed up her face, her voice rising. "You must think I'm really thick. Of course you were enjoying it. Still are as far as I can see. You've not been near me for ages. And boy, am I so glad you haven't."

He took another step closer. "I haven't been near you because you don't do anything for me anymore." His voice rose until he was shouting at her. "You're so fucking frigid. I can't imagine you satisfying any man!"

All her feelings rose to the surface as she clenched a fist and punched him in the face. For a split second he stood stock still; shocked. And then he grabbed her by the hair and pulled her forward into the lounge. He pushed her over the arm of the sofa so she landed on her back lengthwise. The robe parted, exposing her naked body. He threw himself on top of her, knees either side and grabbed her head again.

He clenched his fist and was about to punch her when a blood-curdling scream came from the direction of the door. Anthony launched himself on top of his father and rolled him onto the floor. Flowers in a vase flew off the coffee table and smashed on the marble hearth of the fireplace. Son rained a hail of punches into father; mother screamed in shock.

"Anthony! For Christ's sake ..." Charlie struggled to free himself from his attacker.

"I told you last time ..." More effort and struggle. "Come near Mum again ..."

Finally Charlie rolled Anthony off and onto his back then turned and held him down.

"Calm down!" Charlie shouted. "Anthony! Stop!"

The boy struggled a bit longer but his anger finally subsided.

"I gave you a free shot last time," Charlie said. "No more."

Belinda, stunned initially, drew the robe around her and jumped on Charlie's back, her arm around his neck in a stranglehold, pulling.

"All right. All right … enough!" he said.

Slowly, all three began to relax and slacken their grip on each other. Belinda got to her feet, breathing heavily, then Charlie slowly stood. Anthony wriggled and jumped up.

"No!" Belinda shouted. "Anthony, no. Leave it. Your father's leaving."

Anthony was breathing hard, staring at his father, pure hate in his eyes.

Charlie looked from his son to Belinda, a chastened expression on his face. He shrugged his jacket back into shape before making halting progress to the door. "I'm sorry," he said, He disappeared into the hall and they heard the front door opening and closing.

Anthony looked to his mother, his expression softening. "Did he hurt you?"

Belinda chuckled. "I'm all right. But I did smack him in the face." She shook her fist loosely. "Quite a good one, if I say so myself … but it bloody hurt."

Anthony's face broke into a broad grin. He walked forward and hugged Belinda. She wrapped her arms around him and they stood motionless for a few minutes, tears dripping down her cheeks.

"You have to report this," Anthony finally said, pulling free. "It can't go on, Mum. This is the second time that I know of."

She wiped her face with both hands. "It is," she said. "But I don't want to cause any more trouble. I don't want to make things worse."

Anthony looked incredulous. "How can they get any worse?"

"Let me get dressed and we'll talk in a bit."

# 22
## Wednesday1st August 2001

"And so, ladies and gentlemen, without any further preamble, I'd like to introduce your new DCI, Rupert Hemingford," DCS Flynn concluded.

A short burst of applause broke out and Hemingford stepped forward. At six foot three, he was a few inches taller than Strong, slim and with mousy brown hair cut neatly short. "Thanks for those generous words," he addressed Flynn, before facing the assembled CID officers. "I hope to meet you all on a one-to-one basis over the next few days but from what Chief Superintendent Flynn has told me you're a very talented bunch and I should be pleased to have you working with me." His accent was slightly cultured, fairly nondescript southern English. "And please note, my attitude is very much working together with you, rather than you working for me. I look forward to that very much."

Luke Ormerod bent down and whispered into Strong's ear, "Tosser."

Strong, sitting at a desk, stifled a chuckle and looked round the room to see how the others were reacting to the new man. He wasn't as quick to make judgements. If the man had made it to the rank of DCI at the age of thirty-six then he obviously had some qualities that appealed to the higher ranks, even if much of it was political.

"And don't forget, my door is always open. Thank you."

DSs Kelly Stainmore and Jim Ryan stood together by the next desk to the right. Although looking at Hemingford, Stainmore didn't seem to be paying full attention. DCs Malcolm Atkinson and John Darby were standing by a bank of filing cabinets whilst Trevor Newell and Sam Kirkland stood in front of the desk to Strong's left.

Another polite burst of applause and Hemingford disappeared with Flynn.

"I see he's been on the standard team building course they've all been on," Ormerod sneered. "*My door is always open*," he mimicked.

"Give the man a break, Luke. He's only just walked in. He's only saying the same sort of things I would."

"Difference is, we know you mean it, guv." Ormerod turned away, content to have made his point.

Atkinson and Darby joined Ryan and Stainmore and mumbled a few words before dispersing to their respective work stations.

Newell and Kirkland turned to Strong. "So what do you reckon, guv?" Kirkland asked.

"Early days," was all that Strong felt able to add.

Sergeant Bill Sidebotham appeared at the door and scanned the assembled detectives. Eventually, he spotted his target and waited until Strong caught his eye. He gave a nod and disappeared back into the corridor. Strong rose and made his way as discreetly as possible in pursuit.

In the corridor, Sidebotham looked serious. Strong knew there was something amiss as his usual demeanour was a smiling jovial character.

"Colin, I've got a woman and her son downstairs … will only speak to you," he said.

"Who?"

"Gave her name as Belinda Chamberlain."

*  *  *

Strong held out a hand to Belinda after he walked into the interview room where Bill Sidebotham had placed her and Anthony. "Mrs Chamberlain, how can I help?"

She shook it gently. "Belinda, please."

"He attacked her again," Anthony interceded. "He was on top of her about to punch her in the face."

Belinda turned to her son. "Anthony, it wasn't as straightforward as that."

"I saw what I saw," he said belligerently.

"You weren't there from the start."

Strong could see the frustration building in the lad's demeanour. "Perhaps if you would come with me, Belinda, and we could have a conversation as you would want to," he said. "Anthony will be fine in here." He looked to the boy. "Perhaps a drink … tea, coffee or a cold one?"

Anthony sullenly shook his head. "Make sure you tell him everything," he said to his mother.

"I'll talk to your mum and then we'll take a statement from you. Is that okay?" Strong said.

"Suppose," he shrugged.

Strong led Belinda upstairs to the Soft Interview Suite, reserved for sensitive questioning of victims of crimes such as rape or sexual assaults. He left her alone for a few minutes whilst he grabbed Kelly Stainmore to sit in with him.

Once seated on comfortable sofas, Belinda, having declined a drink, began telling Strong and Stainmore about the events of the night before. He let her tell the story without interruption until she concluded at the point where Charlie had left.

"Okay," Strong said. "Thanks for being so frank about all this, Belinda. Now I would like my colleague DS Stainmore, Kelly here, to take a formal statement from you. Are you quite sure you'd like to do that?"

She looked surprised. "Are you trying to talk me out of this?"

"No, not at all. It's just something we have to make certain, that's all. Don't worry." He smiled. "You've done the right thing."

Ten minutes later, Stainmore was taking Belinda's statement as Strong and Ormerod sat with Anthony.

"There's nothing to be frightened of Anthony," Strong said after introducing his colleague. "Your mother's having a statement taken by another of my colleagues."

The boy looked disbelievingly. "Is that when you talk her out of it?"

"Not at all. We take domestic crime very seriously. Certainly I do, as do my colleagues." Strong glanced to Ormerod who nodded agreement. "But before we can take any action, we need to have written statements. Now, is it okay if you tell us, in your own words in your own time, exactly what happened last night?"

Anthony proceeded to tell how he'd arrived back home, spotted his father's car parked outside and rushed inside. When asked why he'd 'rushed' he said he'd been fearful of what his father might do to his mother. He went on to relate how he'd entered the flat and heard his parents arguing. He appeared at the living room door to find his mother on her back on the settee and his father astride, one knee either side. His father had hold of Belinda's head and was poised as if to punch her.

"But he didn't actually strike her, did he?" Strong interrupted.

Anthony screwed up his face. "Who's side are you on?"

"It's not a question of sides," Strong responded in an attempt to answer the lad's natural suspicions. "We just need to be absolutely sure of what happened. It has to be accurate because whatever we record may be part of evidence that will be given in a court of law. If there's any flaw in that evidence, a defence barrister would expose it and any future case could collapse."

"I understand," he said, in a conciliatory tone. "In answer to your question, no, he didn't actually strike her." His tone hardened again. "But he did that night you saw us in A & E."

"So why don't you tell me about that night?" Strong prompted.

"I was in my room, listening to some CDs. Mum had come in from a late shift and Dad was watching TV. After a little while, I heard their voices raised. I couldn't make out what they were saying at first. But they got louder and I started to get worried. As I opened the door, I heard Dad say something about photos. There was a crash of ... like dishes crashing to the floor. Then a scream. I knew he'd hurt her. I ran into the living room and she was getting up off the floor by the door to the kitchen. He was huffing and puffing ... like walking round ... like in circles. I rushed over to Mum and began to help her up."

"And what did your dad say?"

"He was in denial. 'I never touched her,' he said. 'She stumbled and fell against the door frame.' He had both hands on his head, like he was in desperation."

"What did you do then?"

"Mum was sort of mumbling. I couldn't get much sense from her, but I got her onto one of the chairs and put her head back. Then I went into the kitchen and got a cloth, run it under the cold tap and took it back into Mum. I helped her hold it to her head. And then I phoned for an ambulance. Well it was a head injury."

Strong nodded his approval to this course of action. "And where was your Dad during this time?"

"He'd disappeared. Drove off somewhere I think, because his car was gone when the ambulance arrived."

"That's good Anthony, you've done well. But one last thing, did you actually see your father assault your mother on that occasion?"

Anthony seemed deflated. "No," he said quietly.

"That's all right," Strong said. "It all adds to the circumstantial nature of the allegations. We'll see what your mum says and take things from there. Is that okay?"

Anthony nodded, head bowed.

"In the meantime, DC Ormerod here will take a formal statement from you."

The boy eventually looked up at Strong. "Thanks," he said.

\* \* \*

"Colin, take a seat." Hemingford offered a clean, neatly-manicured hand. Strong shook it then sat down opposite the desk and big leather chair he'd inhabited for the past eleven months.

"I've heard a lot about you. All good," the new DCI added quickly.

I'll bet, Strong thought. Aloud, he said, "I'm sure you'll learn the rest in due course, sir."

Hemingford laughed, nervously. He'd been briefed about his past record, he was sure. "Can we drop the 'sir' thing too, Colin. I'm Rupert. I feel it helps to make the team feel comfortable." Another modern concept, Strong thought. He wasn't sure how the rest of the team would react.

"Okay, Rupert." Strong's eyes quickly took in the few personal items that the new man had brought to the office, most notably a couple of framed awards on the wall behind his head. "How do you think life in the north will suit?"

Hemingford grinned. "I'm sure it'll be just fine. I know how friendly the people can be." He shifted his posture in the chair then continued, "I just thought we might have an informal chat ... get to know each other a bit. Now I know we had a group get together earlier, for want of a better phrase, but I just wanted to hear how you view the current situation, Colin."

"What do you want to know?"

Hemingford was sitting forward with both hands on the desk. As he spoke he used them to accentuate his various points. "Well, Detective Chief Superintendent Flynn tells me the number one case the team are looking into at the moment is this spate of distraction burglaries involving elderly people."

"That's right. DS Stainmore and DC Ormerod are leading that one. We're looking at the possibility that someone from Pinderfields Hospital is involved."

"And what's the logic behind that?"

Over the next few minutes, Strong explained how they had arrived at that decision.

When he'd finished, Hemingford asked what he thought of Kelly Stainmore and Luke Ormerod.

Strong's hackles rose. "I'm a firm believer in people making their own minds up. I'm not going to comment on any of my team in that respect."

"Look, I see you as my right hand man, Colin," he responded. "I'm just trying to hit the ground running, so to speak. But I respect your view. I'll be talking to all the team individually over the next day or so." He leaned back in the chair. "Anyway, what's occupying your attention at the moment?"

Strong related his dealings with the Chamberlains and how Belinda had made an accusation of serious assault against her husband.

"Always a bit messy, these domestics, Colin."

"No more than any other assault."

"So what's your next move?"

"I'll be interviewing Charles Chamberlain under caution and review the matter after that."

Strong could see Hemingford's expression change. Flynn's already had a word with you on ACC Wadsworth's behalf, he thought. "I'm not sure if that's wise, Colin," he said.

"I'm not sure Mrs Chamberlain would agree with you, Rupert," Strong replied sarcastically. "Especially if you had seen her face last week."

Hemingford sighed. "I'm sure you'll be diplomatic."

"Never anything else, Rupert." Strong stood up. "If that's all, I want to make some phone calls."

Hemingford also got out of his chair and held out his hand once again. "I understand your disappointment, Colin, but let's try and work together."

Strong looked at the proffered hand for a beat, shook it, turned and left the office.

# 23
## Thursday 2<sup>nd</sup> August 2001

Sammy was well aware she'd only get one chance at this. One attempt to obtain the information that may or may not shed light on exactly what dark deeds were taking place at the council with regard to the Lofthouse Development.

Susan had observed Faulkner's secretary's lunch breaks for the past two days and hoped she was the creature of habit she appeared to be.

Just before twenty-five past twelve, Susan looked to Sammy who took a deep breath to steady her nerves and nodded back. The drizzly rain had been coming down all morning and they quickly crossed the road to step inside the town hall building. Sammy shrugged off her coat and handed it to Susan. If her subterfuge was to succeed, she had to give the impression of having arrived internally.

A couple of minutes later, Sammy knocked on the door to Bernard Faulkner's office and opened the door. Brenda, his secretary, had tidied her desk, was on her feet, arm out, about to take her coat off the stand.

"Oh sorry," Sammy said, "are you off out?"

"Can I help you?" Brenda asked.

"I'm Sarah from IT. I've got a report of a fault on Mr Faulkner's PC. I know he's back on Monday and we were scheduled to come then but I've finished my other tasks and I thought I'd come and take a look now, if that's okay?"

"Well, I'm not sure … with Mr Faulkner still on holiday …"

"I just thought if it could be rectified now, then when he's back next week, it would be less disruptive."

"I can see that … it's just …"

"He won't know I've been in."

Sammy could see Brenda weighing up her options. "Well …I suppose it'll be alright," Brenda finally said. She opened a desk drawer, took out a key and unlocked the door into Bernard Faulkner's inner sanctum.

"Could you just lock his door again and leave the key in here" Brenda indicated the top drawer of her desk.

"Sure, no problem." Sammy smiled and indicated the coat stand. "You'll need your umbrella, I think it's still raining."

With Brenda gone, Sammy walked into Faulkner's office and took in the room's interior. In contrast to the plain walls and single plain window of Brenda's office, this room was different class. Oak wood panelling lined the walls and the two windows were finished with genuine leaded glass. A large oak desk and leather chair were the focal point, four other chairs were dotted around the room. She sat down in his seat, fired up his computer and waited for it to come to life.

Out in the street, Susan, tucked into a doorway, observed Brenda leave the building, open up an umbrella and walk down the street towards the centre of town. She watched until she disappeared from view then took out her mobile and texted Sammy.

The computer was slow and finally prompted Sammy to enter a password. She looked around the tidy desk then opened a drawer. On a post-it note stuck to a diary was what she'd hoped to find. So much for security measures, she thought. She tapped in the symbols and waited. Another message appeared to let her know the password would expire in six days and did she want to change it now? She grinned and began typing. Her new password was accepted and, she thought, IT help or no on Monday, he would have problems accessing his files.

A text announced itself on her phone and she read what Susan had sent. If she was as much a creature of habit as Susan suggested then Sammy would have thirty-five minutes before her return. Not a great deal of time if there was a lot of material to copy.

The screen settled down and Sammy opened up Faulkner's email. Plugging in a blank memory stick she began the lengthy process of copying the various folders of his emails. Whilst that was happening, she pulled out a notebook from her bag and began to look through his drawers for any other useful bits of information. The desk diary yielded several nuggets. She noted down one or two email addresses, family birthdays and other personal information that may help should she need to second guess any other passwords. A card with an odd symbol and the words *Talisman Club* was between a couple of pages. She turned it over. The rear was blank. It was an establishment she'd never heard of but imagined it was probably some private members' gambling club. A message appeared on the screen indicating the copying exercise was complete. She dismissed any further thoughts on the card from her mind and carefully placed it back in the diary.

Brenda had reached the sanctuary of The Ridings shopping centre. Under cover and reasonably warm she wandered aimlessly into Primark to see if anything jumped out at her. She'd bought a paper in Smiths and would aim for Morrison's at the far end to pick up a few bits of shopping and a sandwich she would eat at her desk when she got back. A couple of tops looked interesting but she couldn't find one in her size. She checked her watch and decided to leave and make her way towards the supermarket. As she strolled along the walkway, not paying much attention, a voice called to her. "Hi Brenda."

She looked over and saw a man she recognised from work. "Hello, Tom," she greeted. She was about to walk on when she hesitated and turned to him. "Oh Tom, thanks for sending down one of your young girls just now."

Tom looked puzzled. He ran the Council's IT department. "Sorry, you've lost me," he said.

"Sarah turned up just before lunch."

"Sarah? We don't have anyone called Sarah." Tom frowned. "I've got Carl pencilled in for Monday morning on Mr Faulkner's computer fault."

Brenda could feel her cheeks colour. "Oh, ignore me," she flustered. "My mistake. You're IT aren't you? Sarah's from another department altogether."

Tom gave a nervous smile before continuing on his way.

She felt sick. Who was that who had talked her way into her boss's office? More importantly, what was she doing? She had to get back, and quick. If anyone found out about this, she'd lose her job. And she liked her job. She liked Mr Faulkner.

Sammy was still trawling through the computer files. Whenever she came across anything interesting, she made a copy onto the memory stick. A lot of the folders appeared fairly boring; minutes of meetings, internal memos, expenses. Finally, tucked away in a fairly non-descript folder, she came across a sub-folder labelled 'TD'. Only when she opened that up did she realise it referred to Thistle Developments. Another one to copy. Then there was the folder headed 'Personal'. That had to be worth copying, she thought. Just then, the familiar ping of an incoming text message sounded. It was Susan. 'Get out quick!' it said. The files were still copying and the message said '4 minutes remaining'. God this machine was really slow.

Was Susan panicking? She called her back, "What's up?" she asked.

*"The secretary's on her way back up the street. You need to get out now,"* Susan hissed.

"I thought you said she doesn't come back for another …" Sammy looked at her watch. "… fifteen minutes?"

*"I don't know but she's about fifty yards from the main door."*

Sammy checked the copy message on the computer screen. "I need another five minutes in here. Do something, Suz." She ended the call and began closing drawers and tidying the desk, making sure everything was back where it was.

Brenda was alarmed. What was she going to find? Should she grab hold of Security? But that would expose her own stupidity. She hurried on up the street, brolly in front of her, shielding her from the worst of the rain. Only trouble was, she kept bumping into passers-by. After the third apology, she folded the umbrella away, faced the drizzle and strode up the street, back to the Town Hall as fast as she could. She was so intent on her own thoughts, she never saw the young woman cross the street in front of her and stop.

"Hi," the woman said. "It's Mr Faulkner's secretary, isn't it?"

"Er … but yes. Who are you?" She looked from the woman to her goal, the doors of the building.

"I was just wondering when would he be back?" Susan was standing immediately in front of Brenda.

"But … oh, Monday," Brenda was flustered. "If you'll excuse me, I'm late."

"So would he be available for interview next week sometime?" Susan persisted as they danced around one another on the pavement.

I … I would think so but ring the office on Monday and we'll see what we can do … er Miss …?"

"er, Robson. I'm from Yorkshire Life."

"Yes, yes, okay. Call us on Monday." Brenda finally skirted the woman and hurried on up the steps and in through the big doors. She wasn't sure what would face her. Would the woman still be there? If she was, what would she do? She hoped there wouldn't be a violent confrontation.

Susan only hoped she'd bought her friend enough time. And that Brenda hadn't noticed she had an extra coat draped over her arm.

"Come on, come on, come on," Sammy pleaded with the computer. Finally, the copy was complete and she pulled the memory stick from the machine and set in motion the instructions to shut it down. Her notebook was closed and placed back in her bag just as she heard movement outside.

# 24

*"I tell you, it's fantastic. Just you and all that nature. Mountains, lakes, not to mention lovely pubs."*

*"Burrit's so bloody boring, Pat. Ah'd rather watch paint dry. I mean what d'you do all day, sittin' beside an open lake, the wind whistlin' off the mountain, an' all you've got for company is some bloody orange float bobbin' on the water."*

The conversation from the porter's room drifted down the corridor as Stainmore and Ormerod approached the open door.

"It's a waste of time talking to you," Patrick Whitaker said to his colleague as Stainmore and Ormerod appeared at the door.

"Can I help you?" the other man asked.

"It's Mr Whitaker we'd like to see," said Stainmore. "Is there somewhere we could talk?"

"Can you give us a minute, Billy," Whitaker said.

"I've got to go up to X Ray anyway." Billy stood and hurried from the room. Ormerod thought he recognised the face but focused on their target.

"Is this about my mother again," Whitaker asked Stainmore.

"I'm afraid we're here on another matter, Mr Whitaker," she answered.

He looked nervous as Ormerod closed the door. "Oh yes?"

"Can you tell us what it is that you porters have to do on a daily basis?"

"How do you mean?"

"Well, your normal duties. What would they be?"

"All sorts really. We take patients from department to department. From A & E up to the wards, if they're to be admitted. Take patients who're not so mobile from some of the outpatient clinics to X Ray. Stuff like that."

"And you're the sort of bloke who enjoys that kind of work?" He looked puzzled, but Stainmore continued. "You know, interacts with the patients."

"Mostly they're okay, yeah. Some welcome a chat, others are a bit past it but ... what's this about?"

Ormerod flicked open his notebook. "What kind of vehicle do you drive, Mr Whitaker?" he asked.

"A Vauxhall Astra, why?"

"And could you tell me where you were on 19$^{th}$ April? It was a Thursday."

"A Thursday? Probably here," Whitaker responded.

"What about Wednesday 25$^{th}$ April?"

After this and other dates of 3$^{rd}$ May and 16$^{th}$ July had drawn similar responses, Stainmore joined in. "Would it surprise you to know that you were actually off-duty on all these dates?"

Whitaker looked flustered. "Well if I was, I'd either be at home or fishing somewhere. I can't remember what I were doing back in April on a specific day."

"Okay, Mr Whitaker. Thanks for the moment." Stainmore said. "We'll be in touch if we need any more information."

Outside in the car park, Stainmore posed the question of Ormerod, "What time does he finish his shift, did his boss say?"

Ormerod checked his watch. "About half an hour. He's off at two."

She unlocked her car and they got in. "Right, let's try one more thing," she said and started the engine.

*   *   *

After his meeting with Hemingford yesterday, Strong had called the offices of Chamberlain Associates to be told that Charles was in London for a meeting that afternoon and was staying overnight. He wouldn't be back in the office until this afternoon. That suited Strong. For a start it meant that Belinda should have an incident free night.

He put his head round the door of the CID Room just after lunch and checked who was there. Malcolm Atkinson was studying his computer screen and Trevor Newell and John Darby were discussing a statement that Trevor had taken from one of those arrested for car theft the previous week.

Darby looked up as Strong entered. "All right, guv?" he enquired.

"Where's Kelly?" he asked.

"Out with Luke. I think they've got a break on those distractions."

"And Jim Ryan not around either?"

"Court, guv," Newell answered. "That GBH case. The serious assault on the priest."

Strong nodded, disappointed he couldn't take his preferred detectives with him. "Are you busy at the moment, John?"

"Not especially."

"Well get your jacket and come with me."

Darby slipped his arms in the sleeves. "Oh, before I forget, guv, you were asking about a development at Lofthouse?"

"Anything interesting?"

"Not really. Just another big out of town shopping development that's planned for just off the M62. To be honest, I don't know how they all survive. I mean, there's only a limited amount of money people can spend."

The conversation progressed as they descended the stairs. "But what stage is it at? I haven't seen any activity there. But there again, I haven't been past for a month or two."

"Only got final planning approval last month. Not sure when work will start."

"You did a bit of building work in the past, John."

"Did a bit with my uncle's building company, yeah."

"How much do you reckon a scheme like that would be worth?"

At the rear door to the car park, Darby paused and sucked his breath through his teeth.

"You sound like a cowboy builder," Strong remarked. "I'm not asking for a quote, just your gut feel."

"Must be near to one hundred million all in."

Previously Strong had walked the short distance to Chamberlain's office, but today he took a car. On the way, he briefed Darby on the purpose of his visit. And more importantly, for him to keep quiet unless Strong invited him to say something.

"And resist the temptation to ogle the receptionist's tits, John," Strong concluded as he pulled into a visitor slot near the entrance.

Darby looked put out. He was even more put out when they walked in and he saw the woman behind the desk who looked about sixty with grey hair in a bun. "You were joking?" he said quietly to his boss.

"Mr Chamberlain, please." Strong showed his warrant card.

"You'll have to excuse me, sir," the receptionist said, lifting the phone and checking for an extension number. "I'm only filling temporarily."

Strong looked to Darby and raised his eyebrows.

Chamberlain asked her to send the detectives through and met them at his office door. "Inspector Strong," he sighed. "This is becoming boring now." He turned back into the room.

"I'm afraid this is more significant, sir," Strong said. "We've received a serious complaint against you and, as you'll no doubt be aware, we have a duty to investigate that complaint."

Chamberlain flopped down on his seat. "Oh, what is it now?"

"Two nights ago, that would be Tuesday, the 31st July, did you visit your wife Belinda at home?"

Chamberlain looked to the ceiling. "Of course, I might have known."

"So did you, sir?"

"You know I did, because she's told you. He leaned forward. "Look, we had words. It was just another argument. Purely domestic."

"That's not quite how it was put to us. Mr Chamberlain, we'd like to talk to you at Wood Street."

Chamberlain looked surprised. "You're arresting me?"

"Not unless we have to, sir," Strong responded, a satisfying feeling spreading through him.

Chamberlain lifted the phone and dialled a number. It was his solicitor and he asked him to meet him at Wood Street as soon as he could. Satisfied with the answer, Chamberlain stood up and put on his jacket. "Let's get this over with then," he said, resignedly.

*   *   *

Stainmore pulled her car to a halt kerbside about fifty yards from Whitaker's front door. Ormerod sat beside her in the passenger seat. The first thing that caught their attention was the white Ford Transit van parked nearby.

"So what now?" Ormerod asked.

"We wait," she said. After a pause, she continued, "Last time I called here … you know, to talk to Whitaker about his mother, the front door was opened by his son, Frank I think he said he was. Anyway, a young lad maybe around twenty." She looked at Ormerod. "I thought it was just nerves, the way he was guarded when he opened the door to me. And then, when he realised it wasn't him I'd come to see, he couldn't get out quickly enough."

Ormerod was nodding, his attention firmly on the street. "So we have a stocky bloke who could have had contact with all the victims and a younger lad … how tall?"

"About three inches shorter."

"A shorter slim lad who gets a bit nervous when police come knocking on the door." He gave his moustache a stroke. "Interesting to say the least."

Before Stainmore could comment, a dark blue Astra approached from the opposite direction and parked in front of the Transit. Patrick Whitaker got out quickly, locked up and hurried to his front door.

"Do we make a move now?"

"Give it a minute, Luke."

A minute was all it took for Frank Whitaker to emerge from the flat and trot towards the Transit.

"Stop him," Stainmore instructed, opening her door.

Whitaker junior spotted Ormerod approaching, jumped into the van and tried to start the engine but he was too late. Ormerod wrenched open the door and grabbed the keys from the ignition.

"Not in a hurry, are we son?" the detective said. "Because we'd like a word. Police." He flipped open his warrant card. "Why don't you come and join your dad."

Frank Whitaker became compliant. Outside the van, Ormerod held him by the arm and locked the door before leading him back to the front door where Stainmore waited.

"It's Frank, isn't it?" she asked. The youth nodded. "Invite us in then."

Ormerod allowed Frank to open the door with his key but put a finger to his lips and gripped his arm tighter to indicate he wouldn't be best pleased if he shouted out to his father.

Their footsteps sounded on the bare wooden treads as they climbed the stairs to the first floor flat.

"Frank," Patrick Whitaker said from above, "I thought I told you to piss off in that van before ..." The three figures emerged into the hallway and Whitaker senior broke off. "Shit," he said quietly.

"Shit indeed, Mr Whitaker," Stainmore said. "Why don't we carry on with our chat from earlier."

Whitaker turned and led them into the living room.

"Not dashing off anywhere important, were you?" Ormerod asked Frank.

Frank shook his head and said nothing. "He was just going to get a few bits from the shop, that's all," Patrick responded.

"Make yourselves comfortable," Stainmore said to the men. "Sit down."

Both complied as Ormerod walked around the room.

"I was wondering if you'd had a chance to think what you were doing on those dates we spoke of?"

" Er … well, in April, I'd have probably been at home …" Patrick stuttered, "… or doin' some shoppin' I can't really remember." His attention followed Ormerod as he prodded about the detritus on the mantelpiece. "That May date, I think I was in Leeds and the last one a few weeks back, I'd have been fishing."

By now, Ormerod was looking at the contents of a fruit bowl that stood on a sideboard. It contained no fruit, just odd keys, receipts, a corkscrew and some opened letters, junk mail mostly.

"Here, don't you need a warrant for that?" Patrick asked, growing agitated.

"We can easily get one, Mr Whitaker … if that's what you want," Stainmore replied.

He turned his head when she responded and Ormerod opened the middle drawer of the unit. Whitaker heard him do that and jumped up. "Just a minute," he said, "that's private."

Ormerod pulled out a long box and opened it. He held it up showing a row of medals on display. "A relative of yours?"

"Er … yes … on my mother's side," Whitaker mumbled.

"And he was Francis Eric Parsons of The Green Howards, was he?" Ormerod looked to Stainmore then back to Whitaker. "I think we'd better continue our discussions at Wood Street," he said.

# 25

Brenda rushed up the stairs and scurried along the corridor to her office. Opening the door she looked round. Her room was empty but the door to Faulkner's office was ajar. She walked slowly towards it, her breathing heavy. She stopped and listened. All was quiet except for the faint traffic noise from outside; that and the sound of her own blood pounding through her ears. Another couple of steps and she gripped the handle. She swung the door open, fully expecting 'Sarah' to come rushing past her. Nobody. The office was empty. She held her breath and walked over to her boss's desk and took in the correspondence file she'd been adding to all week, the desk-tidy and the framed photographs of his children. All seemed as it had been earlier that morning. Her hand dropped down and felt the computer stack on the floor below the desk. Warm. So, she had been using it, whoever *she* is. Brenda finally exhaled and began to relax. Whoever she was had gone and there was nothing she could do about it now. She only hoped that there had been no damage done. A knock on her office door made her jump.

"Hello."

Brenda recognised the woman's voice as her accoster of a few minutes ago out in the street.

"I'm sorry to bother you again," Susan called from the doorway, as Brenda walked back into her own room, "but I was wondering if you could direct me to the Head of Planning's office?"

Brenda shrugged off her coat. "Er … yes. Of course."

Susan adopted her best concerned look. "Is everything okay? You seem a bit flustered."

"No. It's just that … oh, nothing. Never mind." The secretary hung her coat on the free-standing wooden coat rack behind the door and ushered Susan outside. "Planning is next floor down. I'll show you."

As Susan turned away, a flash of movement from inside Brenda's office caught her attention. She put a hand to her eye and rubbed it, hoping Brenda hadn't noticed her surprise.

They began to walk along the corridor towards the main stairs.

"I'm sorry if I seem to be taking up a lot of your time …" Susan purposely walked slower than Brenda. "You must be busy."

Brenda gave a nervous smile. "Yes. But I'll be busier next week when Mr Faulkner's back."

By the door to the Ladies toilet, Susan stopped and faced Brenda. Over her shoulder she caught sight of Sammy's head popping out from the office doorway momentarily. "I just need to call in here," Susan said. "There's no need to show me where Planning is." The slim figure of Sammy crept out of the office down the corridor and disappeared in the opposite direction to take the rear stairs. "Next floor down, you said. I'll find it. And thanks a lot."

"If you're sure." Brenda appeared distracted once more.

"You've been really helpful. Thanks." Susan pushed open the door to the toilets stepped inside and checked she was on her own. She ran a tap, looked at herself in the mirror and let out a sigh of relief.

"Christ that was close," Susan said. They were back out on the street and Susan was helping Sammy put on her coat. The rain had stopped but it was still cool.

A big grin was on Sammy's face. "I've been in tighter scrapes than that. Besides, you need a bit of stress to make life interesting."

They began walking down the street in the direction of Westgate railway station. "But not that interesting. I've had enough stress to last me a lifetime, thank you very much." Susan was quiet for a few seconds. "She'd obviously thought about things and worked out something was wrong. I don't know how but she must have realised you weren't who you claimed to be. Anyway, how come she never spotted you?"

"Rule one, Suz, when you enter somewhere unfamiliar, always suss out where you can hide if you need to. A bit like you see in films where the characters always need to sit facing the door."

"So, go on, where did you find?"

"There was a big cupboard on the side wall. It was a bit tight but I managed to squeeze myself below the middle shelf and hold the doors closed. I must admit I thought she'd hear me breathing … but then someone came knocking on the office door and she left."

It was Susan's turn to smile. "Glad I was of use. I wondered if you'd had time to get out. She was in a rush." She turned to look behind them, still nervous that Brenda might also have worked out a connection between the two of them. But there were only some shoppers and a few office workers returning from their lunch breaks. "So what did you find out?"

Sammy unzipped her bag and pulled out the memory stick. "Here, you'll need to check this out. There's plenty on there."

Again, Susan looked around before secreting the stick in her pocket. "I'll have a look when I get back to the office." She increased her pace. "Come on. We need to catch the ten past."

# 26

Strong drew to a halt in the car park to the rear of Wood Street police station just as Stainmore and Ormerod turned up with the Whitakers.

Strong got out from the driver's seat and opened the rear door to let Darby and Chamberlain out. As he did so, Stainmore did likewise for Ormerod and her suspects. Stainmore and Chamberlain exchanged glances.

"DS Stainmore," Chamberlain acknowledged.

Patrick Whitaker stood up behind her, Ormerod supervising Frank Whitaker on the other side of the car.

"We meet again, Mr Chamberlain," Stainmore responded before looking at Patrick intending to lead him into the station. His puzzled expression interested her. "Something wrong?" she asked him.

His face quickly resumed normality. "No."

With Patrick and Frank Whitaker booked in and sitting in separate interview rooms, and Chamberlain safely ensconced in another awaiting his solicitor, Stainmore took the opportunity to tell Strong why they'd brought their suspects in.

"Great," he said. "Get yourself a search warrant and see what else you can find. And don't forget the van."

Stainmore nodded. "I see you've got something interesting on our esteemed friend Charles?" she asked.

"An assault complaint from his wife."

"Bastard."

"I'll see what he has to say when his solicitor turns up."

\*   \*   \*

With the search team going through Whitaker's flat, Stainmore and Ormerod began their interview of Patrick

Whitaker. A duty solicitor had been called and was sitting at the suspect's side. The sealed evidence bag containing Frank Parson's war medals lay on the desk between them.

"Mr Whitaker, can you tell me how these medals came to be in your possession?" Stainmore began.

Whitaker drew a breath then responded, "I found them."

"Really? So why was your first reaction to their discovery that they belonged to a ..." she opened her notebook and ran her finger down to the appropriate point and began to read, "... a relative on my mother's side?"

"I was confused."

"So if you found them, where about exactly did you come across them?"

"When I were fishin'. A couple of weeks ago. Down by Newmillerdam."

Newmillerdam was one of Wakefield's best known beauty spots. There was a large lake with wooded surround and paths all around that were popular with dog walkers, ramblers and families. On the road that passed by, a number of cafes, pubs and ice cream vans were poised to cater for visitors. You could also fish in those lakes.

"How did you find them exactly?"

"Well, half way round the big lake, that's one of my favourite spots ... when I was setting up my chair and rods, I just saw this box, in the long grass near the edge. So I picked it up and looked inside."

"And you didn't think to hand it in?" Ormerod joined in. "You didn't think Mr Parsons might be missing them?"

The solicitor put a cautionary hand on his client's arm.

Whitaker gave him a quick glance then shook his head nervously. "I didn't think."

Ormerod smirked. "Do you really expect us to believe that?"

He wrung his hands and looked down to the desk. "It's what happened."

"And can anyone confirm that?" Stainmore asked.

Before Whitaker could answer a knock on the door interrupted them. Trevor Newell's head appeared and indicated the corridor.

Stainmore made the appropriate announcement for the tape suspending the interview, followed him outside and closed the door.

"Call from Whitaker's flat," Newell said, "they've found some jewellery they think could be a match for a couple of the victims."

"Good. How long before we can get confirmation on that?"

"Possibly later this evening. But that's not all …in Whitaker junior's van, a flat cap and … a false moustache." Newell grinned.

Stainmore smiled and nodded. "Little and Large."

Back in the room, she resumed the interview. "Okay, Mr Whitaker, let's stop the fairy stories, shall we."

He looked puzzled.

"We've found items of jewellery in your flat that we suspect belong to a number of victims of distraction burglaries." She paused and stared at him. "Furthermore, in the van parked outside and registered to your son, Frank, we discovered a flat cap and a false moustache."

Whitaker looked down onto the floor.

"The description we have for the lead perpetrator of those burglaries matches you, wearing a flat cap and moustache. The second perp is a close match to Frank. What can you tell me about that?"

"I think, sergeant, some time with my client would be appropriate," the solicitor interceded.

Ten minutes later, the duty solicitor announced that Whitaker was prepared to make a statement.

Stainmore began to write.

He made a full confession to five burglaries committed over the period from April through to July in West and South Yorkshire. He had spoken to all victims in his capacity as porter at Pinderfields and obtained background information from them as well as addresses.

He was at pains to point out that Frank was coerced by him into taking part.

"We'll see what your son has to say when we take a statement from him, Mr Whitaker," Stainmore responded.

They were about to wrap up the interview when she thought of something else. "I am sorry about your mother," she said, "but when we spoke about that at your flat before, you told me she was planning an operation."

Whitaker looked to the solicitor whose face wore a puzzled expression. After a pause, he answered. "It's what she said."

"And you told me she was doing a cleaning job for, what was it you said, 'some bloke with money'."

"That's right."

She decided to take a chance and pursue her line of thought. "I couldn't help noticing your reaction when we arrived in the car park earlier."

Whitaker lowered his head. "It was nothing," he mumbled.

"Mr Whitaker … Patrick, is there something else you want to tell me?"

He looked up to the ceiling, took a breath then focused on Stainmore. "That bloke the other officers were bringing in …"

"What about him?"

"Chamberlain, you said."

"Go on."

"He looks as though he's got a bit of money. I'm sure that was the name Mum mentioned … Chamberlain … you know when she were talking about her little cleaning job."

*   *   *

Chamberlain's solicitor arrived within twenty minutes of Strong placing him in the interview room. He was afforded a further ten minutes alone with his client. Finally, the questioning began. Darby sat silently beside his boss whilst Strong took Chamberlain through the complaint he'd received from Belinda before he asked Charles to comment.

Chamberlain sighed, as if the interruption to his day was totally unjustified. "She was hysterical," he began. "She was accusing me of all sorts of nonsense. And when I didn't react ... she actually punched *me*. I could have *her* charged with assault."

"That would be interesting," Strong said.

"Exactly. But I don't want to go down that route. It would be just her word against mine."

"Unless you had a witness?"

Chamberlain gave a sad smile. "You're referring to Anthony, obviously."

"He has also given a statement."

Chamberlain leaned forward on the desk between them. "But he didn't actually witness anything."

Strong flicked through some paperwork he'd brought with him in a plain file. "We think he did. He claims you were kneeling on top of your wife on the settee about to punch her."

Chamberlain gave a quick glance to his solicitor then faced Strong. "So he never actually saw any assault. And that's because there was no assault, apart from Belinda on me."

"How did you get into that position, Mr Chamberlain?"

"She stumbled, fell over the arm of the chair. I tried to stop her falling and she grabbed me pulling me over too. I landed on top. That was when Anthony appeared. He obviously mistook what he saw."

The solicitor gave a quiet cough and sat forward in his seat before speaking for the first time. "Mr Strong, my client has given you an honest account of what occurred. I put it to you that there was no assault, quite the reverse. My client was assaulted by his wife and in trying to restrain her, they both fell onto the settee which gave a false impression to their son."

"Well thank you for that," Strong said, with a hint of sarcasm.

There was a knock on the door, Stainmore looked in and apologised. "Could I have a quick word?" she said.

In the corridor, she told Strong what Whitaker had said about his mother and Chamberlain.

"Doesn't really help with anything though, does it?"

Stainmore slumped against the wall. "I know ..."

"Only you still have a nagging feeling ..." Strong prompted.

"What if she was attempting to blackmail him?" She pushed herself back upright. "And he's lying about having access to her house. Was she a participant in their deviant games? The cause of death could be either way round."

"But we've absolutely no proof," Strong said. "I haven't got enough to charge him here either. His word against his wife's. The son's statement isn't strong enough." He looked to his shoes and thrust both hands in his pockets. "I don't like the shit but I don't think I can do anything about it." He looked at Stainmore. "Anyway, a good result with Whitaker father and son. Flynn will be chuffed."

"I just thought you should know."

"Thanks, Kelly."

Strong rejoined Darby, Chamberlain and his solicitor in the interview room.

"Just one other thing, Mr Chamberlain," he said. "Denise Whitaker ..."

"God's sake,," Chamberlain protested, "I've already told you all about her and how she cleaned for me."

"Was she trying to blackmail you?"

Chamberlain spluttered. "What! You really need to rein in this vivid imagination of yours, Inspector."

"So she was never a participant in your activities?"

A look of distaste appeared on Chamberlain's face. "Please ..." He looked to his solicitor.

"I think, Inspector," the solicitor said, "this fishing trip is at an end. If there's no further questions regarding the complaint of assault on my client's wife, I think Mr Chamberlain should be allowed to resume his work."

## 27

Souter glanced up from his desk when Susan appeared through the stair door.

Seconds later, sensing her at his shoulder, he spoke without looking at her. "Where have you been till this time?"

"Information."

He turned round to find her holding out the memory stick. He looked at it then saw her grinning. "What's that?"

"Take a look. Plug it in."

"Woah, just hold on. I'm not going to plug a memory stick into this computer. Not without knowing what's on it and where it came from. These things can have viruses, not to mention files can be traced you know."

She made a point of checking there were no other members of staff at the adjacent workstations before she said in a low voice, "Files from Faulkner's computer."

He looked shocked. "How the … never mind." He stood up, grabbed her by the elbow and led her to the stairs.

Out in the near privacy of the car park, Susan related the tale of Sammy, with her complicity, gaining entry to the Council Leader's office and the close shave they'd had getting out.

"Shit," he said once she'd finished. "What if they identify the two of you?"

"How would they? Nobody would recognise Sammy and I'll stay away from the place."

Souter's mouth hung open. "Are you serious? I thought you were intelligent, Susan. You spent a fair bit of time talking to his secretary. And have you never heard of CCTV?"

Susan looked hurt. "Of course I have. I didn't see any."

"No, you won't." He turned away and shook his head then spun back to face her. "Don't you remember last year when Sammy's friend was missing? Sammy and me went to see the CCTV manager and check the coverage of the Market for the night she disappeared. They have coverage everywhere; especially in the Town Hall. As soon as Faulkner realises he's been infiltrated, he'll instigate a security check. You might be lucky, but there's a fair bet the CCTV manager would remember Sammy."

Susan composed herself. "Sammy looks totally different now to the cheap-looking girl she was then. But it's done now. We have copies of the files and Sammy took notes on other details she thought might be useful. So, the question is, do you want to know what we've got or not."

He held her gaze for a few moments then looked away. "All right. But not here. You two had better come round to my flat this evening after work. Make it seven, okay?"

"I'll text her."

"In the meantime, let's get back and do what we're supposed to be doing." He strode off towards the office doors, Susan close behind.

*   *   *

It was ten past seven when Susan and Sammy knocked on the door of Souter's flat. He let them in, a concerned look on his face.

"Have you mentioned who I think was behind the incident down in the car park?" he asked Susan, once the girls had sat down on the sofa. He was still on his feet.

Susan looked to Sammy. "This Kennedy character, yes."

"I've come across twats like him before," Sammy said. Her body stiffened in a defiant gesture. "He doesn't scare me."

"Well he should," Souter said sharply. "He's a few leagues higher up than that 'twat', as you so eloquently describe him, who was after you for some ridiculous rent money last year." He was referring to the pimp who, after throwing Sammy out of her room, had attempted to extract money from her.

Sammy seemed to deflate.

Souter sat down on the easy chair. "Look, I don't want to put you two, or Alison for that matter, into any more danger than you already might be."

"You really think this is a serious threat?" Sammy looked earnest.

He rubbed his chin then sat up. "Kennedy phoned the day after the attack. Just to make sure I got the message. And yes, he did refer to you guys."

"Okay, but there's nothing to arouse Brogan's suspicion that we're still investigating this though, is there?" Susan said.

"And all we're doing is having a look at Faulkner's files," Sammy added. "Nothing to connect with Brogan ... yet."

Souter leaned back in the chair. "I'm still not sure about this."

"Well, we've got it now." Susan waved the memory stick in front of her. "So we may as well have a look."

"Don't worry," Sammy said, "I can do an anti-virus check on it before we open anything up. And provided we don't copy anything onto your hard drive, no one would be able to tell we've looked at those files."

Souter jumped up. "Okay, okay, you've worn me down. Let's do it."

He switched on his PC in the corner of the lounge and waited for it to settle down. Sammy sat at the office chair and plugged in the stick. No viruses were detected and she began by opening up the email files. "I didn't think I'd have time to copy the archive files," she said, facing the screen, "but I managed to get the inbox, sent items and a few other folders on there."

Souter and Susan gathered on either side of Sammy.

"So how far back do these go?" Souter asked.

"January this year," she answered, eyes never leaving the monitor. "We'll have a look at the inbox first and see if anything interesting turns up."

After half an hour, they'd progressed as far as the end of April. Souter was jotting down notes of anything that might be of interest. So far it was a pretty meagre list. One thing they had discovered though was Faulkner's personal email address. He'd forwarded one or two messages on to that.

It was an email dated the second of May that first aroused Souter's interest. That was from Kenneth Brogan thanking Faulkner for his time the previous day, concluding that he, Brogan, would be delighted to discuss further any assistance he could offer in respect of the project they had discussed.

"I don't suppose you got hold of his diary on this stick did you, Sammy?" Souter asked.

She looked questioningly at him. "How long did you think we had in there? I only had time for these folders and a couple of other ones I thought might be useful."

"Okay, let's carry on. That icon there means he's replied, doesn't it?"

Sammy nodded, made a few clicks on the mouse and brought up the Sent Items folder for the same date. "Here we are," she said. "A polite response looking forward to discussing matters further."

Susan disappeared into the kitchen and reappeared ten minutes later with three coffees. In the meantime, Souter had noted two other email communications between Brogan and Faulkner. And then, on May the fifteenth, an email from Charles Chamberlain. *"Further to our little chat last night at T,"* it read, *"I would be interested in facilitating your proposition but would be very wary of how you deal with KB. Amber light on this one. There could be alternatives. Regards C."*

Souter read it twice and leaned back in his chair. "A bit cryptic, that," he pondered.

"Doesn't look as though he replied to that," Sammy said. "And 'T', what the hell's 'T'?"

"I have an idea," Souter said, "but let's see what else appears."

By nine o'clock, they'd been through the emails received and sent up to the present. There had been a number of other references to 'T'.

"So come on then," Sammy said, "what's your theory on 'T'?"

"*Talisman Club*," he replied.

"Of course ... I saw a card for that tucked in his diary."

"Did you now."

"Can't say I know it," Susan joined in, "But how come you've heard of it?"

"Colin mentioned it to me a couple of weeks ago. In fact, we were talking about the woman who'd been found dead in Normanton. You remember ... she'd been dead for over a year."

"I do, yuk," Sammy said.

"Anyway, he just seemed to throw it in. I'm not sure if he was still talking about that case or if his mind had moved on to something else. Was there anything on the card? A number, address or anything?"

"Nothing. Just a symbol on the front and the words, '*Talisman Club*'. I turned it over and it was blank."

Souter seemed lost in thought for a second. "I wonder ... I might have to have another word with Colin. In the meantime, I think we've done enough for tonight."

# 28
## Friday 3<sup>rd</sup> August 2001

It was mid-morning and Strong was sifting through the statements that Stainmore and Ormerod had taken from the Whitakers yesterday. The search of their flat had proved fruitful and the medals had been formally identified by Mr Parsons. Luke said the old man had had tears in his eyes when he'd shown them to him. They were hopeful that several other items found would be identified by the victims or their relatives later today. He smiled to himself, satisfied that his team had worked hard to get a good result.

A brief knock on the door interrupted his thoughts. DCI Hemingford and Detective Chief Superintendent Flynn entered and closed the door behind themselves.

Strong glanced up. "Looks serious," he said.

"Good result on those distraction burglaries, Colin," Flynn said.

Strong leaned back. "Thank you, sir," he said. "Good work by Kelly and Luke too."

"Indeed."

There was a moment's awkward silence before Strong spoke. "Was there something else?"

Flynn coughed. "This Chamberlain business …"

"Ah. Let me guess, he's had a word with Giles again."

Flynn screwed up his face. "Colin … you know how this works …"

"Only too well, sir." He turned to the DCI. "And what about you, Rupert? Are you familiar with how things work?"

Flynn's tone stiffened. "There's no need for that, Colin. The fact is there is no case to answer, as I understand it."

Strong frowned. "No case to answer? Have you spoken to Mrs Chamberlain? Listened to what she's said? And their son who was there at the time?"

"But he didn't actually witness anything, though, did he? The fact is there is no evidence. We all know how these domestic violence cases go. They'll be kissing and making up in no time."

Strong stood up from his chair and shook his head in disbelief. "I can't believe you just said that. You haven't been involved. You didn't see her in A & E the other week."

"No I didn't. But again there was no evidence that she'd been assaulted."

"Last time we spoke on this subject you asked if she'd made a complaint, which she hadn't. She has now, though. And we're duty bound to investigate that."

"So have a word. We don't have enough evidence to pursue this any further. It would be better for all concerned if she withdrew her complaint."

"Better for who? Mrs Chamberlain or you?"

"Just fucking do it!"

Strong pulled himself up into a straight position. "I will not be pressured into persuading a victim to withdraw a complaint."

Their gaze held for several seconds before Flynn turned to Hemingford. "Rupert, I'd like you to pay a visit."

"Sir." Was it Strong's imagination or did he pick up the faint smirk that crossed the DCI's face very briefly.

Flynn turned his attention back to Strong, pointing a finger. "And you ... I'm making allowances here. Be very, very careful."

With that, he opened the door and strode out, Hemingford close behind.

\* \* \*

Susan came out of the examination room with a broad smile on her face. It was her last orthopaedic outpatients' appointment to sign off her treatment for her broken leg from last year.

"Good news?" Belinda asked.

"All signed off, no adverse effects," she said.

"That's great, I'm really pleased for you, Susan."

"Have you got much more to do?" Sammy asked.

Belinda glanced at her watch. "You were the last patient and the clinic officially finishes at six. I'll have a little bit of paperwork and that's me, off home." Her expression saddened.

"Is everything okay?" Sammy asked.

"Oh, it's … well it's not a happy place these days."

"Well you finish off what you've got to do and we'll take you for a drink," Susan said brightly.

"Oh no, I couldn't …"

Sammy looked directly at the nurse. "Why? Have you got something better to do?"

"Besides," Susan added, "I'd like to thank you in some small way for what you did last year. This …" she indicated her leg, "is the result of all your top class care."

Belinda considered for a second. "Okay you two, you've talked me into it. Give me ten minutes."

Twenty minutes later and a few streets away, the three women were sitting at a corner table in a pub, drinks in front of them. Several office workers and a few of the nursing staff were enjoying an early evening drink before making their journeys home. Susan told of how her first year at university had gone and how Souter had managed to fix her up with a summer job on the Post. Sammy spoke of her gratitude for the help Souter and especially Alison had given her in obtaining a job for her where Alison works. Finally, the girls brought the conversation round to Belinda's situation and how they'd last seen her in Pinderfields A & E.

Suddenly, Belinda's eyes filled. "I'd rather not …" Her voice faded.

Susan leaned in closer and took hold of her hand. "We only want to help."

Belinda pulled a tissue from her sleeve and dabbed her eyes. "I'm sorry, it's just …"

Susan interrupted her. "Do you remember when I was on the ward? And you were on night duty. That first time we spoke, I mean really had a conversation. I'd been crying. I got upset at the stupid situation I'd gotten myself into. I didn't want to talk about what happened to my Mum, then my Dad. But you said it would be better if I didn't keep it to myself. You didn't judge me. You just listened. Afterwards, well I really appreciated it."

Belinda sniffed, wiped her face and looked around at the other drinkers. No one seemed to be taking any notice of them. She leaned forward on the table and began the story of what had happened since she discovered her husband had a house she knew nothing about.

Sammy interrupted her flow when she mentioned the roll of film. Her eyes widened and she asked what the participants had been up to.

"Just a healthy bit of BDSM," Belinda responded. There was a moment's silence before all three erupted in laughter.

"And it was Colin Strong who came to see you about it?" Susan asked once they'd regained their composure.

"Him and a DS Stainmore, yes."

"He's a nice guy," Sammy said. "Him and Bob are best mates."

"I know," Belinda said. "That's why, when it all blew up on Tuesday I went specifically to see him at Wood Street."

"Why, what happened on Tuesday?" Susan asked.

Belinda related the events of this week. "But then today," she continued, "I had another one come to see me." She became upset again. "Hemmingway, or something like that. And he tells me they can't do anything about it. Not enough evidence. Even though Anthony was there."

Susan and Sammy looked at each other. "Never heard of a Hemmingway," Susan said.

"Wanted me to withdraw my complaint."

Sammy looked thoughtful. "Bloody funny handshake brigade, Police are well known for it."

"Well I know Charlie's friends with some high up copper, Giles Wadsworth. I'll bet he's been calling in favours there," Belinda said.

"Here, he wasn't one of those in the BDSM club was he?" Sammy chuckled.

"No, definitely not. Can you imagine?" Belinda laughed.

"Might have been handy though … and you had the photos to prove it," Susan added.

Sammy looked away somewhere over Belinda's shoulder into an indistinct distance.

"Sammy," Susan said, "Are you okay?"

"Belinda, have you ever heard mention of a *Talisman Club*?"

She looked puzzled, then thoughtful before finally shaking her head. "No, can't say as I have. Why?"

"Oh nothing really. Just a thought."

The conversation drifted away from Belinda's problems as the girls spoke of their excitement of their upcoming holiday. Finally Belinda, declining the offer of another drink, stood and said her farewells, thanking them for cheering her up.

After she'd gone, Susan and Sammy decided to have one more before making their way back to the flat.

Once Susan had returned with their drinks, Sammy asked, "Are you thinking what I'm thinking?"

Susan slurped some lager. "About the *Talisman Club*, you mean?"

Sammy nodded.

"Do you think Belinda's husband is running some sort of private members sexual deviants club from that other house?"

"Would be interesting, wouldn't it? We know her husband is in contact with 'fat arse' Faulkner and I saw that card in his drawer."

Susan chuckled at the reference to the council leader. "And if Bob's made the right connection, was that woman in the bath involved with it?"

# 29
## Tuesday 7<sup>th</sup> August 2001

At an assembly not far from Wood Street Police Station, in the offices of Wakefield District Council, Souter, Susan and Janey sat alongside a large number of newspaper and TV journalists, awaiting the press conference. He'd nodded to a couple of reporters from the Nationals he'd met on previous occasions and wondered how much importance they would place on what was to be announced. He also recognised a couple of faces from BBC North and ITV's Calendar team.

When Janey had mentioned the MEPs that were expected to show up this morning to 'big up' their involvement in securing funding for the prestigious project, the name of Stuart Hamilton made an impact.

"He's the brother of Lady Morag Hamilton, the wife of Kenneth Brogan," Souter had told her.

"That guy you challenged at the planning meeting the other week?" Janey queried.

"The very same."

That tied in with what Sammy had discovered in Faulkner's emails in a folder marked 'TD', meaning Thistle Developments and references to meetings with the local MEP, Andrew Marsden.

A raised platform with microphone stands was the focus of the assembly and after a few minutes, an entourage swept onto it. Bernard Faulkner led the delegation and Souter recognised the following two men from photographs he'd studied online as Andrew Marsden and Stuart Hamilton, the MEPs. Close behind was the local Labour MP with Michael Pitchforth, the Head of Planning and another man Souter didn't know bringing up the rear.

As he expected, the announcement was heavily political, with the Labour MP attempting to give himself and his party credit for pursuing the scheme, whilst the Conservative MEPs were trumpeting the fact that it was they who had been instrumental in securing significant EU funds to allow the scheme to proceed. The fifth man in the group was introduced as Samuel Appleyard, WDC's soon to retire Chief Civil Engineer.

Questions were invited from the assembled media. Most gave sufficient opportunity for the politicians to milk as much kudos as possible. Only one journalist Souter didn't recognise questioned the need for yet another out of town shopping development. When given the expected answer that it would benefit all local residents, bringing much needed jobs to the area and boosting the local economy, the journalist followed up by asking which faceless developer would actually benefit financially from the scheme. The stock answer was only to be expected; it would be a partnership between WDC and a developer who would be selected with the best interests of local tax-payers in mind.

Shortly after, the press conference was wound up, pressures of other engagements for the politicians the given reason.

"I thought you might have put your head above the parapet and asked something controversial?" Janey asked Souter as they stood to leave.

"Really? I thought this was your story, Janey."

Susan just smiled.

"I'm just going for a pee before we head back," Souter announced. "I'll see you in Reception."

Souter was washing his hands at the sink when a figure entered the toilets. He glanced in the mirror and thought he recognised the face. Dressed only in shirt, tie and trousers with no jacket, the man obviously worked in the council offices. As he dried his hands and the man was at the sink washing his, Souter looked over again. This time, he was sure. "Joe?" he said. "Joe Webster?"

The man looked at Souter for a second before breaking into a broad grin. "Bob Souter, as I live and breathe. How are you mate?" He held out a wet hand before realising what he'd done. "Sorry, let me dry these first. I see your name now and again in the papers," he said before the noise from the warm air dryer drowned all further conversation out.

Souter's thoughts went back a quarter of a century to the last time he'd seen his former classmate as they prepared to leave school and face an uncertain future. Joe had been proficient in maths and science and, as far as he could remember, he'd gone to study something fairly academic at Manchester University.

The dryer stopped and Webster turned to him, a serious expression on his face. "Are you here for the press conference?"

"It's just finished." Souter was surprised to see his old schoolmate walk up the line of cubicles and check no-one was in them.

"What do you make of it?"

Souter was puzzled. "How do you mean, Joe?"

"There's something not right here," he said, giving another furtive glance around the empty toilets.

Just then, the sound of the outer door opening could be heard before two other journalists entered. "Hello, Bob," one of them greeted.

"All right, Jim," Souter acknowledged and led the way out into the corridor, Joe following.

Once there, Joe placed a hand on Souter's elbow. "Are you around for a bit?" he asked.

"I was going to head back to the office with my colleagues, why?"

"No, that's okay. I'll catch you around sometime."

Souter looked at his watch. "What time do you have lunch?"

"Half twelve, normally. You don't fancy a pint then?"

Souter grinned. "Read my mind. Where do you suggest?"

"How about The Talbot and Falcon down by the bus station?"

Souter screwed up his face. "That's a bit of a shit hole, isn't it?"

Webster smiled. "But guaranteed no one from here will be in. About twenty to one. See you." With that, he turned in the opposite direction and took the stairs.

\* \* \*

Janey and Susan had returned to the office to draft an article on that morning's announcement for the evening edition whilst Souter made his way into the Talbot & Falcon pub just after half past twelve. He collected his pint and sat at a table just inside the door. A few savoury characters were drinking in the back and two couples were sitting at another table near the bar.

Five minutes later, Joe Webster appeared.

Souter stood and shook his friend's hand. "What can I get you?" he offered.

Once they'd settled down at the table, drinks in front of them and food ordered, Souter began the conversation, "So, you're a council employee?"

Webster nodded, taking a sip of his lager. "Senior Engineer."

"Was that what you did at Manchester?"

"I studied Civil Engineering. When I left I was fortunate enough to get a position with a small consultancy in Leeds. I joined the Council here about eight years ago now."

Over the next few minutes, Souter obtained a potted history of his old classmate. He'd married a girl he met when he worked in Leeds and they now had two children, a boy of twelve and a girl of ten. He showed him a photo of Kathy, his wife. In return, Souter told him of his life since leaving school, missing out one or two elements he didn't feel his friend needed to know.

Once their food arrived, Souter turned the subject to this morning's events in the Council offices. "You're obviously not happy with things where you are, Joe. Why is that?"

"I tell you, the politics is horrendous."

"But in case you hadn't noticed, we've got a Labour government now, so this lot here must be in their element. I mean, you could put a monkey up for Labour and they'd vote it in round here."

Webster gave a grim smile. "I'm not thinking of those sorts of politics, I'm talking job politics. All the walking on egg shells in case you upset the wrong person, political correctness and all the little fiddles and schemes they all seem to have going." He waved a fork to enhance the point. "No, I'll be honest with you, Bob, I'm looking round for somewhere else at the moment. I've had enough of local government. The pay's better in the private sector too and I don't want to be branded as someone with no ambition."

Souter took a deep breath and leaned back. "Wow. You are discontented, aren't you?"

Webster shrugged and ate another forkful.

Souter watched as two scruffy lads came into the bar and ordered two pints of lager. They glanced round the room but their attention quickly returned to the young barmaid as she poured their drinks, content to have a bit of banter with her. Satisfied there was no one taking any interest in their conversation, he leaned in closer to his old school friend. "When we met this morning, you indicated there was something amiss with this scheme. Is this one of those 'little fiddles and schemes' you just mentioned."

Webster paused, placing his knife and fork down on his plate. He seemed to be considering not only what to say but whether he should say anything at all. Finally he spoke hesitantly. "You're a journalist, right? This is off the record."

"Go on."

"The final report on the soil conditions on this site at Lofthouse, the old NCB land ..."

"What about it?"

Webster again was hesitant. "The picture it paints … it's far worse than I'm sure it is."

"What makes you say that?"

"I did a lot of work on the site surveys. The contamination wasn't that great. I've only just seen the final report that was submitted with the application for EU funding." He shook his head. "It doesn't seem to be the same site to me."

Again Souter furtively glanced around the pub. Voice low, he asked, "Are you saying that the report was doctored?"

Webster nodded. "Had to be."

"But why do that?"

"The only reason I can think of would be to increase the amount of money we could get from Europe to budget for the remediation works."

"Remediation? What's that?"

"Site clean up, removing contaminants and making the site safe in plain English."

"And that would benefit who exactly?"

It was Webster's turn to lean in closer. "Well, I've been thinking about that. You've seen that slippery bastard Faulkner?" Souter nodded. "Well I wouldn't trust him as far as I could break wind. Then there's my boss, Sam Appleyard. I used to think he was okay. But that report couldn't have been altered without his input. At the end of the day, it's his name on it. And, let's face it, the old bugger retires in a couple of months."

"A contribution to his pension fund?" Souter queried.

Webster smiled. "You may say that … I couldn't possibly comment."

"But they wouldn't be able to just trouser money from this, though surely?"

Webster looked surprised. "No, of course not. But, if whoever gets the contract has close connections with them, then …"

It was Souter's turn to smile. "And have you got some idea who that third party might be?"

"Judging by your reaction, Bob, I'd say you have already."

"Another?" Souter indicated Webster's empty glass.

"Best not. I'd like to move on on my own terms and at the time of my choosing, if you get my drift."

"Doesn't have to be a lager? If you're not in a rush, I fancy another."

Webster settled for a J2O and a couple of minutes later, the conversation resumed.

"So you think Faulkner's bent then, Joe?"

"As arseholes! You don't get to his position without shitting on people and pocketing a few bob along the way." He took a sip of his drink before continuing, "There was something going on with his computer this week too."

Souter hoped his face didn't give anything away. "His computer?"

"Yes," Webster chuckled. "Actually, do you remember a skinny lad a year below us ...Jezza, we called him ..."

"Jez, Jeremy Bullen, yep. He's one of your security bods these days, isn't he?"

"That's right. He's actually head of security now. But how did you know that?"

"He helped me with something last year."

"Mind, he's not skinny any more. Built like an outhouse now."

Souter smiled. "I know."

"Anyway, he was telling me this morning that Faulkner seemed to be locked out of his work computer."

Souter felt his blood rush. "Oh?"

"Nothing much in that, except he'd been on holiday last week and found out his password had been changed in the meantime. Faulkner gave his secretary, Brenda, a bit of a third degree and it turns out some young woman talked her way into his office last week, claiming to be one of the IT team. Next thing, Faulkner calls in Jezza to see if he can spot the culprit on CCTV. No idea what she might have been after but ... I just wondered with the timing of everything ...it's a bit strange, isn't it?"

Souter shrugged.

"Especially with everything else that's going on at the moment."

"You think it's connected with Lofthouse?"

"Maybe." Webster was quiet for a minute then chuckled. "But he's so thick, he uses his kid's names and dates of birth for his passwords so he won't forget." He stood up. "Anyway, I must get back."

Souter stood as well and held out a hand.

Webster shook it. "Good to see you after all these years, Bob."

"You too, Joe. But listen, can I ask you one small favour?" He took out a business card and passed it over.

Webster looked at it for a second then slipped it into his pocket. "If I can."

"Would it be possible to get a copy of that Site Report you were on about?"

Webster sighed. "If I do, you can't link it to me."

Souter held up both hands. "Absolute discretion. But could you also identify what results you think have been … adjusted?"

Webster shook his head. "Christ, you don't want much, do you?" They held each other's gaze, before he smiled. "Leave it with me, I'll see what I can do."

# 30
## Friday 10<sup>th</sup> August 2001

Souter was looking forward to a cosy night in with Alison, so the phone call from Jeremy Bullen, or Jezza, as he knew him, was a bit inconvenient. He hoped it wouldn't take too long. He had an idea as to what he wanted to talk about but was surprised he wanted to meet in a pub in Wakefield. The Black Horse was on the corner of Drury Lane and Westgate, opposite one of the jewels of the city, the Theatre Royal. Over the road stood another icon of the city's entertainment scene of earlier times, Unity Hall, now sadly in need of some of the loving attention lavished on the Theatre.

He'd spent the last half hour in the office studying the reports that had accompanied the funding applications for the Lofthouse Project that Sammy had managed to obtain from Faulkner's computer. They certainly made interesting reading; the sums involved were huge. She'd found it in a folder marked TD, for Thistle Developments.

He was a few minutes early of their meet time of six-thirty and was ordering a pint. Bullen appeared at his shoulder as he was about to pay.

"Just a pint of lager for me, Bob," he said.

A few minutes later, they were sitting in a quiet corner of the front room. Bullen had played for their school football team with them when he was a skinny fifteen-year-old but was now a very muscular character that you wouldn't want to get the wrong side of.

"How are things then, Jezza," Souter began. "Got promotion since I saw you last year I hear."

"Thanks," he said and sipped his pint. "The old head retired at the end of last year. I applied, didn't think I'd get it but …" Bullen grew serious. "Anyway, I was just thinking about our last meet the other day."

"Oh yes." Souter raised his glass, more to avoid eye contact with the man than anything else. "Sorry," he said, glancing to the bar, "Did you want any crisps?"

Bullen shook his head, eyes on the table, "It took me a while to think where I'd seen her before," he said then looked straight at Souter. "When you came to see me last, you were with that young street walker. What was her name now?"

"Oh you mean the girl whose friend had gone missing?"

"That's her, yes. I quite liked her really. And I was really sorry to hear how it turned out with her friend." Another gulp of lager. "But d'you know what brought her back to mind?"

Souter shrugged. "Dunno. You saw that piece in the Post I did last week about …" He stopped.

Bullen was smiling and shaking his head. He slowly pulled out an envelope from the inside pocket of his jacket and passed it to Souter.

Souter tried his best bewildered look but he suspected what was coming. He took the envelope and pulled out the photographs from inside. They were stills taken from CCTV cameras, obviously inside the Town Hall.

He studied them for a second or two. They were good quality. The first was a front view of Sammy walking down a corridor. The second was even better. Bullen had obviously zoomed in on her face and shoulders. Her long blonde hair looked far healthier than the straggly, lifeless mane she sported a year ago but there was no mistaking it was Sammy. "You think this might be her?" he asked.

"I've nothing to compare it with … unless I saw her again." Bullen looked round to the bar. A couple in their thirties, office types, had come in and were being served.

"But what's so interesting about this?" Souter asked. "A young woman who looks a bit like someone you might have met once before walking down a corridor?"

Bullen smiled. "You know, don't you, Bob?"

"You've lost me now, Jezza." Souter replaced the photos in the envelope.

"Look, can we be honest with one another?" Bullen leaned in closer. "Bernard Faulkner, Leader of the Council …"

"Go on."

"Prize arsehole and bent as one too." Souter remained silent, allowing Bullen to continue, "Someone talked their way into his office last week when he was on holiday. We suspect they looked through his computer files, at the very least."

"And what would they have found, do you think?"

"A man like that … he has secrets he'd rather keep secret."

"And you think this girl was involved?"

"Matches the description given by Faulkner's dozy secretary."

"Have you shown her these images to confirm?"

"Not yet. I thought I'd do a bit of investigating on my own first. You're the obvious first port of call."

"Me?" Souter was thoughtful but he could see Bullen was weighing him up too.

Eventually, the man opened up. "Look, Bob," he said, "nobody really likes the pompous sod, and if someone's got something on him …" He glanced around the room again before his voice went very quiet. "There's rumours about lining his own pockets, doing favours for 'appreciative' friends. And with this big Lofthouse scheme breaking …"

"Are you saying you might welcome his downfall?"

"A lot of honest people might."

"If, and let's just talk hypothetically here, if this woman was 'assisting' that possibility, how would you propose to deal with these?" He tapped the envelope with a finger.

Bullen shrugged. "There might have been a fault on some of those cameras, the focus might have been faulty. We have problems with the CCTV system from time to time."

Souter considered for a few seconds, studying his old team mate. "Okay," he said, "this is the situation ..." For the next few minutes, Souter explained the background to the incident. "But I didn't know they were doing this. Not until they brought the files to me," he concluded.

"So you have something on him?"

"Nothing solid as yet, just circumstantial."

Bullen studied the beer mat, turning it one way then the other before he finally responded. "Look, this is difficult for me. I'm paid to ensure there are no breaches in security. But ... if this big greedy bastard is turning us all over, everyone who pays council tax, then in my book, that's a breach of security too."

Souter nodded. "Not quite in the league of T Dan Smith and John Poulson ... or not yet, as far as I know." He could see the puzzled look on Bullen's face. "Back in the sixties, up in Newcastle, Smith was the council leader and involved in redevelopment schemes with Poulson an architect, born in Pontefract interestingly. Anyway, huge political scandal when it all came out, Smith and Poulson done for fraud in the early seventies."

"That vaguely rings a bell. Christ, you think we might have something like that here."

"Let's not get ahead of ourselves, Jezza. All we have are a few rumours." He paused a second. "But listen, about the girl ..."

"What girl?" Bullen replied. "We couldn't get any useful images off the CCTV."

"Another?" Souter reached for Bullen's empty glass.

"No thanks, Bob. Got to go. Said I'd take the little one out for a kick about in the park."

Souter smiled. "I'd best get myself off too."

"The big man stood to leave. "But listen," he said, "it'd be good to maintain contact on this."

"Sure."

# 31
## Thursday 16<sup>th</sup> August 2001

"Only three more days to our holiday, Suz," Sammy said. "Are you getting excited yet?"

"I'm beginning to," Susan grinned. "It's actually two more sleeps. You know like when you're a kid and you're counting down to Christmas?"

Susan had finished work and met up with Sammy in Leeds for a breeze around the shops. They were doing some final shopping for clothes, sun creams and anything else they felt they would need for their week long break to Majorca. They'd been all round Albion Street, The Headrow and the Merrion Centre and had got almost everything they'd set out for.

"I think we need a drink to put us in the holiday mood," Sammy suggested as they walked along the street with their purchases.

"What about that place the other side of the hospital where we've sometimes been? They sell San Miguel on draft," Susan said.

Before they realised, they were walking past the hospital itself. "Seems like a lifetime ago since I was in there, Sammy."

"Over a year now." Sammy hesitated and bent down to look across to a car parked in the staff car park.

"What's up?" Susan asked.

Sammy pointed. "Isn't that Belinda's car? Looks like her in the driver's seat, just sitting there."

Curiosity aroused, they strolled over. Sure enough, the woman was sitting motionless with her head in her hands. Susan gently tapped on the window. Startled, Belinda looked out. Mascara had run a little way down her tear-stained cheeks.

Susan looked to Sammy who ran round the front of the car and opened the passenger door and got in. Susan got in the rear and sat behind Belinda.

"Belinda? What's happened?" Sammy asked.

The nurse reached down into the floorpan, opened her handbag and pulled out some tissues.

"Who's upset you?" Susan gently rubbed the woman's shoulder from behind.

Belinda wiped her face and blew her nose. "Oh, ignore me, I'm fine." She looked to Sammy. "I should be happy. Anthony got his AS Level results this morning; four A's and a B; better than he expected."

"Well that's good news," Sammy replied. "I never even passed my cycling proficiency test."

"Susan chuckled. "You did. Don't put yourself down."

Sammy looked serious again. "But you're not fine. So come on, spill."

That brought a semblance of a smile from Belinda. "I got a letter this morning from a firm of solicitors. I know them, of course. One of Charlie's friends." She turned in her seat to face Sammy and look to Susan who had moved across in the back seat so they could all see each other. "He wants a divorce."

"Is that really such a surprise?" Susan asked. "Especially after our last conversation the other week."

"But I'd have thought you could divorce him after finding out about what went on at that other house."

"It's just … well you never think it could happen. I suppose deep down I was hoping we could sort it. It's obvious he's not been happy with me for a long time."

"Best off without him though," Sammy said. "I've seen loads like him. Cheating on women like you." She took Belinda's hand. "And don't forget, if it wasn't for your efforts, bringing up the kids and all, keeping the house in order, not to mention bringing in some money, he wouldn't have been able to build his career, never mind indulge himself in all that unsavoury stuff."

Belinda started crying again then leaned towards Sammy and hugged her. "What would I do without you

…" She turned and put an arm over Susan's shoulder. "… both of you."

"Right," Sammy said decisively, "What we need is a drink and formulate a plan of action."

"But I can't," Belinda pleaded. "I'm only on a break. I don't finish my shift for a while."

"You're sick," Susan said from behind. "I can tell."

Sammy nodded towards her friend. "You should trust her, she used to be a doctor," she added.

Belinda looked from Sammy to Susan and back again. Finally, she pulled out her mobile phone and made a call.

# 32

Flashing blue and red bounced off adjacent buildings, fire appliances and other vehicles in the dim light of dusk. The uniform, recognising Strong, raised the plastic police tape to allow him to drive into the restricted area. Leeds Road was closed in both directions and diversions were in place around back streets. A small knot of onlookers had gathered at either end of the cordon.

The stench of destruction invaded Strong's nostrils when he stepped from his car. Station Officer Gavin Blake broke off from giving instructions to one of his firefighters to come over to him. "Colin," he greeted, taking off his glove and offering a hand. "Bit unusual this one but, there again, nothing surprises me anymore."

"Good to see you again, Gavin." Strong shook his hand. The two had worked together on a number of suspicious fire investigations over the years.

"We're clear of here. Once we discovered it, we called you boys. The fire is out and I'm assured the building is structurally sound."

"Let me get kitted up and you can show me what you've found."

A few minutes later, suited and booted in full forensic gear, Strong followed the fire officer to the smashed-in front door of the terraced house. The room window was shattered, its plastic frame partly melted onto the cill and down the brickwork. Blackened masonry above was evidence of smoke belching from the opening.

Inside, Blake switched on a heavy duty torch. The beam swept around the front room illuminating the scorched ceiling and sooty walls. In the middle of the room, the remains of a three-piece suite had collapsed in on itself. Between the settee and the fireplace was the spot identified as the seat of the fire.

Blake focussed the torch light on what appeared to be a pile of rags with a wire leading from it. "The remains of an iron, still plugged in," he said. "Sitting on a pile of clothing. That's where it started."

"Deliberate?" Strong asked.

"I'll let you be the judge of that. Scenes of Crime should be here any minute. I'm sure they'll be able to give you the full story. But, combined with what's up here ..." he indicated the steep staircase rising up between the front room and the blackened kitchen.

Carefully, they ascended and, at the top, Blake stood aside at an open doorway and handed the torch to Strong. The room was obviously above the sitting room. He shone the torch into the darkness. The beam picked out a naked male, head hooded, body slumped forward, wrists and ankles shackled to a frame bolted to the far wall. Strong took a couple of steps in to the room. "Shit," he said quietly.

"I know what you mean," Blake agreed.

"No, it's just this looks familiar, Gavin."

"You've seen this before?"

"No, I don't mean the death ... it's just ..." Strong left the rest unsaid. Leaning forward, he could finally see the smoke blackened holes cut into the hood at the nostrils. Tape covered the mouth.

"Scenes of Crime are here, chief," a voice from below announced. "We'll help them set up some lights next."

"Thanks, Tom," Blake shouted down.

Strong turned to leave but paused at the doorway. He glanced down at the lock. "This key was in here, on the outside?" he asked.

"And locked," Blake confirmed.

"Well this is suspicious at the very least," he said. "Let's clear out of SOCO's way."

Outside, Strong pulled his face mask clear and greeted Doug Norris, the senior SOCO man he had worked with many times.

"Hope you haven't contaminated my locus," Norris said, a broad smile on his face.

Strong held his arms wide. "Look at this, I'm all kitted up. Overshoes as well. You'd be proud."

"Is it suspicious?"

Strong moved closer and lowered his voice. "Some poor sod naked and shackled to a frame in a locked room when a fire starts on the floor below? I think that counts as suspicious in my book, Doug," he said, grimly. "I'll be interested in what you find."

"It's going to be a long night, then." Norris turned and made his way inside.

A familiar figure approached. "Guv," Stainmore said.

Behind, DCI Hemingford followed. "Something to interest us, Colin?" he asked.

Strong repeated the information he'd just given Norris.

"Any idea whose property it is?"

"Luke's checking with the council, although it's a bit difficult out of hours. But apparently you can view the Electoral Register online these days. Meanwhile, nothing like old-fashioned police work. We need to knock on a few doors."

"I'll instruct uniform to make a start," Hemingford responded.

"In the meantime, Kelly, are you busy with anything?"

She looked to the DCI who turned and strode away. "Not really, guv. Why?"

Strong watched Hemingford approach a uniform. "I'd like you to come with me on this next visit. I'm sure we've seen that location upstairs before."

# 33

On the short drive towards the address that he remembered, Strong described how the sight he'd just seen in the house resembled closely the scenes in the photographs brought in for developing by Belinda Chamberlain.

"You think it's Charles Chamberlain, guv?" Stainmore asked, a surprised look on her face.

"Firstly, I'd like to confirm the address of this property where she found the roll of film. And secondly, I'd like to see if Mr Chamberlain is at home. After all, it may be some other poor sod who thought he was going to have some fun."

They parked up in St John's Square and got out. Strong looked to the Chamberlain house but there were no lights on. His knocks on the door and ringing of the bell went unanswered.

Back in the car, they sat in silence for a moment, broken when Strong's phone rang. "Yes, Luke," he said and listened for a few seconds. "Okay, let me know if you do find anything." He ended the call. "No one listed on the Electoral Role for that address," he said,

Stainmore looked at him for a second then spoke. "So where to now, guv? LGI?"

"Yep," he responded and started the engine.

Up in the Orthopaedics Ward, Strong and Stainmore approached the nurse's station. A nurse in her thirties with short dark hair, wearing a dark blue uniform with Sister Logan on a name badge, looked up from some paperwork she was discussing with a colleague. "Can I help you?" she asked. "Visiting time is long gone."

"I'm looking for Belinda Chamberlain," Strong said quietly, discreetly showing his warrant card.

"Is there something wrong? I mean, she's not here. She went off for her break then called me to say she was ill."

"What time was that?"

"She went off about seven-thirty and called me about half an hour later."

"She seemed quite upset earlier," Sister Logan's colleague added.

"So neither of you have seen her since she went off the ward for her break?" Strong persisted.

The nurses both looked worried. "Is she all right? She's not in any trouble is she?" Sister Logan asked.

"No. Everything's fine. We just need to speak with her, that's all." Strong thanked them for their time then he and Stainmore returned to their car.

*   *   *

The house was in darkness when Belinda arrived home. That was a good sign, she thought. At least he wasn't here. Anthony was staying at Simon's again. It was good his parents were so understanding. With that thought, she lifted the phone and dialled their number. Simon's father answered.

"Hi, it's Belinda Chamberlain here. I just wondered if I could have a quick word with Anthony?"

"Anthony? I'm not sure he's here," the man responded. "There again, I've not been in long. Let me check."

Belinda felt the rush of blood as the first doubts began to bounce around her head. He told her this morning he was going to Simon's and would probably stay over.

The sounds of the phone being picked up crackled through the handset before a female voice came on the line. Hello, Belinda," she said. "I'm afraid Anthony's not here. Simon says he hasn't seen him for a couple of days. Were you expecting him to be here?"

Panic. "No, no, it's my mistake. Sorry Chris, I've had such a lot on recently, I didn't read the note on the wall chart," Belinda lied. "Sorry to have bothered you."

She rushed to his room and opened the door and switched the light on. Everything normal, but no Anthony.

The doorbell rang and she went to answer it.

\* \* \*

Returning to St John's Square, Strong pulled into the same spot by the kerb where he'd parked before. Looking up to the house, there was a light in the hallway and then he saw a room light come on.

"Should have more luck this time," Stainmore commented, following her boss to the front door. The ring was answered quickly.

"Belinda, can we have a word?" DI Strong said.

She looked flustered. "Well … yes, come in."

They followed her into the lounge. "You remember DS Stainmore?"

"Yes. Yes, of course. I'm sorry, I've only just got in." She shrugged off her coat and made for the kitchen.

"Late shift?"

"Yes," she said from the other room. "Can I get you a drink? Tea or a coffee? I'm making one for myself."

"No, not for me thanks." Strong exchanged glances with Stainmore.

"I'm fine too."

"I've just put the kettle on anyway, if you change your minds," she said, coming back into the lounge. "So how can I help?"

Strong took a breath then began. "When we spoke to you about the roll of film you took to be developed, you told me you discovered it in a house your husband owns."

Belinda furrowed her brows. "That's right, I did."

"Can you give me the address?"

A look of concern swept over her face. "Of course," she said and related a number on Leeds Road, Outwood.

Again Strong and Stainmore exchanged glances. "Do you know where your husband is now, Belinda?" Strong asked.

"I've really no idea. He's not been staying here for a while. Not since … well, you understand. In fact, he sent me a letter this morning through his solicitor."

Strong nodded. "I think I get the picture." He took a step towards the woman. "I think you'd better take a seat," he said, gently leading her to the sofa.

"Why," she said, slowly sitting down. "What's happened?"

"I'm afraid there's been a fire at that address."

She covered her mouth with her hand for a second. "What are you telling me, Inspector?"

"We've found a body."

Both hands to her face now. "No! Not Charlie?"

"We don't know," Strong responded. "At the moment our investigations are still at an early stage. But we may need your help later."

"Identification, you mean?"

Strong nodded again and Belinda crumpled into a sea of sobs. He turned to Stainmore and indicated the kitchen. She walked through and began to make the tea that Belinda had intended for herself.

Just then, sounds of the front door opening and closing were heard.

Belinda looked up at Strong through tear stained eyes, a shocked expression on her face. That quickly morphed to one of relief as Anthony walked in.

"What's happened now?" the boy asked. "Has he thumped you again?" He looked at Strong.

"Anthony, I think you need to look after your mother now."

He rushed to his mother's side on the sofa.

"Have you seen or heard from your father recently?" Strong asked.

"Not since last week. Why?"

Strong repeated what he'd told Belinda as Stainmore reappeared with a mug of tea for her. "At the moment, we don't know who was in the house. We just have to look at all scenarios," he went on.

Anthony had his arm around his mother. "Don't worry, Mum," he said. "With any luck, it won't be him."

"In the meantime Mrs Chamberlain … Anthony, if you do hear from Mr Chamberlain, I'd like you to call me, anytime." Strong handed a card to each. "We'll be in touch as soon as we know any more."

Belinda wiped her eyes and looked up at Strong. "Thanks, Inspector."

"We'll see ourselves out," he said, leading the way.

They walked back to the car and got in. Strong put the key in the ignition but paused to look up at the house and puff out his cheeks. "Sometimes this job is shit, Kelly," he said. "That lad's world will be turned upside down shortly, if I'm right."


Once the police had gone, Anthony stood and made his way into the kitchen. "I'm starving," he said. "Have we got anything interesting in?"

Belinda followed him, hands around her mug of tea and stood in the doorway, watching him open and close cupboards then the fridge in a search for food. "Anthony, you don't seem too concerned that Dad might have been involved in that fire."

"He'll be all right," he said over his shoulder. "He always is. Can I have this pizza?" he pulled a cardboard package from the freezer.

"Of course you can." She watched him for a few moments as he set the oven and unwrapped the deep pan margarita. His attitude puzzled her. "Where have you been tonight?" she eventually asked.

"Simon's. I told you, celebrate our results."

"I thought you said you were staying over."

"I said I might but I changed my mind."

She knew he was lying but decided now was not the right time to confront that. She had too many other thoughts buzzing around her brain.

# 34
## Friday 17<sup>th</sup> August 2001

DCI Hemingford called for attention as he strutted into the CID Room. Conversations quickly died away as he looked around the room. "Okay, everyone," he said. "Last night's fire in Leeds Road, Outwood. First call to the emergency services from a passer-by timed at 20:12. Fire fighters on the scene at 20:23. Discovered in an upstairs bedroom, the body of a male, naked apart from a hood over the head with holes cut for the nostrils and his mouth taped. Any news on identity?"

"DI Strong and DS Stainmore are at the mortuary now, sir," DC Ormerod reported. "They have a strong suspicion as to who the victim might be which is why they chose to attend."

"What news from Forensics?" Hemingford went on.

"Still at the scene first thing this morning," DC Darby replied. "The fire investigators confirmed the seat of the fire as being in the sitting room immediately below the bedroom where the body was found. Apparently an iron was left switched on, on top of a pile of clothes."

"A slow burning fuse," Hemingford added thoughtfully.

Ormerod's mobile began to vibrate in his pocket. He removed it and answered the call from Stainmore. "Yes Kelly," he said then listened for a few seconds. "Okay, I'll tell him." He ended the call and looked to Hemingford. "DS Stainmore, sir. She and DI Strong are convinced our victim is Charles Chamberlain, principal of Chamberlain Associates, the legal firm in town."

"Right. But we still need an official identification. Kelly and Colin can handle that with Mrs Chamberlain as soon as the mortuary is ready. In the meantime, what have we got on door-to-door?"

DC Sam Kirkland gave a brief summary of what little the door-to-door reports had revealed so far. "Uniform are still making enquiries, sir and we should have most of that complete by lunch-time," he concluded.

"Okay, thanks," Hemingford said. "I'm going back down to the crime scene. DS Ryan, can you set up here as an incident room and organise information on the boards, all the usual procedures? DC Kirkland, keep the pressure on uniform. DC Darby, chase up forensics. I need something to work with here. DC Ormerod, background checks on our victim. Right, let's go to it."

Hemingford made to leave but was accosted at the door by Detective Chief Superintendent Flynn. "Rupert. Something to get your teeth into, eh?"

"Yes, sir."

Flynn turned and led Hemingford out into the corridor. In a low voice he asked, "Is it true who our victim is?"

"He still has to be formally identified but DI Strong and DS Stainmore are at the PM now. They seem in no doubt."

"Hmm. With his … friendship with ACC Wadsworth, this will turn out to be high-profile. So, don't forget, any resources you think you might need, come and see me."

\*   \*   \*

"Why are you looking so pleased with yourself?" Souter asked Janey Clarke. She'd just rushed in to the news room with a big smile on her face.

Bag down on the floor and computer switched on. "Having a fireman as a boyfriend has its compensations," she jibed.

"What you get up to in the privacy of your own home, I don't want to know … all those fireman's lifts. I can just imagine the contortions you get yourself into." Souter shook his head, as if trying to clear it of unsavoury images. "In fact, no, that's a horrible thought."

"Very bloody funny, Mr Souter," she called from the other side of the workstation screen. And then her head appeared over the top of it. "Nothing to do with what me and Tom get up to in private, it's the inside info he can provide when a juicy story breaks."

Souter looked away from his computer screen towards Janey. "Oh, yes. And what juicy story would that be?"

"It's mine and I'm keeping it that way." She disappeared to sit in front of her keyboard.

Souter stood and walked round to stand behind her chair as she typed. "Go on," he said, "You've got my attention."

Over the course of the next few minutes she banged out the basis of the story for that evening's edition of the house fire in Leeds Road Outwood with the unknown male victim found in mysterious circumstances. "I'm not allowed to say how they found him," she said, "but it is a good one." She then went on to report that the cause of the fire was suspicious and believed to have been caused by an iron setting fire to some clothing.

"Can you reveal that at this stage?" Souter asked.

"Tom didn't say I couldn't, only not to mention how they'd found the victim."

"I'd have thought if it's suspicious, the police would want to keep a lot of information to themselves at the moment, especially how it started." Souter shrugged. "Anyway, sounds like a good story for you, Janey." He knelt down by her chair. "So go on then, just between you and me … and Tom, how was he found?"

\* \* \*

The middle-aged receptionist who had been the gatekeeper last time they visited was talking on the phone when Strong and Stainmore walked into the offices of Chamberlain Associates.

"I'm sorry," she was saying, "but Mr Chamberlain is not available today." A pause. "No I don't know when he's expected back." She put the phone down and it immediately rang again.

Before she could answer it, Strong introduced himself. "Is Mrs Matthews in?" he enquired.

"She is, but she's very upset."

"I understand that but we do need to speak with her."

"Just a minute," she said, stood and walked through the door to the main offices.

A minute later, she reappeared, Anita Matthews following behind.

"If you'd like to come through," Anita said, face puffy and apparently struggling with emotion.

She led them through to the meeting room and offered them drinks, which they refused.

"You've obviously heard the sad news," Strong began once they were seated

Anita nodded. "It's just awful. Belinda rang me about an hour ago. We can't take it in. Are you absolutely sure?" She waved her hands. "I'm sorry, that was a stupid question."

"That's okay, Mrs Matthews." Strong said, "You've had a shock and we don't always think logically at these times."

She gave a faint smile.

"Unfortunately, we do have to ask a few questions," he continued, "And we will have to look at a lot of things here."

She nodded. "Of course."

Stainmore opened her notebook as Strong began.

"Can you tell me the last time you saw Mr Chamberlain?"

"Yesterday," she struggled and dabbed her eyes with a handkerchief. "Yesterday afternoon; when I left the office. That would have been around four-thirty."

"And was everything as normal?"

"Yes. He said he'd be in a bit later this morning, around eleven, as he had a meeting first thing."

"He didn't say who with?"

"No, but it should be in his diary." She stood. "Oh, I'll have to …"

"No, that's fine. We'll take care of that later," Strong interrupted, holding up a hand.

She sat back down.

"And that was the last time you spoke to him? Yesterday around half past four?"

"Yes."

"Now, we have to ask this, but can you tell me where you were yesterday evening between, say six and nine?"

"Was that when ... Oh, God." Another wipe of the face. "I was at home. I cooked myself something to eat as I watched the news and ate watching *Emmerdale*. After that, I caught up with a few emails, then watched a programme about house restoration from nine."

"Thanks for that. Now could you just give me an idea of who works here and what their job titles are?"

As it turned out, the law firm was smaller than Strong had imagined. Stainmore began to write as Anita gave him a quick outline of the company's history. Charlie and two friends from University had worked for a number of other practices until Charlie decided to go on his own and invited the other two to come in with him, albeit as junior partners. One of those friends was Bill Matthews, Anita's late husband. She inherited his ten per cent share of the business. The other partner had left two years ago and Charlie had bought him out. He'd decided to retain ownership of the rest of the business himself and subcontract out to other practices any work he felt appropriate.

Strong was surprised. "So all this set up," he swept his hand around, "is no more than ... a front?"

"No, inspector. There's nothing untoward with how we're established here. What's important is reputation. And Charlie's reputation is ... was, the best. That's why his clients keep him, I mean kept him."

"Do you mind if we have a look in Mr Chamberlain's office now?"

"I'll show you," she said.

"That's okay," he said. "It's only next door. And in the meantime, DS Stainmore here can take a formal statement from you, if that's okay?"

Strong opened the door to Chamberlain's office and paused at the threshold, taking in the details. Everything seemed neat and tidy, no paperwork left out on the desk or the meeting table. He walked round to the other side of the desk. Even the waste paper bin was empty. The desk was inlaid with leather and had three drawers on either side along with a large central one. A computer stack stood below and a keyboard and screen sat on the desk to one side. He would arrange for the computer to be taken away and examined shortly.

In the meantime, he slipped on some latex gloves, opened the desk's central drawer and pulled out a leather-bound diary. Flicking through, he stopped at today's date. *10:00 Bernard WDC.* He thought for a moment. Bernard? And then it came to him; Bernard Faulkner. Next on his visiting list then.

He opened and closed the side drawers, one at a time, to reveal the usual stationery and accessories, notepads, stapler removers, holepunch and other similar items. Then, in the bottom right, below a pack of envelopes, he found them. He picked them up and looked at them closely. Six of them. He slipped them into a plastic evidence bag before moving on to the first of two four-drawer filing cabinets. A quick rummage through revealed files for various clients and projects that Chamberlain had been involved with; some well-known clients and one or two projects that Strong had heard of throughout Yorkshire. He'd get some uniform assistance to list them later. For now, nothing jumped out at him.

When he walked back into the meeting room carrying Chamberlain's diary and the evidence bag, Stainmore was completing a few details of Mrs Matthews' statement. He slowly and deliberately placed the plastic bag on the table in front of Anita. Clearly visible were the front faces of the *'Talisman Club'* business cards. Stainmore looked to her boss.

"Can you explain these, Mrs Matthews?" Strong asked.

She looked away. "I think you know what they mean," she replied.

"Indulge me."

She took a deep breath and exhaled. "The *Talisman Club* is ... was ... Charlie's name for the ... activities at Leeds Road. He thought it was a good idea to have them printed to give to members. It was all informal, but he just liked the idea."

Strong remained standing and slowly phrased the next question. "So why do you think it would be when we spoke to Mr Chamberlain a couple of weeks ago, he denied all knowledge of it?"

Anita stiffened. "You'd have to ..." and then she seemed to remember, "I've really no idea. But it might be because he didn't want to tell you any more about what is a private matter."

"Unless it's relevant to his death," Strong said, before turning to Stainmore. "Are you finished?"

"Yes, guv."

Anita shuffled in her seat to face them both. "Oh there is one other thing you should know about," she said.

"And what's that?" Strong responded.

"That first time you came here, asking about the photographs ..." she hesitated and looked down at the table for a second. "... Anthony came storming in about ten minutes after you'd left."

"Go on."

"He was angry. It was just after his mother had been discharged from hospital. He punched his dad. He blamed him for what happened to her."

"Not surprising," Stainmore threw in.

"But he said if he went near her again, he'd kill him. In a fit of pique, he also said he didn't consider himself Charles's son, or Charles his dad."

Strong looked to Stainmore then back to Anita. "Well thank you for that," he said and opened the door.

Stainmore followed his lead and stood up.

"And by the way," Strong paused in the doorway, "we will need you to identify all the participants from those photographs. We'll see ourselves out."

# 35

Strong made the short walk from Chamberlain's offices to the Town Hall. Stainmore was on her way to speak to Patrick Whitaker. With the strange find in Chamberlain's mouth and the fact that Whitaker had remembered him as the possible benefactor that Denise had identified, he had to be checked out.

Strong strutted into the ground floor corridor of the gothic style building, his footsteps echoing off the terrazzo floor and high ceiling.

"Hey, Colin," a familiar voice called from behind.

Strong turned to see the large frame of Jeremy Bullen about ten yards down the hallway.

"Thought it was you," he said. "What brings you in here?"

"Take me to your leader," Strong said with a laugh. "Hello, Jez." He held out a hand. "No, seriously, I'm here to see Bernard Faulkner."

Bullen shook hands with a firm grip. "Oh, him," he responded, raising his eyes heavenward. "He's two floors up. He's still not bellyaching about someone bluffing their way into his office is he?"

"Did they? When was that?"

"A couple of weeks ago when the big bastard was on holiday. But you don't know?"

"News to me. I'm here to talk to him about something else."

"He probably doesn't want anyone outside to find out. Look, do me a favour will you, don't mention it unless he does."

Strong grinned. "Don't mention what?"

"I'll let you get on," Bullen said, turning away. "We'll have a pint sometime."

"Look forward to it."

Strong made his way up to Faulkner's office and walked into the secretarial ante-room.

"Can I help you?" Faulkner's secretary asked.

Strong produced his warrant card and asked to speak with Faulkner.

"Can I say what it's about?" She was already picking up her telephone.

"I'd rather discuss that with Mr Faulkner, if you don't mind. But I wouldn't be here if it wasn't important."

She seemed to colour and made the call to her boss to announce Strong's presence.

A few seconds later, the door to the adjacent office opened and a tall portly man wearing rimless glasses stood in the doorway. "Inspector," he said, "Come in."

Strong followed him into an office that he thought had probably changed little since Victorian times, apart from the obvious telecommunications items. He sat in the chair Faulkner indicated opposite his oak desk. He wouldn't be surprised if all the furniture was antique.

"So how can I help you," Faulkner enquired.

He took out his notebook, more for effect than to consult. "Do you know a Charles Chamberlain, Mr Faulkner?"

Faulkner looked puzzled. "Charles, of course. Why? What's happened? He was supposed to be here for a meeting this morning but he never turned up. I've tried calling the office but all they tell me is he's not available."

"Did you know him well?"

"We'd done business in the past. Yes, I think I could say we knew each other well." The councillor leaned forward on his desk. "What's happened?" he asked earnestly.

"I'm afraid Mr Chamberlain was found dead last night."

Faulkner looked visibly shaken. "But … how?"

"There was a fire."

The colour drained from his face. "Oh God. This is terrible. What about his wife and family?"

"It didn't occur in the family home. They're all safe and well." The expression on Faulkner's face gave Strong the impression that he didn't actually mean that. "But you said you were expecting him for a meeting this morning," he went on, "Can you tell me what that was about?"

"Er, yes." He nervously rummaged through a few papers on the desk in front of him. "We were going to discuss what role, if any, he could play in connection with our Lofthouse Redevelopment."

"The old colliery site?"

"Yes."

At that point a commotion was heard in the outer office. Faulkner's secretary's voice could be heard to say, *"He's with someone."*

The door flew open and a white-haired man in his mid-fifties, just below six feet tall and markedly slimmer than Faulkner burst in. "Bernie, have you heard …"

"Michael," Faulkner interrupted. "Let me introduce you to Detective Inspector Strong."

"Oh, sorry," the newcomer stuttered, "I didn't … sorry."

Faulkner was on his feet. "Inspector, meet Michael Pitchforth, our Head of Planning."

Strong also got up and held out a hand.

Pitchforth shook it limply, avoiding eye contact..

"Were you to be involved in this morning's meeting, Mr Pitchforth?" Strong probed. "With Mr Chamberlain?" Pitchforth was definitely distracted. "I mean, with this concerning one of the largest projects the council has dealt with and you being Head of Planning."

Pitchforth looked from Strong to Faulkner and back again. "Well, yes."

"And I'm assuming from your reaction just now you've heard about Mr Chamberlain?"

Pitchforth looked to the floor and shook his head. "Only just. It's shocking," he said, "Absolutely shocking."

"Did you know Mr Chamberlain well, Mr Pitchforth?" Strong asked.

"He's been involved with several projects of ours over the past … I don't know … ten years, I suppose. So professionally, I'd like to think I know ... sorry, knew him, reasonably well."

Strong looked from one man to the other. "When was the last time you'd spoken to or seen Mr Chamberlain?" he asked them both.

Pitchforth answered first. "I've not seen Charles since we dealt with that Bullring issue and that must have been back at the end of last year. I was looking forward to catching up with him this morning."

The news also seemed to have hit Faulkner hard. Harder than Strong thought normal. He gave the impression his mind was on other things too. "Obviously, I spoke to him last week, Inspector," he finally responded. "To arrange today's meeting."

"And did everything seem normal to you when you spoke? Nothing troubling him? On his mind?"

Faulkner slowly shook his head, forehead creased in thought. "No. He seemed like he always did."

"And there's nothing else that's occurred recently that you would think out of the ordinary?" Strong watched Faulkner closely.

No mistaking a slight reaction from the man. He had the impression he was about to say something meaningful when he reacted, shaking his head, jowls wobbling. "No, I can't think of anything," he replied.

Strong then took out a business card but paused as he passed it to Faulkner. "Oh, that reminds me ... does the name *Talisman Club* mean anything to you?"

Again, another reaction on Faulkner's face. The eyes widened slightly and he seemed to tense. "No. Never heard of it," he said.

Still with his card held out to Faulkner, Strong turned his head to Pitchforth. "What about you?"

"Means nothing to me either, Inspector," Pitchforth said. For what it was worth, Strong thought he was telling the truth.

"Well if you think of anything else, gentlemen, please give me a call."

Finally, Faulkner took the card and Strong walked to the door. "Thanks for your time," he said.

*   *   *

All available officers were assembled and waiting in the CID room for the six o'clock briefing. Jim Ryan had done a good job of posting all necessary photographic information on the boards which Strong was studying. Ormerod stood by his shoulder. "Initial thoughts, guv?"

"Not enough info, Luke. The sponge phallus was a surprise." he said, referring to the find in Chamberlain's mouth at the PM.

Ormerod laughed. "Can't be connected with the body in the bath though, surely?"

Unsmiling, he turned to look at his DC. "Kelly's never really been happy with what happened to her but ..." He shrugged.

Hemingford stormed into the CID room, the evening edition of the Yorkshire Post in his hand. "Right, which of you lot has been talking to the press?"

Silence descended like a winter fog. Puzzled looks were exchanged.

He held up the paper, folded at the appropriate page. "*The fire*," he quoted, "*is believed to have been started by an iron left on a pile of clothes*." He paused to look around the gathering. "*Police are treating the death of a man found in an upstairs bedroom as suspicious*. Too bloody right we are. But I'll ask you again, who's been talking to the press?" Another hard stare at all the officers present, many shaking their heads.

Eventually Strong responded to break the atmosphere. "That sort of information could have come from the Fire Service. They'd know how the fire started."

Hemingford's anger seemed to subside. "We wanted as much detail as possible held back on this. Only the person who started the fire would have known how they did it. Now, everyone does. At least they didn't describe how Chamberlain was found." He sat on a desk by the side of the whiteboard. "Okay, where are we with this?"

Over the course of the next ten minutes, various members of the team contributed information to the briefing. Strong confirmed that the identity of the victim had been formally established and the initial findings on cause of death. Doug Norris, the Scenes Of Crime officer reported on his assessment of the fire scene. Working with the Fire Service, the seat of the fire was confirmed as the ground floor sitting room where a pile of clothing with an electric iron placed on top had ignited, all as mentioned in the newspaper. That had spread to the adjacent sofa. However, that had not burnt beyond salvation as with all burning in this situation, the clothing and material itself falls in on top of the fire and effectively preserves some of it.

"So what you're saying is that we can retrieve some forensic evidence from here?" Hemingford asked.

"Exactly." Norris responded. "We're examining the remains in the lab at the moment. With a bit of luck, we can extract DNA from them."

"How long for that?"

"Next week some time."

"Make it as soon as," Hemingford said. "So who can we compare those samples to? Who are our suspects?"

Jim Ryan took them through the photos on the board indicating names of those closest to the victim. There were also blanks for other friends and associates of Chamberlain who had yet to be identified.

Stainmore reported on her initial investigation into Patrick Whitaker, whose estranged mother cleaned for Chamberlain. He'd given an alibi that, for the time of the fire, he was on duty at Pinderfields.

The briefing finally ended with tasks allocated to various officers.

# 36
## Saturday 18<sup>th</sup> August 2001

At the briefing the previous evening, Stainmore was charged with checking out Patrick Whitaker's alibi. She'd been down to Pinderfields and spoken to a number of the A & E staff who were on duty on Thursday evening. But they'd struggled to remember if he'd been with them all shift. A check with security of their CCTV footage showed him leaving the hospital at 18:47 through a loading bay door and returning the same way at 20:12.

After she'd returned to Wood Street, Strong decided he would accompany her to Whitaker's flat on the Lupset estate. He was driving.

"What did you reckon to Luke's assessment, guv?" Stainmore asked.

Before they'd set off, Luke Ormerod had had a quiet conversation with Strong and Stainmore to voice his concerns about Hemingford's attitude when questioning Belinda. He thought the new DCI had adopted an unnecessarily hard line. He'd reduced her to tears at one point, accusing her of being involved somehow.

"To be fair, Kelly, she wasn't at home when we called on Thursday and the hospital told us she'd gone off sick. So I suppose, she's offered no alibi for the relevant time frame."

Stainmore was staring out of the window. "And, so far as we know, she would have the strongest motive of those we know about." She looked back to Strong. "But you've spoken to her quite a bit recently. You don't think she's capable, do you?"

"Who knows what pressures she's been under from Chamberlain. It must have been a shock, finding out what he's been up to, never mind seeing the photographic evidence. But … no, my instinct tells me not."

Pulling up outside Whitaker's flat, Stainmore indicated the white Ford Transit belonging to Frank, with Patrick's blue Vauxhall Astra parked in front. "With a bit of luck," she commented, "they're both at home."

Patrick Whitaker answered the door himself, the disappointment obvious on his face. "What now?"

"Can we come in, Mr Whitaker?"

He sighed heavily and led the way up the stairs. "Close the door behind you. We don't want anybody just walking in off the street."

Up in the living room, there was no sign of Frank.

"You're son not in?" Stainmore asked.

"Out with his mates."

"Where was he on Thursday night between six and nine in the evening?" Strong enquired.

The line of questioning threw Whitaker for a second. "He was doing a job. Removals. Some old girl on Wrenthorpe was being moved into an old folk's home off Batley Road. He knew the granddaughter and helped them out." He looked at Stainmore. "I told you before, he's not a bad lad."

"But what about you Mr Whitaker," Strong went on, "Thursday between six and nine."

Again Whitaker addressed his answer to Stainmore. "I told you yesterday, I was working. A & E."

"That's true to a point, Patrick." Stainmore picked up the thread. "But you weren't there all shift."

Whitaker's gaze avoided the officers.

"We have evidence to suggest you left the premises from about ten to seven until just before a quarter past eight. Right smack in the middle of the period we're looking at."

"You must be mistaken. I told you, I was working."

"Get your coat, Mr Whitaker," Strong said, "we'll continue this conversation at Wood Street."

\* \* \*

In interview room two, Whitaker sat nervously at the table. "Can't I have a fag?" he asked.

"Health and Safety now, Mr Whitaker. You'll find most public buildings are 'no smoking'. Rumour has it, it'll be banned in pubs soon." Strong cast a quick smile to Stainmore and, still on his feet, placed tapes in the recording devices.

Whitaker shook his head.

"But, if you tell me the truth about Thursday night, then I could arrange for you to have a cigarette break out in the yard."

Whitaker rubbed his hand down his face. "Look, can I have a private word?" He looked to Stainmore who was poised, notebook open ready to write down the salient points of the interview.

"Anything you want to say to me, you can say in front of DS Stainmore," Strong responded.

Whitaker screwed up his face. "Please Mr Strong," he said, "Man to man like."

"Kelly, can you see if you can get us some coffees?"

Stainmore rolled her eyes, stood up and left the room.

Strong sat down opposite Whitaker. "Okay, what's so delicate that only I will do?"

Whitaker leaned forward, arms on the table in a conspiratorial gesture. "This is difficult. Not for me but for somebody else." He drew a deep breath but Strong remained silent. "Can I trust you to be … discreet?"

Strong smiled. "I'm a policeman, Mr Whitaker." He leaned forward, his face inches from the suspect. He thought he knew what was coming but decided he wouldn't make it easy for him.

"I was with someone else," Whitaker said.

"A woman?"

He nodded.

"Married?"

"Yes."

"You realise, I'll have to speak to her."

"Which is why I wanted to talk like this."

Strong took out his notebook. "Go on."

"She's a ward clerk at the hospital. Gloria. Gloria Redfearn."

"I'll need some contact details?"

"She works on the Maternity Unit. She should be there today, extra hours. It would be good if you … didn't need to call on her at home. Her husband wouldn't be too understanding."

"Where does she live?"

"One of those terraced houses just over the road and a bit lower down from the hospital."

"Handy." Strong nodded and checked his watch. "So you reckon she'll be at work now?"

"Should be, she was going in to catch up on some paperwork. They've been busy recently."

Stainmore came back into the room at that point with three coffees.

"Can we just look after Mr Whitaker for a little while, Kelly? Hopefully, I might be able to save us some time and effort."

"Must have been something interesting he said then?" She looked put out and placed the drinks on the table.

Strong took a big slurp of his coffee, put the cup back down and gathered his notebook. "I won't be too long," he said. "If you don't mind, we'll accommodate you in a cell, Mr Whitaker. You can take your drink with you."

\*   \*   \*

Just under an hour later, Strong walked into the CID room and sought out Stainmore. With a slight movement of the head towards his office, he attracted her attention. Inside, door closed, he rested against the desk. "We can let him go, Kelly."

"Why? What did he tell you?" She looked disappointed.

"Turns out he's been giving one to a ward clerk who works at the hospital and has the convenience of living over the road. When the shifts work out and her old man's out, as he was on Thursday evening, our romantic charmer slips out and slips her one."

"Genuine?"

"I never mentioned why I was asking, just that I needed to know if she could confirm his whereabouts for the times in question. At least she had the good grace to look embarrassed."

"The slimy little …"

"Come on, Kelly, he's not married, she is."

"Still though."

"I know what you mean." Strong pushed himself up. "So what does that leave us with now?"

"Well I spoke to the daughter of the old girl who was being moved by Whitaker junior on Thursday and that checks out. He pitched up after work around six and they didn't finish until ten."

"Well, just to cover all the bases take DNA samples from the Whitakers. Forensics can run a check with any evidence from the Chamberlain fire and release Patrick.

# 37
## Monday 20<sup>th</sup> August 2001

"Okay ladies and gents, listen up please." Hemingford called the briefing to order, standing in front of a display board. At the top in the centre, a photograph of the victim, Charles Chamberlain. Felt tip pen lines connected to one side with Belinda's name and below hers, two boxes with the children's names, Anthony and Grace. To the other side, a box with Anita Matthews name. Below, the names of Patrick and Frank Whitaker had been written in red.

Hemingford briefly summarised the facts as known so far. Chamberlain had been tethered to a wooden frame bolted to a wall in the first floor bedroom of a terraced house he owned on Leeds Road, Outwood at some point before twelve minutes past eight on Thursday evening. A fire started in the sitting room immediately below the bedroom. Cause of ignition, an electric iron placed on clothing, mostly women's underwear, which spread to the nearby settee. Cause of death, asphyxiation due to smoke inhalation. Unusual aspects, apart from the victim being naked and restrained, was the presence of a phallus-shaped sponge placed in the victim's mouth prior to being taped up, all prior to death. Also, when firemen arrived the door was locked with a key still on the outside of the door.

"So what else have we got?" Hemingford asked. "Colin?"

"There was a tenuous connection between the victim and those two up there." Strong pointed towards the board. "Patrick Whitaker's mother, Denise, our body in the bath case, cleaned the property for Chamberlain up until some time around May last year. As some of you

248

know, she was living as a man and had, in her bathroom some … male genitalia, made of sponge."

"Same as found in the victim's mouth?" Hemingford looked surprised.

"Yes. But we've checked on father and son and they're both out of the frame. Their alibis for the time of the fire hold up."

DS Jim Ryan joined in. "We've been to his offices and checked through most of the files. Techy boys have his computer but so far, nothing out of the ordinary or unusual has come to light."

"Luke and I have spoken to the wife," Hemingford pointed to Belinda's photo. "and the son. Mrs Chamberlain disappeared from her shift at the LGI around six, claiming to be unwell but wasn't home until …?" He sought Strong out once more.

"She wasn't at home when we first called on Thursday evening at five past ten. We called again at five to eleven, by which time she was there."

"And all she's told us is that she was unwell and sat in her car until she felt able to drive home," Ormerod added.

"Not exactly a convincing alibi," Hemingford commented. "Anything else?"

"Fire officer's report confirms what you mentioned earlier, sir," Darby said, "and forensics are running tests on the clothing that started the fire. Apparently they can obtain DNA of the regular wearer, especially if it involves collars, cuffs, waistbands, that sort of thing, where sweat might accumulate."

"Do we know what the garments were?"

"Women's I believe, bras and knickers." Darby had a smirk on his face. "But with some of those photos we saw, it's a toss up whether they were worn by women or blokes."

Strong quickly moved the discussion on. "What about the victim's clothes, personal effects, mobile phone?"

"Good point, Colin," Hemingford responded.

"Found in the other bedroom, sir," Darby answered. "Neatly folded on the bed with his suit hung up on a hanger. It looks like he was staying at the house. We found some more of his clothes in the wardrobe and drawers in that bedroom. His mobile was in his jacket pocket. Again, that's been sent off to Technical Support."

"Personal effects?"

"Wallet, credit cards, keys, all with us as evidence," Darby added. "And we've brought his car in for forensic examination. It was parked in a side street."

"Can you chase up their report on the phone please, John. Be interesting to see who he called and who called him in the hours leading up to the fire." Hemingford's gaze switched to DC Kirkland. "Sam, anything from door to door?"

Kirkland shook his head. "Nothing out of the ordinary, sir. The victim's car had been seen regularly outside the property but nobody reported any unusual activity on the evening of the fire."

Hemingford sighed then switched his focus to DS Ryan. "Jim, can we get a time-line marked up here too?" He turned to face the board again. "And what about this one," he said, pointing to Chamberlain's PA. "What has she had to say?"

"We interviewed her on Friday morning," Stainmore picked up. "Reckons she was at home alone on Thursday evening. But she's coming in shortly to go through those photographs that Mrs Chamberlain had taken in to be developed the other week. I think this time she'll be willing to identify who was involved. Again, that should give us more background to the victim."

"As long as she doesn't identify the Chief Constable, we'll be okay," Hemingford quipped.

Ormerod glanced at Strong and made a face, as if to say, *'Fuck, he's cracked a funny.'*

Strong just smiled.

"Right, you should all know what you're doing. To it," the DCI instructed.

*　　*　　*

"Thanks for coming in, Anita."

Anita Matthews was seated at the table in the front interview room where Stainmore had brought in drinks in styrene cups for them both.

"Didn't have a lot of choice, did I?"

"But you do want to help find out who murdered Mr Chamberlain though?"

Anita let out a deep breath. "Of course. There doesn't seem much point in keeping secrets anymore." She looked intently at Stainmore and pointed towards a folder of photos on the table. "Do you think one of those here was responsible?"

"The point is, we don't know. But we do have to explore all avenues. In my experience, the perpetrator is normally known to the victim and finding out as much as we can about them will help."

Anita held her gaze for a moment then lifted her coffee and took a sip. "Okay, let's do it."

This time, Stainmore had the full images to show her. She opened the folder and began. Ten minutes later, she had an interesting array of names. Anita also thought that the photographs had probably been taken prior to May 2000. One of the men involved had moved to Bristol around that time and another had died in January this year. Both were clearly identified. Also prominent was Bernard Faulkner. Anita informed her that he was very much into sadism and used to throw himself into those activities, rather too enthusiastically for Anita's liking. "Horrible man," she opined. "But Charles obtained a lot of work through him. Faulkner's secretary was also named, with her proclivities more on the masochistic side. "Ideally suited, I suppose," Anita said. "She always seemed subservient to him. Maybe even a little bit frightened of him, I suppose." Other names included a female head of department at a secondary school in Barnsley and a number of prominent local businessmen.

Once Anita had left, Stainmore knocked and entered Strong's office.

"Well guess who **are** members of the *Talisman Club* then, guv?" A smile played around her lips.

Strong looked up from some paperwork on his desk. "Let me guess," he said, leaning back. "Would one be a certain leader of a council, not far from here?"

"Got it in one. Plus his ever faithful secretary."

Strong's eyes widened. "Ooh, interesting."

"Brenda Morgan, spinster of this parish." She placed the list on his desk in front of him.

He picked it up and read.

"She also said, as far as she knew, there hadn't been a meeting of the club for several weeks. But there again Chamberlain had been staying there since his difficulties with Mrs Chamberlain."

"D'you know, I knew Faulkner was lying," Strong said.

"But there again, he was moving his lips, guv. And he is a politician."

"Cynical as ever DS Stainmore." A thin smile appeared on Strong's face. "Right," he said, standing up. "I think it's time we paid Mr Faulkner another visit."

\* \* \*

Grace returned to the lounge and studied her brother.

"How is Mum?" Anthony asked, without looking up.

Grace had travelled up from Southampton a couple of days ago. She bore an uncanny resemblance to her mother when she was of a similar age, except she was a couple of inches taller at five foot nine. Same shaped face with attractive cheekbones and long blonde hair. She was enjoying her work with a firm of accountants in the city where she'd been for almost a year. She'd also settled in well to the flat she shared with two other girls she'd met on the course. The chances of her returning to Yorkshire were slim; until the events of this week.

"She's asleep," Grace replied. "Do you want something to eat?"

"I'm fine." Anthony was slouched on the settee watching television. Grace deliberately stood in front of it. "I'm trying to watch that," he moaned.

"What are you not telling us?"

"I don't know what you mean."

"The night of the fire - where were you?"

"What's it to you?"

"Nothing," Grace shrugged. "But Mum's up there worried to death that you had something to do with it."

He sat himself up straight. "But how do we know *she* didn't?"

"Anthony! How can you possibly think that."

"Well I didn't, all right?"

"No it's not all right, Anthony. Dad's dead - murdered and you'd stormed into his office a few days before with some crazy accusations that you were going to kill him."

"They weren't accusations. He hit Mum. You don't know, you weren't here. It was only me that was around to pick up the pieces. Mum was really upset."

Grace knelt down in front of her brother and took hold of his hands. "I know. And I'm sorry I wasn't here." She blinked and a tear fell down her cheek. "I'm hurting too," she said, quickly wiping it away with her sleeve "But you must see how it looks. She told me you were supposed to be at Simon's that night." She looked him in the eye. "But you weren't, were you?"

He looked away. "It wasn't me, okay."

"So what are you hiding?"

He pulled his hands free and stood up. "I'm going out."

"Where …?" but her voice trailed away. She knew he wouldn't say anything else unless he wanted to. And now the front door slammed and he'd avoided answering … for now.

*   *   *

"Apparently Faulkner's in London today," Strong said. "Some meeting with government, staying overnight." He'd strolled into the CID room.

Stainmore was looking at some plastic evidence bags on Ormerod's desk. "He and the subservient Brenda?" she wondered.

"No, on his own. He'll be back at lunchtime so we'll go and see what he has to say about the goings on at Leeds Road then." He indicated the bags. "Something of interest?"

"I don't know. It's just …" She held up a bag containing a set of keys. "These look unusual."

She returned to her own desk and opened a drawer with an envelope containing two bunches of keys. "These are the two sets of keys we found in Denise's house." Selecting one ring, she held it up. "Now we know this set, the ones we couldn't identify at first, were for Chamberlain's Leeds Road house. He confirmed that when we spoke to him." She now took the other set over to Luke's desk. And these are for Denise's house. I meant to hand them back earlier. I remembered they looked quite unusual. You see these deep cuts at either end of the key itself. Now if I put it against these…" She held Denise's key alongside one of those found in Chamberlain's room. "Not only was he lying when he said he'd never heard of her originally, he was forced to admit that she cleaned for him. Then when pushed on whether he'd had a key to her place, he wondered why we would think he would have a key to her house. He knew she lived in a house. And now …" Strong could see the patterns on both keys were the same. "… we find he'd lied again, and he did have a key to her house."

Strong looked from the evidence bag to Stainmore. "And you think …?"

"It is possible he was there when she died. We can't prove it, but why lie all the time unless he'd got something to hide."

"And you always had a gut feel that there was something not right with the Whitaker case."

"But the evidence wouldn't prove anything and now he's dead."

# 38
## Tuesday 21st August 2001

"Mr Faulkner," Strong began, "last Friday, we spoke about the tragic events surrounding the death of Charles Chamberlain."

He and Stainmore were seated opposite the Council Leader in his office in the Town Hall. Brenda had fussed around when they'd first appeared and was now elsewhere making teas and coffees for them.

"What a shock, a real shock," Faulkner responded. "If I can help in any way …"

"I appreciate that and I think you may be able to."

At that point, Brenda knocked and entered with a tray containing mugs of coffee for Faulkner and Stainmore, a tea for Strong, a milk jug, sugar bowl and some biscuits on a plate. She placed it on the desk, removed the items, lifted the tray and turned to leave.

"Thank-you, Brenda," Faulkner said.

"Actually, Brenda." Strong looked to the woman. "Have you made a drink for yourself?"

She appeared to be taken off her stride. "Er … yes, it's on my desk."

"Well bring it through and join us, if you would."

Now Faulkner looked bewildered. He pushed his glasses further up the bridge of his nose. "But …"

Strong held up a hand. "Bear with me."

Brenda returned with her mug and nervously sat on the edge of the one remaining seat.

Strong addressed Faulkner. "Could I just ask you, when was the last time you saw Mr Chamberlain?"

The man puffed out his cheeks. "Oh well, it must have been a few weeks ago now."

"I know you told me you'd spoken to him on the phone the week before last, when you arranged Friday's meeting."

"Yes, that's right."

"But you haven't actually seen him for several weeks?"

"Yes. Yes, that's correct."

Strong turned to his secretary. "What about you, Brenda? Is it okay to call you Brenda?"

She gave a thin smile. "Yes, that's fine. I'm Brenda Morgan," she offered.

"So when was the last time you may have seen Mr Chamberlain?"

She looked flushed. "I … I don't really know Mr Chamberlain."

"Sure?"

"Inspector, where is this leading?" Faulkner interrupted.

Strong reached in his pocket and pulled out two cards and passed one each to Faulkner and Brenda. Strong's attention was on Faulkner whilst Stainmore studied his secretary. "You do recognise this, don't you? Both of you, I mean."

Brenda looked up alarmed. Faulkner looked away.

"I don't need to remind you that this is a murder enquiry." Strong leaned forward onto the desk. "Now last time you told me you'd never heard of the *Talisman Club*. New information has come to light. You might want to reconsider your answer."

Finally, Faulkner looked at Strong. "Look, this has nothing to do with Brenda here. If we could just have a word in confidence."

He turned to the woman. "Oh but I think it does have something to do with Mrs Morgan?"

"Just tell them, Bernie. They obviously know."

Back to Faulkner. "Well?"

The Council Leader leaned forward, both arms on the desk as if taking Strong into his confidence. "Look, this is only a bit of adult fun … consenting adults … not harming anyone."

Strong leaned back and looked to Stainmore. "Now where have we heard those phrases before?"

"Can't think, Sir."

"So, let me ask you again, when was the last time you saw Mr Chamberlain?"

Faulkner looked to his secretary. "About ten days ago. Thursday before last. There was a meet at Leeds Road."

Stainmore had been taking notice of the woman's reactions. It seemed as if she was about to say something before Faulkner had jumped in. "Brenda?" she asked.

"Yes, a week past Thursday," she confirmed.

"Sure?" Stainmore persisted.

Brenda seemed to stiffen, sitting straighter on the seat. "Of course."

Strong looked from one to the other. "You both attended?"

"Yes," Faulkner responded, "Brenda was with me."

"Who else would be able to confirm that?"

"Really ... I don't know if ..."

Strong was becoming irritated. "Mr Faulkner, we've already had most members of the club identified. We even have some photographic evidence."

Faulkner looked to his secretary, visibly shaken. "Well, there was Anita, of course." Strong nodded. "Bill, Bill Watson. He owns a garage out Batley way. And his friend Charlene, I think she's called."

"Anyone else?"

"Sam," Brenda offered, "Sam Appleyard."

*　*　*

"Anthony, I'm getting sick of this. I know you weren't with Simon on Thursday evening," Belinda said, raising her voice a touch.

For what seemed like the twentieth time she was trying to elicit something resembling the truth from her son. Not only had she to cope with the death of her husband and all the circumstances surrounding that, plus the recent discoveries of the secret life he seemed to have been living, but she had what she considered to be the unnecessary worry that Anthony may have had some involvement in the incident.

"Well I was and I don't care what you think," he responded, a defiant glare on his face.

"Hey, don't you speak to Mum in that tone of voice," Grace defended.

They were sitting in the lounge of their St Johns house. Belinda had stood up and switched off the television. Anthony had been engrossed.

"Funny how the police are satisfied. It's only you who seems to be making an issue of it."

"So not only are you committing perjury but you've got your mate to lie for you as well." Grace was determined to pile on the pressure.

"You know nothing." His face twisted into an angry expression.

Belinda put up a hand to Grace who was about to retort. "So tell me," she said in a gentler voice.

His head dropped as he avoided eye contact.

"Please, help me understand," his mother persisted.

He looked up at her. "I wasn't anywhere near that house." A tear dropped from an eye. "And I wasn't doing anything wrong." He stood up and walked to the door.

Grace made to stop him but Belinda impeded her. "Just leave things for now," she said. "He's not going to tell us any more." They could hear the front door closing as he left the house.

Belinda sat on the settee next to her daughter and looked to the ceiling.

"Come on, Mum, he might not be involved but he's hiding something."

Belinda knew she had a point. "The only comfort I have is that the police are satisfied with his story."

"But what if they dig a bit deeper? His mate Simon might not be so solid. And then …"

"You know they took DNA samples? Me and Anthony."

"You said."

"What if they find traces of his at the house? How's that going to look?"

It was Grace's turn to calm thoughts down. "But he didn't know about the place until, well …"

"I don't know, Grace." Belinda got to her feet. "Anyway, I'm tired. I'm going for a lie down," she said and walked from the room.

\* \* \*

"Impressions, Kelly?"

"We're still not getting the full truth. Brenda seemed to be about to say more on a few occasions." Stainmore zipped up her jacket as they made the short walk back to the station from the Town Hall.

"He definitely pulls her strings," Strong agreed. "I thought he was married though?"

"What's that got to do with anything? His wife's probably some timid creature past the menopause that helps out in a charity shop."

Strong laughed. "You paint a vivid picture, Kelly. She's probably at home working for a sex chat line that he knows nothing about."

"Ha!" It was Stainmore's turn to laugh. "We don't know, but he's a slippery bastard, that's for sure."

"Anyway, we need to track down the others. He said this Sam Appleyard was their Chief Engineer but not in the office today. Can you track down those other two, the garage owner and his bit of stuff." They were back at the station, Strong tapped in the security code and held the door open.

"I'll check it out," she said as they walked down the corridor.

# 39
## Wednesday 22nd August 2001

Next day, Anthony had left early for his summer job in Waterstones. Grace decided she needed her hair trimmed and had gone to a little basement establishment on The Bullring. And so Belinda was alone with her thoughts in the St Johns house once more.

She drifted aimlessly from the lounge through to her bedroom. And it was *her* bedroom now, she considered. No longer *their* bedroom. It hadn't been *their* bedroom for some while. Not since that day she discovered those legal papers in his bedside drawer. God, that seemed ages ago now. The piles of pennies and two pence pieces were still on top of her chest of drawers. She looked at them and felt anger. They were the instigators of this whole chain of events. She walked over to them and swept them off onto the carpet, some bouncing off the walls, landing behind the chest, some behind her bedside cabinet.

Then she sunk to the floor, tears flowing, loud sobs. She turned onto her side and hugged her legs close to her body.

She couldn't think how long she'd been like that. She may have fallen asleep for a short while. But she suddenly snapped herself back to reality. She pulled herself straight, got to her feet and made for the bathroom. Splashing water on her face for a minute, then gently drying herself with a towel, she looked in the mirror. Somehow she would sort this. If that meant protecting her family from any more harm, then she would do whatever it took.

She opened Anthony's bedroom door then stepped over the threshold. For a boy, the room was remarkably tidy. He'd always been orderly. Even much younger, when he collected model cars, he would always return them to their boxes and store them in shoeboxes, out of the way, under the bed when he wasn't playing with them.

His wardrobe doors were closed, no clothes scattered around like other lads his age, bed made, drawers closed and everything put away. On his bookcase, all books were placed spine out, fiction on separate shelves from non-fiction, another for his school books. Grace was the untidy one. Even now, when she'd only been back for a few days, she had clothes strewn around her bedroom, the open suitcase on the floor.

So what had Anthony been up to when the fire took hold? She didn't think he would ever tell her. But what if he had been as angry with his father as he had been three or four weeks ago when he'd gone round to his office and actually punched him? What if he had been angry enough to set the fire? She couldn't let anything happen to him. He'd got his whole life in front of him. And she couldn't let him waste that for the sake of what his father had been up to.

She returned to the lounge and searched out last night's evening paper. Flicking through the pages and finding the number she was looking for, she picked up the phone and dialled.

# 40
## Thursday 23rd August 2001

"Cracked it, Colin," Hemingford said, big beaming grin on his face. He was strutting up the corridor towards Strong, Luke Ormerod in his wake.

Strong was confused and his expression said so.

"Belinda Chamberlain has just confessed to starting the fire that killed her husband," the DCI announced as they all swept into the CID Room.

Ormerod's expression showed he didn't share the enthusiasm of his boss.

"She confessed?" Strong was in disbelief.

"DNA from the clothes, bras, knickers and blouses, all came back as a match to her. They were her clothes."

"Doesn't mean to say she'd taken them round to the house though?" Strong suggested.

"Popular misconception, Colin, that fire destroys all evidence. Besides, she'd received a letter from his solicitor that morning saying he wanted a divorce. So, in a fit of pique, she decided that he couldn't have everything, so she decided to destroy the place."

Strong's face set hard. "With him upstairs? So how did he manage to manacle himself to that frame."

"She lured him into thinking she was interested in that. Then locked the door on her way out," Hemingford continued.

"And the sponge phallus?"

"Didn't mention that."

Behind him, Ormerod gave a slight shake of the head and looked away.

"Do you mind if I have a word with her, sir?" Strong asked.

"As long as you don't try and talk her out of it and spoil my first case." Hemingford grinned and walked out of the room. "Just need to report the good news to the Superintendent."

Once he'd disappeared, Strong addressed Ormerod. "You're not convinced either, Luke?"

"I wasn't at first, guv. She spoke about the iron on the clothes and … well, thanks to our newspaper friends, everyone knows that. But she could tell us that he'd been manacled to the frame and that the door was locked."

Strong scratched his temple. "But she didn't know about the sponge," he said quietly, as if in thought. "I've got to talk to her Luke. Where is she now?"

"In the cells, guv. Do you want me to come with you?"

"I suppose you better had but just let me do the talking."

The custody sergeant unlocked the cell door and walked away a few yards. Strong entered, hands in his pockets and leaned against the wall. Ormerod remained by the door.

Belinda Chamberlain looked to have shrunk from the woman he'd spoken to only a few weeks before. She glanced quickly up at Strong then away again. Her eyes were moist, swollen and bloodshot.

"Belinda," he said gently, "what have you done?"

"I've told the other one. I put the iron on the clothes, switched it on and left."

"But why?"

"I wanted to destroy the place. If he hadn't bought it … if I hadn't found out about it." She let out a deep sigh. "That's not true. Whether I'd discovered his nasty little secret or not, he'd still have had it, wouldn't he?" She rubbed her nose with the sleeve of her cardigan. "I was going to wreck his car too but, in the end, I couldn't be bothered."

"And you knew he was upstairs."

"Of course."

He pushed himself away from the wall and looked down on the woman. "You know what?" he said, "I don't believe a word of it."

She looked directly at him and held his gaze for a second, before turning away.

"I think I know you better," he said. "Why are you doing this?"

"Just leave me alone." She lay down on the hard bunk, faced the wall and pulled herself into the foetal position.

\* \* \*

"I just don't get it, though ..." Strong was dishing up some chilli-con-carne onto beds of rice in bowls on the kitchen work surface. "Why would she do that?"

Laura poured some red wine into two glasses on the small dining table in the kitchen. "What makes you think she didn't?"

Strong brought their evening meal over to the table.

"Nearly forgot," Laura said, "there's bread in the oven."

Once settled at the table, Strong resumed the conversation. "I've spoken to her several times now. When she was brought into A & E, when Bob was there and next morning I bumped into her coming out. I like to think I'm a good judge of character and I just don't think she's capable of murder."

"I didn't think she was charged with murder?"

"Well, that's the charge. If she hadn't said she'd shackled him to the frame and just said she'd let herself into the house, placed the iron on a pile of clothes and switched it on, she would probably have been charged with manslaughter."

"But you said that she'd received a letter that morning from her husband's solicitor saying he was starting divorce proceedings. That might be enough to make her do something she wouldn't normally do."

"From Luke's reaction, I think Hemingford has been applying the pressure and she's finally cracked." He took a sip of wine.

"But, who knew how he was found?"

"I'm still trying to work that one out. But there was one final detail she never mentioned."

"Oh?"

"Sorry, Laura, I can't even tell you that." He paused for a mouthful of food. "But I think there's more to it. Why would she put her hands up to something like this?"

Laura put down her fork. "Okay, let's say this was me. She's been married for, what, twenty-odd years, two children, a boy and a girl?" Strong nodded. "Daughter off the scene, at least as far as this is concerned, and the boy at home." She cut herself a piece of bread. "Well, there's only one answer. If you think she wasn't involved and has made a false confession, then she's covering, taking the rap, however you want to describe it, for someone else. And if it was me, the only people I'd do that for would be family. And the only one on the scene is the lad. He's your focus."

"That's what I was thinking. I'll ask Luke what reaction they got from Anthony when they questioned him."

Laura had picked up her fork again and taken another mouthful. "But what's really getting to you, Colin ..." She pointed her fork to reinforce the point. "... is the new guy. You don't like him, do you?"

He pulled a face. "It's not that exactly."

"So what is it, exactly?"

"I think he's swallowed this confession too easily. Either that or it's an easy win for his first major case."

"So keep digging around. It's not like you to give up so easily."

# 41
## Friday 24th August 2001

Alison sat on the toilet in a cubicle on the 4th floor of her office building and stared in disbelief. But that wasn't strictly true. Her body had been telling her for some time that this may be the case; she'd felt tired more recently, her breasts were tingly and she'd felt nauseous first thing in the mornings. But here it was in blue and white. The tell-tale colours of a positive test. She didn't need to see a doctor to confirm it, she knew already. Twice she'd missed which would make her, what, about ten weeks?

She'd nipped out at lunch-time to Boots, avoiding Sammy. She didn't want her to see what she was buying. And now, here it was, all her concerns realised. God, thirty-seven and pregnant. What will Bob say? He'll be over the moon, won't he? But will he? Of course he will. No, wait, she can't tell him, not yet. He won't want her going to the States; and that's been a long time coming. It's such a great opportunity, six weeks over there; big swish offices in the World Trade Center; great views over Manhattan, not to mention the work experience. She'd been looking forward to it already. Promotion options should open up for her when she gets back too.

But then ... she looked back down at the stick. Ten weeks ... that would mean about sixteen weeks when she was due to fly back. That would be okay wouldn't it? Her head was in turmoil. Bob should know. She'd tell him tonight. But there again ...

The noise of the toilet door opening made her hold her breath. Then footsteps entered and walked up the line of cubicles.

"Is that you in there, Alison?"

She recognised the voice and let out her breath. "I'll be out in a minute, Sammy."

"Mr Bates has just come down. He wants to run through a few things before you head off next weekend."

She stood, wrapped the stick in paper tissue, placed it at the bottom of her bag then flushed the toilet. "Be there in five," she said.

\* \* \*

That evening Souter opened the door for Alison and they finally stepped into L'Italia. The waiter showed them to a table for two in a quiet corner towards the rear.

"At least we made it through the door this time," Alison said, a cheerful expression on her face.

The waiter handed them each a menu and asked for their drinks order.

"A pint of Peroni, please and ..." Souter looked questioningly to Alison.

"Just an orange for me." She looked up at the waiter. "Have you got a J2O?"

"Certainly, madam." The waiter nodded and left.

Souter was surprised. "I'd have thought you'd have gone for some nice Italian red?"

"It's just what I fancy," she said and buried her head in the menu.

A few minutes later, the waiter returned with their drinks and they were ready to order. Souter plumped for minestrone soup to start and a pizza for the main – large. "Well I'm hungry," he said in justification. Alison declined a starter and chose a steak for her main.

"I hope Sammy and Susan are having a good time," Alison commented, once they were on their own again. "Over half way through their holiday now."

"I'll bet they are."

He didn't fool Alison. She could tell there was something on his mind. "What's wrong?"

"You saw the paper today? The Outwood fire?"

"Oh, yes. That was terrible. That poor man. And it's his wife who did it." Alison looked shocked.

He leaned in close and spoke quietly. "The thing is," he said, "remember when I was in A & E …"

"Difficult to forget."

"I know. But did you remember, they brought some woman in to the next bay?"

"Yes and when her husband appeared Colin had to step in to stop things getting ugly."

"That's right. Well … she's the accused and he's the victim." He leaned back.

Alison put her hands to her face. "No!"

"Yes. And it gets worse." He swallowed some lager. "Susan will be disappointed; Sammy too."

"How so?"

"She's Belinda, that nice nurse who worked on the Orthopaedic Ward when Susan was in. Sammy liked her as well."

"Jesus."

"I know." The conversation paused as the waiter brought his soup.

"The thing is, I can't help thinking that I've had something to do with it?"

"What? You mean you were at the fire?"

"No, not like that. It's just … I don't know, maybe something was said out of turn."

"You've got me," Alison said, a perplexed expression on her face.

Souter sampled a spoonful of his minestrone but didn't expand.

Alison studied him for a second then, head down, she began to say, "Actually, I've got something …"

Simultaneously, Souter began, "Anyway, I wanted to … sorry, what was it?"

"It's okay," she said, looking up nervously. "You go first."

"I was only going to say I booked my tickets today."

"New York?" Alison looked surprised.

"Yep. I fly out on 30th September and back on your flight on 14th October."

"So you're okay with me going?"

"Of course. Why wouldn't I be?"

"No … well that's great," Alison said, hoping her expression didn't give anything away. "I hope you'll not be too bored because I'll still be working that first week, I've got the last week free."

"In New York? Bored? You kidding?" He finished the last of his soup. "So what were you going to tell me?"

"Oh, nothing much, only that Mr Bates the office manager gave me all the details of what I'll be doing for them while I'm over there." She smiled nervously. "And, of course, all the security arrangements for getting in and out of the building. They're pretty hot apparently, since that nutter tried to bomb it about eight years ago."

Further conversation was interrupted by the waiter collecting Souter's empty plate.

# 42
## Sunday 26<sup>th</sup> August 2001

Alison opened the door to the boisterous girls just after eight on the Sunday evening. Both bounded into the living room, Susan holding a carrier bag that appeared to be full of gifts. "Hey," Sammy said excitedly, "have you missed us?"

Alison's smile was strained. "Of course we have." She hugged Sammy then did the same to Susan.

"We brought you something back." Susan held up the bag.

"Aw, you shouldn't have, not for us."

"But we wanted to. Without you two, we wouldn't have … well, you know how we feel," Sammy added.

Alison lifted out the two bottles of wine and some other gift bags. "I'll put the kettle on," she said and disappeared into the kitchen.

Souter walked towards them. "Had a good time?" He gave both girls a hug.

"Oh yeah, brilliant," Susan replied then gabbled on about some lads who'd fancied them all week and they'd had fun trying to avoid.

Souter sat back down on the settee, looking subdued.

Eventually, Sammy nudged Susan and their good humour subsided.

"What's wrong?" Sammy asked.

"Something's happened, hasn't it?" Susan joined in.

Souter rubbed his face with both hands. "You'd both better sit down."

Over the course of the next five minutes, whilst Alison returned with hot drinks, he summarised the events leading up to Belinda Chamberlain's arrest for arson and murder, as Strong had advised him the charges would be.

The girls looked at one another, shocked expressions on their faces.

"But that can't be right," Susan protested. "When was the fire?"

"The Thursday evening before you went on holiday."

Again another exchange of glances. "But we were with her at that time, having a drink in a pub near the hospital," Sammy said.

"Are you positive?"

"Of course. We'd been shopping, for the holiday, you know, and we spotted her in her car, parked up outside the hospital. She was upset."

"So why would she admit to doing it? Doesn't make sense."

Alison put her mug down on the coffee table. "You've got to speak to Colin," she said. "They can't proceed if you two can give her an alibi."

"I'll speak to him in the morning." Souter leaned back on the sofa and took a deep breath. "I can't help feeling I've contributed to this in some way," he muttered.

Susan looked at him strangely. "What do you mean by that, Bob?"

"I'm not sure but ..." He bent forward. "Were you there in the newsroom on the Friday morning when Janey was talking about the fire?"

"No, not me, why?"

"No, you're right, it was only the two of us. She was telling me details about the fire. Apparently, she's going out with one of the firemen that attended."

"And?"

"She mentioned how it started and I did query whether she should put that information in the report she was writing. But then I persuaded her to tell me some of the other details that she didn't include in the article."

# 43
## Monday 27<sup>th</sup> August 2001

"Come through," Strong beckoned, holding the door into the station open for Souter, Susan and Sammy to pass.

"You're looking fit and well again, Susan," he said as they made their way down the corridor.

"Thanks. Now totally discharged from treatment," she replied. "Had my last appointment at Orthopaedics three weeks ago."

Settled into Interview Room One, drinks declined, Strong faced the three of them.

"You said you had something important to tell me?" Strong began by way of introduction. "I mean, it must be if you're all in here on a Bank Holiday, especially with the weather outside."

"It is," Souter affirmed.

"About Belinda Chamberlain, you said? But you do realise I'm not involved in that case now. DCI Hemingford is leading the investigation."

"Then he needs to know that she didn't do it … couldn't have done it." Susan blurted out. She and Sammy did an impression of a double act routine as first one, then the other, interrupting themselves, told him how they had been away for a week on holiday, returning only last night and were shocked at what Bob had told them. They went on to tell the story of their encounter with Belinda on the evening of the fire, relating that they had taken her for a drink and a chat to cheer her up because she was upset at receiving a letter from her husband's solicitor about divorce proceedings.

"What time was all this?" Strong asked when they'd finished.

"We spotted her about seven o'clock and she left us around a quarter past ten. We seemed to have a lot to talk about and the time just flew," Susan said, looking at Sammy for confirmation.

"That's right," the other said.

Strong leaned back and put his hands behind his head. "I was never convinced by her confession," he said after several seconds' deliberation. "What I can't work out is why."

"But Susan and Sammy's statements will be enough to get her released, surely?" Souter said.

"They'll need to make formal written ones. I can organise someone to take them now. I'll take this to the new man." He grinned. "That'll piss him off. Thought he was on an easy win on his first big case."

"But, as you say, Col, why would she put herself in that position?"

Strong resumed a normal seated position. "Got to be covering for someone."

"Who? Her boy?" Souter surmised. "He was a bit pumped up at the hospital that night, if you remember?"

"I do," Strong agreed, "but his alibi for the evening checks out. Apparently he was with his schoolmate."

Souter looked from Susan to Sammy. "Lover then? Was she involved with someone?"

"No, I can't believe that," Susan responded.

Sammy shook her head.

"You can't always tell," Strong said. "That's why they get away with it. People keep them secret. It's only when they make a mistake and get caught out … Anyway," he got to his feet. "I'll get someone to take those statements, if that's okay?"

"While they're doing that, can I have a quiet word, Col?"

"Sure."

They both made their way out into the corridor.

# 44
## Tuesday 28<sup>th</sup> August 2001

"Oh, by the way, have you heard?" Janey Clarke slipped on her coat as she loaded her bag behind the low partition. "They've just announced that Thistle Developments are the preferred developer for the Lofthouse Project. Work probably due to start in the new year."

Souter and Susan exchanged quizzical looks. Susan had arrived a few minutes earlier. She was about to enquire if he'd heard any more following their visit to see Strong the previous day when Janey had stood up, ready to leave. They were lounging by Souter's workstation in the Post newsroom.

"Has that just been announced?" he asked.

"Press release first thing this morning. I'm just on my way to speak to Bernard Faulkner. Going to do an interview and a piece for the evening edition. See you." She strolled off towards the stair doors, a smug look on her face.

They watched her disappear before he sat down on his chair.

"How are you this morning?" Susan asked.

"I'm okay," he replied, but she could see that wasn't really the case.

"What was all that clandestine chat in the corridor with Colin about yesterday?"

"Just some other information that helped with Belinda."

"What other information?"

Souter sighed then finally decided he'd have to tell her. "The night before she went in to 'confess', she rang me."

Susan looked surprised. "So you knew she was going to do that?"

Souter made a face. "Of course I didn't. But I didn't think anything about it until I found out what she'd done."

"What do you mean?"

He nodded towards Janey's empty work station. "It involves Janey too. Apparently, she's knocking about with one of the firemen who attended the scene."

"I know, you said. But she's actually pulled a fireman?"

"Don't sound so surprised. Anyway, when she wrote the piece on the Friday after, she mentioned that the fire had been started by an iron left on a pile of clothes. But it was what she didn't report that was interesting." He then explained how Chamberlain had been found in the upstairs bedroom.

"I get it," Susan seemed to cotton on. "That info was never in the public domain but you told Belinda about it when she called you."

Souter nodded.

"Hence she could tell the police that when she confessed and that added weight to what she said.

"But there was one further piece of information that I didn't know at the time. Colin told me yesterday. And I can't tell anyone else, not even you."

"Okay, I can see that. But what do we do now? It was obvious she was covering for someone."

Souter looked at his watch. "Give it until later this afternoon, then you're going to make a phone call."

*   *   *

Belinda arrived home just after two in the afternoon. Grace had collected her from New Hall Prison in Flockton about ten miles to the west of Wakefield, where she'd been remanded in custody. Despite Grace probing her mother for answers, Belinda had refused to be drawn as to why she'd made a false confession. For the last fifteen minutes of the journey, Grace had resigned herself to the fact she'd have to change her tactics if she was ever to get to the truth.

Belinda sat on the sofa in the lounge as Grace made tea. She looked ashen and years older since Grace had last seen her mother. Life inside New Hall, even for only a few days, had made its impact. She finally spoke, "Where's Anthony?"

"Out somewhere," Grace answered.

"Not surprised."

Grace brought in a mug of tea for her mother and one for herself and sat down next to her.

Belinda cupped her hands around her mug and sipped gently. "How's he been coping with all this?" she asked.

"Hardly seen him to speak to. I think he's avoiding me." Grace looked to her mother. "You know I confronted him last week?" she said. "About him lying about being with Simon?"

Belinda looked alarmed. "What did he say?"

"He just insisted the fire wasn't anything to do with him and avoided every other attempt I made to get him to talk."

"I didn't want him to know that I knew he wasn't with Simon." Another sip, then she turned to Grace. "But the police must be satisfied that he was, so Simon must have lied for him too. Otherwise ..." She turned away and a tear ran down her cheek and dripped off her jaw.

Grace placed a hand on her mother's knee. "Oh Mum, I'm sorry I wasn't here to help you with all this."

Belinda put her mug down and wiped her face with the back of her hand. "You've got your own life now," she said, before the telephone interrupted.

"I'll get it." Grace got up, walked over to the phone and picked it up.

\*   \*   \*

Hemingford stood in front of the whiteboard and pointed. "Right, Charles Chamberlain ... what do we really know about him?"

The full squad were the audience in the CID Room.

DS Jim Ryan and DC Sam Kirkland gave a succinct resume of who the victim was, his business connections and family.

The DCI was obviously still infuriated. "What I still can't understand is how the hell did the wife know how he'd been found if she was never in that room."

"That was never in the papers," Ormerod agreed.

"Can only be one of the firemen on the scene." Strong suggested.

"She managed to speak to one of them then, is that what you're saying?" Hemingford pressed, the taut atmosphere palpable.

Strong held out his arms. "Or someone who knew one of them. You know how gossip gets around." A few nods and mumbles. "Anyway, this isn't getting us anywhere. What about some of the other leads we were exploring?"

The tension in the room subsided. "Okay, Colin," Hemingford said, "What about this *Talisman Club* thing then. What do we know about that?"

Strong gave a brief outline of the informal, private gatherings that took place at the house and those so far known to have been involved.

"Have all known 'members' been interviewed? Whereabouts for the evening in question?" Hemingford asked.

Strong looked to Stainmore. "We've spoken to a number of them but we have a few more to get through. No-one without an alibi so far."

Hemingford turned his attention to Darby. "John, didn't you say his mobile was being analysed?"

"Yes, sir. Most calls in and out on the days before the fire were to named recipients on his connection list, nearly all business. But there were two calls on the 16$^{th}$ that came from an unregistered mobile. We've not been able to trace that yet."

"Well keep on it." He looked to DS Ryan. "And Jim, what news from the investigation into his computer?"

"Again, nothing to arouse suspicion," Ryan replied. "All emails seem to be business related and nothing out of the ordinary."

"And nobody saw anything on your door-to-door enquiries, Sam?"

Kirkland shook his head. "Afraid not."

Hemingford began to pace in front of the board. "Right, well get back out there and visit the neighbours again. Someone must have seen something out of the ordinary on that evening. Somebody must have visited the property. Christ, people walk dogs, kids play out. We need to get that breakthrough here." He pointed at various officer in turn. "Look again at his business records, computer, phone. That woman of his, Anita is it? She must have something else to tell us. Let's go to it."

\* \* \*

"Come here," Susan said and wrapped her arms around Belinda in a bear hug. Sammy joined in too. All three were engaged in a tearful reunion. Grace had opened the door to them at the St John's Square address and Belinda had walked up the hallway to meet them.

That afternoon, Susan had called Belinda at home. Strong had told Souter that they were releasing Belinda at lunch-time and gave him the contact number. Souter had come with the girls, and he and Grace were left like embarrassed spectators.

Belinda broke free. "Come on through," she said, wiping her face and leading the way to the lounge.

"We couldn't keep quiet and let you be in prison," Susan said, once they'd all sat down.

"I know. I didn't want to involve you. It was stupid of me to think you'd not come forward."

"Once the girls had made statements," Souter explained, "they checked the CCTV footage from the pub where you were on the Thursday evening and that corroborated your version of events."

"I've caused an awful lot of trouble, haven't I?"

"Have the police given you a hard time?"

"That Hemingford bloke, have you met him, Bob? He wants me to come in to Wood Street tomorrow for 'another chat' he says."

"I know Colin's not keen on him," Souter replied. "You will be taking a solicitor with you though?"

"She has to," Grace jumped in.

"But anyway," Sammy spoke, "Why did you say you were there?"

"Come on, you know we're going to gang up on you," Susan said with a smile.

"Grace, why don't you make our guests some tea," Belinda said.

"Mum!"

"Okay, okay." Belinda wiped her face again and composed herself. "You probably know why already. In a word, Anthony."

"You think he was involved, or worse still, set fire to the place?" Sammy asked.

"I don't know what to think. What I do know is that he lied to me ... is still lying." She related the facts as she knew them and her fears about her son.

Grace added her concerns that her brother seemed secretive. "I suppose they all go through that phase," she offered in conclusion.

"Would you like Susan and me to have a chat with him?" Sammy wondered.

"He might talk to us, not being family," Susan added.

Grace and her mother looked at one another. "Might be worth a go," she said. "We've got nothing to lose."

# 45
## Wednesday 29<sup>th</sup> August 2001

St John's Square was quiet at just after ten o'clock at night. The street lights cast a warm glow over the pavement and front gardens and a gentle breeze rustled the leaves of the trees on the church side of the street. Souter had swapped places with Susan, who was now in the driver's seat of his Escort. Sammy was in the rear, alongside him. The radio on low. Waiting. Belinda had rung him earlier to tell him that Anthony was due to return at ten. This was their best opportunity.

Just after a quarter past, a tall, lanky figure appeared around the corner, hands thrust deep into his trouser pockets.

"That's him," Souter said. "Are we all ready?"

"Let's do it," Sammy responded.

Souter waited until the boy was about to turn into his path. He got out of the car, walked round to the passenger door and held it open. "Anthony Chamberlain?" he asked. "We'd like a word."

The boy looked at Souter, then to the car and made a face. "Oh come on, I've told you all I know."

"It'll only take a minute. Just clear a few things up."

Anthony shrugged, stepped forward and got into the front passenger seat. Souter closed the door and stood outside.

"What? What the fuck is ..." Anthony looked alarmed at Susan in the front then at Sammy behind. "You're not police. I'm out of here!" He pulled the door handle but Souter pushed it closed again.

"You can either talk to us or to the police," Susan said, "The choice is yours."

"I know who I'd rather talk to," Sammy added.

"Look, Anthony," Susan's tone softened, "Your mother helped me a great deal last year. I'd like to think of her as a friend. I know what she did, she did for you. I think you owe it to her to be honest."

Anthony shook his head and Susan could see he was fighting with his emotions.

"Anything you say to us in here ... tonight ... will stay in here," Susan continued.

"We promise," Sammy said. "We won't even tell him outside, if that's what you want."

For nearly fifteen minutes the girls tried every means to persuade Anthony to open up, but he stuck to his story that he was with his friend, Simon. Finally, Susan got out of the car, shrugged and shook her head at Souter.

Disappointed, he opened the passenger door and let the boy out.

As Souter drove the girls back to their flat, they discussed how the conversation had gone. "Alright, we'll have to approach this from a different angle," he finally said. "I'll try and arrange something similar. I still think you two are the best means we have of getting at the truth, though."

# 46
## Thursday 30<sup>th</sup> August 2001

Belinda had given Simon's address and a description of him to Susan. She'd also rung his parents with a story of wondering whether Anthony had left his trainers at their house recently. Apparently, Simon was out, taking some books and CD's back to the library on Balne Lane for his mother and himself. He'd set off about half an hour before and usually spent a fair bit of time browsing when he was there.

Susan was at Alison's house along with Sammy and Souter when Belinda had rung to tell her this. Quickly organising themselves, the three of them left Alison to continue preparing for her upcoming trip to the States on Sunday.

The ugly concrete structure of Wakefield's Balne Lane Library could have been a legitimate target of Prince Charles' views on architecture. It performed its function well, however.

They spotted Simon studying the rack of CD's on the second floor.

In a well-managed manoeuvre, Sammy and Susan approached him from different sides.

"Hi Simon, how are you?" Sammy asked.

He turned and looked surprised.

"It is Simon, isn't it?" Susan asked from the other side.

"Who are you, what do you want?"

"You're friends with Anthony Chamberlain, aren't you?" Sammy continued.

His eyes narrowed. "What of it?"

The girls began a practiced routine. Sammy: "Best friends, some would say."

Susan: "Do anything for him."

Sammy: "Keep secrets."

Susan: "Even lie."

Simon put his hands up, palms out. "What is this? Leave me alone."

Sammy: "We will when you tell us the truth."

Susan: "You see, Simon, Anthony's mother was extremely kind to me recently. And when I heard she'd lied to the police - made a false confession - I was puzzled at first. But then I got to wondering why would she do that? And the only explanation that made any sense was that she was covering for someone ... someone she really loved. And that someone could only be Anthony."

Sammy: "Except Anthony maintained he was with you on the evening of the fire that killed his father."

Susan: "But he wasn't, was he? Your Mum told Mrs Chamberlain she'd not seen too much of him recently. You were at home but Anthony wasn't with you."

Sammy: "Do you know what the penalty for perjury is?"

Simon's head looked as if he was following a match on Wimbledon's centre court, turning from one to the other. Finally, he raised both hands to his face, closed his eyes and shook his head. "Okay, okay," he protested. "Not here."

Souter had been loitering by an adjacent section, browsing some videos. He looked up as they made to move away and caught the slight shake of the head from Susan as the three of them walked away.

"We can get a coffee or something downstairs," Sammy suggested.

A few minutes later, Simon was sitting at a Formica-topped table opposite Susan and Sammy, a Coke in front of him and coffees alongside the girls.

"So what's the big problem?" Susan asked.

Again Simon appeared to be agonising over what to say. "Look, whatever I tell you, promise me you won't tell Anthony's Mum, or anybody else for that matter."

"That's a pretty big ask when we don't know what it is," Sammy said.

"The fire had nothing to do with Anthony. I know he was pretty pissed off with his Dad and what he'd been up to but trust me, he wasn't anywhere near."

"But you weren't with him, so how would you know?

Simon looked down and studied his hands. After a moment he spoke quietly, "I was covering for him. But I knew where he was."

"I hear what you say but to convince us, you're going to have to tell us a good bit more. You need to tell us where and what he was up to."

He looked up at Susan. "I told you, I only covered for him."

Sammy looked to Susan. "Unless it's totally illegal, I'm fairly sure that what you tell us will remain between us here."

Susan nodded agreement. "Of course."

"But it just doesn't involve Anthony. I mean someone else could lose their job if it ever came out."

Susan was becoming exasperated. "Look Simon, you're going to have to trust us."

A deep breath was the noisy precursor to Simon's next statement. "Okay," he began, "Anthony's been having … having it away with one of our teachers."

Sammy and Susan looked at one another in shock before smiles began to form.

"I know what you think, and I do too," Simon went on, "Lucky bastard. Miss Weaver's a cracker."

"Miss Weaver?"

"She only came to the school this year. She teaches history."

Susan let out a deep breath. "How old is this Miss Weaver?"

"Anthony says she's twenty-one."

"And you're sure he was with her that night?"

"She's got a flat in Smirthwaite Street, not far from the school. He goes there regularly."

"We are going to need her to confirm that."

Simon rubbed his hand over his head in an angry gesture. "You can't. If this gets out, they'd know it was me who told you. Anthony would kill me." He stopped, realising what he'd said. "I didn't mean that, not literally. But she'd lose her job."

Susan leaned in closer to the boy. "Simon, if this is true, it'll go no further. Stick to your story that you were with Anthony and ... well, just hope that nobody else suspects anything."

He writhed in discomfort. "I shouldn't have said anything." He stood up. "I've got to go."

They watched him strut out of the cafeteria area before Souter joined them.

# 47
## Friday 31st August 2001

"Anthony?"

"Not you again. Look, leave me alone." Anthony turned to walk away.

Souter had wandered into the Waterstones store in The Ridings. He caught sight of him at the rear where the lad was sorting some books on the Transport and History shelves.

Souter took a step closer to him and in a quiet voice said, "I know about Miss Weaver,"

Immediately, Anthony stopped what he was doing and slowly turned to face him. "What?"

"I said I know about …"

"How? Who told you?"

"Doesn't matter. Was that where you were the evening of the fire?"

Anthony's head dropped. "Shit!"

"You could say that. But I'll make a deal with you. Let me talk to her, confirm what you say and, as far as I'm concerned, I'll say no more about it, certainly not to your Mum. If she asks, all I'll say is that you were with a girl."

The conversation paused as they danced around an elderly gent who passed them by in the narrow aisle. "But then I've got to say who. And that's another lie to unravel." Anthony looked distraught.

"Just say it was someone you met when you were out with Simon one night. Not from round here. Whatever, it's over, you're not seeing her any more. Simon was doing what a mate does, covering for you."

Anthony looked up at Souter. "She's going to another school in the new term."

"Miss Weaver?"

Anthony nodded.

"That could be handy," Souter said. "How do you feel about her?"

"It's getting too awkward."

Souter had a faint smile playing on his lips. "But the sex was great though, right?"

Finally Anthony lost the sullen look. "Fantastic." He smiled.

They held one another's gaze for a second. "So how does my idea sound?" Souter asked.

"It'll be over anyway when she finds out that you know about us. But I've got no real choice have I? I didn't want to lie to Mum, but I couldn't tell her the truth. And when she went and made her statement, I wondered if it was true - that she'd got so angry with Dad that ... Anyway, I'm glad it had nothing to do with her. Things just got out of hand and I couldn't say anything."

Souter studied the boy. "Have I your word that you were with your teacher that night?"

"Of course."

"Okay, I'll leave it for you to sort things out with Miss Weaver in your own time and in your own way. I won't make things any more difficult for you by going round to talk to her. All right?"

"Thanks."

The book Anthony had in his hand caught Souter's attention. "Look at this," he said, taking it from him and examining the cover photograph. "I remember these engines coming through Doncaster when I was growing up. My Dad was interested in trains and he used to take me to see them. You could feel the throb of the big diesel engines vibrating through the platforms. And I can still hear the distinctive sound they made. Deltics, yes, that's what they were. I remember they were on some of the top named expresses; Flying Scotsman, ten o'clock out of Kings Cross and ..." He paused as he remembered another named train. "The Talisman, that was four o'clock from London." He opened the front cover and was shocked. "How much?"

He gave the book back to Anthony. As he made to leave, he turned back. "Hey, don't be hard on Simon, he's a good mate. It's just my girls can be very persuasive when they want to be."

\*　\*　\*

"I thought you'd be wanting to spend as much time as possible with Alison before she jets off to exotic places instead of supping pints with me in a noisy pub." Strong wiped the froth from his top lip after slurping from his pint.

Souter grinned. "Oh, I'll be seeing her later tonight, don't you worry about that."

They were sitting at a table in Henry Boons on Westgate just beyond the railway bridge having met up after work. It was a busy place and suited their mood.

"Besides, I'm not sure you can class New York as 'exotic'."

"Beats the arse off Wakefield though. When is it she actually goes?"

Souter put his glass back down on the mat. "Sunday. I'm taking her over to Manchester."

"You're going to miss her." Strong said it as a statement rather than a question.

"The truth is, I don't really want her to go." Souter glanced at his friend. "I mean, it's a long way … on a plane … and there have been some disasters in recent years. Lockerbie, Kegworth."

"Come on, Bob, it's the safest form of transport."

"No, it's just …" He looked down and adjusted his glass on the beer mat. "I'll worry." He looked up and faced Strong. "She's the best thing that's happened to me."

"I know." Strong took a sip of his beer and attempted to lighten the mood. "Well I hope you'll behave yourself while she's away."

Souter spread his arms. "I'm a changed man, Col. And anyway, she'll have her spies on the case, Sammy and Susan."

"You're a lucky man, Bob."

"I know. Anyway, how's life with your new boss? Any progress on the Chamberlain fire?"

Strong had another sup. "It's stalling. We've had nothing new since we released Mrs Chamberlain."

"What about the son, Anthony?"

"No, I thought about that, but his alibi's water-tight apparently. His pal says they were together that night watching music videos."

Souter felt inwardly relieved. "So what about his BDSM club members? I mean, that would be taking masochism to a new level."

Strong smiled. "You wouldn't believe who's involved with that."

"Oh, I would, Col."

"But apparently their last 'meeting' was the week before." Strong squinted at his friend. "Anyway, how do you know? More importantly, who do you know is involved?"

"It's my job, just like it is yours. I probably don't know everyone but I do know it involves some senior council officials." Souter held up his glass. "Another?"

# 48
## Sunday 2nd September 2001

Souter watched Alison get dressed that Sunday morning and immediately wanted to drag her back into bed. God, how was he going to manage for six weeks without her? Well, four by the time he met up with her again in New York. He admired her shapely legs before she put on her fitted trousers then felt disappointed as the lovely rounded breasts disappeared within the confines of her bra. Was it just his imagination or did they seem a bit bigger these days?

She caught him looking. "Pervert," she said with a cheeky grin. The effect on him was noticeable. "And you can put that away," she said and laughed.

"Don't go," he said.

She stopped buttoning up her blouse. "Are you serious?"

He sat up. "Of course. I don't want you to go all the way over there - on your own."

"I can't not go. Not now. The office would be mad with me."

"Sod the office."

"But it's my job. My career." She sat back down on the bed and looked at him through sad eyes. "If you'd said this before, I would have pulled out of this trip."

He leaned forward, took her head in his hands and kissed her. "I know. Ignore me, I'm being selfish."

"No you're not. You're worried, I understand that. But it'll be fine, trust me." She stood. "Anyway, you'll be with me in no time." She smiled at him and continued to button her blouse.

Again he had an uneasy feeling that her smile didn't quite reach everywhere it should.

"Come on," she said, "I don't want to miss the flight."

On the drive over to Manchester Airport, all sorts of random thoughts had gone through his head. "I wonder when it was that they stopped calling it Ringway?" he contemplated.

"Ringway?"

"Yes, I remember as a kid that's what they called Manchester Airport."

"What made you think of that?"

"Dunno. Just something that sprang to mind."

"Well never mind all that rubbish," she retorted. "You just be careful while I'm away. And don't get into any trouble."

"As if."

"I've told Susan and Sammy to keep an eye on you. I know what you're like." She giggled and at that point he immediately wanted to stop the car, right there, on the M62 and rip her clothes off.

He watched her progress through the security screens, and felt a pang of jealousy as some overweight woman in a uniform ran her hands over Alison's body. Clear of all the formalities, she put her jacket back on and picked up the rucksack she'd decided to use as hand luggage.

What a lovely arse, he thought, as she bent down to adjust a shoe.

She turned towards him one last time and blew him a kiss. 'I love you,' she mouthed then disappeared from view.

Suddenly, a huge lonely feeling descended. And then a sense of foreboding. What if that was the last he would ever see her? His thoughts darted back four years to the last time he'd seen his son, Adam. That was just before his ex-wife took him off to Canada. He'd lost him too when he'd drowned, two years ago now. Just seven years old. A lump came to his throat and his eyes were full. Guilt was the next wave of emotion that swept over him. Guilt that it had been some time since he'd thought of

Adam. But that was down to Alison; and that was a good thing, surely.

He pulled his handkerchief from his pocket and wiped his face. Before he could replace it, the strains of *Scotland The Brave*, the ring tone on his mobile, snapped him out of the dark places he'd just visited.

*"She get off all right?"* Sammy's voice enquired.

"Just gone through security," he struggled to say.

*"Are you okay?"*

"What? Oh yeah. Just had a sneezing fit, that's all," he lied.

*"Well, don't forget you're coming to us for tea tonight."*

"How could I?" he said with a chuckle.

*"Susan and me are going to cook you up a storm!"*

"Great. I'll see you both later." He ended the call and instantly felt better.

# 49
## Monday 3<sup>rd</sup> September 2001

The Redoubt seemed quiet when Souter pulled into the car park at the side. There were only two other cars. Joe Webster had called him that afternoon to say he had some information for him. They'd settled on the pub as being sufficiently 'off the plot' where no one from the council offices was likely to frequent.

Webster was sitting on a bench seat in one of the back rooms, pint of lager on the table in front of him. Souter entered and signed a drinking motion to his old school friend but Webster indicated he was fine with what he had. A couple of minutes later, after a bit of banter with the landlord, he was sitting on a stool opposite him.

"Are you okay?" Souter asked.

"I'm just nervous about all this, Bob."

Souter took a sip of his Tetley's. "Why? Have you spoken to anyone else about your suspicions?"

Webster shook his head and lifted his pint. "No." A drink of his lager and he replaced it onto the beer mat. "It's just ... these are powerful blokes."

"Faulkner might be a big fish in the little pond of Wakefield local politics," Souter opined, "but I wouldn't describe him as a 'powerful' man."

"Nor me. Or Sam Appleyard for that matter."

"That's your boss, right?"

Webster nodded. "Not even Pitchforth, the Head of Planning. No, it's who they've managed to get themselves into bed with that concerns me."

The door to the pub opened and the chatter from three men swept in. Webster glanced across nervously.

"Eh up, lads," the landlord could be heard saying, "Usual?"

Souter looked over to the room doorway towards the bar then back to lean in closer to his friend. "What have you heard?" he asked.

Raucous laughter erupted from the bar, interrupting their concentration.

Webster smiled briefly then grew serious. "I suspect you've probably heard the same." He leaned forward on the table and lowered his voice. "Have you ever heard of Thistle Developments?" Souter nodded. "Then you can probably tell me more about their owner Kenneth Brogan than me you."

"You've heard his name mentioned then?"

"Not him specifically but Thistle. I overheard Sam talking to Pitchforth about them getting involved. They didn't seem too pleased about it and it wasn't supposed to be common knowledge – not until they were announced as 'preferred developer'." Webster looked to the doorway again but the group were laughing and joking with the landlord at the bar. He resumed his story. "So I did a bit of digging on the internet and discovered Thistle is run by Brogan. All their work's been north of the border up till now."

Souter nodded. "I know. But did you also know that Brogan's brother-in-law is none other than Stuart Hamilton, that Scottish MEP that was at the announcement?"

"Christ. No wonder there's a lot of hushed conversations going on." Webster took a large swig of his pint. "I spoke to an old uni mate who works for Glasgow City Council and he told me to be careful. Thistle have an unsavoury reputation, he told me."

Souter leaned back and stretched. Sitting on the stool wasn't the most comfortable arrangement. "I'd heard that," he said. "Anyway, what have you got to substantiate your suspicions that they doctored the site conditions report?"

Webster drained his drink and partly unzipped his jacket before bringing out a large brown envelope.

"I'll get you another," Souter said, rising to his feet.

"Just a half, Bob. I'm driving."

When Souter returned with replenished glasses a few minutes later, Webster pulled out some paperwork from the envelope. He nervously looked to the doorway then unfolded an A3 size drawing and spread it on the seat beside him, the table and his body blocking anyone who might enter from seeing. Souter repositioned his stool to the side of the table not only to reinforce that barrier but so that he could see more clearly.

"This is a map of the old colliery land with all the old buildings shown where they were when the pit was working," Webster said in hushed tones. "This chain link line is the extent of the site. Now you see this area I've shaded …" He circled a section of about ten percent of the total area bounded by a dotted outline. "… This was the extent of the contamination my findings indicated."

"Right," Souter said, "I follow that."

Webster folded the drawing away and opened out another. This also depicted the site. "Now this version is the one that ended up in the official report." He looked across at Souter who was studying the new plan. "On this one, you can see that the contaminated area is about seventy-five per cent of the total area."

Souter's eyes widened. "Bloody Hell," he said quietly.

"Exactly."

He looked at the engineer. "But are you sure your initial findings are correct? You didn't make a mistake? Or someone else discovered a greater area? I'm not doubting you, Joe, I'm just looking for any other explanation."

"No doubts at all. I saw the original draft some months ago."

"And you've got your site results safe somewhere?"

"On a memory stick at home." He took a sip of his drink. "It's in my bedside drawer if anything happens to me."

Souter looked at Webster's serious face before it broke into a grin. "Only joking," he said. "But that's where it is."

Two elderly men had come into the pub and were heading into the back room with their drinks.

Webster folded up the second plan and placed it back in the envelope.

"All right, lads," one of the two newcomers greeted.

Souter turned to face them. "Better now we're in here," he returned with a smile.

The two sat down near the doorway and began to chat away.

Back to look at his friend, Souter resumed the conversation. "Have you got anything I can take with me?"

Webster pulled out a memory stick from his pocket and discreetly handed it to Souter. "I managed to make a copy of the final report for you yesterday lunch-time," he said in a quiet voice. He gave a quick glance to the two men who were engrossed in their own chatter. "Also on there are the figures as they should be."

Souter slipped the stick into his pocket. "Thanks for this, Joe." He leaned in close once again. "But listen, in your opinion, how much of a financial difference have these adjustments made to this project would you think?"

"Could be as much as four or five million."

"Christ! That is big money. So how much is the scheme worth overall?"

"They're bandying figures of around a hundred and ten million for the whole thing." Webster cast another concerned glance to the doorway and drained his drink. "Anyway, I'll have to go now, Bob. Kathy'll have my dinner ready and the kids'll want a bit of time with me." He stood, put the envelope back inside his jacket and zipped it part way up.

Souter got to his feet and held out a hand. "Thanks for this, Joe. I'll keep you informed if I hear anything else."

"Just be careful, Bob. See you."

He sat back down and watched his friend disappear through the doorway, tapping his pocket to feel the outline of the stick he'd just been given. He didn't let on that he'd already had a version of the final report, courtesy of

Sammy and Susan's escapades, just in case the one Joe had given him differed again. Check it out tonight at home and print off the reports in the office tomorrow, he thought. In the meantime, he felt peckish. He'd walked down to the pub and would pick up a takeaway on the way back to his flat. He drained his pint and called in to the toilets on his way out.

Emerging through the door to the car park, it was still a warm sunny evening. A strange noise made him stop and turn. A 'hiss', almost like a tyre deflating, came from behind a car then stopped. Now a groan. He walked to the back of the first vehicle and looked down.

Joe Webster was lying half propped up against another car. For a split second, Souter struggled to take in the scene. His jacket was open, blood oozing through his shirt from his stomach. Both hands were held against himself in a vain attempt to contain it.

"Joe!" Souter exclaimed. "What the hell's happened?" He dashed to his friend, pulling out his mobile phone as he did so. "Ambulance," he said as the emergency operator came on the line. He relayed the situation and his location to ambulance control. "Looks like a stabbing," he concluded.

Webster made the hissing sound again, his face screwed up in pain.

Panicking, Souter stood up and dashed back inside the pub. "Quick, I need help!" he shouted, grabbing some beer towels from the bar. "Someone's been stabbed out the back. Ambulance is on its way."

The landlord followed him back outside. "Keep an eye on the bar," he instructed the young lad who'd been serving alongside him.

Souter knelt by Webster and held some towels to the man's stomach. "What happened Joe?"

"Some bloke ... didn't see ... just the pain."

"Ambulance is coming."

The landlord had his mobile to his ear. "Best call police an' all," he said.

"Tell Kathy ...I love her," Webster struggled.

Souter put a hand behind his friend's neck. "Tell her yourself," he replied.

From the direction of the city, sirens could just be heard.

"And Megan ...and Tom too."

He assumed they were his children but he'd never mentioned their names before. "Hold on, Joe, I can hear the ambulance coming."

"I'm ...scared Bob."

"Stay with me, Joe."

He was mumbling now in an incoherent attempt to talk.

"Save your strength." Souter watched as Webster's eyes grew dull. "Hang on in there. Joe! Joe!" It looked as though a mist had covered his eyes and they were still; unseeing. "Joe, come on."

"Okay, sir, we'll take over now," a deep unfamiliar voice interrupted.

Souter felt himself being lifted under the armpits on to his feet and gently led away. Flashes of reflective jackets and blue lights meant help had arrived. Too late.

Souter was staring onto the table in the front snug of The Redoubt, cupping a small brandy in his hands when Colin Strong walked in. He didn't look up.

"Bob," Strong said, gently. He stood for a second but there was no reaction so he sat down beside him.

Behind the bar, the landlord held up a pint pot to Strong but he shook his head.

"He's gone, isn't he?" Souter eventually said, still focusing on the table. "How are his wife and kids going to cope?"

"Don't worry about that. We'll be speaking to them." Strong stared at the door before turning to his friend. "What happened, Bob?"

Slowly, Souter turned his head. "You know who it was, don't you? Joe Webster. He was in our class at school."

"I know." Strong leaned back on the bench seat, folded his arms and looked to the ceiling. "Have you just met up with him again?"

"Bumped into each other at the council offices the other week. He's an engineer there."

"And did you 'just bump into him' tonight or was your meet arranged?"

"You got a ciggie, Will?" Souter called out to the young lad behind the bar.

"Don't smoke," the lad replied. "D'you want one?"

There was an expression on Souter's face that emphasized the illogicality of Will's question.

"I'll get you one," he said.

"He called me this afternoon," Souter eventually answered. "He had some information he wanted to give me." He paused. "Well, that's not strictly true. I'd asked if he could find something out for me … and he had."

Before Strong could follow up, Will was back at the bar. "Here," he said, holding out a packet of cigarettes and a cheap disposable lighter. "Old Frank says there's a couple in there and the lighter's nearly empty. You're welcome to them."

Souter stood and collected them from the barman. "Tell him I appreciate that."

"Thought you'd given up?" Strong said once he'd sat back down.

"I had." He gave a weak smile. "Just like that line in *Airplane*, 'Looks like I chose the wrong day to quit smokin'," he added in a mock American accent. He lit up, took a deep draw and exhaled a large plume of smoke.

Involuntarily, Strong placed a hand on the breast pocket of his jacket where the still-unopened pack of cigars was tucked. Then he took his hand away. "So what information did he get for you?"

"Oh, it was nothing, just some council details, that's all."

Strong looked directly at his friend. "You're lying to me, Bob. Now Joe's been murdered, that's for certain. I'm not sure what the motive is, if any at the moment. But for me to do my job properly, I need to know every detail leading up to this tragic event."

Souter avoided eye contact and took another long drag of his cigarette, blowing the smoke to the other side, clear of Strong.

"So what did he get for you?" Strong repeated.

Eventually, Souter looked at his friend. "It was to do with the Lofthouse Development. Joe had done a lot of the work on the initial site survey. His interpretation varied considerably from the final report that was presented to the EU for funding."

"Would that be sensitive enough to warrant someone shutting him up?"

"I don't know."

"Where is this information now?"

"He had it in a brown A4 envelope that he held inside his jacket when he left."

Strong thought for a second. "I don't remember seeing any brown envelope with him."

"No," Souter replied, "neither did I."

# 50
## Tuesday 4th September 2001

Strong had been allocated SIO, the Senior Investigating Officer, for the investigation into the murder of Joe Webster. Detective Chief Superintendent Flynn had deemed that Hemingford had enough on his plate with the stalled investigation into the fire that killed Chamberlain. All officers would still be involved with the fire investigation but a small number were allocated to work with Strong on the stabbing.

After Strong concluded his first briefing on the case, he took Stainmore with him to collect Kathy Webster, Joe's widow, to formally identify his body. It was another difficult episode, made more painful for Strong by the fact that he and Joe had been classmates at secondary school. He'd said that he would need to ask some questions and take a formal statement from Kathy at some point but understood if she would want some time beforehand. She insisted that that happened as soon as possible and wanted to go with them to Wood Street to give that information.

He found it difficult dealing with Kathy Webster. She wanted to know what progress he was making in his enquiries. Truth to tell, he had very little to go on. There was no CCTV at The Redoubt pub, the landlord had seen nobody strange in the place at the time and, so far, no witnesses had come forward who had seen anything useful. The post mortem carried out earlier that morning confirmed a single knife wound to the abdomen which had punctured the aortic artery and he'd bled out very quickly.

"I understand you were in the same class at school?" she had asked him.

"That's right, but I'd not seen Joe since we left."

"But he was with someone who had been at school with him, wasn't he?"

Strong told her about Bob Souter and how it was Bob who had found Joe and tried to help, but the injury had been too severe.

He told her he was expecting Souter to come in at some point that morning to make a formal statement and give Strong the opportunity to probe his friend for any piece of information that might help find out who was responsible and why.

With a promise to keep her fully informed as soon as he found anything out at all, he offered for Stainmore to drive her home. She declined, saying she'd some business in town and would make her own way back.

As he was escorting her through the main entrance, he spotted Souter sitting on a hard plastic chair.

Souter stood as his friend appeared. He recognised Joe's wife from a photo he'd been shown on that first meet in the Talbot & Falcon pub.

"Mrs Webster … Kathy," he said. "I'm so sorry."

Strong spotted her unease. "Mrs Webster, this is Bob, Bob Souter. He was with your husband when …"

She looked straight at the journalist, her eyes filling with tears. "Did he suffer?"

"I don't think so. He … he told me to tell you … that he loved you," Souter struggled to say.

Strong could see the pain on his friend's face, and that he was near to tears. "Look, why don't you both come back inside for a few minutes?" he suggested.

Kathy shook her head. "I've got to be somewhere now, but …could we meet later?" she asked Souter.

Souter wiped his face with his hand. "Sure," he said and pulled out a business card. "You can get me on either number."

She gave a weak smile. "Thank you," she said quietly. With an appreciative nod to Strong, she walked through the main doors and disappeared down the ramp into Wood Street.

"How was it this morning?" Souter asked Strong once they'd settled into the uncomfortable chairs in Interview Room 1.

"Difficult. I know I've accompanied relatives to identify bodies before and it's never easy but ... remembering Joe from years back, well ..."

"And nothing to go on?"

Strong straightened in his seat. "That's what I'm hoping to find out, Bob. So, come on, what do you know?"

Souter shrugged. "There's not much more I can add to what I told you last night. Joe and I bumped into each other - in the toilets, oddly enough, a few weeks back when I was at some press conference in the Town Hall." Souter then proceeded to tell his friend what Webster had suggested regarding adjusted findings in connection with the site survey for the proposed Lofthouse Redevelopment Scheme.

Strong's ears pricked up at one point. "Who did you say his boss was?"

"Appleyard. Sam Appleyard."

"That's interesting," Strong pondered.

"You know him?"

"Only that his name came up with something else."

"Like what?"

"Another investigation."

"Come on, Col. I might be better placed to help you if I know a bit more. Which investigation?"

Strong sighed and considered whether to answer or not. "Well, I suppose it was you who told me what it meant." He snapped forward in his seat as if to emphasise the point. "But you can't print anything on this."

"Now you have got my full attention."

"He's one of the members of this *Talisman Club* that Chamberlain ran."

Souter's eyes opened wide. "Shit, so he could have been involved in Chamberlain's death too?"

"Look, I didn't say that, only that his name's come up in connection with that investigation." Strong was keen to refocus the interview. "Anyway, you say he showed you these drawings and figures that seemed to show some alterations to the survey?"

"Yes. He had two drawings of the site in the envelope along with his figures."

"But did he give you a copy?"

Souter hesitated. "No. He just showed them to me."

"I hope you're not holding back on me, Bob? Because this is serious. A man was murdered."

"And don't I know it. Christ, he died in my arms, Col. Have you any idea how that feels? Not just another human being but someone I knew. Someone I'd only been speaking to a few minutes before."

Silence hung like a shroud for a second or two as Strong held Souter's gaze. Finally he shook his head. "I've attended plenty of deaths, but I can't say I've ever experienced life extinguishing."

Strong shook his head then stood up. "I'll get us some drinks. I think we need a break."

Ten minutes later, proper mugs of tea on the table, rather than the vending machine variety, they resumed the interview.

"You don't seriously think Joe's death can have anything to do with this commercial scheme, do you, Col?"

"I just don't know, Bob. We've got very little to go on at the moment. No witnesses, no weapon, nothing significant."

"It's more likely to be some yob off his face on drugs or something. Somebody tried to mug him. Joe grabs the envelope because he doesn't want to give it up. They think there's something more important in it, grab it and rush off."

"So why haven't we found it then? If that was the case, they'd have thrown it away when they realised it was just some drawings and figures. Nothing they could sell."

And so the conversation went round and round, Souter keeping quiet about the memory stick until he'd had a chance to review it and Strong suspicious that he wasn't being told everything. Finally, they had a formal statement from Souter which he signed.

# 51
## Wednesday 5th September 2001

Alison had called the previous night from New York. Souter couldn't be more pleased to hear her voice. He decided not to tell her about what happened at The Redoubt but he knew she could tell something had occurred. 'Just a bit of a row at work.' He didn't want to go into details. 'Nothing to worry about,' he'd concluded. Her excitement at being in the States quickly overwhelmed her curiosity as to what Bob was concealing. God, he wished she was here so he could share his pain. But he was happy for her to be experiencing new adventures. And after all, he would soon be there with her. Only three and a half weeks to go.

She was full of all the exciting new places she'd been taken to. The hotel was in downtown Manhattan, basic but comfortable. Colleagues in the office had organised tickets for a Broadway show next week and she thought she'd spotted an actor from one of the TV shows she'd seen back home.

He'd arrived at his desk early and reviewed the files on Joe Webster's memory stick. The two versions of the site plan were there as were two versions of the table of results. Coordinate points in one column and values of various contaminants in others. He was at the printer collecting hard copies when Susan approached.

"How are you, Bob?" she asked.

"Still a bit raw, if you must know." He had his back to her as he shuffled the papers into a neat pile then placed a large paperclip around them.

She placed a hand on his shoulder. "Do we need to talk?"

He straightened up, put a hand in his pocket and drew out a handkerchief to wipe his face. Gently, she turned him towards her and hugged him. "We do," she said, answering her own question.

They found a vacant meeting room and sat down.

"This has to be about Lofthouse, doesn't it?" Susan asked.

"No other explanation I can think of." He spread the drawings on the table in front of them. "This is what he showed me on Monday." He proceeded to explain what Joe had told him and how the value of the works had probably been increased by four or five million pounds.

"Christ, that's worth killing for," Susan concluded. "So who do you think are the chief beneficiaries?"

"Joe reckoned Faulkner and his boss, Sam Appleyard on the council, at least. But there may be one or two others with a vested interest in lining their pockets. And finally, Brogan. He must be in line for the biggest share. Janey reported on their 'preferred developer' status last week."

Susan looked thoughtful. "Don't forget all the political hangers-on too, Brogan's brother-in-law, Hamilton. Possibly Marsden, the local MEP."

"If I remember correctly from Janey's report last week, I still think the council are dangling the carrot to Thistle. I don't think there are any contracts in place."

"Extra pressure for none of this to come out then, Bob. So what's our next move? Spill all this to Colin?"

"*Our* next move? No, you need to keep well away from this, Susan."

She studied him hard. "Could it be the same guy who attacked you? The man in the leather jacket, Kennedy?"

"I just don't know. I didn't see anybody and from what Colin said when I saw him yesterday, they haven't been able to trace any witnesses either."

"And let me guess, you haven't mentioned the Brogan / Kennedy thing to Colin?" His face told her the answer. "Christ what are you like? What would Alison say if she knew? She'd tell you to give all you know to Colin."

A knock on the door interrupted them and Janey poked her head around. "Strategy meeting you two?"

"What? Oh very funny."

"Pardon me for having a sense of humour. Anyway, there's a call for you," Janey said, indicating Souter. "A Kathy Webster, says it's important."

# 52
## Thursday 6<sup>th</sup> September 2001

The Websters lived in a recently built stone detached property in Ackworth, just off the main Doncaster Road. The front room curtains were partly drawn despite the warm sunshine; a respectful gesture, Souter thought. Kathy answered his ring on the bell herself. "Come in," she greeted.

He stepped inside and apologised that he was a few minutes earlier than the time she suggested when she called him yesterday.

Kathy Webster looked to be around forty with shoulder length dark hair, tied back and was dressed in a blue floral pattern blouse with dark blue trousers.

An older woman with a strong resemblance to Kathy appeared at the lounge door.

"This is my mum," she said. "She's come to stay with me for a while."

Souter acknowledged her.

"This is Bob Souter. He was at school with Joe. He was with him when …" She wiped her face with a tissue as she struggled to hold her composure. "I'm sorry."

"No, listen, don't apologise," he said.

"It's too soon, love." Her mother put an arm around her shoulder.

"It's okay, Mum. I'll be fine. I need to speak with Bob, if you can give us some time."

"If you're sure?" The woman studied her daughter for a few seconds before retiring to the lounge and closing the door.

Kathy led the way to the rear facing kitchen. "The kids are at my sister's. I thought it best," she offered by way of explanation.

"How are they coping?"

"Still in shock, especially Tom." With her back to him at the sink, she filled the kettle. "Tea, coffee?"

"Tea for me, thanks. He's twelve, isn't he?"

Kettle plugged in, she turned to face him. "Yes. Megan's ten." She waved at the breakfast chairs. "Please, sit down," she said then sat down herself opposite him. Head down, she nervously fiddled with a teaspoon. "The police have said they have no motive at the moment and it sounds as though they've precious little idea." Then she looked up at Souter. "So I wondered if you could shed any light on it for me."

He puffed out his cheeks. It was a question he knew she'd ask but he still wasn't sure how he would answer. "The only logical explanation would be if somebody attempted to mug him when he left the pub."

Her expression showed she didn't believe that. "I was hoping you'd be honest with me," she said.

He was puzzled. What did she mean? How much of Joe's work was she aware of?

The kettle boiled and she rose to make their drinks. "Did he tell you how we met?" She held up a milk carton.

"Er, yes and … yes," he responded.

She put his mug of tea down on the breakfast bar in front of him and stood leaning against the sink, cradling her own. "What exactly did he say about that?"

This was perplexing. "Well, that he worked for a small consultancy in Leeds and he met you there."

A slight smile played on her lips and he could see for the first time how attractive Kathy was. "Let me guess, you think I was a receptionist … or a typist in the same office."

Souter felt his cheeks redden. "Well …"

"Would it surprise you to know I'm actually a qualified civil engineer?"

"He never told me that."

She gazed off down the hallway. "Oh yes. It was a deliberate move on my part when we married that I'd put my career on hold for a bit. The kids and all."

Souter nodded and took a drink of his tea. "That was selfless," he said.

"But it looks as though I'll have to resume that now. I was thinking maybe in a year or two, when Megan had gone to secondary school. Joe and I had discussed … well, that's not important now." She resumed her seat and sipped her drink. "But what it does mean is that I'm well aware of Joe's misgivings over this big project he was working on."

It was becoming clear for Souter. He thought he might be protecting Kathy from an unthinkable truth, but she probably knew more than he did. "Lofthouse, yes. He showed me plans of the site and spoke about how his findings may have been altered."

"No maybe about it. And those drawings were in the envelope that's never been found?"

"Yes."

"Did he give you anything electronically?"

"A memory stick, yes."

She pulled a similar one from her trouser pocket and placed it on the surface. "Like this one?"

"Yes. He told me he'd left one in his bedside drawer if …"

"If anything should happen. Yes he told me that too." She lifted her mug and drank some tea. "So, Bob. Back to my original question, what do you think happened?"

Fifteen minutes later, Souter had told Kathy most of what he suspected about the old colliery development project and the roles of the main players. He held back on some details, like the incident in his car park and who he thought was responsible for his assault.

He could see her deep in thought as he concluded his accounts. "So you drew Joe into all this?" she said.

This pained him. "No. He came to me and said he was uneasy about what had been going on. He told me he was looking for another job because it made him so uncomfortable."

Kathy relaxed slightly. "I know. He had a couple of interviews lined up next month."

She stood up and took their empty mugs to the sink. When she faced him again, her eyes were moist. "So … at the end … what exactly did he say?"

When he'd relayed what occurred, she picked up the memory stick. "I'll be talking to DI Strong tomorrow," she said.

"I did tell him what Joe had shown me but I didn't say he'd given me the memory stick. I wanted to see what was on it first."

"I'll be telling him all about Joe's work concerns and explaining the contents of this. But just so's you know, I won't be saying anything about having spoken to you about this."

"Okay."

# 53
## Friday 7<sup>th</sup> September 2001

"Guv, a Mrs Betty Williamson downstairs to see you," Sam Kirkland announced.

Strong was at his desk poring over statements from the pub customers and landlord. "Betty Williamson," he repeated. "Who's Betty Williamson?"

"Something about the stabbing at The Redoubt."

"Come on then, let's hear what she's got to tell us."

Betty Williamson was a short stout woman who looked to be in her seventies. Her heavy patterned coat was unbuttoned. She wore sensible lace-up shoes, had a scarf around her neck and wore glasses. The white hair in a tight perm completed her image.

"Mrs Williamson," Strong said, "I believe you've got some information for us. Would you like to come through?"

Strong led the way to the Ground Floor interview room, the woman following and Sam Kirkland bringing up the rear.

With a refusal for any refreshments, Betty was keen to tell her story.

"I just thought it were a bit of an argument," she began. "It wasn't until I saw the paper this week that I realised what I must have seen."

Strong decided that although the woman was completely coherent, he might just have to tease out the relevant information. "Can we start at the beginning, Mrs Williamson."

"Betty, call me Betty, love," she said. "Well, I were on the bus into town, I live down bottom of Lupset, you see, and I were going to meet my friend, Mary. I were on top deck on the left hand side and as we slowed down to go round that bit of road around St Michael's Church, I saw these two blokes in The Redoubt car park. They looked like they were arguing. And then this one punches the other in the stomach. Leastwise that's what I thought. Until I saw the paper."

Strong looked to Kirkland and, for the first time in this investigation, he wondered if he was about to get a break. "Can you describe the two men, Betty?"

"The one who were punched ... well stabbed, I suppose, he looked about forty, smart haircut, average height and build. He'd got a brown jacket on. The other, he had his back to me, so I didn't see his face. He were shorter and thinner, maybe skinny, you might say. And he were in jeans and a black leather jacket."

Strong leaned forward onto the table. "And what time was this?"

"I were meeting Mary at the top of Westgate at seven, and I got on the bus at twenty-five to, so it'd have been around quarter to seven on Monday."

"And what exactly did you see." She looked irritated, so he held up a reassuring hand. "I know what you said just now but I want to be sure you tell me every last detail, because it's vitally important, Betty. Take your time."

He saw her sit up straighter in the chair, obviously feeling good about herself and no doubt flattered that she was contributing crucial information to a murder enquiry.

She continued, "As we got to the pub and the bus slowed, I glanced over and saw the man in the leather jacket rush up to the other one. He looked a bit surprised. I think he'd just come out the side door. Then the one in the leather jacket makes to grab something that the other one has tucked in his jacket."

"Did you see what it was?"

Betty gave the question some thought. "It might have been an envelope. I think it was something brown, like his jacket."

"Did the smaller man get hold of this envelope?"

"Not at first. So then he seemed to punch the other man. The last I saw, the man, you know the one who got stabbed, he fell back."

"And then?"

"Well that were all I saw. The bus had moved on past The Redoubt and was turning the corner. And where they were, they were in the car park at the other side."

"I know you said this man in the leather jacket was shorter than the man who was attacked, but did you get any impression of his age?"

The woman frowned. "Maybe the same as the other man. As I said, he had his back to me so I couldn't see his face."

"And did you notice anything about the attacker? Anything at all, I mean, you say he rushed at the victim, Was there anything in the way he moved? Did he have a limp, that sort of thing?"

Betty shook her head. "No, nothing like that. The only thing I thought at the time was that he was fast. I think he'd have taken that man by surprise. I don't know, maybe he'd been a boxer, lightweight, you know."

Strong stood. "Mrs Williamson … Betty, you've been a great help. Do you think you could just give a formal statement to my colleague here?"

She smiled. "Of course."

\* \* \*

Later that day, Kathy Webster called in to Wood Street to speak to Strong. She'd rung earlier to tell him she had something important to show him.

He listened intently to what she had to say and looked at the contents of the memory stick. With her professional knowledge, she took him through the drawings and figures contained in the files. When she finished, she gave him permission to copy the files onto another device so he could log it as evidence.

"Does this help?" she asked.

"Well, it's circumstantial but it may be crucial if we can connect other things here. I can tell you we have located a witness who has made a statement on what she saw from a passing bus at the time of the attack and we're pursuing that as a major line of enquiry at the moment."

With a promise to keep her informed of all developments, he escorted her back to the reception area.

As he climbed the stairs again, Luke Ormerod called from along the corridor. "Guv, you need to see this," he said, heading back to his desk.

Strong joined him and looked over his shoulder at his computer screen.

"Strathclyde just sent me this." Ormerod leaned back so his boss could get a clearer view. "Photos of William Kennedy, for the past two years thought to be working for Kenneth Brogan, principal owner of Thistle Developments."

Strong read out loud the text on the screen. Height, five feet eight; weight, eleven and a half stone. And if I'm not mistaken, it looks like he's wearing a black leather jacket."

# 54
## Monday 10<sup>th</sup> September 2001

The rain was drumming on the roof as Souter and Sammy sat in his Ford Escort in a pull-in almost opposite the gated entrance to the long-abandoned Lofthouse Colliery. The heavy clouds had helped to bring a premature darkness to the end of the day. It was cold and miserable outside but the engine was running in an attempt to maintain some heat. The lights were off and the wipers intermittently swept the screen so they could watch for any activity.

"Are you sure this is where they meant?" Souter asked. "It looks derelict and desolate over there."

"It's what the message said, and I don't think there's any other way in." Sammy pulled her coat tighter around her neck.

Souter checked his watch again. Five past eight and another double-deck bus whooshed past, rocking the car and sweeping a wave of water up and over the driver's side window. When the vision cleared, a large dark Mercedes saloon drew to a halt by the entrance gates. He gave Sammy a gentle nudge.

A large man in a long dark overcoat stepped from the driver's seat, rummaged in a pocket and approached the gate. He unlocked the padlock and pulled the chain free before pushing one of the gates open. Dashing back to his car, he drove through, leaving the entrance clear.

Sammy reached for the door handle but Souter placed a hand on her arm. "Hold on," he said. "That looked like Faulkner. There was someone else with him but I couldn't make them out." He looked across at her. "I think that's only half the delegates. We wait."

A few minutes later a large black 4x4 slowed and turned into the entrance. After a moment's stop, it drove on up the tarmac driveway and into the darkness.

"Okay," Souter said, "Now we go, but phones on silent."

They crossed the road and made their way through the gate and up the drive. They could make out the two cars they had seen enter at the end of the road, parked outside the old brick building he assumed was once the main offices. They kept to the right-hand side where a number of brick structures lined the route which would offer cover should other vehicles appear.

By the time they reached the old offices, a number of lights were shining inside. The windows had timber battens fixed across from the outside to deter vandalism. That was to their advantage as they could peer in without much chance of being spotted. Souter recognised Bernard Faulkner and Sam Appleyard, Joe Webster's old boss, sitting on some chairs around a large table. Neither looked happy.

If they were to learn anything, they needed to get inside so they could hear what was being said. Route one by the front doors the main players had used was too risky. Souter indicated the side of the building and led the way around the back. As he made his way round the perimeter, he kept looking up at the various windows they passed. All were in darkness and all seemed secure. Finally, he stopped at one that was gently flapping in the wind. It looked like the size of a toilet window. He glanced at Sammy and pointed to it. She nodded then stood with her back to the brick wall and held out her clasped hands at knee level.

"You're kidding," Souter whispered.

"Get yourself in and you can pull me up," she replied so quietly he struggled to hear.

He shrugged then carefully placed his left foot in her hands, gently pressed down then launched himself towards the cill. At the second attempt, he pulled himself over the edge and paused, half inside, half out. A torch from his coat pocket revealed a scene of devastation. It had obviously been the gents but the cubicle partitions were smashed from the walls and the pans and cisterns were in pieces. The only fortunate aspect was that boxing, presumably to conceal pipes, ran immediately below the window where the wash hand basins had once been fixed. That appeared to be intact. Carefully, he twisted himself inside and managed to turn himself around before lowering first one leg then the other onto the top of the timber boxing. Slowly, he let his weight settle onto it. It held. And now he was in the reverse position of where he had been a few moments ago, half inside, his stomach on the cill with his upper body outside and his arms stretched out. In this position, he pulled Sammy towards him and gradually in through the window.

Once safely inside, he allowed himself a smile and mouthed to her, 'I'm glad you're not fat.'

She punched him gently on the arm.

A stale stench from the open drains permeated the room. Torch off when they got to the back of the door, he listened. Silence, so he gingerly opened it. Outside, the corridor was in complete darkness in one direction but, towards the front of the building, a dim glow could be seen. Slowly, silently, they headed that way. They could hear a murmur of indistinct voices. At the corner, those voices became clearer.

\*　\*　\*

Susan was becoming increasingly worried. She'd had a bad feeling about the situation from the time she listened to the voicemail on Bernard Faulkner's mobile phone. It had been left by Kenneth Brogan confirming a meet at the old colliery, the site of the new development. '*Things need to be sorted*,' he had said. She was pacing the lounge of the flat, turning things over in her mind.

One night, over ten years ago now, she heard her mother's voice asking her to keep an eye on her Dad. The only thing was, her mother had died of cancer a few months before when she was fourteen. She began to suspect she was more receptive than most to phenomena she couldn't explain or understand. Two years later her Dad displayed the first signs of the dementia that was to eventually envelope him. Last year she encountered two young schoolgirls who spoke to her after she had fallen into the basement of a long-abandoned farmhouse. Their bodies were later discovered hidden in another section.

This feeling was the same, but different. Nobody was speaking to her, she just had an overpowering feeling of dread. Ever since Bob and Sammy decided they would go to the venue for the meeting. She told them it was a bad idea. But when they insisted it was the only course of action, she told them to be careful. Now they'd been gone for over an hour with no word, her anxiety and sense of foreboding was increasing.

She promised Bob she wouldn't but she felt she had to try and call him on his mobile. She dialled the number and heard the ringing tone. It rang for several seconds before the call was cut. Next she tried Sammy's. Same result. Now she was panicking.

\* \* \*

"I want out of this," an unfamiliar male voice could be heard.

"It's a bit late for that now, Sam," was the reply from the unmistakeable cultured Scottish accent of Kenneth Brogan.

Souter realised Sam must be Sam Appleyard.

"Just give me my fee and we can forget all about it," Appleyard went on.

"But you altered the survey. In fact, as it stands, you're the only one who's done anything wrong."

"Don't give me that. I had nothing to do with Chamberlain."

"Ah, Charlie, the deviant. But you were there, my friend."

"I had nothing to do with his death. It was your moron here who set the fire."

"Who are you calling a moron?" a rough Glaswegian voice joined in.

The sounds of a brief scuffle were heard before Brogan spoke. "Calm down, Wullie. This'll get us nowhere."

Souter and Sammy looked at each other. She pointed to him. 'That's who ...' she silently mouthed. Souter nodded and put his finger to his lips. A dim flashing light in his pocket drew his attention. Moving back around the corner, he pulled his mobile from his pocket, spotted Susan's name on the screen then cancelled the call. Back with Sammy, the conversation proceeded.

"And young Joe Webster? Why stab him?" Appleyard challenged. "He would have been happy with my job when I retire next month."

"You're right. I didn't condone that. But he was talking to that journalist Souter. And he's still sniffing around. We might have to take care of him too."

Sammy's phone began to flash and she repeated Souter's actions. Susan again.

"But back to me. The deal was I get my fee when the funding was secured. You have that now. Two hundred and fifty grand is a small price to pay for the potential millions you'll make," Appleyard said.

Sammy went to put her mobile back in her coat pocket but missed the opening. It clattered to the concrete floor.

"What was that?" Brogan sounded startled.

Souter looked to Sammy, alarmed.

"I'll check it," Kennedy answered.

Footsteps, then the sound of a door opening.

Fear swept over Souter and, gripping Sammy by her arm, he turned and shuffled them both back down the corridor. He pushed her into a side room just as Kennedy appeared at the corner.

Kennedy paused then glanced down at the mobile phone abandoned on the floor. Reaching inside his jacket, he pulled out a handgun. "I think we've got company," he shouted back to Brogan and the others.

*    *    *

Strong pushed the doorbell to the flat and waited. There was something wrong and he had to get to the bottom of it. She'd been late in that morning and had left early before he'd had a chance to talk to her.

A minute later, he heard footsteps on the stairs then the door opened.

"Guv?" Stainmore looked surprised. "What are you doing here?"

"I've come to see you, Kelly."

"Oh." She seemed embarrassed. "Personal or professional?"

"I know there's something on your mind. I need to find out what." He held his hands out. "More importantly, I need to help you."

"I'm fine, honestly, guv."

"Well drop the 'guv' and invite me in."

She considered for a moment then held the door wide.

Strong led the way upstairs to her two-bedroomed flat whilst she closed the door behind them. Along the hall and into the lounge, he took in an empty wine bottle on the floor below the coffee table and a full glass of white wine on top.

"Drink?" she offered from the doorway.

"No thanks, Kelly, I'm okay."

She sat on the settee and picked up her glass. "Sit down," she said. "Don't mind if I do though?"

Strong slowly sat in an armchair to the side. "I'm worried," he said.

"What about?"

"You."

"Why? I'm alright."

He looked at her with raised eyebrows. "I can see different. I know you've done some great work recently but I can tell you're not the Kelly who first became a DS."

She avoided his gaze and didn't reply.

"Look, we've known each other, what … five or six years?"

"Nearly."

"Can we be honest with one another?" She nodded and he continued, "You've seemed lethargic in recent months, you're also feeling cold and it's September. And …"

She looked up. "I know, I've put on weight, my hair looks like shit and my skin's crap."

"I am worried about you," he repeated.

"So was I but I think I've gotten to the bottom of it."

"Oh?"

"I've been meaning to tell you. I saw my GP last week. He's run some tests." She took a sip of her wine. "That's where I was this morning."

"And?"

"I've got an underactive thyroid."

"That's great … I mean, that you've found out what it is. And it's a simple treatment, right?"

"A pill a day for the rest of my life, yes."

"So when did you start taking the medication?"

"This morning. I haven't felt much difference yet but the doc says it kicks in fairly quickly. He also said it probably made me depressed too. He's right, I have felt down for a long time. And this doesn't help." She held up her wine glass.

Before he could say any more, Strong's mobile began to ring. He pulled it from his pocket and answered.

\* \* \*

Susan considered her options. That didn't take long, she could only think of two. The first was to drive down to the site herself. No, she didn't think that was really a choice, especially if her friends were in trouble, and she felt they were, she'd just be complicating things. That left only one thing to do. Picking up her mobile again, she dialled a number. It was answered on the fourth ring.

*"DI Strong."*

"Mr Strong … Colin, it's Susan here, Susan Brown."

*"Hello, Susan. Are you okay? What can I do for you?"*

"It's Bob … and Sammy …" She then proceeded to tell Strong where she thought they were and why. "I just have this feeling that something's going wrong."

Strong was silent for a moment. *"Is this like one of your premonitions?"* he finally asked.

"Sort of."

*"Where are you now?"*

"At my flat."

*"Okay, you stay there. I'll check out the old colliery site."*

The line went dead and Susan was left wondering what use she would be stuck in the flat.

\*   \*   \*

Strong ended the call, a serious expression on his face.

"What's up?" Stainmore asked.

"That was Susan."

"The young woman from the schoolgirls' case last year?"

"Yes. Apparently Bob, you know my journalist mate, and Sammy, the young girl who's friend was found dead last year …"

"I remember."

"They've gone off on a mission to witness some secret meeting between council officials and some dodgy developer at the old Lofthouse Colliery site."

"So why did she call you?"

"Because it involves a character by the name of Brogan who Bob mentioned to me a little while back and he's connected with some dangerous thug by the name of William Kennedy, the one we're looking to speak to in connection with the Webster stabbing. I think they might be walking into a dangerous situation." He stood up. "Look, I'm going to have to go."

She put her glass down on the coffee table and also got to her feet. "Well I'm coming with you."

He held up both hands. "No you can't. Besides, how many have you had?"

"This is my second and I've hardly touched it. I'm not arguing. I'm riding shotgun." A grin appeared on her face as she walked to the hall and picked up her jacket. "Come on then. What are we waiting for? Perhaps the medication *is* kicking in."

\* \* \*

Kennedy pulled a torch from his pocket and shone it down the corridor. It picked out nothing more than some metal ceiling grid and broken tiles that had dropped onto the floor from above. That and some stones and paper strewn around by kids no doubt when they explored the buildings before the site was secured.

A sick grin formed on his face as he slowly walked down the corridor. Several doors led off either side and every one he came to he kicked open with a large boot. Each time the torch beam swept around an empty room. Until he came to an office on the left hand side.

Souter and Sammy were behind the door, flat against the wall, breath held, when the door shuddered open. The beam of light shone around then left. Souter relaxed a fraction before the hand appeared again. He decided he would have to take direct action and slammed the door against Kennedy. The torch flew from his hand and Souter dashed around the door to grapple with his nemesis.

Ron Boyle's words came flooding back to him. *Wiry, deceptively strong and violent with it.* Although he was taller and heavier than Kennedy, the tables were quickly turned and the man who'd already tipped him into his own car boot had him face down on the floor with both hands behind his back. The fight left Souter when he realised the muzzle of a gun was pressing against his cheek.

Sammy stood motionless, pressed to the wall unable to move with fear. She'd seen the gun in Kennedy's other hand.

Kennedy looked up at her. "Fetch that fuckin' torch over here!" he barked. "Try anythin' and your friends brains will be spread all ower this flair."

Carefully and deliberately, Sammy followed his instructions and passed the torch to him, her eyes never leaving the gun.

Kennedy had hold of both of Souter's wrists when he pulled his weight off him. "On yer feet. An' make it slow," he commanded.

One halting movement at a time, Souter stood up.

Out in the corridor, Kennedy shuffled them both towards the corner then on into the meeting room where Brogan, Faulkner and Appleyard were waiting to see what had happened in the darkness.

"Look whae it is," Kennedy introduced.

Faulkner and Appleyard looked shocked.

"Well, well, Mr Souter. You really are beginning to irritate me," Brogan said. "And, if I'm not mistaken, one of your lovely friends. Miss Grainger, Samantha, how lovely to see you."

Sammy cringed, not only at his tone but the fact he knew her full name.

"What the hell's going on, Kenneth? Who are these two?" Faulkner asked, but his attention was focused on what was in Kennedy's hand.

"Sit doon," Kennedy said and shoved Souter and Sammy towards some chairs on the other side of the table.

Souter sat down and gently pulled Sammy into the adjacent seat.

"Bernard, I'm surprised you haven't yet made the acquaintance of the renowned Yorkshire Post ... what is it? ... Crime and Home Affairs Correspondent, Mr Robert Souter. The young lady ... well, I'm afraid I'm unable to give much information on her position. Apart from being in deep trouble here." Brogan smirked.

*　*　*

On the drive to Lofthouse, Strong gave instructions to Stainmore. She was on the phone to the control room first, then the CID office. Luke Ormerod answered.

"Ask him to check out Kenneth Brogan and William Kennedy." Strong said. "From memory, Kennedy has previous for violence. And get the Armed Response Unit to meet us."

She did as asked then looked at Strong. "You really think it's that serious?"

"It could be, Kelly. There's big money at stake here."

The rest of the journey was carried out in silence until Stainmore's phone rang. "Yes Luke." She listened for a few seconds. "Hold on," she said, then to Strong, "Apparently the ARU is on another shout over in Bradford. Something kicked off about an hour ago and they're attending. And as regards Kennedy, quite a violent record but no mention of using a firearm. Brogan's clean, as far as he can find out."

"Shit. Tell him to round up whoever he can and get up to the old Lofthouse Colliery and meet us there. Soon as."

Stainmore passed on the message and ended the call.

Five minutes later, they approached the site entrance. Strong slowed and pulled in to block the gates, killing the lights and switching off.

"That looks like Bob's Escort over there." He indicated the car parked about thirty yards up on the opposite side on the grass verge.

"How do you want to play this?"

"I think I need to have a quick look first, see what is actually going on. You stay here and wait for Luke."

"But guv ..."

"Don't argue Kelly." Strong opened the door just as a Nissan Micra drew to a halt behind his. "Bloody hell," he said. "I told her to stay at the flat."

Stainmore turned round in her seat. "Who's this?"

"Susan Brown." He got out and approached her car.

"What's happened?" Susan asked as she got out from behind the wheel.

Strong restrained her. "Nothing. Everything's fine as far as we know, Susan." He put his arms around her and guided her to the rear door of his Mondeo. Opening it, he said, "Just sit in here a minute, will you. You know DS Stainmore, Kelly?"

"Hi Susan," Kelly greeted from the front seat.

She seemed reluctant but Strong gently eased Susan in and closed the door.

Zipping up his jacket and flicking up the hood he set off up the drive.

*　*　*

"Look, we don't want any part of this nonsense," Faulkner said.

"Nor me," Appleyard concurred and stood up.

"Sit down," Brogan said, all the more effective as he only raised his voice a touch. "Nobody's going anywhere just yet."

The engineer complied, looking increasingly worried, glancing at the gun several times.

"You've given us a real headache, Mr Souter," Brogan went on. "I've no doubt you've been listening to our conversation for a little while now. So I imagine you've heard more than is good for you."

Sammy held Souter's left arm tighter. But he didn't respond to Brogan immediately, his mind rapidly sifting through any ideas that might get them out of this situation. He thrust his right hand into his coat pocket and pulled it tighter around him. "What do you want then Brogan? This whole scheme is about to unravel in front of your eyes." He decided a brazen approach was best, hence the use of the man's surname. Meanwhile, his right hand gently fumbled about in his coat pocket.

"The thing is … Souter," Brogan responded, "I haven't actually done anything wrong. In fact, my company isn't yet in contract for this scheme. The only parties who might be open to prosecution are the council officials sitting next to you."

Kennedy, still with the gun aimed at Souter and Sammy, stood by the side of his boss grinning like a lunatic.

In his seated position, Souter's pocketed hand was obscured from Brogan's view by the table. He turned his mobile the right way round and pressed a few buttons. He only hoped his memory didn't let him down and he was managing to connect with the number he wanted.

"In actual fact," Souter said, "I could help you here."

"And how could you possibly do that?" Brogan smirked.

\* \* \*

Half way up the drive, Strong's mobile began to vibrate in his pocket. He'd silenced it before setting off. He paused and pulled it free to see Bob's name come up on the screen. "Hello, Bob?" he answered quietly, before realising his friend wasn't actually speaking to him. But he could hear the conversation from the meeting room. He listened as he made his way carefully towards the building at the end of the driveway where two cars were parked.

He approached the lighted windows that had battens fixed across. Inside he could see two men standing, one well-dressed in a Crombie overcoat. His was the first voice he had heard through Souter's phone call. To his left, a smaller skinnier man in a leather jacket and jeans stood, eyes focussed on the other people seated around a meeting table. But it was what he held in his right hand that alarmed Strong. The hand gun was pointed at Souter and Sammy who had their backs to the window. Side-on at the table were Bernard Faulkner and another older man Strong didn't recognise.

If he was unsure as to the seriousness of the situation on the way here, he was in no doubt now. He turned and scuttled back down the drive to where he'd left Stainmore and Susan, all the while listening to events unfolding in the room in the old offices.

*   *   *

"For a start, as you say, the only people who've done anything wrong are these two here." Souter indicated the council men.

"Just a minute …" Faulkner protested.

Souter interrupted him. "And I'm sure the readers would welcome a juicy story involving council officials lining their own pockets courtesy of a controversial commercial scheme."

Brogan smirked. "Very true and possibly very creative of you. However there is one person here who might not like your logic and plan of action."

Kennedy looked puzzled.

"What did they used to say in the war … oh, yes, that was it, 'Careless talk costs lives.' Well thanks to the careless talk of our esteemed engineer here." Brogan waved a hand in Appleyard's direction. "I'm sure you heard him speak of … other matters."

"No idea what you're talking about," Souter said.

"Very good, but I'm sure Wullie here doesn't believe you. After all, he has more to lose than anybody after what you overheard."

Kennedy stiffened. "What d'you mean, boss?"

"The unfortunate incident with Mr Chamberlain, Wullie," Brogan explained.

Kennedy looked put out. "Ah didnae ken you'd clamped him up in that bedroom. Ah wis only meanin' tae create a bit o' damage. A warnin', like."

Souter only hoped the mobile phone link to Strong was working. "So it was you who set the fire where Charles Chamberlain died?"

"It wisnae deliberate."

Brogan put a hand on Kennedy's arm. "Trouble is Wullie, the courts might not see it like that."

"Ah just wanted tae frighten him."

"But Wullie wasn't responsible for what was in his mouth?"

Kennedy looked perplexed.

"That's never been …" Brogan's angry expression melted into a grin. "I found it in the bathroom. I can only imagine the purposes it might have been used for."

Souter decided there was no mileage in pretending he hadn't heard what had been said about his schoolmate. "But then there's Joe Webster," he pressed on.

Brogan nodded. "So you heard that too?" He turned back to Kennedy. "You see the trouble they think you've created Wullie?"

Kennedy looked amazed. "But it's whit you wanted me to do."

"I didn't tell you to kill him."

\* \* \*

Back at the car, Strong dived into the driver's seat, phone still clamped to his ear.

"Who is it?" Stainmore asked.

"What's happening?" Susan joined in.

Strong covered the mouthpiece, still listening intently to the audio link from the old colliery offices. "We have a big problem," he said. "Brogan and his nutter sidekick are holding Bob, Sammy, Faulkner, the council leader, and some other bloke at gunpoint."

"I've got to help," Susan said and struggled with the door handle.

"Calm down, Susan, the child locks are on and you're going nowhere," Stainmore said, "This is a job for us."

"And where is Luke?" Strong asked, hand still shielding any sound to the phone.

On cue, a car drew to a halt in front of them. Luke Ormerod, John Darby and Trevor Newell piled out.

Strong leapt out to greet them. Stainmore did likewise.

"What have we got then, guv?" Ormerod asked.

Still listening on his phone, Strong brought all his officers up to speed quickly with the situation evolving a hundred yards or so from the gates.

"Still no update on the ARU, guv," Stainmore added.

"And we're the only officers I could round up," Ormerod stated, "But uniform are sending a couple of units as well."

"Okay, we'll have to play the hand we've been dealt, then. But tell uniform, no lights or sirens when they get close. I don't want to create any more panic in there." Strong thumbed in the direction of the driveway. "Kelly, stay with Susan."

"No way. Trevor can sit in. I'm with you lot."

Strong considered a second. She was the most senior of the other officers, after all. "Okay," he said. "Trevor, can you make sure Susan stays in the car until uniform turn up. If there's a female officer, swap over. All phones on silent for the rest of you."

\* \* \*

"You told me tae deal wi' him." Kennedy was indignant.

"Not permanently," Brogan came back. "I've told you before, you go way too far sometimes. You shouldn't take what people tell you too literally."

"Not having a little falling out are we?" Souter began to speak in a stronger Scottish accent.

Brogan spun round. "Shut it Souter. I know what you're trying to do."

"You see, Wullie, if I can call you that, your boss here will let you carry the can for all this mess."

Brogan took a step closer to Souter. "I've told you already …"

"Naw," Kennedy interrupted, "Ah'd like tae hear whit he's got tae say."

"Hang on a minute, I've looked out for you these past few years. I've kept you out of places like Barlinnie. Why would I want you to go back there? Can't you see what he's trying to do? He's trying to sow seeds of doubt with you."

"It's working though, isn't it?" Faulkner suddenly joined in.

Souter was glad of his intervention.

"Go on," Kennedy said, gesturing with the gun.

"I can believe you didn't mean any real harm to anyone with that fire, Wullie, but what happened with Joe Webster?"

"He wouldnae gi' me the envelope."

"The one he had inside his jacket?"

"Aye."

"Was that what you were asked to do? Get hold of it.

"Well … no … naebody knew he had it. Ah didnae ken mysel' until Ah saw him tuck it in closer under his jaicket."

"But there was no need to stab him though?"

"Ah just wanted tae frighten him. All he had tae dae was hand it over."

"Shut up, Wullie," Brogan said. "You're just digging yourself in deeper."

Souter decided to push a bit further. "So what did you do with the knife?"

Kennedy smirked. "Ah, yae see, I'm no' as dumb as ye a' think I am. That's ma insurance plan."

"How do you mean?"

"It's hidden in his car," he said, indicating Brogan.

\* \* \*

The heavy rain had stopped as Strong, Stainmore, Ormerod and Darby made their way hurriedly towards the main building. Just before they got there, Strong signalled to stop. He was listening intently to the conversation being relayed over his phone from a few yards away. "John," he said in a whisper, "Make sure those cars aren't going anywhere; the four by four first."

Darby nodded, walked towards Brogan's car and tried the door handle. Locked. Undeterred, he made his way to the front, fiddled about with the bonnet and managed to release it. Head inside, he rummaged around, before reappearing, a wide grin on his face then moved on to the Mercedes.

In the meantime, the others approached the lit window. Inside, the figures were still unaware of the activity outside. Stainmore and Ormerod spotted the gun in Kennedy's hand, looked at one another, then at Strong. He squatted on his haunches, back against the brick wall below the window and beckoned them to join him. Darby was still fiddling with the Mercedes bonnet release.

"What's the plan?" Ormerod whispered.

Strong held up his hand as he concentrated on the events unfolding on the other side of the wall. Suddenly …

\*   \*   \*

"It's where?" Brogan retorted. "In my bloody car?" He waved a hand towards Appleyard. "He was right, you are a moron."

"Just a minute …"

Suddenly … outside, a car alarm sounded.

"Whit the fuck …"

Faulkner was on his feet. "That sounds like my Merc," he said, trying to see out of the window.

Souter stood too and put a hand to the glass to shield out the room light.

"Sit doon!" Kennedy yelled. "Ah'll sort this. You all stay here." At that, he left the room and stomped down the corridor.

Faulkner joined Souter at the window. "There are some cars at the end of the driveway blocking the entrance."

"Let me see," Brogan said, pushing the council leader out of the way. "Fuck," he said and dashed for the door.

\*   \*   \*

Strong killed the connection with Souter's phone and spoke to the others, "Take cover, Kennedy's coming out." They all got to their feet and scattered, Ormerod around the corner of the building, Darby crouching down behind the Merc whilst Strong and Stainmore managed to get to the other side of Brogan's four by four.

Strong peered through the windows of the car and saw Kennedy appear at the doors in an agitated state. And now, he had a clear view of the gun. With the light behind, Kennedy's eyes swept the area in front of him. The Mercedes orange indicators were flashing and the horn was giving a loud warning. Kennedy seemed to see the cars blocking the entrance for the first time and Strong heard him curse.

With the noise from the car alarm to cover him, Strong dialled control. "I don't care what they're attending to, we need that ARU here now, it's urgent. And where's that uniform back-up? Tell them to move it, this is a serious situation."

Stainmore gave her boss a nudge. He followed her gaze to see the muzzle of a gun pointing at them, and the demented look on Kennedy's face.

"Ah don't remember yous two bein' invited," he said. "Get up!"

"Take it easy," Strong said, slowly getting to his feet, Stainmore beside him. "We're police officers and you need to think very carefully ..."

"Hey!" Ormerod shouted from the corner of the building. "Armed Police! Drop your weapon!"

Kennedy turned towards him and that gave Strong the chance he needed. From behind, he struck Kennedy's wrist, knocking the gun to the ground. Stainmore went to grab it but was knocked out of the way when Kennedy, grappling with Strong, swung him round into her and onto the ground. Strong was surprised by Kennedy's strength and swiftness of movement. He managed to put a hand on the gun barrel as Kennedy took hold of the handle. Together, they struggled on the wet ground, twisting it one way then the other. As they both managed to stand up, Stainmore joined in and tried to wrestle the gun free. Again, they fell to the ground, a tangled heap. Just as Ormerod arrived to lend his strength, a shot rang out. Everyone seemed to freeze.

Brogan appeared at the doors, took in the scene and held up his hands. "Are you police?" he asked.

Kennedy took advantage of the distraction, got to his feet and made a dash for it.

"After him, Luke," Strong shouted, then looked down at Stainmore, motionless on the ground.

From the main road, the sounds of sirens and flashing blue lights. Trevor Newell had moved Strong's car to allow the marked vehicles to enter and was sprinting up the driveway with them.

John Darby moved in to arrest Brogan as Souter and Sammy appeared behind. "What's happened?" Souter asked. "We heard a shot."

On the rain-soaked tarmac, Strong cradled Stainmore's head in his lap. He'd opened her jacket and was holding his hands to her chest in a vain attempt to stem the blood flow. "Get an ambulance. Get a fucking ambulance," he cried, to no-one in particular.

"Stay there," Souter instructed Sammy and ran to help his friend. He pulled his mobile from his pocket and dialled 999, as a number of other officers had probably done. He knelt down by Strong and lifted one of Stainmore's wrists and felt for a pulse. "She's still with us," he said. "A bit erratic and weak."

"Help me stop the bleeding, Bob," Strong said.

Souter scrunched up Stainmore's jumper and pressed down alongside Strong.

"Why Kelly? Why?" he said.

For the first time he could remember since they were boys, Souter saw his friend cry, tears rolling off his cheeks.

# 55
## Tuesday 11th September 2001

Strong had been in the Leeds General Infirmary since the middle of the night. He'd arrived with Stainmore and the paramedics in the ambulance; insisted on travelling with them. They'd worked on her on route and she'd been taken straight into the operating theatre where a team of surgeons was waiting.

He looked a mess, despite attempts to clean himself up; hair unkempt and blood stains on his jacket. He paced the corridor outside, accosting any medical personnel entering or leaving through the double doors. He knew they were doing their best but his frustration rose to the surface. Fortunately, Luke Ormerod was on hand to pull him off a man in theatre scrubs who had just come out.

"Guv, let them do their jobs," Ormerod said. "They'll tell us anything as soon as they can."

Strong visibly deflated and sagged onto one of the uncomfortable plastic chairs. Ormerod sat down next to him. "Faulkner and Appleyard are in custody, as is Brogan," the DC said quietly. "Hemingford is interviewing them himself. Flynn is visibly upset, but he's in there too."

"What about that other bastard?"

"We're still searching the site for Kennedy. There's a lot of old buildings and such for him to hide, but the site's secure. He won't have got away."

Strong looked at him. "You can guarantee that, can you?"

Ormerod looked down.

"Sorry, Luke. I didn't mean …"

"That's okay, guv."

"So what have those two from the council said?"

Ormerod sat forward in his seat, arms on his knees. "There was a meeting of the *Talisman Club* called by Faulkner for the night of the fire, under pressure from Brogan, he says. Faulkner, his secretary, Brenda, and Appleyard lured Chamberlain upstairs and secured him to the frame. Then Brogan stuffed the sponge in his mouth. Faulkner reckons they were only going to leave him for an hour or two. But Kennedy had set the fire and when Faulkner went back to release him, the place had gone up."

"Kennedy. That fucking nutter." Strong looked to Ormerod. "You know he stabbed Joe Webster?"

Ormerod nodded. "We recovered a knife from Brogan's car, as you said."

Strong was on his feet again, thoughts back with Stainmore. "Why the hell did I let her come with me?"

"You can't beat yourself up." Ormerod stood beside his boss. "Look, have they said anything at all?"

"One of the doctors said the bullet went through her lung and missed her heart by millimetres." Again he fixed Ormerod with his gaze. "If she dies, how can I ever face her parents?"

"Jim Ryan's bringing them in now." Ormerod put both hands on Strong's upper arms. "But it's not going to come to that. Kelly's strong. She'll pull through."

"I'd have agreed with you if it was the Kelly Stainmore of a couple of years ago. But recently, she's … well, she's had some problems."

"I must admit, she's not looked a picture of health."

"She's just started medication for an underactive thyroid. That's why she'd put on weight, her skin looked rough and her hair …"

The doors burst open and two men, obviously members of staff dressed in shirts and trousers, appeared, halting the conversation.

"You two colleagues of Miss Stainmore?" the older of the two enquired.

"I'm DI Strong. I was with her last night. How is she?"

"I'm Mr Pettigrew, the senior cardiologist here, part of the Major Trauma Team." He proffered a hand which Strong shook. "She's been in theatre for ..." He checked his watch and Strong did the same. Ten-fifteen. "... just over seven hours," he continued in a cultured English accent. "We've managed to remove the bullet and re-inflate her lung. She was lucky it missed major blood vessels, but she's not out of the woods yet. We'll get her up to the High Dependency Unit shortly. The next forty-eight hours will be crucial."

"So what are her chances?"

Pettigrew puffed out his cheeks. "Well, she's survived the surgery, that's the first step. She's young enough, but, like I say, the next forty-eight hours ..."

"Can we see her?"

"Once she's gone upstairs, it'll be up to the nursing team. She'll be wired up to the machines and sedated for some time. But you'll be able to look through the vision panel, at least." He placed a hand on Strong's shoulder. "If you'll excuse me, I have other patients I need to attend to."

"Thanks doctor," Strong said.

"Come on, guv, let's get a coffee or something," Ormerod suggested. "You look as though you could do with one. And it'll be a little while before Kelly gets settled in upstairs."

"Yeah, you're right, Luke. Let's go."

On the way, Strong's mobile rang. He looked at the screen before answering.

\* \* \*

About half a mile away in the Yorkshire Post newsroom, Souter was pensive as he studied his computer screen. The lack of sleep didn't seem to have affected him. He and Sammy had been taken to Wood Street to make statements, finally being released at four in the morning. The events of the previous night had made the nationals as well as the front pages of the Post, although the detail was lacking. Photographs of the main players would accompany Souter's later account for the evening editions. Susan was with him, still shocked but excited at the way things had unfolded. She'd made a contribution to the reporting, pulling some background information together on the councillors.

Sammy had been shaken up quite a bit but had decided to go into work that morning. Souter would give her a call later to check how she was coping.

Before he completed the updated story, he had one important phone call to make. He'd called the hospital about DS Stainmore's condition and, as he expected, had been refused any information. West Yorkshire Police were also reticent to comment. He dialled Colin's number.

He wasn't sure his friend would answer but he did. Strong told him what Mr Pettigrew had said. He agreed that Kelly's condition was best described as critical but stable.


Just after half-past twelve, Souter and Susan entered the pub about a ten minute walk from the offices. He'd called Sammy and they'd arranged to meet for some lunch. Souter was at the bar ordering a pint for himself and an orange juice for Susan when Sammy appeared at his shoulder.

"Can I have a dry white wine please, Bob?" she asked.

"Course you can." He added her drink to the order.

A few minutes later, food choices made, they were all seated at a table by one of the large windows.

"So how have you been?" he asked Sammy.

"Trying to keep my mind off last night." She looked anxious. "Just can't believe how close we came to …"

"Hey, don't linger on it. It's Kelly Stainmore we need to think about now."

"Have you heard how she is?"

Souter repeated his conversation with Strong.

Sammy looked shaken. "I liked her. If you remember, it was her I first spoke to about Maria last year."

"Well, let's just hope she pulls through."

340

The food order arrived interrupting the depressed conversation.

They were quiet for a while as Susan added some black pepper to her lasagne, Sammy cut up her pizza and Souter squeezed tomato sauce over his fish and chips.

Susan finally broke the silence. "Have you heard from Alison recently?"

"Spoke to her early on Sunday morning," Souter said, as he finished swallowing some fish. "She's really enjoying it. They've all been so nice to her, took her out to the Statue of Liberty on Saturday and she was going to Long Island on Sunday."

Sammy, who appeared to be playing with her food rather than eating much, joined in. "Ten days she's been out there now, isn't it?" she asked.

"She flew out on the second, so ..." he counted on his fingers, "yeah, today's day eleven, I suppose."

"Not that you're missing her or anything." Sammy laughed. "How long before she's home?"

"Well, we'll be back overnight on 14th October, touching down next day but," he had a huge smile on his face, "I'll be seeing her on the thirtieth of this month. Only nineteen days to go."

"And you can't wait," Susan added. "Which of the Twin Towers is she based?"

"80th Floor of the South Tower," Souter said. "She says the views are magnificent." He swept the last of his chips around the plate, scooping up tomato sauce. "Someone took her to the top the first day she arrived but it was a bit hazy. Still saw for miles though." He took the last bite and placed his knife and fork on the plate, a satisfied grin on his face.

"Can't wait to see the photos," Sammy said.

Souter checked his watch. "We need to get back, Susan. Will you be okay this afternoon, Sammy? You haven't eaten much."

"I'll be fine, yeah. I wasn't feeling too hungry." She looked up and smiled, but Souter could see she had been affected by everything that had happened the night before. "Plenty to keep me occupied," she went on.

As they all stood up to leave, she looked at Souter. "Listen, let me know if you hear anymore about Kelly Stainmore."

With assurances he would, he gave her a big hug. Then he and Susan headed back to the Yorkshire Post offices as Sammy departed in the opposite direction.

*   *   *

DS Ryan arrived with Kelly's mother and father. He took them directly to HDU where the senior nurse in charge took them into her office to bring them up to speed with Kelly's condition.

Strong and Ormerod were waiting outside Stainmore's room. "How are they taking it?" he asked his DS.

"Worried shitless, I'd say. I think this is their worst nightmare, something happening to their daughter."

Strong shook his head. "We've got a duty of care … I've got a duty of care, for my officers and I've let her down."

"You can't say that, guv. She insisted on coming with you. If she hadn't …well, there was nothing you could have done."

"I should have ordered her to stay put." Strong turned away and walked over to a seat near the room's vision panel, thankfully more comfortable than the ones outside the operating theatres.

Ryan and Ormerod exchanged looks. "He's taking this personally, Jim," Ormerod said in low tones.

Ryan merely nodded.

A uniformed constable then appeared, introduced himself and said he'd been appointed to patient security for the first shift. He took up position by the room door.

Ormerod's phone rang and he turned away to take the call.

Stainmore's parents reappeared from the office. "I'll take you in to see Kelly now," the nurse said, leading them to the room.

Kelly's father paused at the door, recognising his daughter's boss. "Mr Strong," he said. "I understand you were with our Kelly last night."

Strong stood and approached the man. "I'm so sorry, Mr Stainmore."

"Please, call me Jeff. I understand you took care of her after it happened until the paramedics arrived. They tell me you might have saved Kelly's life."

"No, I ..."

"She has the greatest respect for you Mr Strong. She always talks about you and how much she admires you. Thank you."

The two men held each other's gaze for a second before Jeff Stainmore joined his wife in Kelly's room, sitting at her bedside.

"Guv," Ormerod said excitedly, "You won't believe what's going on."

Strong snapped his attention back to his DC. "Not more trouble?"

"Not here," Ormerod replied. "I think we need to find a television. Apparently, two planes have crashed into the Twin Towers in New York. All Hell's breaking loose over there."

"Are you sure?" Strong looked incredulous.

"They're speculating it's no accident."

Strong pulled out his mobile phone. "Christ, just when I thought the day couldn't get any worse." He dialled a number.

Ryan gave a puzzled look to Ormerod who shrugged his shoulders. "Not our jurisdiction, guv."

"Engaged." Strong said. "It's my mate, the one we rescued last night. His girlfriend is on a six-week secondment to their US office." He re-dialled. "Based in the Twin Towers."

"Shit," Ryan said.

"Exactly." He turned away. "Hello, Bob?"

# 56

When Souter and Susan walked into the newsroom, the tense atmosphere was overwhelming. Chandler and the Editor were standing in the middle of the room, looking at the television screen on the wall. The volume had been turned up. Pictures of a tall, smoking building were being broadcast.

"What's going on?" Souter asked Janey Clarke who, like the other journalists, was on her feet, attention focussed on the live television pictures.

Without turning to look at him she said, "It looks like a plane's just crashed into one of the Twin Towers in New York."

Souter looked to the television and his stomach lurched. His legs buckled. Susan made a desperate attempt to stop him collapsing to the floor but it was too late. Most of his meal reappeared too.

John Chandler and Janey Clarke turned round immediately and bent down to help him. Susan pulled out a chair from a nearby desk. Between the three of them, they managed to sit him down. Janey went off saying she'd get a glass of water and some paper towels.

"Bob! Bob, can you hear me?" he heard Chandler say.

Of course I can fucking hear you, he said to himself. Aloud he said, "Yep. Yes, I'm alright."

"You're obviously not alright," Chandler responded.

"I think it's Alison," Susan said quietly.

"Alison?" Chandler queried.

"She's there." Susan indicated the television. "She's working in one of the towers. Been there for ten days."

"Oh Christ." The colour drained from Chandler's cheeks.

Janey returned with a glass of water and one of the cleaners followed with a mop and bucket.

Souter took a drink. "What's happening there?" he asked. "I need to see." He stood up but staggered. Chandler steadied him.

They listened for a while as the television news presenters gave an account of how they had reports of at least two plane hijackings. One of those planes had crashed into the North Tower, somewhere below the one hundredth floor. Several times they repeated footage of the actual impact.

"Susan said Alison is out there. Do you know exactly where?" Chandler asked.

"Her firm has offices in the South Tower. Floor eighty." Souter turned away quickly and pulled his mobile phone from his trouser pocket. "I need to hear she's okay."

Chandler and Susan turned with him. "I'm sure she'll be fine," Chandler said. "They've said they're evacuating her building now." He indicated the TV with his thumb.

Souter dialled a number, listened for a few seconds then pulled the phone from his ear and studied the screen. "Network busy," he said and tried again.

"It's bound to be," Susan suggested. "Everybody will be trying to get hold of their friends and relatives."

"Still busy," Souter said, having tried again.

A sudden gasp drew everyone's attention back to the television.

"What? What?" Souter said.

"Fucking hell!" one of the Post journalists exclaimed. "A plane's just flown into the other tower now. What the fuck is happening here?"

"Let me see. Oh Christ! Alison ... Oh, Jesus Christ, it can't be ..."

Chandler put his arm around Souter's shoulders, steadied him once more "He can't see this," Chandler said. "Let's get him up to my office." He began to lead Souter towards the door.

"I can't ..." Souter protested, attempting to get a clearer view. "I need to get hold of her ..." He fumbled with his mobile again.

"Let's get you up to Mr Chandler's office first, Bob. We can try and call her from there."

Souter couldn't remember much about the next few minutes. Somehow, Chandler and Susan forced him out of the newsroom and up one floor into the deputy editor's office.

Sitting on the leather settee, Souter struggled to see the display on his phone through the tears in his eyes.

"Let me keep trying, Bob," Susan said and gently took the mobile from his hand.

Chandler produced a black coffee from somewhere. "Drink this," he said.

"What am I going to do?" Souter sobbed, spittle trailing down his chin. "What *am* I going to do?"

Susan dialled Alison's number several more times with the same result. Just as she was about to try again, the mobile rang.

"It's Alison," Souter said, jumping up and grabbing his mobile. Tears in his eyes meant he couldn't see the display clearly. "Alison? Are you okay?" he said into the phone.

*"Bob, it's me, Colin,"* came his friend's voice.

"Bob? Why are you calling? I thought it was ..."

*"Alison, I know. Look, I've just heard. Where are you?"*

"I can't get hold of her, Col. I'm trying all the time but I just can't get through."

*"You probably won't until all this settles. God knows when that'll be. But where are you now?"*

Souter composed himself. "I'm in John Chandler's office. I saw the planes strike. It was awful. They hit the building Alison's in."

*"Look, I'm just walking into the cafeteria here at the hospital. They've got the TV on. From what they've been saying, they were evacuating the buildings. She's probably out on the street now."*

Souter pulled the phone away from his ear to speak to Chandler. "John, can we have that TV on?"

"I'm not sure it's ..." Chandler began.

"I need to see," he said firmly.

"Okay." Chandler switched on the small set sitting on top of the cabinet by the side of his desk.

Pictures of the smoking buildings filled the screen.

"They're both on fire, Col."

*"I can see that."*

The phone rang on Chandler's desk. Souter looked across expectantly.

"I've got to go. I need to keep trying to get hold of her."

*"Okay, mate but stay positive."*

Souter ended the call as Chandler covered the mouthpiece of his desk phone with his hand. "Someone called Sammy's downstairs asking to see you."

"Can I fetch her up?" Susan asked. "She's a close friend of all of us."

Chandler nodded and Susan left the room.

They listened as the commentators described the scene and surmised all sorts of theories as to what was happening and why.

Sammy came bursting into the room "Oh, Bob," she sobbed. "What's happening? They're all in bits in the office."

Souter stood and they embraced.

"Did they manage to speak to anyone in New York?" he asked.

"I think one of the bosses got through to someone over there just after the first plane hit but no one's been able to contact them since."

"Makes sense," Susan said. "All the land lines would have been damaged. Did anybody try mobiles?"

Sammy shook her head. "Have you tried to get through on Alison's?"

"I'm still trying." Souter dialled Alison's number yet again.

\* \* \*

"We got you a coffee, guv," Ormerod said when Strong's call had ended and he'd finally joined them at the table.

"What news?" Ryan asked as Strong put his mobile away.

"The man's all over the place. He hasn't been able to get hold of his girlfriend."

"I doubt he will for some time." Ryan indicated the large television on wall brackets at the far end of the cafeteria. "According to them, they've closed down the telephone networks. Fear of terrorists using mobile signals for their own ends, apparently."

"Terrorists? They think it's a terrorist act?"

"I don't think they know much at all at the moment, but you know how these journalists go," Ormerod put in. "Sorry, I didn't mean …I know your mate's a journalist, I …"

"It's alright, Luke." Strong waved a hand, his attention not wavering from the screen. "I know what you mean."

By now, all activity had come to a standstill in the cafeteria. Staff had swelled the numbers of customers transfixed by the unfolding drama. Strong had a feeling this was one of those moments in history where everyone would know where they were, when they looked back to this day; just like the moon landings.

Strong finally sipped his coffee and winced. Ormerod and Ryan had already finished theirs.

"Shall I get you another?" Ormerod asked.

"No thanks, Luke."

Ryan stood up. "I'm going back upstairs to see how things are," he said, then made his way out.

After he'd gone, Ormerod stared at his boss. "She will be okay, you know."

"Who? Kelly or Alison?"

"Both."

Strong shook his head, attention focussed on his DC. "I don't know, Luke. I should never have agreed to her coming along."

"But she grabbed the gun."

"And if she hadn't, I might be lying downstairs in the mortuary now. She saved my life. And yet everyone says I've saved hers. It's my fault."

Ormerod leaned forward on the table. "You can't blame yourself. The only ones to blame are the bastards we have in custody."

Before Strong could respond, there was a collective gasp uttered by the people watching events in New York. He and Ormerod both stood to see what was happening. In disbelief, they watched the South Tower slowly collapse in a huge dust cloud.

"Was that …"

The television commentary confirmed which tower had just gone down.

"Fuck," Strong said, quietly. "That was where Bob's girlfriend was based."

"Guv," Ryan came rushing in.

"I know, we've just seen it, Jim."

"What?" He looked to the screen, then back to the DI. "No, not that. It's Kelly. The machines have all gone off upstairs. Something's wrong."

# 57

In Chandler's office, Souter and his boss, Susan and Sammy were transfixed to the small television screen. There was a collective intake of breath which seemed to suck all the oxygen from the room. It was held as they watched the South Tower fall in on itself and a dust cloud like a nuclear explosion fanned outwards and upwards from the base.

Sammy gripped Souter's arm tightly, hid her face in his chest and gave a sob. Chandler froze, jaw open, while Susan covered her mouth with a hand, tears welling in her eyes.

Sammy straightened up. "That's …" she began.

"Alison's building, yes," Susan continued for her.

Chandler opened a drawer in one of the filing cabinets by the side of his desk. A whisky bottle was produced with two glasses. He poured a generous measure and walked round to where Souter was sitting. "Here," he said. "Drink this."

Souter took the glass and, without looking at its contents, gulped it down in one. He turned to Sammy sitting alongside him. "Why me?" He looked pleadingly at his young friend. "What have I ever done to anyone? All I ever wanted was to have a soulmate, hopefully one day a family."

Tears rolled down Sammy's cheeks.

"I told you about Adam," he continued. "What happened to him."

She nodded, wiping her face with her hands. Susan, struggling to keep her emotions in check, gave Sammy a tissue.

"I was hoping … maybe one day … you know?"

"I know, Bob," Sammy said. "But Alison didn't tell you though, did she?"

Souter looked questioningly at her. "Tell me? Tell me what?"

"She wanted to but she thought you wouldn't let her go."

"Let her go? Why?"

"She was pregnant."

He felt confused, puzzled. "No ... when ... I mean, why didn't she tell me? She knew how much it would mean to me. She told you but not me?"

Sammy dabbed at her eyes with the tissue. "She was going to tell you when you went to that Italian restaurant."

His thoughts began to clear. "She didn't have anything to drink. I wondered ... but why not tell me?"

Sammy took a breath. "She was worried how you would take the news."

"Worried? Why? That would have been the best news I'd ever had."

"I know. But she thought she'd tell you when you got to New York." Sammy wiped her nose and sniffed. "I think she thought it would be more romantic."

"And now she's gone ... with our child."

Sammy put her arms around him and sobbed.

Susan squatted down in front of the pair and put her hands on Souter's face, turning it to face her. "Look at me," she said. "Alison's not dead, Bob. She's not, I can feel it."

\*　　\*　　\*

When Strong, Ormerod and Ryan reached the High Dependency Unit, Kelly's mother and father were holding each other, sitting on two of the chairs. Strong glanced into the room and saw a team of at least five medical staff working around Kelly's bed.

After a few minutes, the senior nurse came out and spoke to Kelly's parents.

"What's going on," her mother asked. "The alarms just went berserk."

"We think Kelly is still bleeding internally. The team have managed to stabilise her and she'll be going back down to theatre now."

As the nurse was talking, the door opened and Kelly was wheeled out and along the corridor to a waiting lift. Various tubes were in place and a team of three accompanied her.

"In the meantime, Mrs Stainmore," the nurse continued, "has your daughter any underlying medical problems you are aware of?"

Kelly's mother looked puzzled. "No. What sort of problems?"

"It's just a routine enquiry. I mean, is she on any medication you know of? Does she suffer from any blood disorders for example?"

She shook her head. "No, nothing like that. Not that I'm aware of."

"Okay. Now look, please try not to worry, she's in the best possible hands. There's a relatives' room where you can wait. You may be more comfortable there. I can take you and I'll come and tell you whenever we have any news."

The nurse led Kelly's parents down the corridor and disappeared.

Strong and Ormerod looked at one another.

"I'm not religious, guv, but I'm praying," Ormerod said.

"Look, you two get back to Wood Street," Strong said. "I'll stay here and talk to Kelly's mum and dad."

"You sure?" Ryan asked.

Strong nodded and watched as his two officers walked along the corridor and disappeared through doors at the end.

A minute later, the nurse reappeared.

Strong approached her. "Excuse me," he said, "You were asking about Kelly just now."

"Sorry, you are …" She stood by the office door.

"I'm Detective Inspector Colin Strong, Kelly's boss."

"Well I can't tell you any more than you overheard."

"No, I understand that. But you were asking about her health."

The nurse studied him for a second then opened the door. "Take a seat for a moment DI Strong."

As she sat behind her desk, Strong closed the door behind him and sat down opposite. "I don't know if it's of any help," he began, "but I've been concerned about Kelly, DS Stainmore for some time."

"In what way?"

Strong took a breath. "She's appeared generally run down, seems to be lethargic at times, depressed at others."

The nurse began to jot down brief notes.

"She put weight on, her skin didn't appear healthy. Anyway, she told me last night that she'd been diagnosed with an underactive thyroid."

She looked up at him. "So is she on any medication, do you know?"

"She said she'd just started yesterday morning. A pill a day. Apparently."

The nurse nodded. "That would be the usual treatment. Thanks, Inspector. I'll pass your information on to the medical team, in strict confidence, of course."

He stood. "So, in your experience, Nurse ... Walker." He strained to look at her name badge. "How do you think she's doing."

She gave the question a moment's consideration. "I really wouldn't like to speculate. All I can tell you is that she has a first rate team attending to her now. We'll have a better idea after they've operated and stopped the bleed. But look, thanks for this, I best get down there and let them know." She walked to the door and held it open.

"Thanks," Strong said, and followed her out.

\* \* \*

"I don't think the world will ever be the same again," Chandler said, almost to himself.

"It certainly won't be for Bob," Susan said quietly.

"This is history in the making. God knows where this will lead us." Chandler was focussed on the television screen.

Susan looked round at Bob and Sammy, hugging each other on the sofa. Bob was staring blankly into space, Sammy, face puffy, eyes red and tears still streaming down her face.

Turning back to Chandler, she said, "I honestly feel she's okay."

"I hope you're right, Susan."

Despite her optimism, grief weighed heavy in that office.

\*   \*   \*

About a mile away, the anxiety was unbearable.

It had been an hour since Stainmore had been wheeled into theatre for a second time. Luke Ormerod had ignored his boss's instructions and let Ryan return to Wood Street alone. Whatever he'd said, Ormerod knew Strong would need his support. He met up with him again, looking lost outside the empty room of the HDU.

"Any news?" Ormerod asked.

Strong shook his head. "Nothing since they all left."

"You know there's been another plane crash? Into the Pentagon now?"

"Christ, are we in a dream here?" Strong wondered. "What the Hell's going on?"

After a moment's pause, Ormerod put his hand on Strong's elbow. "Come on," he said, "At least let's get to where the action is." He started to lead them down the corridor, intending to make their way to the operating theatres. They got as far as the Relatives Room when Nurse Walker reappeared, her expression impossible to read.

"Excuse me …" Strong began.

"Can I just speak to Mr and Mrs Stainmore first," she interrupted him, walking past the two of them, into the room and closing the door behind her.

Strong and Ormerod waited for what seemed like hours but could only have been a couple of minutes before a loud wail was heard.

"Oh Christ, no. Don't let this be," Strong whispered to Ormerod.

Finally the door opened and the nurse led out Jeff Stainmore hugging his wife tightly. Her head was buried in her husband's chest as she gasped and sobbed. He spotted the detectives and a grim smile broke on his face. "They think she'll be okay," he said. "But it was touch and go for a while. She's coming back up now."

Strong sagged against the opposite wall and looked to the ceiling. Silently he mouthed, '*Thank you Lord,*' as tears streamed down his face.

# 58
## Friday 7<sup>th</sup> December 2001
## Gran Canaria

Colin Strong sat on the balcony of the first floor apartment, enjoying his coffee. The sun shimmered and sparkled off the Atlantic Ocean. The small ferry was just returning to the harbour from the first of its round trips down the coast to nearby resorts. The day promised to be warm and sunny yet again with temperatures into the mid-seventies. He and Laura had rented the place for three weeks; they were due home for Christmas.

The break had certainly done him good. Ever since Kelly's shooting, he'd struggled to sleep. Nightmares most nights. Images of a deranged Kennedy, face contorted into ugly grimaces. Kelly leaping on him and then a gunshot. That was when he invariably woke, drenched in sweat.

No matter what his colleagues said to him by way of support, he couldn't help blaming himself for what had happened. Facing Kelly's mother was the worst. It was as if she could see deep inside his soul, view his guilt as clear as the bloodstains on his clothes. Jeff Stainmore presented the opposite picture. He warmly gripped his hand as Strong left the hospital that day. "Thank you," he had said. Thank you for what, Strong thought? Thank you for getting my only daughter shot and almost killed?

Two days after Kelly's shooting, they'd found Kennedy's body. On that dark wet night, in his rush to escape, he'd fallen through the rusted cover of a settlement tank and drowned. The foul drains were blocked and it had backed up. An unimaginable end, but an appropriate one, for such a nasty little shit, Strong thought.

Faulkner was facing charges in connection with attempted fraud. His financial position was being investigated with a fine tooth comb. Thanks to the evidence provided by Kathy Webster, Appleyard was facing charges in connection with his falsifications of the site survey findings. The pair of them and Brenda Morgan could still face manslaughter charges related to the death of Charles Chamberlain. He'd been an obstacle – looking to put the council off dealing with Thistle. Pitchforth appeared to have taken no part and distanced himself from their actions. Brogan was wriggling. Expensive lawyers were putting forward his previously expressed views that he'd done nothing wrong. Others had invited him along to the last meeting of the *Talisman Club* and he was as shocked as anyone at the outcome. Kennedy was not working under any instructions he'd ever given him. The other aspect was that Thistle Developments had not signed any contract with the council and so could not be held responsible for what had occurred. It was more than likely there would be some form of official enquiry into the Lofthouse Development and, for the time being, the whole scheme was on hold.

DCS Flynn had told Strong to take sick leave. He'd resented that initially but Laura had insisted he take time off because she could see how much he'd been affected by all that had happened.

He had had time to think and he was giving serious consideration to changing lifestyles completely. To that end, their holiday rental could be a first step. He was keen to move things on further.

On the table in front of him sat an unopened letter. It had arrived the morning they had left to come on holiday. He didn't need to open it to know who it was from. Maybe now was the time.

Laura came out on to the balcony with her drink as he picked it up. Slipping his finger in the top, he ripped the envelope apart. As he knew, it was from Bob.

"What does he say?" Laura asked.

Strong read the note then put it down. "He's getting married next month and he'd like me to be his best man."

"That's great isn't it?"

"I'm really glad things have worked out for him. He was in a terrible state for days before he heard from Alison. Just good fortune that she was suffering from morning sickness and hadn't left her hotel room that day."

"I know. And, at last he has a baby to look forward to." She looked to her husband. "But you're still hurting? You blame him too?"

"Partly. He should have told me all he knew about Brogan and Kennedy and all the rest of them. Put together with what we'd found out, maybe that confrontation at the old colliery wouldn't have occurred. Kelly wouldn't have been shot."

Laura drained her coffee. "You can't think like that, Colin. Otherwise it's going to eat you up. Kennedy was responsible, not Bob, and certainly not you. And if Kelly was sitting here now, she'd say the same. In fact, when she starts back in the New Year, ask her."

Strong merely gazed out to sea.

She glanced at her watch. "Come on, get yourself ready. That estate agent will be here in half an hour to collect us. He says he has a couple of nice villas for us to view."

THE END

*Enjoy TALISMAN?*

*Then please review on Amazon, Goodreads etc.*

*Have you read more in the series?*

*See the next few pages …*

Book 1 TROPHIES

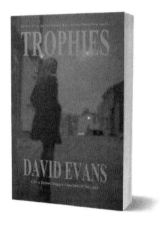

By the turn of the millennium, memories had dulled. But the discovery of a trophy case at the scene of a murder leads to the realisation that a series of attacks on women over the previous twenty years had gone unconnected. DI Colin Strong is convinced there is also a link with one other notorious unsolved crime. His best friend from schooldays, journalist Bob Souter, has returned to Yorkshire and begins to probe. Working separately and together in an awkward alliance, they seek the answers.

Available through Amazon:

Getbook.at/Trophies

Book 2          TORMENT

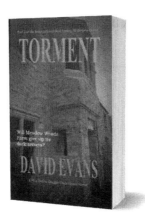

A message left in error on a young woman's answerphone is the catalyst for uncovering some dark deeds. Three young women are missing; luxury cars are being stolen; and just what did happen to two young schoolgirls, missing since the 1980's?

DI Colin Strong and journalist Bob Souter are drawn into murky and dangerous worlds

Available through Amazon:

Getbook.at/Torment

Book 4          TAINTED

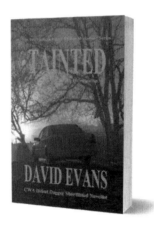

A botched attempt to extort money has tragic consequences.

An embarrassing DNA match to an unsolved rape and murder twenty years before means DI Colin Strong has to use his best diplomatic tactics.

Simultaneously, journalist Bob Souter is tasked with writing about that same case to re-focus public attention. Will the newspaper's actions help or hinder the police?

Meanwhile, Strong's team has two separate murder enquiries to run.

Available through Amazon:

https://getbook.at/Tainted-DavidEvans

Printed in Great Britain
by Amazon